"FARE WELL, SIR JOHN,"
SHE MURMURED UNEASILY.

Reaching for the door latch, Maria turned finally toward the Highlander to bid him good-bye.

John put his hands on her shoulders, turning her around and pulling her close. "Nay," he whispered. "You'll not escape me quite so easily."

She looked up into his deep blue eyes in surprise.

"But . . ." The words died in her throat as she felt his hands slide up the side of her neck, then cradle her face.

His gaze shifted to her mouth, and he brushed the full lower lip with his thumb.

"What are you doing?" Maria whispered foolishly.

"I am going to kiss you again."

"Against—against my will?" she asked shakily.

"Nay, lass, not against your will," he whispered, slowly lowering his head. "But perhaps against your better judgment."

His mouth covered hers, and within her chest a shower of sparks rained down.

The Beauty of the Mist

May McGoldrick

A TOPAZ BOOK

TOPAZ
Published by the Penguin Group
Penguin Books USA Inc., 375 Hudson Street,
New York, New York 10014, U.S.A.
Penguin Books Ltd, 27 Wrights Lane,
London W8 5TZ, England
Penguin Books Australia Ltd, Ringwood,
Victoria, Australia
Penguin Books Canada Ltd, 10 Alcorn Avenue,
Toronto, Ontario, Canada M4V 3B2
Penguin Books (N.Z.) Ltd, 182–190 Wairau Road,
Auckland 10, New Zealand

Penguin Books Ltd, Registered Offices:
Harmondsworth, Middlesex, England

First published by Topaz, an imprint of Dutton Signet,
a division of Penguin Books USA Inc.

First Printing, April, 1997
10   9   8   7   6   5   4   3   2   1

To our parents,
for sharing with us the beauty of life.

Prologue

Antwerp, The Netherlands
March, 1528

L et the Scots come.

Like the wings of a wounded raven, the black cloak fluttered madly about the running figure. Maria, Queen of Hungary, paused, panting heavily and pressing her exhausted body into the dark shadows of the shuttered, brick town house. The flaring light of the torch that lit the street glistened off the wet stone of the alley, and the young queen tried to melt even deeper into the blackness. Straining, Maria could hear no sound of pursuers in the cold night air. Her jade eyes flashing, she peered back past the torch toward the gloomy walls of the palace, towering above the roofs of the sleeping town.

Turning away, she could see the one finished spire of the cathedral rising before her. Unfamiliar with the twisting streets and alleyways of this town—or any other—Maria gazed up at the landmark she'd been told to follow.

The houses and shops crowded her on every side, and as she ran, the cold, damp air stabbed at her lungs. The sky above began to lighten, and she pushed herself onward, her feet flying over the slick stones.

At the end of the twisting way, she slowed before entering the open plaza around the cathedral. Beyond the stone walls of the huge church, black in the predawn light, lay the harbor. She had to reach it before life in the palace began to stir, before the tide turned.

There, by one of the stone quays, a longboat waited. A longboat that would take Maria to her aunt. To the strong seaworthy ship that would carry them far from an abhorrent wedding.

She ran across the empty plaza, hugging the walls of the cathedral. She would make it to the harbor now. She could smell the brackish water of the river already.

Let the Scots come, she thought defiantly. Let them come.

Chapter 1

A gilded cage is still a cage.

John Macpherson, Lord of the Navy, stood with his back to the smoldering fire and watched in restrained silence as the young king with the fiery red hair halted his restless pacing at one of the glazed windows overlooking the open courtyard of Stirling Castle. Following the young man's gaze, he could see that the sixteen-year-old monarch's eyes had riveted on a solitary raven flying free in the gray Scottish skies that surrounded the castle walls.

Across the chamber Archibald Douglas, the Earl of Angus, smoothed his long black beard over his chest as he finished reading the last of the official letters. Folding the document carefully, the powerful lord paused and looked up at the black-clad young man by the window, before dripping wax onto the parchment.

John saw the smile flicker over the Lord Chancellor's face as he lifted the king's royal seal from his desk, pressing it carefully into the soft wax.

"With these letters, Sir John here should have no trouble fetching your bride, Kit . . . I mean, Your Majesty," Archibald corrected himself, seeing the king turn his glance briefly on him.

His face hiding the growing rage within, John Macpherson continued to watch the scene unfolding before him. The king had summoned him to court for instructions on a mission of the utmost importance. But after spending just a few short moments with these two men, John knew that the horrible rumors he'd been hearing

while away from court were all true. Archibald Douglas,
the Earl of Angus, chief of the powerful Douglas clan,
Lord Chancellor of Scotland, member of Regency Council, and the ex-husband of Queen Margaret, had King
James, his stepson, under lock and key.

The chancellor turned to the silent Highlander.

"Sir John, the Emperor Charles is expecting you at
Antwerp before the end of the month. I don't think I
need to tell you that it is quite an honor that he is en-
trusting his sister, Mary of Hungary, to our care for
the voyage."

"Aye, m'lord," John responded, looking at the King
as he answered.

"His Majesty will be spending Easter at Falkland Palace," Angus continued. "But if you need to contact me,
I will be in the south, clearing vermin from the Borders."

The King turned his face to John and their eyes met.

Then John Macpherson saw once again the flash in
the lad's eyes. The same fearless spark that the Highlander had first witnessed years earlier in the fatherless
bairn. James had been only an infant when his royal
father died fighting the English at Flodden Field. En-
trusted to the safekeeping of one brave woman and a
handful of loyal supporters, the Crown Prince had been
whisked across the Highlands while a few stalwart nobles
struggled to arrange for his safe return. And then he
had come back to the arms of the Queen Mother. Still
not yet two years of age, little Kit had been crowned
James V, King of Scotland and the Western Isles.

That was the day John Macpherson had first seen him.
The day of his coronation. A mere bairn sitting on the
high throne of a country in chaos. But everyone who
had knelt before him, swearing their loyalty before God,
had been struck with the clear knowledge that the boy
was a Stuart. Silent, serious, and steadfast through the
course of the ceremony, Kit had shown them all that he
had the blood, the courage, and the intelligence of his
forebears. He was the one who would carry on. The new
king who would rise to save Scotland from her enemies.
The one who would save Scotland from herself.

John watched the King walk toward him, ignoring the chancellor's continuing speech.

The Lord Chancellor. The man who had married the queen in her widowhood solely for the reason of filling the power void that existed in Scotland after the devastating loss at Flodden Field. Everyone in Scotland knew that the union would bring the Douglas family power, and it did. The marriage gave the Earl of Angus control over the young king, and eventually put him in a position of absolute power—to rule in his name.

And from what John had been hearing, since the Queen Mother requested that the Pope annul her marriage to the man, the Lord Chancellor had been tightening his control of the young king—and guarding him fiercely.

John knew, as did everyone else, that there was no one strong enough to challenge the Lord Chancellor. Little more than a year ago, several thousand men had tried at Linlithgow, but they'd failed. And as he cut them down in their blood, Angus had claimed that he was only protecting the Crown.

John straightened as the red-haired king halted before him. The Highlander towered over the young man, but their eyes never left each other's face.

"You think me weak, Jack Heart?" the King asked in a low voice.

Jack Heart. John smiled. He hadn't heard the nickname for some time. Not since the days when the boy king had been under the protection of the Queen Mother. Then, James had been far less restricted in his liberties, and John had taught the lad to sail amid the whitecaps off Queen's Ferry. They'd spent a full summer in each other's company, and it had been then that the young king had learned the name that John had once been called by the sailors of the Macpherson ships. It had become a term of endearment between the two. Though few even recalled the name anymore, even fewer would have dared address the fierce Lord of the Navy in so familiar a manner.

Except Kit.

"Then you agree."

"Never," John answered. "You are not weak, lad. Only trapped."

"My father would have handled it differently."

"Your father was never separated from his people nor imprisoned at your age," John continued with more assurance. "And as much as I loved him as a king, he had his flaws."

"But he was a soldier. My father had courage. As you have courage." James stared at the commander's tartan. "If you were in my position, you would never have accepted this fate."

"But, m'lord—"

"Jack Heart," the young king cut in, "you were barely a year older than I when you stood your ground in the mud beside my father at Flodden Field. You have courage, Jack. You have determination. You have heart. I lack these things, I know. These, my friend, and many more."

"Only in your own eyes, m'lord. In the hearts of all loyal Scots, you are our King and our future."

James gazed up at John, a wistful look flickering across his face. "I don't want to be a disappointment to my people."

"You won't be, sire," John answered in earnest, seeing the lad's distress. The young king almost reached his shoulder now. But he was so young. Too young, perhaps, to battle the evil that perched at his right hand. "You'll overcome this . . . difficulty, and your triumph will win the heart of every Scot. You'll take your throne when the time is right. And then, the accounts of your bravery, the tales of your generosity, the recital of your acts of goodness will far exceed any standard set by your father and their fathers in this land. Always remember this, Kit: Your people see the promise, that is why they want you, and that is why they cherish you."

James looked up trustingly. "I will do my best not to disappointment them. I will slip this trap."

"Like the fox himself." John's eyes shone with affection.

"Like my father." The King spoke softly. A perceptible change came over the young man's face. "Aye, Jack. Then you'll bring her to me."

"If that's your wish." John paused, casting a casual glance at the chancellor, who was eyeing them suspiciously from across the room. "Of course, we could devise other means—other ways to bring an end to this . . . undesirable situation."

The young king smiled sadly, looking down at his untried hands. "If it were only that simple. But if we were to go that way, then it'd mean that others will need to fight my battle. Others like you, Jack Heart. But if I were free . . ."

John waited for him to continue, but Kit changed his course.

"He has given his word to me and to the council that he will gradually step aside after this marriage takes place." The young man gave a quick glance over his shoulder. "It's the best way. I don't wish that any more blood of innocent Scots be shed while any other way exists to settle this unholy affair. This is *my* responsibility, Jack. This is something I can do. I know it might not seem so important to you, but to me it is. This is the first chance for me to show my will, my strength. This means everything to me."

"But at your young age . . . you are willing to marry someone you've never known . . . never seen."

"For the good of Scotland, I will. And it will bring me one step closer to my people." The lad's eyes lit up at the thought. "There will be time enough later to settle the differences . . . once I am free. Please, Jack, I need this chance."

John nodded in response. How could he deny his king's fervent plea?

"Bring her here, Jack." The young man placed his hand on the Highlander's arm. "I will wed her. It's God's will."

The chancellor stalked briskly across the room, and John took the sealed letter from his hand. Archibald Douglas's voice was cool and his gaze steady.

"Keep her safe, Sir John."

John nodded curtly to the chancellor and, exchanging a telling look with the young king, bowed to them both before departing from the chamber.

Chapter 2

The German Sea, off the coast of Denmark

Maria's hands were chafed raw and bloody.
Tucking the oars awkwardly under her arms, the young woman pressed her fingers gingerly against the stinging, red flesh on the palms of her hands. A small billow shifted the open boat, and one of the oar handles lifted, banging her hard under the chin.

"You're certainly no sailor, my girl," Isabel threw out in an effort at caustic wit, though her aging eyes drooped with a deadening weariness.

Maria sadly took in the sight of the woman before her. The loss of blood, the cold, and the exhaustion were taking their toll.

"I think it would be better if you slept, Aunt."

Isabel stretched her sore legs and then, shaking her fingers, tried to fight off the numbness that gradually was settling into her body.

"I can't sleep. I won't. Not with a novice at the oars. If it is my fate to become bait for some half-frozen northern fish, then, by God, I want to be awake." Isabel sighed. "It won't be too long now. I can feel it. The noise you're making trying to row is enough to lead the blackguards straight to us, even in this fog. Can't you hear them behind us? Do you think they stormed our ship just to let us go?"

Maria rolled her eyes, trying to ignore both her fear and the damp, bone-chilling cold. Wrapping her fingers painfully around the wet wooden shafts, she flexed her aching shoulders and started once again to push the small boat through the endless fog.

"Just think of the time you've spent—wasted," Isabel

continued. "In the time to make even one of your elegant tapestries, you might have been learning something useful! Something about the sea! About how to survive . . ."

Maria sighed, feeling the strength drain out of her arms with every word her aunt spoke. With every stroke of the oars. Trying to ignore her pain, and the growing sense of hopelessness that was stealing through her, the young woman forced herself to focus on the sound of the oars slapping against the murky black-green water. But nothing proved effective in shutting out Isabel's continuous stream of conversation.

Shipwrecked. Stranded. Vulnerable.

The thoughts swept over the young woman with a numbing coldness, like nothing she'd ever experienced. Maria fought back her tears as she looked over her shoulder at the dying Spaniard stretched in the bow of the boat. How easy it would be to close her eyes and lie back like him, to let nature take its course. The sailor hadn't moved or even moaned for quite a while. She wondered if he was still alive. He looked at peace. The musket shot that had wounded her Aunt Isabel had found its final resting place deep in the chest of the poor man. Perhaps it would have been better if Maria herself had been the recipient of such a wound. Perhaps, then, she'd be the one at peace, far beyond the cold and the aching muscles and the stinging hands, and the overpowering weariness. She shook her head and tried to rid herself of such morbid thoughts.

Glancing back at her aunt, Maria thought for a moment to ask Isabel to go past her and check on the sailor. But then she decided that even asking her to hold the oars while she herself moved forward to him was foolishness. The thought of unbalancing the boat with the shifting of weight was unthinkable. It could mean disaster for them all.

What her elderly aunt had said was true. Maria was no sailor.

"I think we've been going in circles," Isabel muttered as petulantly as she could manage.

"You're probably correct. And you should add lack of navigation abilities to my list of shortcomings," she whispered, then looked down at the smear of blood spreading from her palms onto the wooden oar handles. Her fingers were stiff and numb and her muscles were cramping terribly. She silently thanked the Virgin Mother that her hands were sticking to the oar handles. It was the only reason her arms had not fallen off. Yet.

John Macpherson peered in vain through the dense fog that enshrouded the *Great Michael.* Turning his eyes upward, he gazed for a moment at the mists that threaded in and out of the rigging, obscuring even the banner that he knew must be hanging limply at the top of the mainmast. In this inconstant March weather, there was no telling when a fog would lift.

Becalmed not long after sunrise, the ship had quickly been surrounded by the enveloping mist. It had rolled in like some heavy fleece and tucked around them. John had taken one last look at his other three ships bobbing on the flat sea a half mile or so away.

As the morning had slowly passed, the sound of muffled cannon fire had signaled a fierce battle being waged far to the south, but John and his crew had heard nothing now for hours. The ship's master turned his gaze to the south once more.

As if reading his thoughts, David Maxwell, the ship's navigator, stepped up to the railing beside his commander. "If we hadn't run into this windless fog, Sir John, we might have found ourselves in the middle of a lovely fight."

"Aye, David," John returned with a side look. "Not exactly the kind of action we were planning on this trip."

"Then as ungodly as this dismal mess seems, perhaps there's something providential in it, eh?"

"Perhaps so, Davy." The Highlander paused thoughtfully, then turned to acknowledge the short, thickset man who was just joining them. It occurred to John once again that throughout the early going of this journey, he couldn't turn around without finding Sir Thomas Maule a step away. Colin Campbell, the Earl of Argyll, had cautioned him about this beforehand, but John had not wished to make changes in their traveling plans. After all, Sir Thomas—despite the extreme possessiveness he demonstrated in matters regarding what he considered his own—was a good man, and the Highlander did not want the aging knight excluded from the honor of bringing home Scotland's next queen.

Truthfully, John knew the problem did not lie with Sir Thomas, in any case. The difficulty lay in the fact that Sir Thomas's bride, who was accompanying them on this journey, was none other than Caroline Douglas, a woman known to all as John Macpherson's former mistress. But as far as John was concerned, everyone was also well aware of the fact that the rocky affair between them had ended long before the lady accepted the hand of Sir Thomas Maule in marriage. In John's opinion, Caroline was now only an old acquaintance. Nothing more.

"Well, navigator," the stocky man queried, "how far to the south do you think those guns were this morning?"

"Hard to tell, Sir Thomas," David responded carefully. "As any sailor can tell you, the fog can do tricky things to the sound. That fighting could have been ten leagues south of us, or two. I wouldn't want to wager my share on a guess about it."

"I should have hoped for a better report than that, lad. But perhaps you're lacking in experience." Sir Thomas Maule turned in the direction of the ship's commander. "And you, Sir John? Would you care to wager on the distance?"

"Nay, I agree with David," John responded, glancing at the navigator's angry face. "We'd be fools to let down our guard completely, assuming them far away. Whoever they were, the chances are that one of them tasted blood and may be hungry for more. And we'd be fools to assume them too close, losing all sense and exhausting our men with extra watches for no purpose. The fog will shield us from them for now. And when the mists lift,

and we get some wind in our sails, we'll have time
enough to decide whether we need to fight. In any case,
we're prepared for whatever action is needed."

"If this were any other mission, Sir John"—Thomas
Maule nodded seriously, patting the long sword at his
side—"I wouldn't mind a little action."

"But on the sea, Sir Thomas, battles differ greatly
from those on the land," David cautioned pointedly, still
bristling from the knight's words. "A strong arm and a
mighty sword are all for naught when there is no solid
ground for your footing."

John held back his smile. The voyage from Edinburgh's seaport at Leith had already taken too long for
his men's liking. Most of them, as pleased as they were
to look upon the pleasing faces of noblemen's wives and
daughters, had little respect for the shallow shows of
courtly behavior by the husbands and fathers. Having
a group of land-dwelling nobles onboard had already
presented a number of problems with the rough and
plain-speaking sailors of the *Great Michael,* though nothing had, as yet, gotten out of hand. But John could only
guess at the problems of discipline that would accompany their trip back to Scotland. After all, they would
have a queen and her entourage to contend with.

"For us who fought in the muck at Flodden, laddie,"
the squat warrior retorted, squaring off with the young
navigator, "no deck made of wood will ever be cause
for alarm."

"Aye, Sir Thomas," John broke in, trying to head off
what he knew could quickly develop into a full-fledged
brawl. "As you say, were this any other mission. But for
now, you might make yourself comfortable. We could
be in for quite a long wait. Thank you, navigator."

David Maxwell, perceiving the hint from his master,
bowed slightly to the two noblemen and detached himself from them. John watched the navigator as he
worked his way forward, the white feather in the young
man's bright blue cap bobbing cheerfully as he stopped
and talked with each sailor that he passed.

"That lad," Sir Thomas began, staring after him, as

well, "he's lacking all sense of rank and position, wouldn't you say?"

John continued to watch his man. "We all have our flaws, Sir Thomas. But David Maxwell is as sharp as the blade of your dirk, and he fears no man. David's as loyal to Scotland as any man alive, though he may be, perhaps, just a wee bit proud of his seagoing mates." He turned and looked at the stocky fighter beside him. "These folk who sail the high seas have as much right to be called warriors and heroes as those who fight on land. But most have not been credited as such."

Sir Thomas rubbed his sausagelike fingers thoughtfully over his chin.

"And being a man who has spent his whole life in the service of his country," John continued, "you know, perhaps better than most, the reasons that drive a young man like him."

The elder man nodded slightly.

"He is the best navigator I've ever seen." John turned his gaze back to the scene before him. "He's been to the New World, and he's gone around Africa, clear to India. David Maxwell is a fine young man, Sir Thomas."

There was not much more to be said. Sir Thomas knew that quietly, discreetly, he'd just been set down a peg, though he was damned if he could figure out just how. These Macphersons, and this one in particular, had a way of making you feel . . . well, muddled somehow.

Sir Thomas turned to watch as two white sea birds, like a pair of ghosts, swooped out of the mists not far above their heads. They circled through the rigging, alighting finally on one of the great wooden booms. There, the two birds sat nervously, as if assessing their unexpected good fortune in finding the ship. Suddenly and without warning, one of the birds, peeking viciously and crying out as if it were being murdered, drove the other from their perch. As the knight continued to watch, the bird glared at the other where it landed not far off.

A bit uncomfortable, he stood beside the giant Highlander. Sir Thomas knew that part of the problem stemmed from a gnawing urge he felt to compare himself with John Macpherson. He knew his wife was comparing them every moment. And it hurt him to accept the truth, since he felt so helpless against it. He lacked the fine looks, the build, the great strength. And he lacked the youth. John Macpherson was in the prime of his life, and something inside the aging warrior made him want to hate the man. Made him want to fight him, to scar that handsome face. But how could he? With what accusation? For what reason?

Sir Thomas's face clouded as he forced himself to bury his feelings inside. They made no sense. Nothing made sense.

Why his beautiful young bride had chosen him—an aging man with a daughter her own age—over this young and striking warrior, certainly made no sense. The fact was that John Macpherson had shared Caroline's bed for years before him, and try as he might, Sir Thomas could not push away the thought that every time he took her to bed, perhaps Caroline was imagining John Macpherson in his place.

And Sir Thomas had heard the murmuring at court. The talk that it was only a matter of time before the Highlander would recognize his loss and go after his longtime lover. But that, too, seemed to make no sense. The man had never shown any hint of such interest. No interest at all. Caroline had remained in their cabin and Sir John on deck. And yet, even that, in a way, irked Sir Thomas. Three days of traveling at sea and the two had not even met.

The situation was beginning to torture him, and he wished they had not come.

John Macpherson looked on in silence as the watch changed. From the forecastle, a half dozen men emerged, saluting their leader before scurrying nimbly up the dripping lines of the rigging to their posts aloft. A few moments later, the sailors who'd been relieved began to work their way down to the deck, disappearing forward into the crew's quarters.

With the exception of Sir Thomas, the members of

the delegation of nobles who were sailing on the *Great Michael* had hardly stepped foot on deck at all. This certainly suited John.

In the few brief instances when he'd joined them below, John had found the conversations consisted of the same idle prattle he'd found in every court in Europe. The last time the Highlander had been below-decks, one of the ranking nobles had tried to engage his opinion on Mary of Hungary and her apparent inability to bear any children by her late husband. A bad sign, the nobleman had whispered gravely to the nodding heads around the table. The future queen, he'd said, shaking his head. Barren, undoubtedly. And what would become of the Stuart line then?

But John had shrugged them off without responding. His duties certainly did not include fortune-telling.

The Highlander had no patience for such drivel and had moved off, hardly concealing his distaste. And, of course, he moved off with Sir Thomas in tow.

Leaning out over the side of the vessel, John eyed the sturdy timbers of the hull and considered the knight for a moment. He knew Sir Thomas was keeping an eye on him. And that was perfectly acceptable to him. In fact, remembering Caroline's style of love play, he had wondered at times if she had already started her games, had begun to make Sir Thomas wild with jealousy. Knowing her so well, John was prepared to respond should the time come, but he was still not sure if her unfortunate husband even knew the game was on.

The Highlander's face grew grim. He knew the going could get rough, perhaps even bloody, depending on Sir Thomas. Indeed, if he could get through his voyage without having to deal with Caroline Maule, he would count the trip as miraculous.

"Tell me, if you would, Sir John, your opinion." Sir Thomas ran his heavy hands thoughtfully over the wet railing. "How is it that the Holy Roman Emperor Charles, the most powerful monarch this side of Suleiman the Magnificent, agrees to let us convey his sister to her new husband?"

"Tradition, I assume," John responded after a pause, glad to see that the man beside him had found an agreeable topic to converse upon. "And the nature of the bargain. If we lose her, there'll be war to settle the affair—along with a certain demand for the return of the first dowry payment that the lord chancellor's presently keeping in Stirling Castle."

The older man hesitated for a moment, searching for the right words for what was on his mind. "It can all be a . . . nasty business. Can it not?" he asked at last under his breath. "Marriage, I mean."

"Many believe that to be the case, Sir Thomas."

"It doesn't need to be, you know." The man continued to stare down at his hands and the dark wood beneath them. "As one who is going through it a second time, I tend to see it differently."

John nodded noncommittally.

"I am inclined to believe that not only royal marriages, but that most betrothals—even among the lowliest—are often ruined by the financial motives that so often bring two families, and hence, a man and a woman, together." Sir Thomas turned and eyed the warrior. "What's your opinion on the topic, Sir John?"

The Highlander knew what he was asking, and he did not mind to speak the truth.

"I have not found this to be the case in my own personal experience, Sir Thomas. But I believe you are correct in what you say. However, I do believe there are exceptions. And once a union is formed, perhaps love can create the truly lasting bond."

"Ah. But what do you think the elements are that foster that difference in a marriage. That give some people such an edge, such a chance for lasting happiness?"

John stared out at the wisps of fog that continued to rise and settle around the ship. Though it halted the progress of his mission, there was real beauty in the mist. If only he knew the answer to the man's question. His face clouded over.

"You are speaking to the wrong man, Sir Thomas."

There was silence. Even though her name had not

been mentioned yet, this was the closest the two had
ever come to discussing Caroline.

"You are the last of your brothers to wed." Sir
Thomas was determined.

John turned and looked at him. "That's true."

"If you truly believe what you've just said, then what
is it that's held you back? Marriage, by all accounts, suits
the Macphersons well. They seem to be among those
exceptions you speak of. They seem to be among the
happy few." The elder warrior's eyes were piercing. "So
why not you?"

The Highlander paused. He wanted to give a quick
answer and put the man's mind at ease. But he couldn't.
How could he speak of the happiness that he saw in his
own brothers' marriages without sounding envious of
their great joy?

He could have asked Caroline to be his wife. Many
thought he would. Their intermittent affair had lasted
nearly seven years. But still, when it had come to the
end, when she'd demanded an answer, taking her as wife
was a choice he couldn't make. He'd let her go.

She was not Fiona, nor was she Elizabeth. Those
women whom John's brothers had been fortunate
enough to wed were rare creatures, and the Highlander
knew it. Caroline was not like them, and what had existed between the two of them was far different from
what he had seen in his family. They shared their moments of physical passion, sure enough, but real love had
never been within their grasp. And passion with Caroline was not a particularly suitable subject of discussion,
at the moment.

"My answer," John said at last, "is that I have not
felt . . . inclined to marry. Not yet."

"Then . . . no second thoughts?" Sir Thomas asked
quietly.

John met his direct gaze. Surprisingly, there was no
hostility in the man's honest face. John knew it was his
right to ask.

"None. None at all."

*   *   *

The loud squawk of a seabird somewhere overhead brought the older woman back to the present.

Isabel leaned forward, hiding a wince and looking concernedly at her niece. My God, she thought, what had she done? The torn and bloodied cloak that was draped over the young woman was in better shape than the creature within. Isabel looked at a bruise on Maria's forehead, and the new one on her chin. She saw the pale skin and bloodless lips. Maria's eyes had lost their shine and had taken on a vacant look. She could hardly believe this was the same princess and queen, the same woman renowned for such flawless beauty. Isabel inwardly cursed herself for seeking out the child, for suggesting that if she was so unhappy, then she should go against her brother's will in the matter of this senseless marriage. Isabel cursed herself for putting her niece into the position of dying on this floating nightmare.

Charles, where are you? she called out silently. For once in your life, react with some decisiveness to your aunt's foolishness. Come after us, my boy. Come after your sister. Come, Charles.

When she broke the silence, her tone was decidedly softer.

"Oh, Maria. I do wish I could be of some help. Surely, one of the other longboats from our galleon will be catching up to us soon."

Maria's eyes shot up at once at Isabel's change of tone. Then she smiled. For all her gruff words and exterior, she knew the older woman to be one of the most loving creatures alive.

"I'd like to think so, too. But we've been rowing in this fog for hours now." She looked around her. Since separating from their sinking ship, they had not seen anything at all. No people, no boats, not even floating wreckage. Nothing. "We don't have any idea where we are or where we're going."

"Don't be silly, child," Isabel chided. "You've been keeping us on a course as straight as an arrow shot. A very good job indeed, considering it is your first time at this sort of thing. We should land in Denmark anytime now."

Maria smiled weakly in the direction of her aunt. "Or England in about a month!"

"Now, child." Isabel scolded half-heartedly while trying to peer through the dense mist.

Maria watched her aunt's expression. At last she had shown signs of awareness, her complaints silenced. For the first time since disaster had found them, it seemed that Isabel was seeing the real danger. In the pandemonium on the burning ship, the men lowering the longboats amidst shouts and panic, there had been no time to think. They had spotted the French warship less than a day out of Antwerp, and then the chase had been on. Their mistake had been flying the Spanish flag—the flag of the Silver Fleet. That had given the French motive enough to attack. Every pirate and privateer in the German Sea knew of the treasure troves of silver and gold that the Spaniards were bringing back by the shipload from the New World.

At the first exchange of cannon fire, the captain had turned their small ship in an effort to flee to the north, hoping the open seas and the high winds would give them the edge. But he had been wrong. The French ship had been faster. From that point on, everything in Maria's mind tumbled together in a whirlwind of action. Shots, swords, screaming men. Blood. She rubbed her cheek against her shoulder and wiped away the tears that were stinging her eyes and spilling over.

"I am sorry, Maria."

The younger woman stopped her rowing and looked at her aunt.

"I am sorry for this. For bringing you with me." Isabel slumped backward and looked skyward. "At my age, you would think I should have more wisdom, more insight into the demons running loose in the world."

"But you do, Isabel. I value your wisdom."

She turned her gaze back to her niece and smiled gently. "I should not have tried to interfere in your future.

I should have left you to the comforts of the life that you have always been accustomed to."

Maria leaned over the oars and tried to get closer to the older woman. This was not the aunt she had always known talking. This was fear of what lay ahead. Thoughts of the end. "Don't say these things to me, Isabel. You and I both know what you did was right."

"But it wasn't. Can't you see?" she cried. "This is the final proof of it. Do you know how many times I have sailed between Antwerp and Spain in my life? Hundreds of times. And only once—twenty years ago—did any ship I was on ever come under attack. But this time—"

"You've had good luck in the past. That's all. My luck is different." Maria tried to gather all her strength. She could not allow Isabel to blame herself. Taking her life in her own hands. Seeing what the world had to offer. These were the very things that she herself had wanted for so long. "My dearest Isabel. We might die here at sea, or we might become fish bait, as you so delicately put it, but know the truth! I would welcome such a death rather than accept once again . . . so meekly . . . the life Charles has negotiated for me."

"Choosing death over a life as the Queen of Scotland!" Isabel rolled her eyes. "You are being too dramatic, child."

"I am not," she said matter-of-factly. "This flight . . . this trip . . . sailing with you for Mother's castle in Castile. This has been the only thing I have done in my twenty-three years of living that has been of my own free will. It's not Scotland that is the problem. Do you know how painful it is to have your life planned from the age of three? I have been told whom to befriend and whom not to befriend, what to do and what not to do, where to go and where not to go. Whom to marry and whom not to marry. And all that . . . twice!"

Isabel could not help the smile that broke across her lips.

"I know, my dear. I know. But all this ordering about you've been subjected to—even twice—has never been able to so much as dampen your spirits. Never!"

"But it has." Maria couldn't stop the tears that were rolling down her face. "This time, this second marriage, this desire of Charles to have a Habsburg on every throne in Christendom. This Scottish business . . . it was my undoing, the stone that crushed me. I cannot go through with it."

Isabel just watched. She'd known it. As agreeable and submissive as Maria had always been, who could be surprised that she might not relish the idea of marrying a second time? And once again to an adolescent, sixteen-year-old king. The idea was unthinkable. To everyone except Charles, that is. He could not see the match as dismal, but Isabel could. And that's why she'd come for Maria.

"If, God willing, we survive this," Isabel said, "you know that your brother will come after you, don't you? If we are lucky enough to reach Castile, he'll lay siege to your mother's castle, if need be."

Maria nodded. "Of course. He'll expect me to honor his agreement. To go through with this dreadful marriage."

"What will you do then, child?" Isabel asked. "We must decide on our plan."

As she continued to pull on the oars, Maria watched the blood trickling from her hands and dripping blackly onto the gray wool of her dress. She could not and would not go to Scotland. She would refuse to marry James V. She would disobey her clever, manipulative brother.

"I will become insane. They will see that I have become what my mother was before me. They call her Juana the Mad. Before I'm through, they'll give me the same title. It will be quite believable. Like mother, like daughter. I will rant and rave and howl at the moon. I'll out-Herod Herod in my madness. I'll tear at my dresses, weave bones in my hair, and run naked in the rain."

There was silence. Maria looked up and saw the wide-eyed expression of her aunt. Isabel was trying to speak, but no words left her mouth. Only a strange croaking sound. Maria watched her mouth open and close again.

"What, Aunt?"

"Run!" Isabel's voice was a raw whisper. "Run like mad."

Maria's head snapped around only to see a huge ship looming just yards away, rising up out of the fog like some ghostly apparition. She had never seen a ship this large. But by the time her weary brain could register the reason for her aunt's fear, it was too late. The small float crashed forcefully against the ship's black hull.

Maria had forgotten to stop rowing.

She was no sailor.

Chapter 3

Like a snake striking out at his prey, the sailor's line shot out toward the pitching longboat.

The small craft bobbed helplessly at the ship's side. Aboard the *Great Michael*, a crowd of seamen lined the rail and hung from the rigging, straining for a clear look through the thick, concealing mists, ready for action. The occupants of the longboat made no move to board the larger ship, and the Scottish sailors waited impatiently, casting quick, questioning glances at their commander for their next move.

"Where in hell did that boat come from?" John Macpherson exploded, pushing through the rugged throng.

"It looks like it's a solitary boat, m'lord," his navigator replied. "And only three men, at that."

"Bring them up!" he ordered sharply.

"Is that wise?" a voice broke in.

John did not even turn to acknowledge the question from the tall, blonde-haired woman who glided quickly to his side. Caroline.

"What happens if they are armed?" she continued. "Even if they pretend to be friendly, isn't it possible they could cut all our throats as we sleep?"

Without answering, John turned his head and frowned threateningly at Sir Thomas.

"Come, come, Caroline," her husband offered gently, taking his wife by the elbow and pulling her from the railing in an effort to avoid any unpleasantness with the angry Highlander. This was not the time or place. "I think Sir John is the man to decide that."

John continued to peer over the side as a number of his men lowered themselves down the ropes.

"*Women,* m'lord!" came the return shout from one of the sailors. "Two women and a man."

The cry drew a slew of astonished men to the edge. John leaned forward, watching as another sailor scurried down the side. "Bring them up! Now!"

"They're bloody Spaniards, m'lord!"

"I don't care if they're the devil's own sisters!" John shouted angrily.

"This one's dead, m'lord," the sailor called up, pointing at the male in the bow of the boat. "He's got a hole in his chest the size of my fist."

"Bring them up!"

"Even the dead one?"

"For God's sake, man!" John fumed, his patience gone. "Aye! Of course, the dead one."

The sailors below, hearing the fury in their commander's tone, hastily secured the boat to the ship and started at once.

Seeing at last that his men were hustling, John stepped back, letting the ship's mate take charge. Turning around, he stopped short at the sight of the delegation crowding around him. For the first time since they'd left port, the noblemen and women had found something entertaining enough to draw them out of their comfortable cabins. Like a bunch of children, they were jostling one another for a better view of the newcomers.

And he didn't like it a bit. His men didn't need the distraction. Not now.

Moving toward Sir Thomas, who was standing with Caroline and his daughter Janet by the mainmast, John spoke to him quietly. A few words were all that were needed to be said, and the aging warrior leaped into action. John knew this was exactly what the knight desired. A chance to be involved and a chance to be useful.

Turning back to the railing, John ignored the cacophony of complaints resulting from Sir Thomas's blunt efforts to usher as many of the women and men as he could belowdecks.

Refusing the offers of help from the pushing throng remaining on deck, the Highlander silently thanked God that so far during this journey they'd been spared any attack at sea. Not that the *Great Michael* couldn't hold her own in any fight, but John was sure that the chaos he would have to deal with onboard would be much more difficult than any enemy assault.

Moving through the crowd, John saw David and the mate carefully helping an elderly woman down onto the deck from the rail. From the blood-soaked cloak, it was obvious that she had sustained an injury. John held back an instant as she took the arm of one of his men and tried to walk a few steps. Not being able to support her weight, however, she suddenly leaned heavily against the sailor and sank slowly to the deck.

John moved hastily to the woman and crouched before her.

"She is wounded," a woman said from behind him. "Her shoulder."

John turned toward the strained voice of the other survivor who had just been brought aboard. He noticed how, once onboard, she politely but firmly rejected the assistance of his men. As she crossed to where the older woman lay, she wobbled a bit, but quickly regained her footing. The lass is a mess, he thought, giving her dripping clothes and jumbled tangle of hair a cursory glance. She, too, sported black spots on her torn, gray dress that he was sure had to be blood, but she didn't appear to be in as grave a danger as the older woman. Whatever their condition now, these women had obviously survived an ordeal far more serious than a row in the cold fog.

Taking his eyes away from the other, John pulled back the blood-soaked cloak gently and looked at the wound on the older woman's shoulder. These two must be survivors of the battle they'd heard earlier today. The older one had received what—from the burn on the surrounding skin—looked like a wound from a musket shot. But the damage was not life threatening, he decided, should the injury not fester.

"Ship's mate," he called over his shoulder, "have the surgeon up on deck to look at her wound."

Then he stood and turned to look at the other woman, who now stood only a step away.

Maria saw him rise and her breath caught in her chest. Crouching before Isabel, the man had not looked as intimidating as he did now. A fierce scowl clouding his swarthy face, he towered over every man on deck. Quickly, she tore her eyes away from him and fixed her attention on her aunt's face. She did not dare to look up.

"And you," he asked shortly. "Any injury?"

"None," she whispered simply, turning and stumbling once more as she knelt beside Isabel.

John looked at the small, water-soaked figure at his feet, and his heart warmed to the bedraggled creature. He'd heard the tremble in her voice. There was a child-like quality about her—an uncertainty—that made him wonder for a moment from what depths she had conjured the strength to survive the ordeal of being adrift at sea.

The gray wool dress that the woman wore beneath her cloak must have been clean at one time, but it was now ruined with dark stains and seawater. Almost as though she could read his thoughts, the young woman pulled her heavy cloak tighter around her, making it nearly impossible for John to ascertain anything more about her.

Laying her fingers lightly on her aunt's cold, limp hand, Maria fought off the desire to run away from the gaze of the giant standing behind her. She could feel his eyes burning into her even as she tended to Isabel. For a brief moment, she thought that perhaps the mariner knew who she was, but her attention was diverted as her aunt began to murmur in her unconscious state. It didn't matter what this man knew or didn't know—there was not much she could do about it, and Isabel needed to be cared for. That was all that mattered.

She seemed quite young, John thought, but a strange bittersweet sensation swept over the Highlander as it occurred to him that nearly every woman he met now seemed to be quite young. The attention she showed to the other indicated that they must be related somehow. Mother and daughter perhaps.

"There is blood on your cloak. Are you certain you have no wounds?"

"None," she responded evenly. "It's the sailor's blood. Not mine."

She did not even turn her head when she answered, but he could see the shiver. The shock, John thought. Being cold and wet and left in a boat drifting at sea can test the mettle of the toughest men.

"Are there other boats coming?" he asked. "Other survivors?"

"None that we saw," she whispered.

"How long were you in the boat?"

"Long."

"How long?"

She didn't answer, only shrugged her shoulders in return.

"Did your ship sink?"

She didn't answer again. As interesting as she was, John found himself quickly becoming tired of speaking to the back of the woman's head.

"Where's the bloody surgeon?" he asked irritably over his shoulder, and moving—as he spoke—to the other side of the injured woman's body. There, he crouched, facing the young woman.

"He's coming m'lord," the ship's mate responded, pushing into the circle.

"Who attacked you and how many ships were involved in the fight?" John asked, forcing his voice onto a more even keel.

Maria stared at her aunt's closed eyes. Isabel was resting, at least. But she still couldn't bring herself to lift her gaze and look at the man. She felt vulnerable, lost, and she fought to hide the tremors that were going through her body. She didn't have to look about her to know that she was encircled by dozens of curious spectators watching her every move, hanging on her every word. Like a prize doe, hunted and injured and brought to bay at last, she felt quite trapped. What were they going to do to them? The giant, the one asking the questions, was clearly in command, and the others obviously feared him. She knew she should, as well. He had called them the devil's sisters.

"I need to know these things." His voice was sharper than he intended, but still John reached over and tapped the woman gently on the shoulder. "How many ships?"

"Just one." Her gaze flitted briefly to his face, but dropped immediately.

Her eyes were the color of bright jade, and John found himself staring as she lowered them. They were the most beautiful color, set in a face devoid of color. The paleness of her complexion only served to heighten the stunning effect of her green eyes.

"A French ship," she continued. "Only one."

John nodded. Looking into her face, he found himself at a loss for words. Letting his eyes turn from the young woman's face to her exposed hands, he could see them trembling as they clutched the older woman's cloak. His eyes traveled up again quickly to her face. She was indeed young, very young. Beyond the pallid, dirty face and a tangle of black hair, he could see there existed a terrified, young woman.

A thin, drunken rattle of a voice could be heard on the outside of the throng of men surrounding them. The surgeon, a member of the Douglas clan and a man that John was sure had been sent along as Angus's spy, slowly approached. He was a puffy, bleary-eyed monk with more of an interest in wine and a soft bunk than the welfare of either his fellow men or their souls. John's face clouded with anger once again as he watched him taking his time in answering his summons.

"We'll talk later," the Highlander growled, standing at once as the surgeon sidled through the crowd. Ignoring the man, John gestured sharply to the mate. "The woman's been out in this damp air long enough. Take her below; the surgeon can see to her there."

"I shall stay with her?" Maria asked, quickly rising to her feet and turning to the ship's commander. The inflection of her words wavered between that of a command and a plea.

This time their eyes met, but only for an instant, before Maria averted her gaze in embarrassment.

"Aye," John responded, "of course. I'll look in on you in a short while. My men will see to your needs. There are still questions that need to be answered."

She nodded, then stood silently, waiting for the men to move her aunt.

There was very little space to clean up, and nowhere to spread out her wet, soiled clothes in the small room adjoining the large cabin where Isabel had been taken. A young boy had entered the cabin right behind them as they arrived and had, without a word, handed her a woolen dress and some linen undergarments. Maria had been thankful for the thoughtfulness of the gesture, but had not really known whom to thank. On deck, she'd seen many gentlemen and women standing about, dressed in the latest courtly fashions. Thinking about it now, she was surprised at the number of women aboard ship. Clearly, it was one of those ladies to whom she owed her gratitude.

Holding up her wet garments, she scanned the room helplessly. From where she was, Maria could hear the murmuring voices of her aunt, who had thankfully regained consciousness, and then the sound of shuffling feet moving out into the corridor. Finally giving up on the clothes, she placed them in a neat pile in the corner. There was a small wash bowl and pitcher set into a board along one wall of the tiny cabin, so Maria carefully swabbed at the painful open blisters of her palms and fingers. Wrapping strips of linen dressing around her hands, she tried unsuccessfully to tuck under the ends of the bandages. Having both hands reduced to nothing more than raw flesh made it almost impossible. Besides, even at this she was a novice. She shook her head with disgust. Unskilled in even the simplest of tasks.

With frustration and disappointment pulling at her, Maria tearfully jerked the wide, forest-green sleeves of the woolen dress down over her wrists. Then, dashing a glistening droplet from her cheek, she yanked open a narrow door and stepped into Isabel's more spacious cabin.

Her aunt's gaze traveled to her at once from where she lay. Maria watched as the older woman put her finger to her lips, hushing her for the moment. The young woman complied and stood back, waiting as the surgeon's boy gathered together the bloodied dressings from the small table.

"You were lucky, m'lady," the surgeon rasped, reentering the spacious cabin. "The ball just grazed you. But your sailor had no chance."

"Then he is dead?" Isabel asked.

"Aye. Dead and gone to his Maker." He glanced back at the older woman. "Sir John wants to know the man's name. For the prayers when we put him into the sea."

"I . . . I don't know it," Isabel said with embarrassment, looking at Maria.

"His name was Pablo," the young woman whispered quietly. Maria had asked him as she struggled to take his place at the oars. But she knew his soul had reached his Maker long before their prayers would.

"Pablo," the man repeated shortly, turning to Isabel. "Very well. Tell me, was it your ship? The one that went down?"

Isabel shook her head quickly in denial. "Nay, it wasn't." She was not about to tell this man any more than was necessary.

"Ah, well." The man started for the door, but then stopped before Maria and pointed to a small bowl of liquid and some clean dressings. "I'll leave these with you. You might change her dressing if it begins to smell badly. And Sir John will be down directly. He appears to be impatient to have some questions answered. But don't worry about your mother, my dear. She is going to be fine."

"She is not—" Maria caught herself. "—not going to die, then?"

"Nay, lass," the man wheezed wearily, before turning

again for the door. "I've given her something to make
her sleep. I'll send the lad back in a wee bit. If you need
me, have him fetch me."

Without any further ceremony, the man shuffled out
into the dark corridor with the young boy at his heels.

Maria waited until the cabin door was shut behind
them, then moved quickly to the side of her aunt's bed.

"They are Scots!" she said, her concern apparent in
her voice.

Isabel patted the blanket next to her, and Maria sat
down at once.

"I can see that, my dear," Isabel concurred, her eyes
taking in the elegant furnishings of the cabin. "And not
just any Scots. No doubt, this is part of the fleet that
your brother summoned to come and take you back to
their king."

Maria surveyed the cabin as well. Though her experience aboard ships was somewhat limited, the size of the
room surprised her. Running her swollen fingers over
the fold of crisp white linen that covered her aunt, Maria
glanced at the rich, burgundy damask drape that hung
around the bunk, and the matching coverlet. A window
seat beneath a small glazed window was covered with
velvet cushions, and carved chairs surrounded a table
that held fine crystal and several plates of cheese and
fruit. An odd discomfort spread through her as she realized where the ship's commander had put them.

"This was to be *my* cabin!" she cried in dismay.

"You aren't going to put your old auntie out, now?
Are you, dear?" The older woman chuckled.

"Don't be silly!" Maria took Isabel's hand. "But what
am I to do? What would they think if they find out who
we are?"

"Does it matter what they think?" Isabel yawned and
stretched her body in the comfortable bed.

"If I am to be their queen . . ." Maria whispered.

"You are right," Isabel agreed, keeping her voice low.
"If you *are* to be their queen, then I'd say, you have
already lost any chance at their respect. After all, you're
supposed to be sitting high and dry in Antwerp, waiting

for them to arrive, not rowing in the open seas in an effort to escape them. But that's assuming you ever do become their queen."

"I can't tell them who I am," Maria said decisively. "I am going to Castile, not to Scotland."

"You . . ." Isabel yawned again. "You are going to Antwerp, my dear. That's where they are headed."

Maria looked at her aunt helplessly. "But I can't. Can you imagine the embarrassment? I wouldn't be able to face Charles. He would never forgive me. Being found adrift at sea by the same people sent to convey me to their home. By the Virgin, the shame that would come of it."

"I thought none of this mattered. I thought you had resigned yourself to accept your brother's wrath."

"I *had* resigned myself," Maria said despondently. "But that was when I thought we could face him from afar. Not when I thought we'd be dragged back and handed right over to him. You know the power that he wields. How persuasive he is. Never in my life have I won an argument with him *tête-à-tête*."

Maria sighed. Though she hated the thought of it, since she was little, her brother had always had his own way. Charles was a bully as a child—he was just a more powerful one as an adult.

"Why can't we go on as we planned?" the young woman pleaded, fighting to keep the note of desperation out of her voice. "I don't want to go back, Isabel. I can't."

Maria watched her aunt fighting off the drowsiness that was overtaking her. "You ruined the longboat, child."

Maria could not help but smile. "You know very well that I don't mean rowing." She turned her head and stared at the small window. "We must find another way. We must be close to Denmark. If we can reach Copenhagen, perhaps we could hire another ship to take us to Castile."

Isabel opened one eye and tried to focus. "But it's too far to swim, Maria. And I'm just feeling warmer. . . ."

Maria watched the smile tug at her aunt's lips before the older woman visibly gave in to the effects of the medicine.

"We have to think of a plan," Maria whispered, mostly to herself. "I can't give up hope. Perhaps we can employ someone's help. There are many on this ship. . . ."

"The commander," Isabel said, her eyes fluttering open a bit. "The Scot. Sir John, they call him. He is a young and handsome man. Certainly as good-looking as any sailor *I* ever came across in my life."

"What does *that* have to do with anything?" Maria asked as she smoothed a silver tendril of hair from Isabel's face.

"Hmmph!" Isabel closed her eyes again. "And to think you've already been married once!"

"Isabel!" Maria protested, a blush reddening her cheeks. But her aunt was fast asleep.

Chapter 4

If there was one thing John Macpherson hated, it was being in the dark.

The wick lamp he was holding created a small orb of light in the gloom of the corridor, and as he lit the lantern hanging on the wall, John nodded to the young sailor guarding the cabin door.

"Any news?"

"None, m'lord," the man responded. "When I took the trencher of food in earlier, the older lady was asleep and the younger one was just pacing the room. She said nothing at all, m'lord. But I heard her latch the door when I went out."

John pushed past the man and rapped on the door.

A flurry of quick steps and the sound of someone struggling with a latch could be heard on the other side. There was a pause and then, as the door was opened slightly, the Highlander found himself staring down into a set of shining green eyes that peered apprehensively back at him.

"May I come in?"

She hesitated a moment, then turned and gestured vaguely into the darkness of the room. "My . . . She is sleep."

"I won't stay long," John said, ducking his head as he brushed past her and into the cabin.

Maria stood uncertainly by the open door, unsure of what to do. She couldn't object to his barging in; after all, this was his ship. With her throbbing hand still on the door latch, she pressed her back against the panel of the cabin wall. Outside the little window beyond the

huge Scot, the gloom had quickly deepened with the
onslaught of night, and the young woman welcomed the
growing darkness. She watched him as he gazed closely
at her aunt, and then at the pile of clean dressings and
bowl of water that sat on the table.

As he turned, the light of the lamp shone clearly on
his dark features. She could look at him from where she
stood without the fear of being noticed. What Isabel had
said was the truth. The man's features could be considered handsome. Extremely so. But in Maria's mind the
fierceness of his expression only served to mask his fine
looks. She let her eyes linger. His massive shoulders
seemed to fill the room. He was a powerful man. His
black hair was worn long, but tied back with a leather
thong. She watched as his eyes carefully surveyed the
cabin.

Sensing that he was being watched, John swung the
lamp back in her direction, and saw the young woman
turn her eyes downward. She was a small thing, hidden
in the shadowy darkness. It occurred to him that she
would melt right into the dark panel behind her if she
could.

Now Maria knew it was her turn to be watched. Once
again, she fought the fear that was rising within her,
making her too apprehensive to look up at him, to return his gaze. The familiar flutter in her stomach told
her that once again she was unprepared—no, incapable
of dealing with life. With real life.

It was true. It hadn't been his looks or his behavior
that had brought out this fear in her. Maria knew it was
something else. All her life she'd been protected, iso-
lated from the company of men. Of her father, Philip
the Fair, she had no recollection. With the outpouring
of her mother's grief after the mysterious death of Philip,
Maria had been taken away and brought up surrounded
by women in a convent in Castile. She almost never saw
her brothers or even heard from them until the eldest,
the Emperor Charles, arranged for her to join her betrothed, the sixteen-year-old King of Hungary—the boy
king she'd been promised to at age three and then wed

to at seventeen. Until the moment she left the safety of the convent walls, Maria had never—aside from her aged confessor—had any occasion to deal with any grown man directly.

Only when she had arrived in Hungary did she realize how vulnerable—how inept—that made her. She had not been prepared to deal either with life or with the people she met there.

Standing silently in the dimly lit cabin, she cursed her own weakness, but kept her gaze riveted to the wide planking of the floorboards. She had learned to mask her fears, in the role of queen. But stripped of those comfortable trappings, the entourage, and the space that ceremony provided, there was nothing for her to hide behind.

John continued to gaze in silence at the young woman standing awkwardly in the shadows by the door. Something about her made him feel uneasy. No question, there was certainly an air of mystery about the two new arrivals. She had mentioned they'd been attacked by a French ship. She must be afraid, considering the fact that Scotland and France had been closest of allies for more than a hundred years. What did she think, that he would hand them over to the same people who had tried to murder them? Aye, that was a possibility, and she did look terrified. Certainly, there was no way she knew what lay in store for them. And aside from the political uncertainties, these days of who is friend and who is foe, the fate of two women found adrift at sea could hardly be. perceived as promising . . . under the best of circumstances.

But from his own perspective and in the minds of those who lived on the sea, the fact that these two had survived such an ordeal was considered purely miraculous. Using their best estimates, the Spaniard in the long-boat had been dead for quite a while. Hours. So the survival of the two women had rested solely in their own hands.

Their own soft hands.

Maria watched as the Scot turned his attention back

on Isabel once again. With the lantern in his hand and his back to her, he leaned over the sleeping woman, seemingly looking for something. Maria summoned all of her courage, determined to move closer to Isabel's side. From the steady breathing, she knew her aunt was still fast asleep. But before she could take the first step, he swung around.

Maria remained frozen where she stood.

He strode across the deck toward her.

She pressed her back against the cabin wall, her hand releasing the latch and clasping her other hand behind her back. She thought his visit finished, so she stared at the shadowy wooden planks, waiting for him to go.

There was a long pause as he came to a stop before her. Maria could feel the heat of the lantern on her face. She pressed her weight against the wall, trying to get away. Why didn't he go? She lifted her eyes to his face.

Even in this dim light, his eyes were clear and deep and blue. Like an ocean wave they pulled at her. Like some small empty shell on the shore, Maria felt herself being drawn down into shifting sands, helplessly falling. Losing herself in the blue depths.

"Wait," he growled.

"What?" She flushed, looking quickly away.

"Wait here." The giant stepped through the door and gave the waiting sailor a quick order that sent him scurrying down the corridor.

Maria let out a breath and glanced nervously toward her aunt. She wished the older woman was awake. Isabel would have been so much better at handling this man than she herself could ever be. Maria peeked back at the door only to see the Scot reentering the cabin.

"I asked you before, lass, when we were on deck, if you were hurt."

As he stopped in front of her again, she dropped her gaze to the crisp white linen of his shirt. "You did."

"And are you?"

"I am not."

John brought the light closer to her face. He saw the dark bruise on her forehead; the short, clean cut on her chin; and the blush that was spreading rapidly on her cheeks. She had the smoothest and the palest of skins. And she still avoided his gaze.

"Why didn't you let my surgeon see to your injuries?"

"They are mere scratches."

John raised the light even closer. "The gash on your chin is oozing blood."

Maria's hand flew to her chin. He caught her wrist, and she grabbed at his fingers with her other hand. His grip was viselike, though, and in a flash of panic, she quickly realized he was not about to release her.

"Let me go," she whispered.

"Mere scratches?" John looked steadily into her startled face, and she abandoned her weak effort to resist. Her other hand fell limply to her side, and Maria looked away from him.

John turned her hand in his and pushed up the edges of the wide sleeve. He cast a critical eye on the bloody and loosely tied dressing on her hand.

Anger and rebellion suddenly shot through Maria as he studied the bandages, and she again tried to yank her hand out of his grasp, but he held her tightly. She shuddered in pain and gave up the struggle.

"Please let me go," she pleaded softly.

"Not until you let me see the extent of it."

"It's nothing serious," she whispered. "A bit of the skin rubbed off."

"Let me see them," he ordered. "Both of them."

For a moment the two stood glaring at one another. What right did he have to march in, taking charge of her well-being? Maria thought angrily. But the commander's silent stare answered her unasked query, and she looked away. He was in charge. In charge of his ship and all aboard her.

John stood patiently. He had all the time in the world. If she had the strength to stand up to him, as close as they were, and hide her one injured hand behind her while the other remained in his grip, then he was game. He could wait. But he knew she wouldn't prevail against his wishes. Not many could.

Maria hesitantly brought her other hand from behind her back. She was tired, and she was in pain. If seeing to her injured hands was what it would take to satisfy the man, then so be it, she thought.

"That's better," he grunted, satisfaction apparent in his voice. Turning her a bit, he placed the small lamp in a wall sconce.

John looked down at the poorly bandaged hands and loosened his grip on them. From the drying bloodstains on the cloth covering the palms, it was obvious that the skin was raw beneath. If he didn't rebandage them now, the cloths would adhere to the wound.

"What you did today took real courage." Pretending to concentrate on her hands, he didn't look up as she lifted her gaze. "I—"

The sailor knocked lightly and ducked into the cabin. Still holding her wrist, John gestured to the table. The man hurriedly placed the clay jar beside the pile of dressings. Then, with a nod at his commander, he left them alone, closing the door on his way out.

Turning to the young woman once again, John found her looking at him with questioning eyes.

He had to think hard to remember what he was about to say. Facing him fully, as she did now, she had the power of an enchantress. Her black hair, pulled tightly back, highlighted rather than subdued her perfect features. And her eyes. They flashed like polished jade. He felt the magic holding him captive.

"I am John Macpherson," he said at last.

She nodded politely, dropping her hands to her sides.

"And you?" he asked.

She threw a panicky glance in Isabel's direction. She was snoring.

"Your name?"

"Maria," she whispered.

"Maria . . ." He waited.

She paused. "Maria. My family name is of no importance to you."

In spite of the note of defiance in her answer, John could read the hesitation and fear in her visage and in her stance. He had to put her mind at ease. No doubt she thought he would try to ransom her back to her family. That was not an uncommon practice with shipwreck survivors. But that was not his intention. And, perhaps because he had just succeeded in bending her to his will, he now felt the need to convince this young woman that she and her companion were in no danger. He had no intention of taking advantage of their misfortune.

"Well . . . Maria. I assume you must be curious about this ship and our destination."

She nodded slowly as she considered her best course of action. It definitely would not do to let him know what she and Isabel already had surmised. The best thing for her to do now was simply to listen, to offer nothing, and to let him talk. She raised her eyes expectantly to his face.

"You are on the Scottish ship the *Great Michael* heading for Antwerp. As soon as this fog lifts, we are only perhaps three days from port, depending on the wind. Once we arrive, you should have no trouble finding passage on another ship . . . to wherever you were originally going. Unless, of course, your original destination was Antwerp." He paused deliberately, waiting for her reaction. He could read the obvious struggle playing across her features as she half turned away from him. "I want you to know you are safe on this boat, lass. You should harbor no fears concerning any treatment you'll receive from me or from any of my men."

"Thank you." She turned her gaze back to him, nodding in acknowledgment. There was no reason why she shouldn't believe everything he'd just said. From the first moment that they had stepped aboard his ship, she and Isabel had been treated with the utmost care and respect.

"Now, if you'd allow me, I would like to see to your hands."

Maria instinctively hid them in the folds of her skirt, her face reddening. If nothing else, the man was tenacious, but it didn't matter how uncomfortable his atten-

tions made her feel. Yet what if he should ask more
questions? she thought. True, the man was kind. And
gentle. And handsome. But so dangerous, she thought.
It was becoming evident to Maria that the more time
she spent with the man, the more difficult it would be
to defy him. Never mind lie to him. And yet, within her,
gratitude vied with discretion for dominance.

"But they are fine," she said at last, of her hands.

"They are not." He came closer. "The dressing on
them is already soaked with blood. If they are not
tended to right now, the wounds will likely become inflamed. You could end up being in much graver danger
than your sleeping companion."

"There's no need, I tell you," she protested. "I can
change the dressing."

"Nay, lass, you can't. But that's not the only thing
that needs to be done." Seeing her retreat, he stopped.
"Of course, if you don't trust me, I could ask my surgeon
to come back and see to them. He has a tried-and-true
remedy that he uses on the sailors whenever they encounter such injuries. And it is quite effective. I'm surprised he didn't use it on your companion."

"I would like that, if you don't mind," Maria responded. Having the old surgeon look at her hands was
the answer. After all, he'd done some good for Isabel.
And honestly, though she would do her best to ignore
the pain, the throbbing seemed to be getting worse. As
tired as she was after the day-long ordeal, somehow she
couldn't imagine getting much sleep with such discomfort. "Perhaps, if it isn't too late to ask him—"

"Nay, that suits me, as well," John lied. "But he cannot tend you here. Perhaps we could take you below to
the galley. There is far less chance there of you waking
up your friend with your screaming."

"Screaming!"

John kept a straight face as he nodded in response.
Her eyes were wide, her complexion paler than before.
"Aye, of course!"

"What does he use?" she asked at last. "Your surgeon, I mean."

"To be truthful, lass, you'd be better off not knowing," he said gravely. He took a half-step toward the door. "I'll just call and let him get started."

"Wait!" she said, a note of command in her tone.

John turned and looked at her expectantly.

Her voice was softer when she spoke. "What is it that he'll do?"

The Highlander hesitated . . . for effect. "He'll seal the wound with boiling oil."

Maria shuddered in disgust and backed up. "That is barbaric."

"Aye. But it works. In fact," he said, glancing over at Isabel, "it has been the standard treatment for gun wounds for . . . oh, thirty years, I'd say. But perhaps he didn't want to listen to your companion's screams."

She shook her head. "Never. I won't let him touch me."

John watched as she pressed her back solidly against the wall. "Then you'll allow me to look after you?"

"Is your treatment any better?"

"Aye, some."

"Let me guess." She looked at him doubtfully. "You'll cut off my hands to spare me the pain before pouring boiling oil on them."

"Now, that's barbaric." He cringed, mocking her. Seeing her expression relax, the Highlander continued, a slow grin tugging at his lips. "Nay, I won't use boiling oil. The oil may be needed for other . . . more important uses on the ship."

"I see." Maria struggled to quell the sudden urge to laugh. The boyishness of his smile made a vast and surprising difference in the Scot's fierce looks. It gave them a gentleness. Maria wondered at herself. It was absurd to entertain the feelings that were running through her—the softening that she could feel inside. She placed the back of a hand against her forehead. Perhaps she was becoming feverish.

"Since your oil is so valuable," she continued, "then I suppose you'll just cut my hands off."

"Nay, that won't do. Far too messy."

"And you expect me to trust you," she blurted out, "after telling me what you'll not do, but hiding what you intend to do!"

"Aye. What else!" John took a step closer and stretched out his hand in invitation.

"Such an answer won't do. Not at all." She remained where she stood. "I need to know more of what you're planning. Who knows? Your surgeon's remedy might be a blessing relative to what you have in mind."

"Trust me. It isn't." John smiled at last at her stubborn refusal. "I plan to apply a remedy to your hands," he said gently. Still holding his hand out to her, it suddenly became quite important to him that he have her trust. "And I promise, it won't hurt . . . much."

"Then you must plan on knocking me unconscious, since I can't imagine anyone touching my hands without causing me extreme agony."

John looked at her wide-eyed expression. "A moment ago, they were 'mere scratches.' Now we're talking 'agony'! Which is it, lass?"

"Well, I . . ."

"There are a number of folks on this ship that I'd like to knock unconscious." He saw the confusion playing across her features. "But you aren't among their number."

Maria waited a moment, looking as he gestured once again for her to respond to his outstretched hand. The giant was not going to give up. Truthfully, he'd exhibited more patience than she'd expected. Finally, she yielded with a sigh and laid her hand, palm up, in his.

"Aye, that's the spirit." John turned and led her to the table. Pulling out a chair, he gestured to her to sit.

Maria sat down apprehensively, her back straight as a longsword.

The Highlander grabbed the lantern from the wall sconce and brought it back to the table. Then, after searching unsuccessfully for another lamp, John remembered the storage cabinets in the adjoining servant's quarter, the one that the younger woman was now occupying. Striding wordlessly across the room, he opened the door and stepped into the darkness of the next cabin.

Aside from the linens and other luxuries supplied for the return voyage and the future queen, the storage compartments built into the walls contained a variety of necessities, as well. Searching in the darkness of the small space, John let his fingers travel over the smooth wooden surface of the cabinet doors to where, he knew from memory, a number of wick lamps and candles would be found.

As he lay one hand on the smooth wooden ledge beneath the cabinets, his fingers brushed against a metal object, causing it to slip off the edge before he had a chance to catch it. Whatever it was, the falling object made a clinking sound as it hit the plank deck at his feet.

Cursing under his breath, John crouched, feeling around for it. His hands ran along a length of the polished floor until his head banged against a door. Backing up, he cursed again as the sleeve of his shirt caught on a cabinet latch.

Grinning sardonically at himself in the darkness, he sat back on his heels. What a picture I must make, he thought. The Lord of the King's Navy, crawling around like some bungling half-wit in the pitch-black bedroom of a young woman I've just somehow managed to fish from the sea. He sighed heavily.

No question, something had been tugging at him from the first instant he laid eyes on her. Even on deck, soaked and disheveled, her beauty had drawn him to her: the quiet perfection of her features, the deep jade of her eyes. But at the same time, a voice inside his head kept cautioning him. She looked young. Too young. She could only be half his thirty-two years. He was a man experienced in the knowledge of the world and its women. But unquestionably, a man pushing past his prime. And, to be honest, he wasn't sure if he still had the patience or the endurance to court a woman as shy and vulnerable as this one.

My God, he thought. She's probably a virgin to boot. Pushing himself to his feet, John pulled open the door to the corridor. Immediately, light from the lantern he had lit earlier illuminated the cabin. Turning, he let his eyes scan the tiny space, pausing on the pile of wet clothing sitting at the far end. There, on top of what appeared to be the dress and the cloak that Maria had worn, lay her wet undergarments. He smiled wickedly as he thought how shocked her expression would be to know he had laid eyes on something so private. Taking a step back to the cabinets, he looked once more for the object that he'd knocked from the ledge.

Directly in front of him John spotted a glimmer of light in a crack between the decking and the base of the cabin's solitary bunk. Leaning down and carefully taking hold of it, he extracted the item from its hiding place. It was a ring at the end of a gold chain.

Straightening himself to his full height, he held the chain up and gazed at the exquisitely fashioned gold ring. The dim light in the room would not let him see more of the design, but of one thing he was certain: What he held in his hand was a wedding ring.

Maria turned and looked again in the direction of the partially open door. She wondered what he could be doing. She sensed that he had gone for another wick lamp, but she had seen nothing of the sort there when she'd changed into the dry clothes.

She wished she could smooth back the loose strands of her thick, black hair. But as time passed, she was finding her throbbing hands more and more useless. She could feel that the loose knot of hair was still held in place with the combs, but she wondered for how long. Glancing down at the square neckline of the borrowed dress, she gingerly smoothed the backs of her hands over the tight, embroidered bodice. She didn't want to dawdle over silly fancies, but somehow, suddenly, it mattered to her how she looked.

What could he be doing? the young woman thought anxiously. Glancing hopefully at Isabel, she found her still blissfully dreaming in another world.

Maria saw the flicker of the candle before she saw the

man. Feeling an unexpected flutter in her stomach, she twisted quickly back in her seat, staring ahead and pretending disinterest.

John placed the candles on the table beside a large bowl of fresh water and began to unroll the dressings. He opened the corked jar, keeping his eyes on her.

It was not unlikely, he decided. The ring. It had to be hers. Thinking about it more rationally, it only made sense. A young woman as beautiful as she would quite naturally be married. Even at her age. But where was her husband? John thought. More than likely he was not on the sunken ship, for she showed no sign of mourning. Perhaps the man was waiting for them at their destination. Of course, that was it, he decided, fighting off the irritation that was creeping into the corners of his consciousness. Some young caballero recently returned from the New World, probably. Pockets filled with silver and gems for his young bride. How foolish to assume that—like so many other treasures being transported on the seas—she would simply be for the taking.

Maria pulled back her face in surprise as the odor from the jar reached her nose. "It's . . . it's rather foul!"

He sat down before her and started unwrapping the soiled dressings on her hands. "I can see you have not spent much time at sea."

"What makes you say that?"

Above the line of the dress, the skin of her bosom, her neck, her face glowed in the lamp and candlelight. John could see the flutter of her pulse at her throat. Her eyes, wide and dark, shone questioningly. Damn.

"This smell is hardly foul. If you were more experienced in sea travel, you'd probably consider it pleasant."

"I like the salt smell of the sea."

"Do you, lass?"

She leaned forward and smelled again. "What is that . . . sharp smell!"

"Turpentine," he responded. "Egg yolk, rose oil, and turpentine."

"I've never heard of this . . . turpentine before," she whispered. "But it sounds like a strange mix."

"Aye, but it works. It's more effective than seawater, and infinitely less painful than hot oil." John pulled away the last of the loose dressings and frowned at the sight of her palms and fingers.

Maria followed his gaze and stared with an odd sense of detachment at her hands. They were no more than exposed pieces of flesh, as raw as newly butchered meat, oozing with blood and pus. To her dismay, and with a feeling of mild revulsion, she noted that some of the linen had already begun to stick to the inflamed wounds.

He looked up, expecting her to faint. Truthfully, he thought, it would be better if she did.

She continued to stare.

"This will hurt."

"You gave me your word that it wouldn't," Maria protested quietly.

"This is worse than I thought it would be," he growled. John stood up, happy to have something he could be angry with, and stalked to a cabinet. She saw him take down a decanter and pour a liquid in a cup. He came back to her and laid them both on the table. "Mere scratches!"

The Highlander sat down and pushed the cup across the table-board. "You'll need to drink this, woman."

"Boiling oil?" she asked, smiling weakly.

"Drink!" he ordered. The young woman began to reach for the cup, but as she did, John saw her trembling fingers. How could she possibly touch anything with those hands? he asked himself. His voice was softer as he continued. "It will not hurt you, lass."

Gently, he lifted the cup to her lips, and she leaned forward, taking a sip. It burned her lips.

"It's strong. Is this turpentine, too?"

John chuckled. "It's whisky. A good Scots drink. But it's probably not strong enough." He held the drink again to her lips, and she reached up, tipping the cup until it was gone. Lowering it, he noticed the amber droplets glittering like jewels on her full lips. Without thinking, he reached out and brushed his finger over them.

His touch was so intimate. Maria knew that codes of behavior dictated that she pull back from his caress, but she didn't. Somehow, here in this cabin, inside the darkened walls, she felt separated from her past. From court. From all she'd ever been taught. Her eyes captured his gaze.

John stared at her for a moment, then withdrew his hand as if he'd been the one injured. She was married.

Maria lowered her gaze in confusion and dismay. She didn't know what was coming over her. Her senses were on fire, and she could feel her face burn. She watched him lift her hands and carefully lower them both in the water.

Tears sprang to her eyes, and she tried to pull back, but he held on. The pain coursed up her arms, but she realized in a moment that she had the strength to bear it.

Gently, the Highlander pressed on the torn flesh with the wet linen, and Maria's mind focused on other things. Her eyes continued to stare, but not at the act of the cleansing itself, but rather at the hands that held hers so expertly. At the difference in size, in color, in the very strength of the fingers that cradled and gentled her injured flesh with the utmost care.

"It must have come unexpectedly."

She snapped out of her reverie and glanced at him questioningly. A searing pain shot into her wrist, causing her to wince.

"The attack on your ship," he continued. "Why else would you be left with only one man to protect you in a battle?"

The sharp pains were increasing dramatically in her hands. She shuddered and went back to staring at them. Each time the water moved, the flesh of her palms sent shafts of hot metal into her wrist and arm.

"Where were you headed?"

Maria didn't look up.

"What port did you sail from, at least?" Receiving only silence as an answer, he continued, struggling to retain a reasonable tone of voice. "They will be looking for you when your ship doesn't arrive."

She pressed her lips tightly together.

John turned back to his task. From the decanter, he poured some of the whisky into the bowl of water, causing her to flinch once again. He'd hoped to take her mind off her hands by involving her in conversation, but she wasn't cooperating.

"You know, lass, there is a possibility we might come across other survivors. Did the vessel have many longboats?"

"A few." She nodded slowly, her eyes never lifting from her hands.

John pulled gently at a section of linen that would not separate from her raw flesh. She gasped.

He felt the flesh tear in his own chest. He'd not thought it possible for Maria to become any paler, but as he looked up into her ghostly complexion, he was certain that she had. Her eyes glistened with pooling tears, but they refused to overflow onto her bloodless cheeks. She continued to look stubbornly at her hands. He'd seen many wounded in battle. He'd tended to many injured on his ship. But none of them had been a woman, and none had been as beautiful or valiant as this one. He watched as another wave of pain shook her frame, but she bore it well.

"Talk about something," he ordered. "Tell me anything, but talk."

"It hurts!"

"I know it does," he growled. "But if you hadn't tried to hide your injury earlier, it wouldn't be quite this painful now."

She said nothing, but tearing her eyes away from her hands, she stared off into the darkness.

"Talk to me, Maria. Trust me, it will help. You must take your mind off your hands. Separate yourself from the pain."

"I can't!"

"Aye! You can, damn it!" he responded sharply, his tone commanding.

She lifted her face, and John saw the tears now rolling

down her face. He reached over for the cup, poured
some more drink, and raised it to her lips.

"Drink," he ordered quietly, and this time she complied with no argument, draining the cup.

With another gentle tug, the piece of linen came away.
A flush of relief swept through him. He was nearly
finished.

"But I don't know what to say," she hiccuped softly.
"It hurts so much."

There was one large flap of skin that needed to be cut
away, and the Highlander pulled his razor-sharp dirk
from the sheath at his belt and laid it on the table. He
suddenly wished she were not as strong-willed as she
obviously was when it came to enduring pain.

"A story," he suggested. "Tell me a story."

"I don't know any stories. What are you going to do
with your dagger?"

He put her hands back on the table. "Think of some
happy moment in your life. Perhaps some time to come.
Or one from your past. I need to cut away that piece of
skin. You won't feel it."

She felt lightheaded. "There have been no happy moments in my life." She watched in horror as he carefully
wiped the blade with the linen and then quickly sliced
the skin. He was right; she felt nothing.

"Think of your husband," he said, gazing steadily at
her. "Think of your marriage."

John took a handful of the ointment from the jar and
gently smoothed it onto the palm and fingers of the hand
that appeared less injured. She didn't deny being married. Her breaths were coming in pants.

"Imagine his face, when he finds out you are alive.
That you survived the sinking of the ship."

She shook her head.

"Try!" he ordered.

"But I can't," she said weakly, her eyes rolling up in
their sockets.

"You have to. He'll be waiting." John smeared the
ointment as lightly as he could on her other hand. "He'll
be waiting when you arrive, his arms open to you. His

heart full of affection. He'll be waiting at the docks to whisk you away. And you'll run to him. Glad to have found him again. . . ."

John paused. She was staring at him, her expression suddenly blank. Even her breathing seemed to have stopped. "Maria?" He reached out and touched her above the elbow, giving her a gentle shake.

Maria's eyes tried to focus for the briefest of moments. "But . . . he is dead!"

John was too late to catch her head as it banged to the table with a thud.

She wasn't married.

Chapter 5

John Macpherson's attention was wandering.

He could still feel the thick black hair uncoiling, tumbling, caressing his arm with the slippery softness of silk. She had been as light as a feather, as beautiful as an angel, and as trusting as the dead.

After all, she had fainted.

Vaguely, the Highlander could hear his navigator speaking, but John's mind was not with him. The two men leaned over the maps spread out on the high worktable in his cabin, and John's gaze followed as David pointed out where he figured they were and what their best course might be for the completion of the voyage. But his mind's eye lingered over another vision.

Once Maria had lost consciousness, John had thought he'd have a much easier time finishing up the dressing of her hands, but he'd been wrong.

After carrying her into the other cabin, the Highlander had remained beside her, sitting on the edge of the small bunk. John had gazed on the young beauty, her ivory skin glowing in the flickering lamplight. He'd sat there for the longest time, unable to tear himself away, even to retrieve the fresh dressings from the other cabin. John scoffed at his own adolescent foolishness, but he remained where he was, turning his thoughts instead to the things that she'd said.

So she had no husband. But for how long had the man been dead? Were there any bairns? Why was she not mourning him? And where was she headed? What relationship existed between Maria and her companion?

But he had no way of knowing any of the answers. Not until she confided in him.

Sitting beside her, John forced himself to look once again at the torn flesh of her fingers and palms. The ointment would do its work. But there were more questions that needed to be answered.

From her steady breathing, he could see that sleep had replaced the fainting spell. A wry smile crossed his face, for John knew the reason for her losing consciousness. It was more likely due to her exhaustion and the strong drink he'd given her than any pain from the application of the ointment. She was remarkably tough. But still, he found himself unable to leave her unattended.

Looking carefully at the bruises and the cut on her chin, he decided that they required no dressing. Even those marks did nothing to mar the beauty, nor to dispel the aura of enchantment that surrounded her.

With her hair spread in cascading, ebony waves over the white coverlet, he'd gazed appreciatively at the steady rise and fall of the softly rounded breasts, the pale skin of her throat aglow in the golden light, the full and sensuous lips. His eyes had lingered over those lips, wondering if the taste of them could be as sweet as he imagined it to be.

John shook his head, clearing his brain of the dream, and glanced out at the gray morning fog still blanketing the ship.

"Sure, she is a bonny lass."

John's eyes shot up to his navigator's smiling face. David's look was full of mischief as he stood across the table, leaning over the maps.

The Highlander supposed he had a great deal to be thankful for. When David had knocked quietly at the cabin door last night, the young navigator had brought with him one of the few serving women aboard. John wondered what his young friend knew of his thoughts.

But with the woman to spend the night looking after the sleeping castaways, there had been no more reason for him to stay. And as he'd parted company with his navigator in the corridor outside the cabin, John had felt a bittersweet sense of relief. This immediate attraction, the pull that he was feeling for her had struck him so quickly. Far too quickly.

"You can ignore me if you like, m'lord," David continued. "But I still say she's a bonny thing. And I don't see you denying it."

"Who?" John asked casually, running his great hands lightly over the chart. "Janet Maule? Nay, David, I don't deny it. I think she's quite bon—"

"Nay!" the navigator broke in. "I am speaking of the lass we picked out of the sea. The one that has you spellbound."

"Spellb—!" John glared at David. "You're daft, man. What makes you say such a thing?"

"Well, in the past hour, m'lord, I've taken you to and from the New World but twice on this chart, and the blasted place isn't even drawn on it. But you've only shaken your head each time over and agreed to everything I've been saying. Now that I think on it, perhaps while I was at it, I should have asked for ten pots of gold and a ship of my own." David grinned at his commander. "You've been lost to the world, I'd say. She has bewitched you."

John knew there was no point of denying that his attention had not been on the charts.

"Very well, David. She is a comely woman, I'll grant you." But that was as far as the Highlander was willing to go. On the other hand, he couldn't let his navigator go on needling him for days on end. "However, I am merely an observer of that beauty, and a distant admirer at that. Unlike a certain navigator of mine, who openly woos a certain Mistress Janet."

"She is not *my* Mistress Janet, for God's sake," the man protested. "And I don't woo her openly. If your lordship continues to talk so casually about this, then there is one navigator we both know who will soon have a father's short sword at his throat."

"Well, David, it won't be the first time." John straightened, glad to have been able to turn the tables on the younger man. "In fact, thinking back on the way you handled the man yesterday, I might have thought you were just waiting for the chance."

"Chance of what?" David protested. "To have Sir Thomas cut my throat?"

"Nay. To cross swords," he answered mildly. "You can't hide it, Davy. You carry a grudge against the man. Admit it, lad. As much as you like the daughter, you dislike the father."

David moved away from the table. " 'Tis true, by 'is wounds. I can't help it. Though it's not so bad as you say."

"But why?" John asked. "What has he done to make you feel so?"

"In truth? Nothing!" David turned and faced his commander before starting to pace the room. "It's just the way that he carries himself. You, Sir John—you're of noble blood, one of the finest families in Scotland. You're of far more noble blood than he. And you are my commander, to boot. But I can talk to you. You treat me as a man. I believe you've given me the responsibilities I now bear because . . . well, because I've earned your respect. I take great pride in that, m'lord."

David stopped and placed both hands on the charts again.

"But Sir Thomas takes every opportunity to remind me that I am a commoner, and that he is noble. And worse, that he's of the Douglas clan. That I am lowly, and he is high and mighty. That I am nothing."

"There are many like him, David. Especially among the Douglas blood. Those of ancient blood who fear good men like you. New men, lad. Men with ability." John stood straight and crossed his arms over his massive chest. "You've surely put up with them in the past, or perhaps it would be better to say you've ably subdued your anger. But what you've felt has never eaten away at you. And this hostility for Sir Thomas is clearly eating away at you now."

David turned and moved toward the open window.

"Could it be, I wonder," John continued, "could it be

that because of your attraction to his daughter, the man's place at court frustrates you all the more?"

"Aye. Perhaps it does." David stared out into the gray nothingness.

There fell a silence that neither would break. John knew very well the battle that raged within the young man. A battle of insecurity that tears at your spirit when you are told you're not worthy enough. It was a battle so similar to the one Caroline had so long enjoyed seeing him fight.

Even born noble, John Macpherson was the third son, following in the steps of two highly successful brothers. The shoes to be filled were large. So large, in fact, that John had often, as a young man, despaired of being able to fill them. Of finding his own place. Of making his own mark. The tradition of the third son joining the clergy never seemed appropriate for him, for the whole family knew John was more pirate than priest. So in a very real sense, he had become the pirate. Sailing under the banner of the Stuart king, or sailing under his own flag, John Macpherson became the most feared warrior sailing the northern seas.

But through the years, Caroline had done nothing but tear him down. A member of the powerful Douglas clan even before her marriage, she had too often found cause to stab at his pride, to remind him of her holdings, of the wealth she had inherited at coming of age.

But his wealth exceeded hers tenfold. His victories at sea and the treasures taken had won him power and prestige. And yet, he'd chosen to keep silent. And he buried his feelings deep within him. All the while, as she continued with her display of preeminence, he'd not said a thing. He'd held back his anger and made no attempt to make her see his true self. John Macpherson had been trained for a life where one's value was tested and proven with every cut of the blade and not by the shrewdness of a sharp tongue.

He endured her arrogance for too long, he thought now. The passion they'd shared for years was not love. But later on, when Caroline eventually resorted to keeping him at bay with the hints of other wooers, John had no longer been able to stand what he'd tolerated for seven years. He'd wanted an end to it all.

Oddly, and quite out of character, Caroline had suddenly wanted a chance to change when faced with the reality of losing him. And he would have given her the chance had she not made it conditional. Suddenly it became essential that he should marry her. She had promised to change, to stop playing him for the jealous fool. But he couldn't. John had shaken his head and turned away. And that had been the end of it all. Or so he'd thought.

"I've been too reckless," David spoke at last. "I've been foolish. She is a lady and I am just a sailor. Just a common sailor."

"A great navigator," John interjected. "The finest there is."

"Still common though. If Sir Thomas were to find out that I've been courting his daughter behind his back, he would skin me alive. And the Lord only knows what he would do to her."

"Your wooing of Janet Maule has been completely innocent—so far as I can see. And she has responded in kind. She is no bairn, Davy. So where's the harm?" John grabbed a decanter from the sideboard and poured out a drink for his man. Though he knew David was resilient enough, he hated to see his navigator so distraught. What the young man had to work through was certainly a challenge, and there wasn't much John could do to help him, other than trying to lighten the mood. "And I don't think it matters much that she is as blind as a wee mouse? She's a bonny mouse, for all that!"

"So you think the fact that she can't see past the length of her arm is the reason she's taken such an interest in me?"

"What else could it be, man?" John nodded. "If she could only see your ugly face—"

"She happens to like my ugly face," David chirped in. "And as far as her sight goes, there is nothing wrong with it as far as I could tell. Aye, she claims that people and things are but a shadow when she looks at them from afar, but that's where I come in. I just place her hand in the crook of my arm and lead her to things she can't make out for herself. That is, if her father doesn't catch wind of it."

"And the chances are, lad, that Sir Thomas will never know anything about it. At least, he'll probably not learn of it while he is aboard the *Great Michael*."

Seeing David's uncomprehending glance, John handed him the cup and then continued. "He is too busy watching and worrying about his new bride meeting me in secret. Little else matters to him, I believe."

"Aye." The navigator nodded knowingly. "Lady Caroline may have married him, but he certainly doesn't have the look of a man who's secure in the match."

"Why do you say that?" John asked, somewhat surprised by the young man's words. He thought he'd been the only one conscious of Sir Thomas's insecurities.

"He seems to be spending a great deal of time in your company, m'lord." David shook his head. "I was wondering if he would ever broach the topic with you."

John looked at him steadily, before answering. "He has, actually, though not directly. And I have done whatever I could to try to put his mind at ease."

"It wasn't enough, though, was it?"

"It's difficult to tell," John answered. "Knowing Caroline, I'd guess that she is probably playing a barrelful of games with the man—jealousy being only one. My guess is that she's working him to her will right now."

The Highlander poured himself a cup and drank it at once. Seeing the look of concern creasing the face of the young navigator, John smiled as he continued. "I am just glad she has him to play with and not me, Davy. But sadly for Sir Thomas, I can see that she hasn't learned a thing."

Maria placed a gentle kiss on Isabel's brow and smoothed back the older woman's hair. The physician's medicine was quite effective. After quickly dropping off to sleep, her aunt hadn't so much as moved a muscle.

She turned toward the servant tidying the room.

"Are you certain? I am not asking too much of you?"

"You are not, m'lady," the young woman blurted out, whirling to face her. "Mistress Janet gave me strict orders to remain in this cabin until she returns."

Maria looked in the direction of her sleeping aunt. "If she awakens, or asks for me."

"I'll tell her you've gone to see Sir John, and you'll be back in no time."

Maria nodded in approval and turned to go. But then her shaking legs and her fluttering stomach slowed her momentarily. Reaching the door, she stopped and took a deep breath. Perhaps this was not such a good idea. Isabel! How was it she let her aunt talk her into this? She turned again and glanced at the sleeping woman.

"Is there something wrong, m'lady?" The young servant moved to her side.

"Nay . . . nay." Maria glanced down at her bandaged hands. The events of the night before were quite sketchy in her memory. Had he stayed in the cabin long? Who had carried her to her bunk? She remembered him asking so many questions. And then she'd fainted. Maria flushed at the thought.

Perhaps going to him now was too forward. *Oh, Isabel! You expect too much of me. I will try, but when will you learn I am not who you want me to be?* Maria reached up with frustration and touched the latch.

"Oh, I am sorry, m'lady. You can't open the latch, can you?" Without another word, the woman opened the door wide and held it for her.

With a tentative nod of appreciation to the serving woman, Maria shyly stepped across the threshold and into the corridor. She waited there for a moment as her eyes adjusted to the dimness. Looking down the narrow walkway, she could see the sailor, who was standing guard at the base of a steep series of stairs, move at once in her direction.

"Are ye needing something, m'lady?"

Maria swallowed hard as she looked at the middle-aged man standing before her. It was a different sailor than the young one who had been there the day before. But all the same, he nodded politely as he addressed her. The amount of civility and respect with which they all treated her had already made her wonder, more than once, if somehow they had learned her true identity.

"I was hoping, if you would be kind enough . . ." She was at a loss for words. She was not accustomed to this. Where was her entourage now? Where were the dozens of women who had been surrounding her for years, the ones who had served as her own human shield. The ones she could hide behind.

The man waited patiently.

"I need to see your commander," she blurted out at last.

The man nodded in understanding. "If ye could wait a wee bit in your cabin, m'lady, I could send after him."

"I would prefer . . ." She tried to build her courage. "I would like to go to him. I need some fresh air, and I thought . . ."

The elder man ran a gnarled hand over his grizzled face for a moment, contemplating the request.

Maria waited, not knowing if there was any more explanation she should give. The sailor, though a few years older, looked like so many others who had sailed with them on their doomed journey. So much like the one who had lost his life in the escape—Pablo, who now rested at the bottom of the gray-green sea.

"Please," she said simply, "I need your help."

The bowed back of the man creaked a bit straighter, and the hard edges of his sea-worn face softened at the sound of her plea.

"I can't see Sir John having any objection to that." The sailor looked up and down the corridor. "But before I can take ye up to him, m'lady, ye'll need to wait here for a wee bit, until I find a mate to take over my post."

Maria nodded as the man scuttled down the corridor.

So they were being watched. She'd thought the guard at the door had been posted merely for their convenience. How foolish of me, she thought. Of course, he would have them watched.

But that was not going to stop her from asking him why. That is, if she could find the courage to ask him *any* of the things she was supposed to ask. Maria looked up as she heard the padding of footsteps coming down the corridor from behind her. It was the young boy. The one who had been helping the physician yesterday and again this morning. The lad came to a halt in front of her.

Maria glanced at the curly, sandy-colored hair and the large brown eyes that were peering at her over an armful of linens. He hardly came to her shoulder, and she wondered how one so young could survive a life so rough as going to sea. He stood silently for a moment, obviously unsure of whether he should address her.

"Are you feeling better, m'lady?" he asked at last.

"Aye, thank you," she responded softly. The boy continued to stand and stare at her. Maria wondered for a moment if she was blocking his way, but even when she pressed closer to the side of the passageway, the lad made no move to go past her. "What is your name?"

"Andrew Maxwell, m'lady. What's yours?" The boy paled suddenly. "Oh, begging your pardon, ma'am. I'm probably not supposed to be so forward."

"That's all right, Andrew." She nodded with a smile. "My name is Maria. And how old are you?"

"I'm nine—well, next year I will be." He straightened his back. "But I am as strong as ten."

She couldn't help but smile as the boy scuffed his foot across the planking of the deck. "And what's your job?"

"I do whatever needs to be done, m'lady." The boy's face pinched up as he pondered what he'd just said. "I am the brother to the ship's navigator."

"I thought since you were helping the physician on his rounds, you must be his assistant, at least."

"That I'm not," Andrew said at once, flashing a look of defiance. "The reason that I help the man is because Sir John has ordered me to. He says that by giving a hand to all who call for it, I'll learn more than just sailing."

Maria nodded seriously in agreement. "That is a wise course."

"But when I grow up, I'm going to be a pilot, like my brother." Andrew paused. "But it's hard work to learn so much."

Maria appraised the boy, her eyes thoughtful.

"Aye. But I'm certain you have what it takes, Andrew."

John Macpherson concurred with his navigator's suggested route. They still had two weeks before their appointed audience with the Holy Roman Emperor Charles at the end of March, but there was no way to tell when the fog would lift. Going by David's calculations, if they remained fogbound for more than a week, then they should take their chances and try to capture some of the light breeze that occasionally sprang up and work their way eastward toward the Danish coast. From there, a messenger could be sent overland through Friesland and the Netherlands to Antwerp and the Emperor's palace with news of their whereabouts. With a fast horse, the man should be able to reach the court in less than a fortnight. The last thing John wanted was to have the upcoming marriage muddled by a bout of bad weather.

"I guess if we need to sit tight, a week won't ruin us," John grumbled, rubbing his hand over his chin.

David nodded in agreement, but John couldn't avoid noticing the grin that tugged at the corners of his pilot's mouth.

"What is it now?" he snapped.

"A week. A whole week, with not a thing to do." The young man's large brown eyes could not hide his mirth.

"We've been stranded like this many times in the past," John said, trying not to rise to the bait. "We'll just have to make do."

"Not like this, m'lord," David chirped. "I don't believe *you* have been stranded like this before."

"What do you mean *me*? What is the difference between this fog and any—"

"A great deal of difference, m'lord!"

John glared threateningly at his pilot as the latter leaned over the maps.

"Would you care to clarify that statement," the Highlander growled, "or are you just happy to rile my temper with riddles?"

"I would say more, if you were not in such bad humor," David complained wryly, busying himself with his measurements once again. "Aye. Considering the circumstances, just forget I said anything, m'lord."

"And you can go to hell, you mouse-earned marmoset," John cursed. "If I didn't know better, I'd say you've taken too many blows to your head, drunk a wee bit too much seawater, and bedded a few too many harbor whores. But whatever's caused it, I think you've lost your mind at last."

David's pained expression was comic, indeed, but John kept the fearsome glower on his face.

"Thank you for your words of support, Sir John." The navigator grinned. "But you know I don't drink seawater."

"Aye, I'll give you that," his commander growled. "I'll even grant that you're not much for the women dockside. But if you think you're going to taunt me . . ."

"Well, m'lord. It's just that, in *this* fog, even a ship as vast as the *Great Michael* seems to grant you no more protection than a longboat."

"You are daft, Davy lad! Protection from whom?"

"Perhaps I am daft, Sir John," David conceded, shrugging his shoulders. "But from what I can see, too many are wanting you, m'lord. Just too many. Your hard-won reputation is simply to be your undoing, in the end."

"Wanting me . . . ?" John snarled impatiently.

David straightened from the table and faced his commander. "Well, m'lord, there's that married lady below, the poor thing, sitting in her cabin, doing little else but dreaming of you and pining away her loss. That is, when she's not tormenting her husband."

"I'm finding it hard to believe that Lady Caroline's been sharing these thoughts with the likes of you."

"Nay, m'lord. Though I do hear a few things from

her sweet-faced stepdaughter," David answered. "The darling Mistress Janet."

"Ahh! Of course. And Mistress Janet shares it all with you."

"Of course! The poor Lady Caroline was once, as everyone in Scotland knows, an active woman. But now she sulks and sighs and flies into rages, cursing the *Great Michael* and all who sail on her, and putting Mistress Janet out of their cabin for no reason at all. Och, it's a terrible fierce thing, I would imagine, newly married to one man, but wasting away for another." David shook his head dramatically. "Truthfully, though, I feel for Mistress Janet—caught in the middle and nowhere to turn."

"Except to you." John nodded skeptically, but he knew deep down that, aside from the badgering, David's words contained a strong possibility of truth.

"Aye. Who else could the lass swing her bow toward. She only began to confide in me when she decided to find out for sure—from someone close to you—that the lady's affections were only one-sided. Janet doesn't have the heart nor the courage to discuss any of this with her father, but still she feels an obligation to do something about it. Nay, it doesn't look good. Only two months of wedded bliss and already second thoughts."

David moved over to the window and sat on a high stool, leaning back against the window casing. John knew he wasn't finished and drummed the table with his fingers impatiently.

"What else, pilot. Out with it."

"Well, m'lord," the younger man continued seriously, "only that you should be at ease knowing I represented you and your feelings truthfully to the lady. I assured Janet that you are not just happy for Lady Caroline, but delighted that she should have chosen as fine a warrior and as upstanding a man as Sir Thomas. I told her that you harbor no regrets, nor longings of any kind for the woman."

"That's very good of you, David. Though I don't think you need to be speaking for—"

"It was a pleasure, m'lord," the navigator interrupted.

"Aye, I'm quite sure it was, all things considered. But—"

"But there's more still, Sir John."

"Oh, is there, now? Don't tell me, you are giving up your trade and taking over the vocation of confessor on this ship?"

"That I am not." David paused for a moment. "Though I'd be willing to wager there'd be a fair profit to be made selling indulgences to the lot we're carrying this—"

"Will you continue?" John growled.

With a nod, the younger man started again. "Well, you know the stalwart Sir Thomas is dogging you whenever you're anywhere to be found. But did you know that you have the good gentleman spending the rest of his day stewing about on deck and trying to find crew men that he can bribe to keep him informed of your whereabouts."

"My whereabouts?"

"Aye, m'lord. At all times."

"He doesn't."

"He does," David said matter-of-factly.

John pushed away from the table and stalked to the window. "The suspicious scoundrel!" Never mind the fact that John would never choose to be alone with Caroline. But he was stunned that the old devil would even imagine he could get John's own crew to betray their leader. "To think I felt badly for the man. I hope the men are taking his gold. I hope they take all of it."

"That they are doing. By the bagful." David nodded. "But that's not all of it."

"Come now, David," John said exasperatedly. "What more could there be?"

"Well, perhaps I won't burden you with tales the men are collecting of all the other young women aboard, unmarried *and* married, swooning and collapsing at the very sight of you."

"By God, I surely am happy to provide entertainment for my men, as well as a lucrative side occupation in Sir Thomas's employ."

"They do appreciate it, Sir John." David paused for effect. "But perhaps, most important, the bonny, green-eyed lass staying in the queen's cabin also speaks of naught but you."

"Maria?" John asked with surprise. "How, I'm afraid to ask, do you know that?"

"The serving woman we left with her last night had other duties early this morning, so Mistress Janet, from the goodness of her heart, took it on herself to see to those two."

"I gave instructions that none of the passengers were to barge in on them yet."

"We've seen to it that your orders were followed to the letter—quite nearly," David acknowledged. "But I knew that surely you couldn't mean Janet Maule. I've heard you say yourself that she is not like the rest of *them*. And someone had to see to their needs this morning. With the younger lassie's hands bound up as it is, how could we expect her to so much as change her clothes without a wee bit of help? Never mind seeing to the older woman. Unless . . . unless *you*'ve been planning to go back and see to . . . ?"

John's fierce glare silenced his man. "Nay, I was not."

"Of course not, m'lord. I never thought so for a moment." David measured for the twentieth time the distance between their position and the Danish coast.

"At any rate," the pilot continued without looking up," Mistress Janet told me that the elder woman is a bit feverish, but all in all she seems to be bearing up quite well. In fact, the physician arrived shortly after Janet did this morning and saw to the old woman's wound again and gave her some more of his sorcerer's brew. So, in the meantime, Janet . . . er, Mistress Janet got a chance to chat with the lass. From what she said to me after she left their cabin—"

David stopped abruptly, looking up and shaking his head.

"I'm sorry, m'lord. I am boring you with this idle prattle." He leaned over the maps with a grim expression.

"In weather like this, it's so damned easy getting off course."

John filled his chest with air and clenched his jaw. He would not wring his friend's neck, as much as he deserved having it wrung. He knew what the rascal was up to.

"I think Mistress Janet and I need to have a talk," he said at last.

"Aye, m'lord? What about?"

"About keeping her confidence with bilge-dwelling sea rats that seem to have taken over this vessel," John retorted. "About not falling prey to her sympathies for every ugly dog and flattering tongue that she stumbles across."

"You surely couldn't mean me?" David asked in false horror.

"I mean no one else, you scurvy rogue! In fact, if I—"

The hard rap on the door quickly brought the two men up short. With a few strides, David reached the door and opened it. A look of surprise came over the younger man's visage, but behind him the Highlander barely concealed a look of disdain.

"Lady Caroline!" David announced, turning with a short bow.

The tall woman stepped into the cabin, breezing past the navigator without so much as a look of acknowledgement.

David turned and glanced at his commander questioningly.

"Stay here, David," John ordered sternly. "And continue with your work. If I'm not mistaken, this shouldn't take long."

The Highlander swung around and faced the young woman now standing across the table. "What can I do for you, Lady Maule?"

"I wish for us to be left alone," Caroline whispered in a hushed tone. "This visit regards a private matter. It is not for the ears of . . . well . . ."

"I am afraid not," John responded curtly, his face now

an expressionless mask. "A private interview in my own cabin is impossible—all things considered."

There had been a number of times Caroline had tried to communicate with him before her marriage. He had refused to respond to her wishes then, vowing to keep his course. Their time together was finished, and he meant to keep it that way.

"Lady Caroline," he continued firmly, "there is naught that we can discuss that David cannot be privy to. He is my second-in-command on this ship."

The flash of anger colored the woman's face. Caroline Maule's eyes were like daggers as she pondered John's words. She stared a moment longer at the Highlander's blank expression.

"Very well," she said at last. "If this is the way you see fit to treat me, then let it be."

John remained where he stood and watched as a familiar pouty look crept into the face of his visitor. It seemed to be eons ago that he'd thought that look charming. "Is there something specific you need to see me about, Lady Maule?"

Caroline looked away from him, her eyes playing over the chart on the table. With a toss of her head, a skein of golden hair cascaded down over one of her high, round breasts, a glimmering contrast to the dark blue velvet of her dress. Yes, Caroline Maule was an extremely beautiful woman. But—somewhat to John's surprise—the woman no longer stirred any of the old carnal feelings in him.

"David and I must continue our work here," John said at last. "So if your visit is of a social nature, I have to request—"

"I am not here on a 'social' visit, John," she retorted at once, interrupting him.

John nodded curtly and waited. But her words and her eyes conveyed different messages. As he waited patiently for her to continue, he watched Caroline's fingers trace the edge of the table while her gaze traveled the length of his body. When her eyes reached his face at last, it occurred to him that her look was calculated to be clearly seductive.

He was not game. "What do you want, Caroline?" John asked shortly, under his breath.

The hint of a smile showed coyly on her face. He knew she'd wanted to get a reaction from him, and she had succeeded.

"Well, the reason for my visit here is that, several hours ago, I took time out of my morning's activities to pay a visit to our two new arrivals." She glided to a chair beside the table and sat down with a comfortable sigh. "But I wasn't permitted in their cabin."

John moved as far away as he could in the room, then turned and faced her. "Is that the reason for this visit?"

She waited a moment before she spoke. Her eyes caressed his body shamelessly, again conveying much more than her words. Caroline turned her gaze back to his darkening face. "That and the rudeness of the old swine who stands guard by that door."

John looked over at David.

"Christie has the watch this morning, m'lord. But he is not one to—"

The wave of John's hand quieted the navigator. He knew that nothing David could say would make a difference in Caroline's perception of anything that might have occurred. She had wanted to be alone with him and she had been rebuffed. So her next ploy was to be offended. And offended she would remain regardless of any argument, explanation, or apology. This was her character.

"Those were my orders," John said to the young woman. "Christie was following orders. Now if one of my men provoked you in any way by the manner in which you were spoken to, or by anything else you found to be personally offensive, then I will answer for that conduct."

Caroline's face grew hard. "He laid his hands on me."

"Christie?" David asked incredulously, stepping forward.

The young woman's beautiful face lost some of its

charm as she found herself the object of two sets of suspicious stares. A sneer curled in the corner of her mouth. "He physically manhandled me, abusing my person."

"That would be a serious charge, Lady Maule, if David and I did not know the man better," John responded, his tone expressing his disbelief. The truth of it was, John knew Caroline better. "Wouldn't it be closer to the truth to say the old man tried to keep you from barging past him, even after he asked you to stop?"

Caroline looked away, tossing her blond hair back over her shoulders.

"Did it not occur to you that the man had his orders?" John pressed.

"So I am to be pushed about by any common, seagoing pig? So long as they serve under your orders?"

"The man was directed to keep visitors out." John returned her stare for a long moment with eyes cool and focused. But when she gave a sudden shrug, turning her face from him in feigned indifference, he snapped and his words cut the air sharply. "In case you haven't realized it yet, m'lady, you are a guest traveling aboard a ship of war. The men on these vessels, like all soldiers prepared for battle, are trained to follow orders. To them, it means naught that you are man or woman, noble or commoner. Christie had a job to do. He prides himself on his loyalty to the King and on his years serving under my command."

"I understand your codes perfectly well, Sir John. But my complaint is that your man's orders seem to have been directed at me and only at me." Caroline stood, tossing her head back in a defiant gesture. "My understanding is that he was told not to allow *me* in!"

"No one is to be allowed in, Lady Maule. Not just you, no one." John glanced at David. "Unless otherwise ordered."

"Unless otherwise ordered by whom, might I ask?" She jumped at her chance.

"Unless ordered by me or by my second-in-command, David Maxwell."

Caroline's face grew hard as she swung around to face the pilot. "That explains it all."

John waved David off as the young navigator stepped forward.

"That explains what, Caroline?" the Highlander queried, drawing her attention back to himself.

"The fact that while I am waiting, while I am being physically ill-treated and humiliated by a common sailor, I witness Janet Maule breeze out of the Spaniards' cabin like she owns this ship." Caroline's voice carried a note of suffering, but her eyes were cool.

David began to open his mouth to explain, but again the Highlander silenced him with a look and a shake of the head.

"Your husband, Lady Maule, has quite generously offered his assistance to our shipwrecked travelers. And Mistress Janet, his daughter, has been most helpful in seeing to the needs of the two women." John glared at the young woman before him. "If you had the compassion or the understanding of either your husband or your stepdaughter, then you would put an end to this childish protest and go on about your business."

A flush reddened Caroline's fair skin as she shot back angrily, "I, too, have compassion and can quite ably see to their needs."

John nodded curtly. "We'll keep that in mind, for the next time we come upon any stranded or castaway travelers. But for the time being I would say—"

"That answer is hardly acceptable, Sir John." Furious now, Caroline leaned forward, gripping the edge of the work table with white knuckles. "I will not allow you to exclude me this way."

"Exclude you?" John looked at her anger with indifference, and his response was razor sharp. "Don't forget, m'lady, you are the very same person who, when it came to bringing these people on board, was so quick to express her fear of having her throat cut in her sleep."

Caroline began to respond, then paused and sank back into the chair.

"That was different," she answered sullenly, averting her eyes. "That was before . . ."

John waited expectantly. "Before what, m'lady?"

Searching for the right words, Caroline twisted her long hair about her fingers.

"Why don't you speak your mind?" he pressed.

She turned her glare on him. "That was before I knew one of them to be a young lady . . . a young lady of some breeding. And before I knew they were of such quality that you would place them in the queen's cabin."

That was it, John knew. And what she'd just said so truly defined the woman.

"Does that make a difference to you, Lady Maule?" he asked. "Does that mean your compassion is only engaged when you learn of the size of someone's cabin or the breeding they exhibit?"

The Highlander watched as she brooded silently. "Would it make a difference if I had told you they are as poor as peasants, that I placed them in the finest cabin because it was the only one available . . . and I didn't think you were about to give up yours. Would it matter if I told you that I couldn't put them in the ship's damp hold because the younger one is a wee, ugly mouse with a wheeze and a terrible cough. Would you still be so eager if I told you she is of no interest to you, or anyone on this ship, for that matter. That she has no beauty, no charm, nor any upbringing of the sort you value. Would you still be interested in demonstrating this 'compassion' you tout so highly? Would you still be so keen on breaking in on their privacy?"

Caroline Maule, her face flushed scarlet, appeared to be at a momentary loss for words.

"Nay, I thought not," he said, taking the brunt of a flashing look of anger. "I would say this visit has concluded, m'lady. For now."

He gestured toward the door and watched her as she smoothly rose from her place.

"My orders remain what they were. And until such time as David or I see fit to burden our visitors with the ample charm—and compassion—of their noble fellow travelers, they will remain in seclusion."

Momentarily defeated, Caroline Maule stood for a long time, glaring at the towering Highlander who had never before spoken to her in such a manner. Finally, as the upset began to sink in more clearly, she turned on her heel and started for the door.

"I would just as soon continue this . . . chat at another time," she said over her shoulder as she paused by the door. "And in a more private setting, for that matter." Then she turned her scowling face to David and waited impatiently.

Like a servant whipped into action, David jumped to lift the latch for the irate woman. But to his utter surprise, Lady Caroline made no attempt, as he pulled the door open, to step into the hall. He peered outside.

There, before them, stood Maria.

Chapter 6

She had beauty, charm, breeding, and more.

From John's position behind Caroline, he could see the young woman standing outside the door, and he found himself fighting an urge to push past the Scottish noblewoman. The look on Maria's face was confident, cool. She looked untouchable, strong.

Maria stood quietly, surprised and a bit taken aback by the scorching gaze of the tall, blond woman blocking the doorway. Arriving at the door that she been directed to, Maria hadn't even had a chance to knock before the door was swung open on its hinges, the room's defender facing her like a lioness protecting her lair. Wondering if she had even found the correct door, Maria quickly glanced over the shoulder of the imposing figure and then relaxed somewhat, having spotted the ship's commander and his navigator.

"I must apologize for interrupting," Maria offered quietly, looking from the woman's fierce countenance to Sir John's expression of . . . what was that look? Welcome? Surprise? Relief? "Perhaps I might come back at a different time."

A long pause filled the air before anyone answered her. The Highlander was the first to respond.

"This is no interruption, whatsoever," he replied heartily. "Lady Maule has concluded her business here and is on her way out. If you'll excuse me, m'lady?"

John tapped Caroline lightly on the shoulder, moving her to one side of the doorway as he stepped past her.

"We have not yet been introduced." Caroline's words were curt.

"I am Maria."

Caroline continued to glare at the green-eyed beauty, and it suddenly occurred to Maria that it was perhaps appropriate to curtsy, a habit she had fallen out of long ago.

"Maria of . . . ?" Caroline queried bluntly, breaking the momentary silence.

"Just Maria," John broke in, drawing Caroline's withering gaze as he held out his hand to the newcomer.

Maria made no move to take the Highlander's hand, but spoke up at once, trying to convey a note of friendliness in her voice. "And did I hear Sir John call you 'Lady Maule,' just now?"

Caroline's steely gaze followed the line of John's outstretched hand back to the young woman.

"Are you any relation to Mistress *Janet* Maule?" Maria continued. "We have been very fortunate to share Mistress Janet's company this morning."

"This is Lady Caroline Maule, the Mistress Janet's mother," John responded breezily, stifling a grin as Maria's gaze snapped disconcertedly back to Caroline's face. "Or, stepmother, I should say. Won't you come in, m'lady?"

Tentatively, Maria lifted one bandaged hand. Without giving Caroline another look, John gently took hold of the injured fingers and drew her past the Scottish noblewoman.

"I am delighted you've ventured out of your cabin, Lady Maria," the ship's commander continued. "I was just about to come and pay you a visit myself."

Maria glanced at the blond woman still standing by the door, and John followed her eyes.

"Oh, aye, Lady Maule," he said in a more businesslike tone, "please be sure to give my compliments to your husband for his assistance in the recovery of this lady and her friend. And if you, ever again, have any difficulty in dealing with my men, I recommend you discuss the problem with Sir Thomas first. After all, I believe we can both trust his judgment regarding such worldly dealings."

As the color drained out of Caroline's face, it occurred to John that if looks could kill, there would be bodies all over the cabin deck right now.

"Would you like David to see—" the commander began.

"Well, this explains a *great* deal." The words, edged with steel, Caroline directed at John, but her look of hostile resentment cut the air around Maria. "Aye, this explains it all, indeed." And without another word, Caroline Maule lifted her chin angrily and disappeared through the cabin door.

Maria stood awkwardly as the two men stared after the woman. Glancing quickly from the face of the navigator to that of the giant Highlander, Maria easily perceived the unsettled look Sir John now wore, a look that suggested the presence of Lady Maule created more of a disturbance than his words to her had indicated.

"I honestly meant what I said earlier," she said quietly. "About coming back at a better time."

John turned his blue eyes on her and lifted her hand, pulling her lightly toward him. "Nay, lass. You couldn't have picked a better time to be here. And you proved to be the champion of the moment, driving all before you from the field."

Blushing furiously, Maria averted her eyes, avoiding his gaze as she turned to look at the other man who had now joined them by the work table. Returning the navigator's direct gaze, she curtsied to him in greeting.

John watched as David blushed an even deeper shade of crimson than Maria as he bowed to the young beauty. The commander couldn't help but smile at what he knew to be the young man's sheer delight at being treated with such dignity.

"Navigator, I believe this would be a good time to go and have a chat with Christie regarding Lady Maule's complaint."

"You certainly don't want me to flog him, do you, m'lord?" David asked, shooting John a questioning look.

"Nay, man, of course not," John responded. "I just

want you to give the man some guidance on how to respond when . . . when . . . well, you know what to do."

"But, Sir John, I heard you say yourself that Christie took just the tack a good seaman should have taken." David remained still, working hard to keep a perplexed look on his face . . . and to keep from smiling. His master's eyes and expression left no doubt that he wanted David out of the room, but the young pilot could not resist playing up the moment.

"David," John growled with barely concealed irritation, "just go and do as you are told."

"Aye, m'lord. The maps . . ." The navigator slowly reached across the worktable for the charts.

"If you want to leave them," the Highlander broke in, his tone becoming overtly threatening, "I can have Mistress Janet hold on to them for you."

"No one holds my . . ." David paused and glance up at the commander. "You're planning to meet with Mistress Janet?"

"Aye, I think that in the light of certain talk that has come to me . . . about certain people . . ." John's glare was unmistakable.

"No reason to bother her with any of that, m'lord. In fact," David hurried on, rolling up his maps with notable speed, "I am on my way now!"

And with his charts quickly stowed under one arm, the navigator gave Maria a bow and beat a hasty retreat.

"Finally," John muttered, hiding a satisfied smile, before turning again to his green-eyed guest.

Maria withdrew her hand from his and walked to the side of the high table standing on one side of the cabin. On a stool beside it, a blue cap sat—the navigator's, she was sure—a white feather poking jauntily from one side. The table and the clutter of papers remaining on it bespoke a real workroom, and the brightness of this cabin was a delightful change from the dark cabins below. The line of open windows at one end made a considerable difference, and looking out, she could just make out the white tops of gray-green swells. The fog was as gray and thick as the previous day, and through the window she could hear the rough voices of men working on the deck above them.

Glancing around the room, she suddenly started. A wide bunk, curtained with heavy blue damask, stood in the corner of the cabin. Stricken with unease at the realization that this was his bedchamber, Maria tore her gaze away from the huge bed.

Around the bed, a number of trunks were stowed in alcoves beneath shelves and cabinets that lined the side walls of the ship. Brightly colored banners and a large plaid cloth were draped festively around weapons and light armor, gleaming in their stowage places. Her eyes were drawn to the coat of arms depicting ships and daggers and a cat with claws outstretched on a large shield that hung from the dark wood frame of the bunk.

The masculine character of the room fascinated her and, at the same time, added tremendously to her discomfort. Maria had never been in a man's private chambers before, never mind alone with him there, and she moved quickly to the windows, her face heating up at the thought.

She didn't turn, but noted the sound of the door closing quietly behind her.

John stood briefly at the closed door, his eyes locked on the straight back of the woman by the window. Her arrival had been quite timely, punctuating one of Caroline's least attractive moments. In fact, in all their years together, John had never seen such an apparent lack of restraint in his former mistress. She had not just stormed angrily away from the confrontation. Her emotions had carried her away.

But the warrior knew that Caroline's retreat was temporary at best. Leaning against the door, he knew he had to devise a plan to keep her running. The fair Lady Caroline had a temperament that required her to rise to every challenge, and John would have to be ready for any eventuality. He was now convinced that the Scottish woman was up to no good. If she decided she wanted him back, there was no reasoning with her. And no telling how far she would go. For Caroline, no question of honor, or propriety, or even marital vows would hold her. Nothing.

Just then, Maria turned slightly and glanced shyly at him. Like a sleeper suddenly drawn from a nightmare into a beautiful dream, John smiled. Aye, perhaps there was a way to keep Caroline from causing too much damage—to herself and to everyone else.

"You're having us watched," she noted gravely.

"Aye, for your protection," he answered.

"From whom?" Maria's eyebrows raised in surprise.

"From visitors the like of Lady Caroline."

The young woman considered, and then nodded in response. She could accept that. "For a moment, I . . . I wasn't sure Lady Caroline would let me pass," Maria said, her face grave.

"Aye, I know the feeling," John responded, crossing the cabin. "I recall once making the grave error of stopping my horse on a bridge with a couple of my men not far from Stirling, to talk to a friar. Lady Caroline and a number of her friends and kin came riding up behind, demanding that we clear her way. She can be quite imposing."

"And what happened?"

"Well, it was awhile ago, but as I recall, I decided that since we were all heading to court, we should only knock down a few of her companions before being gracious and giving way."

John began to smile and then frowned at the memory. That encounter—and the events that followed later that same day—marked the beginning of a chapter in his life he now wanted behind him.

"Have you eaten this morning, Maria?" the Highlander asked hospitably, shaking off the reminiscence.

"Mistress Janet made sure that we were fed, Sir John," Maria answered, looking up at him. In the light of the cabin, the man was even more handsome than she'd remembered. Certainly, none of the fierceness of the day before remained in his dark features. "Truthfully, she has been quite kind."

John strode to a cabinet under one of the open windows and removed a decanter and two goblets. "Then, may I get you something to drink?"

She shook her head politely in response.

John paused, his eyes twinkling mischievously. "Now that I think of it, I wouldn't blame you for not accepting anything from my hand."

"Why do you say that?" she asked, trying to ignore the feeling that his half-smile and side-glance wrought in her.

"Last night I gave you a drink, and you passed out in a matter of moments."

Maria looked in embarrassment at her bandaged hands. It was true. She could not remember a thing that had taken place last night after they sat down at the table in Isabel's cabin. She'd opened her eyes to the dim light of early morn and the pleasant, smiling face of Janet Maule.

"I must admit that, aside from wine, I don't have much experience with spirits such as the one you served me."

"Well, don't give it another thought, lass. I know many a Scot who has ended up an evening of drinking just as you did last night."

"Thank you," she said quietly. "That makes me feel much better."

John stepped closer to her. How different these two women were, he thought. Caroline had blown into the room under full sail and dropped anchor as if the cabin were her own; Maria still stood uneasily by the windows, her cloak wrapped tightly around her. Her stance told him she was still undecided whether to run or to stay.

"So," he said, changing the subject, pouring a cup for her anyway and placing it on the windowsill, "how are they this morning?"

Her eyes followed his gaze to her hands.

"A bit swollen, but I feel no pain."

John glanced up worriedly for a moment, before realizing she was not being completely honest about what she was feeling.

"Tell the truth, Maria," he said sternly, putting his

own cup down beside hers and moving toward her. "Don't you feel even a wee bit of pain? Perhaps a bit of throbbing?"

"Well, I . . ."

"Tell me, lass," he continued, gently lifting one hand and flexing the fingers. "Don't you feel hot bolts of steel running up your arm when I do even this?"

Watching the color drain from her face, John knew Maria was in great pain, whether she admitted it or not.

"Very good," he growled.

"Oh?" she responded, gingerly trying to pull her hand from his grasp. The Highlander held her wrist firmly. "You're happy that I suffer?"

"In this case I am," he answered honestly. "If you still had no feeling, I'd be a bit worried that the injuries were festering."

"I see," Maria murmured. Another thing she had not thought of. "Will they be scarred for life?" she asked, almost as an afterthought.

Turning his own hand, palm up, next to hers, he showed her his own. "Most likely you'll have no scars, but if you don't care for them, or you're truly unlucky, they'll end up looking like these."

She stared at his hand. It was strong, large, and callused, and caused her pulse to flutter and the color to rise in her face.

"But don't despair, lass," he continued, joking. "They're practical hands. Sailor's hands."

"I'll be sure to care for them."

"Has anyone seen to yours this morning?" John asked, looking in to the green depths of her eyes.

Maria shook her head, trying to steady her uneasiness. Without another word, the Highlander reached up and tugged at the tie of her cloak. The heavy garment dropped to the deck at her feet. Too surprised to voice a complaint, she stared at his crisp white shirt.

He knew he'd shocked her by his bold action. But if she wasn't going to make up her mind about going or staying, then he would make it up for her. Releasing her hand, John leaned down and picked up the cloak. Then he hung it from a wall peg. "Didn't that physician of mine visit you in your cabin this morning?"

"He did, Sir John," she answered, her eyes widening as the giant took her by the arm and moved her rather unceremoniously into a chair by the worktable. Maria wondered briefly if this was the way all men treated women outside of the boundaries of court life, or if this was just the Scottish way. She sat down, though, without protest. "He wanted to see to them himself, but I asked him to wait . . . until this afternoon. He told us he would be coming back again then."

John pulled up the only other chair in the room and sat before her. As he reached for her hands, Maria quickly withdrew them, placing them protectively in her lap.

"You don't need to see to them," she said hopefully, looking into his handsome face. "I will allow your physician to change the dressing when he comes back."

But the young woman knew she could not long withstand either his gaze or his outstretched hands.

"There really is no need," she repeated, lowering her gaze to his hands. She hadn't come here to have him see to her dressings. She had a task to accomplish, one she had rehearsed in careful whispers with Isabel before the old woman had drifted off to sleep again. She knew exactly what she had to say and do. But everything Isabel had told her then was becoming far more complicated. Here, alone with this tall and forceful man, she was beginning to forget the words she'd practiced. So close to him, she could smell his fresh, masculine scent. And, as much as she tried to avoid it, she could not help glancing up at his handsome face—at his swarthy and chiseled features, at the black hair swept back from his broad brow, and his deep blue eyes.

Indeed, the longer she sat, the more conscious she became of the continual flush she felt in her cheeks, of the growing heat and chills that seemed to be battling for control of her insides. The longer she sat, the more impossible her task appeared to become.

Laying his hands in his lap, John waited patiently,

quite content for the moment to study her in the light
of day. She was even more beautiful than by candlelight,
her lips even more enticing.

He had assumed her to be a lady, and he was quite
certain that she was. A very proper one. Her bandaged
hands in her lap, she sat erect on the edge of the chair,
clearly discomforted by the present situation, quiet but
alert. Clearly, she had something to say to him; she
wouldn't have come to his cabin otherwise. But whatever
it was, Maria was having a difficult time with it.

John knew she was not unusual in that. He recalled a
journey to Spain, in which he had conveyed the Count
Pedro de Ayala to his home. The old gentleman had
spent a number of years in the court of the Scottish
kings, and together the two travelers had laughed over
the diplomat's witty comparisons of Scottish ways and
those of the rest of Europe. In Ayala's view, John recalled, only Englishwomen enjoyed more freedom than
Scotswomen in expressing their feelings—on whatever
topic was at hand. John himself had never made a study
of it, but he'd been hard-pressed to argue the point.

At any rate, like so many other women John had en-
countered in his travels, Maria was struggling to overcome the distance between herself, as a woman, and
John, as a man. And there was an aloofness that graced
her character, as well. An elegance in her manner that
accented natural beauty, but also served to shield it.

But there was no arrogance, he thought. The arrogance and the vanity that had been displayed in Caroline
Maule seemed to be completely foreign to this young
noblewoman. In fact, her lack of presumption, he knew,
was partly the reason he'd originally thought her so
young.

But perhaps this was all a front, designed to protect
her from potential harm. After all, her position was one
of extreme vulnerability, and John knew she had very
real reason to be concerned. She must be wondering
what fate lay in store for her, for she was completely at
his mercy while aboard the *Great Michael.* And John
had caught glimpses of that curiosity. Perhaps beneath

all the quiet elegance and the reserve, he might find her true self. The real Maria.

He only wondered why he felt so drawn to this notion of bringing out that Maria.

Maria didn't have to look up to know that he was studying her. The silence between them was beginning to unnerve her, but she didn't have the courage to break it. She turned slightly in the chair. This is foolishness, she thought, growing angry with herself. He is just a man. A warrior accustomed to making decisions. She glanced briefly into his face and then lowered her gaze once more.

From the blush that remained on her fair skin, John knew that his closeness made her uncomfortable. But the devil take him, he decided wryly, if he'd pull his chair back and put some distance between them. Proper or not, she had come to his cabin of her own will, and she was just too damned attractive for him to let her off the hook. She wanted something. That's why she'd come. But she was too shy or perhaps too scared to ask. Well, he wasn't about to make it easy for her. The longer it took for her to ask, the better it was, as far as he was concerned. Even if the fog lifted today, they would be at sea for at least a few more days, depending on the wind. And the prospect of having Maria's beautiful face to look at made the thought of this journey enjoyable for the first time.

A second thought drifted into John's mind. Having Maria aboard could keep Caroline Maule at bay. He would have to mull it over. Perhaps . . .

Maria knew she had to break the silence. But while her mind struggled to find the words, her eyes focused on the Highlander's hands again. So different from what she remembered of her husband's soft and delicate hands, John Macpherson's were large and strong. She looked at the soft wisps of dark hair on the back of them, the skin weathered and dark from the sun.

"I've never known anyone so content just sitting and studying hands," John broke in with a low rumbling laugh. He held them to the light, trying to study them

himself. "Aye, quite handsome, they are, I should say.
With such a talent for healing, too. To think that these
are the very same hands which I have to thank for bringing you here to my cabin."

Maria looked up quickly, shaking her head.

"Nay, Sir John. You have it all wrong. The reason for
my visit . . ." the young woman blurted out, her eyes
fixed upon his face. The openness of his gaze on her, his
full mouth breaking into a wide, warm smile made her
breath catch in her throat. Once again, she sat
dumbstruck, lost in the deep, sea-blue of his eyes.
Vaguely, she took in the rest of his face—the skin
around his eyes wrinkled and tan from his broad smile
and from the kiss of the sun. A flame ignited within her.

John lowered his hands to his lap. Her eyes right now
brought to mind the young hawks his older brother,
Alec, still enjoyed training. That is, when his wife, Fiona,
wasn't setting them free. Maria, right now, looked like
she was ready to take flight. When he spoke again, his
voice was low and gentle.

"I was only jesting, lass. You certainly need have no
fear—nor any particular reason, for that matter—in coming here." He looked into her eyes for only a moment,
and then turned his gaze away, nudging one of the cups
gently toward her across the table. "It's not whisky, only
barley water."

Maria reached over and took the cup in her two hands
to drink. She wasn't thirsty. But she was in desperate
need of something to shield herself from his charms, and
from the feelings that were beginning to emerge within
her. Feelings that had hardly flickered in the entire life
of her marriage. Feelings she had begun to think she
might never experience again.

Feelings she did *not* want to experience now.

"Is your companion feeling better?" he asked as she
placed the drink back on the table.

"She is . . . well, no, she is not . . ." Embarrassed,
Maria paused, staring at the cup. Concentrate, she
chided herself. "What I mean is, she is in no pain while

she is sleeping. But when she is awake, I believe she is in great discomfort."

"Aye. Well, that's understandable, I suppose, considering what she has been through."

Maria nodded vaguely. Isabel's words were ringing in her ears. She was to say that Isabel was in considerable pain and that she did not seem to be improving. She was to ask if there was any way the Scots could land the two women on the nearest coast. As in, for example, Denmark.

However, if that request was not received well, then Maria was to lie and say that Denmark had, after all, been their original destination. Considering Isabel's poor health, they would be deeply indebted to the ship's commander. That Sir John would be richly rewarded—with their undying gratitude and with ample financial remuneration. Maria knew very well the words she was to say.

But the Highlander had a way of . . . well, distracting her. One unguarded look at the warrior, and Maria was finding her thoughts a jumble, her words forgotten.

Well, if she was going to relay her message, she knew she'd better do it quickly, before she lost the chance. "I . . . I came here this morning, Sir John, to express our great appreciation—that is, Isabel's and mine—in all you've done for us."

"Isabel!"

Maria looked up in alarm. Had she said too much already?

The Highlander shrugged. "Now, at least, I know your companion's name. And her relation? To you, I mean."

Maria waited an instant and weighed the danger of revealing the truth. But there was none, as far as she could see. Something told her it would be best to stay as near to the truth as she could. She had very little experience with lying, but it seemed that the less one invented, the easier it would be to hold to it later.

"My aunt. Lady Isabel is my aunt."

"And were you and Isabel traveling alone? Or were there other family members traveling with you when your ship came under attack?"

"Alone?" she repeated. He was doing it again—controlling the conversation—and Maria could not allow him to continue. She tried to keep her thoughts focused, but in all her life, she'd never felt as unworldly as she did now. "There were no other family members with us."

John started to voice another question, but stopped abruptly as Maria quickly raised a hand to him. He looked questioningly into her serious face.

"I'll try to explain as much as I can," she said quietly. "But please ask me no more questions now."

"Very well, lass," the Highlander responded, hardly surprised at the young woman's obvious distress. She had no reason to trust him. Her face was turned, and John studied her profile intently. Her eyes were darting nervously about, and he could see her pulse fluttering rapidly beneath the creamy skin of her slender neck.

He'd never provoked this kind of reaction in any woman above the age of sixteen. She seemed afraid of him, and he didn't like it a bit. He wondered if perhaps he'd been, after all, too rough with the woman. Perhaps he was pressing her too hard for information. He needed to choose a new tack.

"But I am afraid if I don't ask you any questions," he continued with a smile, "then we'll sit here in total silence until you—finding naught more interesting in my hands—will realize you've got no reason to stay, and take your leave."

Maria stared at the friendly face. "And what is wrong with that? With me leaving?"

"Quite a bit, I'd say!" John said matter-of-factly. "For one thing, I'd be deprived of your pleasant company. But more importantly, I've your safety to consider."

"My safety?" she cried.

"Aye. Lady Caroline might be standing around the corner, you know. Waiting for your departure."

"But you're guarding my door against such an eventuality."

"Aye," he answered. "*Your* door."

Maria looked uncertainly at him. "You aren't saying I need protection from her while I'm en route?"

"Nay, lass." John leaned his face close to hers, his voice confiding in its tone. "Not you. Now we're speaking of *my* protection."

He certainly had to be jesting with her, but Maria could not discern any hint of it in his face. "Excuse me, Sir John, but you don't look like the kind that needs protection against anything . . . or anyone."

"Ah, but I do," John said, pulling his chair closer and lowering his voice to a whisper. "The truth of it is, while the lady waits around one corner, her husband awaits around the other. Both appear keen on doing mischief at the first opportunity."

"Mischief to you?"

"Aye. To me," John repeated.

Maria stared at him skeptically. "But why?"

John shook his head, then gazed at her thoughtfully. "May I speak in confidence, lass?"

Maria paused, considering his features. She had the sense that he definitely was jesting with her, but beyond the hint of a twinkle in his eyes, nothing in his look betrayed him. Well, there was no harm in having him think her reliable. She nodded, albeit somewhat doubtfully.

"You must promise not to relay this to anyone. Not even to your aunt."

"To whom does this confidence pertain?" she asked quietly.

"To Lady Caroline, of course. And her husband, Sir Thomas Maule."

Maria nodded. "You have my word."

John moved his chair even closer to the young woman's. He fought to stifle his smile as she, in turn, leaned toward him. If gossip was the way to smooth away some of her resistance and fear of him, then, by God, he'd begin inventing tales and slander that would make a tinker proud.

"Sir Thomas Maule," he whispered. "Lady Caroline's husband, you have met him. Haven't you?"

Maria shook her head in response. "Nay, I haven't.

Unless he was one of the faces looking on when you took us aboard."

"He was." John nodded, leaning on his knees. "Well, lass, the man is some twenty years or so older than Lady Caroline."

"Is that bad?" Maria asked curiously. In her case, she had been a year older than her husband and would be seven years older than the Scottish king.

"I can't say it is, Maria, and I can't say it isn't. I suppose it all depends. Lady Caroline is twenty-eight-years old. Still young, but hardly a bairn anymore. The problem lies in the fact that their difference in age does indeed bother Sir Thomas." John watched her expression attentively. She looked so young. "How old are you, Maria? If you don't mind my asking?"

"Twenty-three."

"Are you, now?" John responded, raising an eyebrow. "I am thirty-two."

"Nine years difference. That doesn't seem much for—" Maria stopped abruptly, turning her scarlet face at once toward the bandaged hands in her lap.

This time John smiled openly, but not wanting to lose the ground gained, he reached over and handed her cup to her.

She accepted it gladly and brought it to her lips.

"Aye. Nine years, but where was I?"

She handed him back the cup. "You were telling me about Sir Thomas."

"Aye." John absently examined the empty cup in his hands, and without thinking wiped clinging droplets from the side of the cup with his finger and drew it across his lips.

Maria watched his every move.

"This is a second marriage for Sir Thomas," John said finally, rousing himself.

"I assumed that, Sir John. Mistress Janet is a lovely woman."

"Och, aye. That's right. You know the lass."

"What happened to his first wife?"

"A fever took her. About five years back." John

turned the cup slowly in his hand. "She was a good woman, I should think. Mistress Janet seems to be a young woman brought up with loving care. But this second marriage of his . . ."

"There is no love in the match," Maria said gravely.

John smiled to himself. He loved playing the devil. In truth, he was certain that there was little about the marriage between Sir Thomas and Caroline that hadn't been the subject of endless whispering at court. What he really wanted from this little chat was to learn something more about the green-eyed beauty looking so intently at him now. He wondered what secrets *she* might have to share.

"Love?" John mused. "Well, I don't know. Most folks these days seem to take a view that marriage doesn't have much to do with love. And, to be honest, I don't much hold with that view, but Sir Thomas is a difficult man to call on that account." John placed the cup gently on the table. "I myself have never married, but I wonder if it's possible to love more than once in a lifetime."

Maria stared at him, uncertain of the answer herself.

"You must know what I'm speaking of." John pressed. "You told me you've been married before. Could you ever love again—ever marry again for love—after being on the receiving end of your first husband's love and adoration?"

Maria stared down at her hands. Why had she been so foolish as to bring up the subject of love with regard to marriage. Now she found herself on the spot, and she felt completely unprepared to answer. What could she know about a real marriage? When had she ever felt the love of her husband? When had she ever loved in return?

"You have a fanciful view of marriage, Sir John."

Her expression had turned from grave to despondent in the wink of an eye, and the Highlander knew he was sailing into treacherous waters. But, inexplicably, this glimpse of her emotion drew him irrevocably on.

"How long were you married, Maria?"

She raised her eyes to his face, steadily returning his gaze. "Four years."

"Was it a marriage of love?" John believed he already knew the answer to this question, but he wanted to hear her say it.

Maria paused a moment, then shook her head. "Nay, only a marriage arranged . . . well, for the mutual benefit of our families."

Suddenly, the young woman realized that her knee was touching his, and yet she felt no need—or desire— to remove it. In their four years together, she thought, not even once had she sat with Louis, her husband, alone, in such a conversation as this. Always, there had been others about. Only during his rare and all-too-brief visits to her bed had they spent even a moment alone. She thought now of those distressingly distasteful moments. She had known from the start that Louis had . . . other interests. And then he had led his troops against Suleiman the Magnificent at Mohács, and that had been that.

John saw her withdrawing once again. "Well, lass, for whatever reasons they had for marrying—and whatever Lady Caroline's feelings might be for him, I believe that Sir Thomas is at least infatuated enough with his wife that one might construe his feelings to be love. And that brings us to why he wants me dead."

"Wants you dead?" she repeated, startled by the ominous tone of his voice. "But why?"

"Apparently, he thinks I am having an affair with his wife."

Maria's green eyes narrowed. "Are you?"

John shook his head. "Nay, I have no interest in the woman. I don't believe in carrying on with married women."

"Well, Sir John," she murmured, saying the first thing that came to her mind, "that's . . . honorable." She wondered absently if she could trust his words. He was handsome enough that he probably could choose and carry on an affair with whomever he pleased.

"Thank you, lass," John reached out and brushed the

tips of her exposed fingers with his, watching as she suppressed the instinctive urge to pull them away. "But just because I say it's so, I don't think that is quite enough for Sir Thomas."

The jade green of her eyes glowing with interest, Maria now leaned toward him, capturing his gaze and looking searchingly into his face. "But there must be more to this, Sir John," she said. "I have to assume that the men of Scotland don't make it a practice of hurling charges of such a serious nature at one another . . . unless something has raised their fears, encouraged their suspicions. Why should he suspect you and not the other men aboard this ship? Indeed, why does he not trust his wife? In my country there is great dishonor in a woman being suspected in this way."

"But not a man?" He had to ask.

"You know as well as I, Sir John. Men answer to a different set of standards than women do. But it seems, in this case, this woman's fidelity is the one in question, not yours."

Maria watched in silence as the Highlander stood and walked across the cabin to the window. Pausing there, he turned and looked at her intently, as if trying to decide something. Abruptly, he strode across the floor and sat before her once again. He had her full attention.

"Lady Caroline was, at one time, my mistress," he announced. As the shock registered on her face, John continued, "Before she ever married the man. And our liaison was completely over and done with before their marriage."

"For how long was she your mistress?" she asked under lowered eyelids. Now she could better understand the poor husband's struggle.

John held back his laugh. Her tone and manner conveyed a clear reproach. But seeing Maria come out of her shell was worth the danger of admitting such a thing to her. "Seven years."

"Seven years?" she asked incredulously. "That's longer than the time I was married."

"She was a free woman," John argued, attempting to

defend himself. "And she remained free to spend her time with whomever she pleased."

"Seven years!" Maria repeated.

"And she did have other men in her life," John argued, continuing to maintain his relative innocence. "For each of those years, I spent many, many months at sea. And during those times, she was free to act as she so desired."

"Poor Sir Thomas." Maria shook her head disapprovingly. "The agony the poor man must be going through."

"The agony *he* is going through!" John said, his voice becoming an angry growl. "What of the agony I'm going through."

Maria raised an eyebrow at him. "You don't appear to be in pain."

"You think not, lass?" John protested. "Here I am, being haunted by the husband for something I am totally innocent of. And at the same time, I know that . . . well . . ."

"Know what?" Maria urged him, unconsciously touching his hand.

John moved closer to her and whispered the words. "I know she still fancies me, Maria. In spite of my efforts to discourage her, she wants me still."

"But she is married!" Maria shook her head. My God, she'd led a sheltered life! Up to now.

"I'm starting to think that perhaps her marriage vows don't mean a thing to her."

"But they mean something to you," she huffed, truly wanting to hear him confirm it once again.

John nodded. "Oh, aye. I don't want anything to do with her. I certainly don't love her. I don't care for her. I just want her to keep her distance. Is this too much too ask? In truth, it would bring great dishonor to me and to my family if I were to kill Sir Thomas on our way to . . . well, while we're on this voyage."

"Kill him?" she repeated, shocked.

"Aye, in self-defense. If I am pushed to it."

"Might it come to that?" This was a much more serious matter than she'd thought it to be.

"It very well could," John answered honestly. "The man is known for his temper, for his hot-headedness—and for his lack of trust in his new wife. Depending on Caroline's conduct, we could have war or peace onboard this ship. And trust me when I say it, peace is what I'm praying for."

Maria looked at him. Despite his devilish fondness for teasing, the Scottish warrior seemed to be speaking the truth. The absolute truth. "Why don't you tell her these things? The same way that you've explained them to me. Why don't you explain to her the consequences of such dangerous fancies?"

"I have, Maria. Long ago. And I foolishly thought she understood. But I can see now, I was wrong to think we were finished."

"And you think her husband knows it, as well!" She watched him as he sat back in the chair. "You think he suspects her intentions? You think he suspects you?"

"Sir Thomas would be blind and a fool not to have such suspicions," John asserted with a firm nod. "And he's neither. Aye, the woman is driving him mad with jealousy, and she doesn't know where to stop. He is a man, Maria. Only a man. I know how I would be if I were placed in his position. As men, we are driven by the demands of our honor, of our possessions."

"And women *are* just possessions, aren't they!" she put in sardonically.

That certainly didn't sound good, and John knew it. But he'd spoken the truth of how many men value their wives. Or he thought he had. "You asked a question. I believe the answer is that Sir Thomas wrongly assumes me to be still interested in his wife."

Maria sat back as well, unable to tear her eyes away from him. The man's chin dropped to his chest as he considered the situation. She could see the furrows in his brow visibly deepen. He had taken her into his confidence in a most private matter. A loose tendril of hair freed itself and trailed across his brow. She wished to touch it. He had been so candid; he'd revealed so much. Thinking back over all that had been said already, she felt oddly honored, even thrilled by the thought of being his confidante. But then she paused, the question of his motives flickering through her mind. "Why are you telling me all of this?"

"Because I need your help." The Highlander's gaze was direct. There was no mirth in his expression, nor in his words.

"*My* help?" Her brows shut up incredulously.

"Aye," he answered smoothly. "You could help me greatly in my dealings with these folk."

"But you only met me yesterday. What possible help could I provide?" As exciting as it was to think he was seeking her help and as inviting the prospect of spending more time with him, the truth of it was that Maria had cared very little for Lady Caroline's earlier scrutiny of her. But also, aside from that, Maria wanted to attract the least amount of attention to themselves, especially considering Isabel's condition. The last thing they needed was to become embroiled in some sordid affair between a handsome Scottish sea captain and his jealous ex-mistress. "And how in heaven's name did you ever come up with the idea that I would help you anyway?"

"You don't even know what I am going to ask, and already you are objecting."

"Well, of course. It is all so . . . so . . . ." She shook her head, dismissing the suggestion.

John Macpherson placed his elbows on his knees and leaned toward her. The stubborn set of her jaw and the flash of indignation in her eyes made her all the more interesting to him. Aye, he was drawing out the person within, and he liked what he was seeing. She was quite genuine after all.

"I simply thought we might come to some arrangement, but seeing your hesitation, your quite understandable hesitation . . ." His words trailed off.

"An arrangement?" she asked, her sparkling eyes focused squarely on his face. "What do you mean by that?"

John returned her gaze unwaveringly. "Why did you come to see me, Maria?"

She froze at once; then she opened her mouth to explain, but closed it again. Was she so transparent?

"You came here for more than simply to thank me for saving you and your aunt. You could have done that last night in the cabin or the next time I visited you there." John's eyes drifted to her hands. "And let me see, you didn't come here to allow me to administer aid to your hands, or you would have allowed me to do that by now. So let's see what's left." He let his eyes linger suggestively on her lips, causing her to blush, and then he shook his head. "Nay, having witnessed your disposition and your refined manners, I am harboring no hopes that a romantic venture was your cause for coming." John's eyes bored into hers. "You want something Maria, but I don't know what. Yet I am honest enough to admit that I want something as well. So I don't think it so out of the question to assume, perhaps, that we could . . . well, come to some arrangement."

Her face flushed hot at the frankness of his words, her mind running wild with suppositions about what the Highlander had said regarding wanting something, himself. But this was her chance, after all. He had given her the opportunity. If she could only bring herself to speak the words, then perhaps she could avoid returning to Antwerp. Maria forced herself to remain calm.

"What you say is true," she responded, trying to keep her hands still in her lap as she lifted her gaze bravely. "I came here to make a request. But before I reveal my petition, I need to hear yours first."

John nodded in agreement. "Aye, lass. That's fair enough. These are my terms. I'll tell you how you can help me, but then I'll be needing a decision from you, whether you accept or reject my offer."

There was no charm, no gentleness in the man's face. He was all business. But this was much easier to deal with, so far as Maria was concerned. She nodded at last.

"I want you to become my mistress."

"Your mistress?" the young queen exploded, leaping to her feet and sending her chair sliding violently across the cabin floor.

"Aye," John responded seriously, without moving. "I want Sir Thomas to believe that I have no interest in his wife."

"Sir Thomas? You . . . I could never do such a thing . . . I've never . . ."

The Highlander could not help but smile at the sputtering disbelief that was only now turning into green-eyed fury.

"But only for appearance's sake," he continued in an attempt to head off her anger.

"No! Never!" she managed to stammer out. Maria breathed deeply, trying hard to slow her pounding heart. Wrapping her arms around herself, she turned and looked at the closed door. "I think I—"

"Aye, but before you go, I'd like to explain."

"There is no need, Sir John. You've made your intentions quite clear," she snapped, turning and plucking her cloak from the wall peg.

"You *have* to hear my . . . proposition."

"I don't *have* to do any such thing!" Maria glared at him as she angrily tied the cloak at her neck.

John saw the distrust behind her angry expression. He knew he could probably bully her into listening, but that would only serve to make her fear him. Hardly what he had in mind. "I thought you a reasonable woman," he said.

Her eyes locked on him. "Obviously, you've made a serious error!" The young woman turned and headed for the door.

He leaped to his feet and reached the door before she could get there.

Maria saw he was clearly intending to block her way and a flash of panic raced through her. She came to a stop, staring at the white linen of his shirt. The Highlander said nothing, and Maria slowly raised her eyes to his. "I wish to leave," she said quietly, the waver in her voice only barely discernible.

"Maria, I know my words were impertinent. I apologize for that. But before you leave, I wish you would let me clarify my offer. I only ask you to listen, for a few

moments. Only that." John stepped aside, giving her the
opportunity to escape, if she really cared to. Obviously
disconcerted, the young woman didn't move, but the
commander knew he would need to be quick, before she
decided to march out.

"All I want you to do, lass, is to spend some time
with me. Innocent time," he added for clarification. "The
reason why I used the word 'mistress' is because Caroline Maule's mind runs to that bent. The appearance of
such a relationship is all I'm asking, Maria. That will
be enough."

Maria remained rooted in place, a feeling of foolishness, giddiness even, washing over her. Other than the
mention of the word itself, he'd not implied anything
inappropriate. She had obviously overreacted to seemingly nothing at all. "But it is Sir Thomas who poses the
threat," Maria said. "He doesn't know me, so he'll
surely not believe anything I would say."

"You'll need say naught." John cut her short. "Just
seeing me with you will be enough to put Sir Thomas
at ease."

Maria tried to sort through everything in her mind. It
all had happened so quickly. His request, her temper.
And now, the clarification of his request. She looked at
him straight on. He was still all business. She wished she
could be that calm.

"Please consider it, Maria."

She'd never before needed to consider anything even
remotely similar to this in her entire life. Never. Maria,
the Queen of Hungary, sister to the Holy Roman Emperor—Sir John Macpherson's mistress. Well, not his
mistress in truth, she quickly corrected herself. Was that
any better than being his future queen?

"That's all I ask," John said, cutting into her thoughts.
He could read the struggle in her face. When she looked
up at him, the Highlander nodded gravely. "Now let me
hear what it is you came to ask."

"I came to ask—" She paused and swallowed hard.
By answering him, she knew he might assume that she
would accept the arrangement. "I need to think about

this. What you ask is not . . . well, common to my experience. But if you must know, what I ask is to be taken to Denmark."

"Denmark?" he exploded. "But we are headed for Antwerp."

"Denmark," she repeated firmly. "That is my condition."

John answered her direct gaze with his own. He knew there was no way in hell the *Great Michael* would be going to Denmark . . . unless they were forced to by the fog. Aside from that, there was no way he could justify sailing a convoy of four ships east, two days off course. But there was no reason for her to know that, he decided. And once they reached Antwerp, he would pay her passage anywhere she cared to go.

But only then, he thought.

"Denmark," the Highlander nodded solemnly. "You accept my offer and I'll take you to Denmark."

Chapter 7

The physician turned over the jeweled brooch in his scrawny, yellowed palms. Bringing the bright red stone close to the only candle burning in the darkened room, the man bent over, trying to determine the value of the prize before him.

Caroline Maule moved across the room and snatched the brooch away.

"That's enough, for now." She turned her scowl on the disgruntled man standing with his empty hands now outstretched. "Now start answering my questions, and you shall have it to keep."

The monk nodded irritably at his tall kinswoman, standing only a step away. He wanted a drink. "They are Spanish. That's for certain. And moneyed folk, at that. The old woman's dress had a weave of gold thread in it. Not to mention the jeweled rings that she wears on every finger."

Seeing the small man's eyes wander toward the flask of spirits across the cabin, Caroline rapped the brooch on the table.

"What else? What else?" she snapped. "What do you know of the younger one? Are they kin?"

"Aye, I would assume as much," the physician responded, his gaze again vacillating between the flask and the brooch in the woman's hand. A ring, matching the jeweled brooch, suddenly glinted in the candlelight, catching his eye. "But they're a tight-lipped pair—the lass more so than the lady. Neither has said anything to give away their rank—or all their very worth, for that matter."

"There has to be more!" Caroline stamped her foot. "He's put them in the queen's cabin. He must have a reason. There must be something he is hiding."

The monk shrugged his shoulders. "I'd say you are making more out of it than there is. Though I'm not any friend to the man, the Macpherson is known for such odd kindnesses. From what his men say, even back in the days when he was raiding anything that came his way—English, Spanish, Flemish—no matter; he had too much heart to leave his victims floating in the sea to die. He's smart, too, because there's ransom in saving some, and the spreading of reputation in saving the others. That's why they called him Jack Heart, they say. Why, there's one story that, coming upon a burning ship—"

"Stop, you fool!" Caroline snapped. "I am not paying you to fill my ears with gibberish or with the tales of drunken seamen. I want to know of the woman. Of the younger one. I want to know why he is treating her with such courtesy."

The physician's eyes once again wandered from the flask to Caroline's ring. "Perhaps he's taken a fancy to her. She is a bonny lass."

Caroline turned a deadly gaze on the man. "This is John Macpherson you are talking about. If her skirts were all he was after, he would have just put her in his cabin at once. Nay, there must be something more."

John had never been one for courting or long seductions. Caroline could still remember the first day they met, at Stirling. She had ended up in his bed that day. And they'd been incredible together. His skill as a lover still had the power to make her tremble at the memory, and he'd never failed to appreciate her own talents. Indeed, one place they'd never quarreled was in bed.

"I'd say, Lady Caroline, that for the ring to go with the brooch, I might perhaps be persuading the serving lass to find out what you want to know." The cleric looked at her angry face through slitted eyes. "I'd wager she already knows more than even Sir John about the two of them."

Caroline waved the brooch at him once again and then, with a sneer, tucked it into her skirts.

"Bring me what she knows, and if it's worth more than you've told me so far, you'll get both brooch and ring."

With a quick turn of her wrist, Caroline pulled the hood of her cloak over her head and started for the door. The talk had been a waste of time, and she certainly wasn't about to waste her valuables as well. She should have followed her initial instinct and gone again to John himself.

As she passed into the corridor, a malevolent smile crept across her lips. Aye, that was exactly what she would do, and she wouldn't be foolish enough to go to him as she had earlier.

John was what she was after. This Maria was only a nuisance, and Caroline would sweep her away like so much dust. She was Caroline Douglas, and she would not let herself be distracted by such a petty creature.

John Macpherson was what she wanted. And John, she knew—like a favorite glove.

Maria fought back her embarrassment, and cut in on her aunt's sharp words. "Isabel. Please. I saw an opportunity to keep us from returning to Antwerp. So I took it."

"But at what price?" Isabel snapped. "Where is your head, child? Don't you see the consequences of such an arrangement? Oh, Maria, how could you be so naive?"

Maria sat down heavily on the edge of her aunt's bed.

"I'm not about to do anything wrong. He didn't ask me to do anything dishonorable." Her chin dropped to her chest, and she was certain that whatever it was that had climbed to her throat was sure to choke her. "Sir John made an innocent offer. One that I jumped at— thinking of us—seeing it as perhaps our only possible path to freedom."

"Innocent?" Isabel exploded. Seeing her niece cringe, she paused, forcibly quelling the urge to continue her tirade. As she regained her composure, Isabel took in the sadness in her niece's face, and tried to ignore the pangs of guilt creeping in and replacing her anger. The older woman shook her head. Once again, she could see the reason why the Lord had seen to it not to provide herself with a husband, or bless her with a child. With her lack of patience, she was unfit to be a good mother. Unfit and full of bad advice.

Looking at the distraught young woman, she considered for a moment the mess she'd made of Maria's life. After all, it had been Isabel who sent her off to the Highlander's cabin today. It had been she, Isabel the Foolish with another of her brilliant ideas. Now it was up to her to talk Maria out of it. Foolish, foolish woman, she thought. Nothing more than a foolish old woman. Clearing her throat, Isabel tried to weave a note of gentleness into her tone. "It was wrong of me, Maria, to suggest that you go to him. Even if things had gone differently, even if he'd agreed to take us there with no further conditions, Denmark offers us only a temporary refuge."

"Perhaps so. But it is a refuge. Denmark is one more step away from Charles." Maria took heart in the softening in her aunt's words. "Isabel, please don't think the worst. Let me go through with this. I just can't go back to Antwerp. I can't face my brother. You know, better than anyone, what this means. Aunt, I have broken every rule; I have done the unthinkable. I have escaped Charles's grasp, running from his palace, from his city. I have sailed away from him, only to find myself escaping in a ship under attack. And I have . . ."

Her words faltered, and she reached out, placing her bandaged hand on her aunt's arm. Isabel's face revealed nothing of what she might be thinking, and the elderly woman kept her gaze firmly on her niece's injured hand.

"Please listen," the young woman continued, her voice stronger. "What I have been asked to do by Sir John is nothing compared to what I have already done for the good of my family. This Scot is an honorable man, Isabel. He doesn't know a thing about us, and yet, see how well we've been treated. I believe he means what he says. I believe he wants no more from me than what I have told you."

Isabel slowly raised her gaze to Maria's face. "You've just said all I need to know to prove to you the error in this path. Think of what you've just said—he doesn't know a thing about us. Not a thing."

Maria watched her aunt closely. "Aye?"

"Maria, he doesn't know you are a queen. He doesn't know you are promised to his own king. He doesn't know you are sister to Emperor Charles, the most powerful ruler in the world."

"I don't understand. What difference does any of this make? These are the things we don't want him to know."

"Of course we don't, but think of what it means. In his eyes, we are no different than any other poor soul he might find drifting in the sea. He has no reason to believe that we are anything other than what we tell him we are. He is freed from any constraint other than what normally constrains him. And as a man, those constraints are practically nonexistent, believe me. His mission, his loyalty—these things are irrelevant in his thinking right now." Isabel lifted Maria's chin slightly. "This Scot sees a beautiful woman, that's all. A woman with no attachment, vulnerable and available for his use. I'm surprised he hasn't forced you into his bed already."

Maria shook her head. "You are placing more weight in this than there is. You talk as if his actions must be motivated by vice and malice."

"Nay, I've said nothing of malice," Isabel corrected her. "Your Sir John is just being a man. And interestingly, a man you are quick to defend, my dear."

Seeing Maria flush crimson, Isabel pressed on. "Let me guess what you see in him. And you *have* looked at him, Maria. What woman could avoid it? Let me guess. You have seen charm in his manner, nobility perhaps. You have seen confidence in those dark blue eyes, in the way he moves, in the way he talks. I know you have, child. We both have. And I can't remember when I've seen a better-looking man than this one." Isabel paused, thoughtfully. "But he is a hunter, Maria. One of those who believes the Lord has given him license to take whatever he wishes. He has no need for innocent companions. He can have whomever he wants."

Isabel pushed herself up in the bed, wincing slightly at the weight she put on her aching shoulder. Leaning gently back against the pillow, she sighed before focusing her attention once again on her niece. "And there is nothing innocent, Maria, in what he is after."

Maria looked up as Isabel took her hand.

"Listen to me, child. Women throw themselves into the arms of a man like him. That's what he is used to. No loyalties, no love, no conditions, just pure surrender. That's what he is accustomed to and that's what he'll expect from you."

Maria stood up and stalked to the table, fighting all the while the anger that surged through her at Isabel's words. His bed. All her aunt thought he wanted her for was his bed.

Maria's thoughts went back over the brief encounters they'd had. The Scot was always at ease, always unaffected. The man seemed to be, at least, perfectly comfortable with himself—and with her. John Macpherson was everything Isabel had described and more. Much, much more.

Eyes blazing, lips set in a tight line, Maria turned to her aunt. The young queen's anger was burning within her. Anger that she felt toward Isabel, for being able to see what she herself had been blind to. Toward the Highlander, for his unbridled charm and his forward manner. Toward herself, for being so naive.

But deep within her, tucked far back in the recesses of her mind, Maria sensed a needlepoint of light that refused to go away. It poked at her anger, and at her aunt's assertions. After all, so much of what Isabel had said was merely speculation. Speculation based on the observations of a few brief moments when they were taken aboard the *Great Michael.* And even though Maria had, in her heart, already resigned herself to rescinding the agreement she'd come to with the ship's commander, she still saw it necessary to defend him—and his honor. That little needle of light demanded it.

"He is a user of women, Maria. That sums him up. I know. I've seen more than my share."

"How can you judge him so harshly? After all, consider what he has done for us. We must be fair, Isabel—not condemn him solely because of one woman's weakness." Maria's voice could not hide the disappointment she was feeling at her aunt's harsh words, but also the disappointment with herself. "Isabel, my inability to carry out a simple, well-rehearsed discussion is the cause of these things that you speak of. Honestly, beyond that failure on my part, nothing—not Sir John's words, his actions, not even his request of me—nothing has given either of us any hint of the lack of character you describe. He has been nothing but civil, courteous, and gallant. And he is not the unfeeling seducer you imagine."

"There is no purpose in discussing this with you." Isabel shook her head, straightening the blankets on her lap. She knew there was merit in what the young woman said, but she was too old, too tired, and too stubborn to want to dawdle over the fine points of this. "You are an innocent, Maria, unworldly and completely unschooled in the matters of heart and the ways of men. So let us just end this right now."

"I object to that, Aunt," Maria said in a steady tone, unwilling to give the older woman the final word. "I might not have had the days of courting that other women have. And it is true, I have not been in the company of a great number of men. But I do know as well as you matters that pertain to the heart. And as to the ways of men, no one alive has had their life dictated more severely by men than myself. And, Isabel, I know the difference between right and wrong."

Seeing her aunt ease herself farther beneath the bedclothes, Maria knew that their conversation was rapidly coming to a conclusion. "Aunt Isabel, John Macpherson is not a wicked man."

"I never said he was," the elder woman chirped

quickly. "In fact, in my younger days, meeting someone as handsome and as gallant as he is would have been the answer to my dreams. But, as a young rebel, I never concerned myself much with consequences . . . or with the opinions of future subjects."

Maria watched as her aunt sank more deeply in the bed, the elderly woman's eyelids once again showing the effects of the medicine.

The young queen walked to her side and pulled the blanket up to her chin. Like so many conversations with Isabel, this one would have no resolution nor end.

Then, suddenly, Isabel's eyes sprang open once more. "Maria, your arrangement with the man . . . it is off. Understand? It is off!"

Maria nodded heavily. "As always, you know best."

As he made his way toward the stern of the ship, John glanced up through the heavy fog at the ice beginning to coat the rigging. The light streaming from the lantern hanging amidships seemed to push at the cold shroud enclosing the ship, and reflected defiantly off the glistening droplets clinging to the lines above. There had been no change in the fog that surrounded them, but the temperature had been steadily dropping for hours. And that was a promising sign.

John peered out into the mists.

"Aye, m'lord. My brother Andrew said you were looking for me."

John swung around and faced his navigator. "Aye, David. Fetch your charts and meet me in my cabin."

David nodded at his commander's order. But as he turned to go, the pilot paused, a grin tugging at his lips. "It wouldn't be that the idea of standing fast here for a week has lost its charm, m'lord? All it took was spending one dinner in the galley with the lot of them."

John rubbed his face with his hands and pulled his cloak around him. It was true, he had spent the past few hours in the company of the delegation in the ship's galley. But surprisingly, the time had been passed fairly pleasantly and with no complaints. "It wasn't as bad as

it could have been. Sir Thomas dropped anchor beside
me, and we passed the time talking of land routes and
charts. It wasn't bad at all."

"And what was Lady Caroline doing all the while?"
David needled.

"Thank God, she was doing naught that I know of.
She wasn't there. Sir Thomas said something was ailing
her, but I didn't think to pursue the matter." Not interested in this line of discussion, John turned in the direction of his cabin. "Run and fetch the charts, lad. Sir
Thomas is to meet us there shortly."

"You are telling him our route, Sir John?" David
whistled. "Well, this is a first."

John faced the navigator. "David, the man has
attached himself to me like a growth. If he were any
closer, I'd have to wear him as a kilt."

"Aye, I can see you've a problem." David shook his
head gravely, struggling to hide his mirth. "Well, I'm
glad it's you he's interested in and not me."

"Aye, I'm certain you are. It does make Mistress Janet's time a wee bit more . . . free. Eh, Davy?" John
looked on wryly as the young navigator shrugged his
shoulders and gazed noncommittally into the mist. "The
man does know quite a bit about land routes into the
Netherlands, though. I thought I'd show him the maps
and get his opinion, in case we need to send a man
overland."

David started to say something, but stopped, nodding
with a resigned shrug and heading off to do as he was
told.

"David," the Highlander called after him.

"Aye, m'lord."

"You don't have to be nice to him."

John's hand froze in midair as he reached for the latch
of his cabin door. His eyes narrowed at the realization
that the door itself was ever so slightly ajar. Laying his
hand on the hilt of the razor-sharp dirk that hung from
his belt, the warrior eased the door open a crack.

The only light in the long corridor came from the

flame of a solitary wick lamp, but as John peered into the cabin, he could see that someone had lit a candle. From the angle that the small opening afforded, he could see no one inside.

There was no way David could have gotten there before him. And Sir Thomas, John decided, would have waited outside. Other than the ship's navigator, no one would even consider violating the sanctity of the master's cabin. Thinking of the valuables and the chest carrying the men's pay, John's face darkened at the thought that one of these nobles would have the audacity to enter his chamber.

The Highlander drew his dirk and pushed the door open farther. Whoever it was, they would pay.

The shadow of the damask bed curtain hid her face, but the transparent lace-edged shift concealed nothing else. Stunned momentarily by the sight of the woman stretched enticingly upon his bed, John stood motionless on the threshold, his eyes taking in the perfection of the full, round breasts, the nipples showing darkly through the gauzy material. His gaze traveled appraisingly along the intruder's long and shapely legs, the clinging shift doing nothing to hide her womanly charms.

"I didn't know if you were ever coming back," Caroline said softly, her long, blond hair falling forward as she leaned into the light.

The lines of John's face grew taut and grim at the realization of who it was that had invaded his private domain. Fighting the anger that was gathering in his chest, the Highlander suddenly saw Caroline's face change with a start as she stared past him into the corridor. He whirled, ready to counter the blow from her husband. But the blow never fell.

Maria stood at his elbow, her eyes locked on the woman lying naked on the bed.

Chapter 8

Revolted by her own naivete, Maria felt suddenly quite ill. Taking a quick step backward, she banged heavily into the door before turning in a wild attempt to escape from the room. Isabel had spoken the truth. He was no more than a womanizer and a cheat. And she was a fool to have defended him. A fool to have believed anything he'd told her.

A firm hand grabbed her wrist as she crossed the threshold, and she let out a sharp cry. Twisting frantically to free herself from his grip, she saw the Highlander's imploring face.

"Let me go!" she cried. "Let me—"

John Macpherson's strong hands caught hold of her other hand and he held both, pulling her back against the doorjamb. He looked hard into her angry face, into eyes flashing with obvious disgust. He could feel her body trembling as she gave up trying to pull free of him. His words came out clipped and sharp. "I need your help!"

Maria shook her head from side to side, trying again to twist her bandaged hands out of his grip. "You are hurting me. Let me go."

John cast a quick look down the corridor. No one was coming. Not yet. "Listen to me—"

"I won't!" Maria fought him with all her strength. "Go back to her. Let *her* help you. She is the one waiting for you."

He let go of her hands, but grasped her by the shoulders in a viselike grip. "It is not what it seems, lass. I walked in here only a moment before you. I was caught offguard as surely as you."

"Save your lies for someone else." Maria looked up into the darkening features of the Highlander, and suddenly she felt her knees go weak. His gaze flickered away, and then he focused his eyes on her mouth. Filling her lungs to scream, Maria twisted in his arms, only to find herself suddenly flattened against the doorjamb—his big hand pinning her tightly to the wood. He pushed his weight against her, and she thought her lungs were about to explode.

"Damn it, woman. I'm telling you the truth." John looked into her angry, frightened green eyes, only inches away from his. "I tell you this is all her doing. She is trying to wreak havoc here. Her husband is due to meet me here any moment."

Maria shook her head, unable to speak. She wouldn't believe him. He was crushing her; she had to get away. Turning her head, she tried to close her mind to his words.

"Come, Maria, do you think me a fool? Would I summon Sir Thomas to my cabin while—"

From the far end of the corridor, she heard the creak of the door leading from the deck. She felt him stiffen. She heard the urgency in his words as the footsteps faltered uncertainly.

"He is here!" John whispered, his hand lifting her chin. Her shoulder stung from the grip of his other hand, and she could feel the sea air sweep damp and cold around her feet. The tone of his voice conveyed more an appeal than a command. "Kiss me, Maria. Kiss me."

She tried to turn her head in the direction of footsteps, thinking to call for help. Out of the corner of her eye, she caught a glimpse of the stocky man standing at the end of the hall, the young navigator looking over his shoulder. But as she turned, the Highlander's mouth crushed down upon hers. Maria's eyes widened in surprise as his lips devoured hers.

As the commander turned her slightly, Maria could just see the frown stealing across the aging warrior's face. Then she saw the glimmer of the dagger at the man's belt, and her mind began to race. John's mouth was imprisoning hers, his lips and teeth rough and insistent. But all she could think of was how Caroline's warlike husband would react, once he found his wife naked in the cabin. In this man's cabin.

Her hands were free. She could easily disengage her mouth and scream. If she cried out, the two men would surely come to her aid, she thought. But then what? Maria's mind tried to make sense out of the whirlwind of activity that had suddenly engulfed her. If Sir Thomas came as far as the cabin door, he would unquestionably see his wife inside. And upon perceiving Lady Caroline and her disgraceful situation, wouldn't her husband be bound by the dictates of honor to fight the Scot? He would, she was certain, and then someone would be hurt. Perhaps even killed.

John Macpherson was beginning to feel a bit foolish. Maria's lips were unyielding, her body stiff as a branch, and he knew that she was not going to cooperate. Sir Thomas continued to stand at the end of the corridor; he had to be wondering whether to interrupt or go back the way he and David had come. It had not taken long to comprehend Caroline's motives. But he didn't know if she'd planned on going so far as to be the cause of bloodshed. There was no movement, no sound from inside the cabin. It was too much to assume that the lady wanted her husband dead. But that was exactly what might happen, and John quickly considered what would follow.

In a final effort to stop the imminent battle from happening onboard his ship, John dragged his mouth to Maria's ear and whispered, "Believe me, lass. This is not what I want. I'll have to kill him if he comes any closer."

He felt the change move through her, as if she suddenly understood the situation facing him. John felt her hands move around him of their own accord.

Tightening his arms around the rigid woman and kissing her soft earlobe, he whispered again. "This is Caroline's doing. Help me, Maria."

She had to be insane to go through with this, but she couldn't reject his plea. She hesitated a bit, then closing her eyes to the world and to the shame which she knew she was bringing on herself, she slid her hands tentatively over John Macpherson's shoulder, and yielded to his kiss.

The moment she did, John tightened his grip, pressing the contours of her body against his, and pulling her away from the wall. He gazed into the jade green of her eyes.

Maria raised herself on her toes and curved her fingers around the nape of his neck. Pressing her weight against him, she crushed her lips to his waiting ones. She felt his muscles tighten at her bold act.

A moment earlier, John would have been happy— quite happy—just to drag her into his cabin and close the door. Assuming Sir Thomas had recognized Maria, that would have been enough to persuade the man to leave them and come back at another time. But the Highlander was no longer conscious of what he'd been thinking a moment earlier.

Suddenly, everything had changed. A primitive desire was pouring through his veins. The beautiful woman in his arms was continuing to kiss him, her arms tightening around his neck, her hands pulling at his hair, encouraging him closer. Her soft mouth was teasing, tempting, yielding to his kiss, her body softening to an intimacy that he was all too willing to give. Again, John pressed her against the doorjamb, and his hands shifted, his fingers gliding up over her shoulders, and then burying themselves in the silken mass of her sable tresses.

"Ahem!" The older man cleared his throat discreetly down the corridor.

"We must be early," the other one responded.

Maria heard the pins drop to the floor at her feet. Then she shuddered involuntarily as she felt her long hair tumble around his gentle hands.

The Highlander was sliding his mouth back and forth over her burning lips, urging them to open. Surrendering to his silent demand, she parted her lips. She heard him groan deep in his throat as he took a fistful of her hair, his tongue plunging deeply into the soft recesses of her mouth.

A silent thrill raced through her as hidden desires flooded her. Feelings she never even knew she had suddenly erupted within her. Lost in the seductive play of his tongue, the heat of his embrace and his roaming hands, she responded with newfound ardor. Her body ached for his touch, her heart pounded, and her mind whirled in the heady closeness of his embrace. Maria gave another silent moan of surrender, as she parted her lips more, taking him deeper. She gave all she thought she could, but his searching mouth delved even more deeply for more. And she gave it.

"Perhaps we should go," the young navigator whispered in the distance.

"He was the one who asked me here," the older man answered.

She had never been kissed like this before. She could feel his body, his hips—hard and pulsing—against hers. And like a famished pauper languishing at the sight of the feast, she found herself foundering, her body at one moment filled with sensations of crystalline clarity, and the next with impressions of misty oblivion. And she gave in to his touch, shuddering at the passion, matching his rhythm. Maria moved her fingers along his shoulders, wanting to feel the strength, the magic that she knew he held within.

The giant was caressing her narrow waist, his fingers rising beneath the heavy cloak to the sides of her breasts, pressing the firm orbs through the thickness of the wool dress. She moaned and pressed closer to him. Vaguely, she felt his entire body ignite at the open abandon of her response.

To Maria, this was all a dream. The level of desire, the impending threat of danger, the overwhelming sensuality—these were things she had never experienced, never sought out, never known. She was helpless under the insistent pressure of his mouth and his searching hands. And to her dismay, she welcomed the incredible helplessness. She tightened her grip around his neck and pulled his face down even farther to deepen the kiss.

Maria drew in her breath and leaned her head against the door as his hands gently cupped her breasts through her dress. Then, as the Highlander's lips moved to her earlobe, she angled her head to give him access. When he traced a line with his tongue and his mouth down the side of her neck, she felt her heart stop.

"My God, you are sweet," he murmured hoarsely. "And so beautiful . . ."

It might have been the touch of his searching lips, working themselves inside the neckline of her dress, forcing a needle of consciousness into the pulsing mists of her senses. She didn't know where it came from, but somehow Maria's uneasiness reemerged as she slowly recalled that she was nothing more than a diversion the Highlander was using to deflect Sir Thomas's attention from the woman in the cabin.

In a second, anger and shame flooded through her, replacing the feelings that had controlled her only moments before.

Caroline! Maria stiffened as the commander continued to kiss the skin of her neck, his hands continuing to explore her body inside her cloak with practiced certainty. Quite an audience for him, she realized, sadness adding nothing to her damaged self-respect.

From down the hall, the young man's words reached her. "Well, Sir Thomas, I see we have a change of plans."

Maria knew Sir John was pretending he hadn't heard David's words. Angling his hand across her back, he continued to press his lips against her skin, his tongue teasing and provoking. His hands slid casually down over the curve of her buttock, cupping and pressing her hips to his.

"Aye," the elder man said with a chuckle. "It appears Sir John has something else on his mind."

John broke his contact with her mouth, and Maria felt herself being pulled around behind the huge frame of the Highlander. His attitude was suddenly that of a man caught off guard, and his action that of shielding her. When he spoke, though, his words had a note of amusement in them. "Ah . . . Sir Thomas . . . David. I see you've come. Well, tomorrow's soon enough for what I'd wanted to say to you, Sir Thomas. Till tomorrow, then."

Maria watched the two men move back down the corridor, each of them throwing playful looks over their shoulders.

"I say tomorrow is too soon," the navigator said, loud enough to be heard.

"Aye, lad. In fact, I'm feeling quite tired myself," Sir Thomas said. "I think I'll retire to my cabin and see if Lady Maule isn't feeling a wee bit better."

Suddenly, John felt Maria stiffen behind him. He knew what she was thinking.

"That is Lady Caroline's problem, not ours!" he whispered, taking her hand in his.

Maria pulled her hands away from him as he turned to face her. He took hold of her arms gently and smiled down at her, self-satisfaction written all over his face. Maria disengaged her arms and shoved hard against his broad chest.

"Stop it!" Maria cried softly, looking angrily away from his surprised face. "They are gone. Let me go!"

Stunned by the sound of tears in her voice, John stared down at her. Her face was flushed, though with desire or anger he now had no idea. Her lips were swollen from his kisses, her eyes troubled. He placed his hands on the sides of her face. His blood roared with the hunger he felt for her. The way she had felt in his arms, her exquisite surrender, her response to his touch all drove him with a desire to have more of her. Indeed, for a few moments, he had forgotten that anyone was within shouting distance.

But now she looked as if she was ready to run. Softly, trying to not scare her, he asked, "What is wrong, Maria?"

"She is waiting for you!" she burst out, tossing her head toward the cabin interior without looking in. Shoving at his chest, she tried to get out of the circle of his arms, but he wouldn't release her. "I helped you to send her husband away. Now let me go."

John shook his head to clear it. Maria was right. The problem of Caroline still remained. Caroline, he cursed inwardly, glancing in at the motionless figure on the bed. What was going on in that twisted brain, he wondered. She, too, had witnessed the entire scene, yet had said nothing.

"What I said before about her was the truth," John said, focusing his gaze on Maria. He squeezed her shoulders gently. "I have no reason to lie to you, lass."

Maria turned her head away from him. "I've done what you asked me to do. Now let me go." She needed to get away, to run. Her response to him was now filling her with shame. How could she have been so foolish? Even now, the feel of his strong hands, the smell of the masculine scent, the taste of him filled her senses. Even now, she could feel the brush of his tartan against her skin.

She was such a fool. In spite of everything, she could feel herself being drawn to him again. He was too close. She needed to get away from him.

Slowly, John looked around. He refused to look again into his cabin. He didn't want to see Caroline. He let his hands drop from Maria's shoulders and took a step back. "I'll take you to your cabin."

"That won't be necessary," she snapped, reaching down and picking up the pins from the floor.

Silently, John watched her face with a great deal of interest. The same woman who had melted in his arms only moments ago, was now visibly rebuilding her defenses, forcing herself to ignore his presence as she gathered up her hair into a loose knot on the top of her head.

Maria knew getting away from him should be her first priority, but she also knew that she could not return to her cabin in such disarray as this. If Isabel was awake, she would see through her in a moment.

"I'll walk you back," he said quietly. Then, raising his voice—obviously for the benefit of the woman inside the cabin—he continued, his tone severe. "And I'll be sending a few of my men down here to rid my cabin of all unwanted, and uninvited, intruders."

He offered his arm to Maria, but the young woman ignored the gesture. Avoiding his gaze, she finished tucking the last rebellious strands of hair in place and directed her steps down the corridor.

John followed along behind her, watching the silky mass of hair. In spite of her efforts, the thick, ebony tresses threatened to spill down her back. He still could recall the softness and the fragrance of it. Looking over her shoulder, his gaze lit on the side of her face—on the porcelain skin, a blush subtly tinting the high cheek bones. He remembered the satin feel of it under his lips' caressing assault. It occurred to him that he could no more stop admiring her beauty than he could put from his mind the passion of their kiss, the flutter of her pulse as he tasted the skin at her throat, the press of their hips, and the sultry look in her green eyes. He found himself hardening at the thought of her, his blood rising once again at the stirring in his loins.

Obviously aware of the heat of his gaze on her, she quickened her steps. "There is no need to be rushing, lass," he said evenly as they reached the door leading to the deck.

Without answering, she pulled at the latch. The cold, wet mist slapped her in the face as she stepped out onto the windswept deck, bringing her to an abrupt halt.

"There is *every reason* to rush!" she cried out, whirling on him as he followed her through the door.

His expression, smug and amused, provoked her to new heights of anger.

"I've done what you asked of me." She tried to slow her breathing. "But you should know that what happened below, I did against my will . . . against my better judgment. I . . . I came to your cabin to tell you the arrangement was off, and then you . . . you . . ."

"You're telling me you changed your mind."

"I have. There is no deal," she warned him. "I refuse to spend time with you. I refuse to be any part of this sordid, deceitful game. And I refuse to become the focus of idle talk on this ship. I refuse to be thought your . . . your . . ."

"Lover?" he asked with arching eyebrows.

It sounded so beautiful on his lips. It was not what she'd been searching for, but this word—rippling with the notes of his broad Scots accent—thrilled her deeply, and she stared at the Highlander. The wind was whipping wisps of damp black hair across his handsome face. She hated him.

Quickly she turned and stalked to the railing. The flame in the large covered lamp by the mainmast flickered wildly, and the raindrops that struck the top and sides sizzled violently.

"As you say," she nodded sharply, turning to face him. "So there you have it."

As she stood defiantly before him, her chin raised, droplets of water glistening like diamonds in her hair, John gazed in rapt admiration at the woman. Then, in the span of a moment, the commander realized that—whatever she might say—their earlier encounter had produced unexpected results. Judging from her words and the rigid set of her jaw, the Highlander had no doubt Maria was determined to avoid any further romantic encounter. But her huge, green, dark-lashed eyes were telling him something else. She had been as affected by what had passed between them as he. They had both felt the heat, the passion, and he knew it.

And now, after tasting her lips and feeling her response to him, he wanted more.

John reached out and pulled the hood of her cloak over her head. She recoiled at his forwardness, but he ignored the response. She didn't run, at least, or even voice a complaint at his action.

"I'm thinking, lass, that it may be too late for such second thoughts. But whatever you decide you want to do, standing around in this weather isn't going to help you much. Granted, it's fine weather. Much like what we're accustomed to at home. But not being a Highland lass, you should probably try to stay warm and dry—

until you regain your strength, that is. I'll walk you to your cabin.''

Maria stood gaping at the giant. All the arguments that she had prepared were left hanging on her tongue. She had wanted to discuss business—to bring up Denmark. She was ready, if need be, to make an offer of payment—were he to deliver them there. But Maria also wanted to tell him that he was probably correct in saying that it was too late for second thoughts. That she'd already met her part of the bargain by being seen kissing him in the corridor. She wanted, more than ever, to tell him that now it was his turn to pay.

But before she could utter a word of it, the Highlander took her brusquely by the elbow and started back toward the door leading below. For a moment Maria considered pulling her arm away and making him listen to her, but then she decided against it, for deep inside, the young queen knew that, even if she could force him to stand and listen, she wasn't truly certain she could bring herself to mention their encounter again.

John hid his smile as he led her down the stairs toward her door. The flushed look of her fair skin, the furrowed crease of her brow, showed her inner strife. And what she was thinking reflected in her face like the sun on a pool of water. But it was not the obvious lack of guile that he found so attractive, so much as the fact that she was as drawn to him as he was to her. And for right now, that mattered most of all.

Outside of Maria's cabin door, John spotted the elderly sailor at his post.

"To the galley with you, Christie," the commander ordered. "Tell Cook that you're to have a wee bit of something to warm your insides. And when you've finished, see if you can find your way back here."

Arching one bristly eyebrow, Christie straightened up from his position against the wall.

"Aye, m'lord," the sailor responded cheerfully, giving Maria a grizzled wink as he passed. "Though it may take more than 'a wee bit' to warm these old bones this evening."

Maria watched as the elderly sailor tripped lightly up the steps with an agility that belied his age. Reaching for the door latch, she turned finally toward the Highlander—whose gaze she'd been assiduously avoiding—to bid him good-bye. This would be the end, she thought decidedly. This was the last time she would leave her cabin before the ship docked at Antwerp. Whatever plan she could devise to escape her brother Charles would have to be arranged once they reached Antwerp.

Farewell, Sir John," she murmured uneasily, turning her face toward the door.

The Highlander put his hands on her shoulders, turning her around and pulling her close.

"Nay," he whispered. "You'll not escape me quite so easily."

She looked up into his deep blue eyes in surprise.

"But . . ." The words died in her throat as she felt his hands slide up the side of her neck, cradling her face in his large, firm hands.

His gaze shifted to her lips, and he brushed the full, lower lip with his thumb.

"What are you doing?" Maria whispered foolishly.

"I am going to kiss you again."

"Against . . . against my will?" she asked shakily.

"Nay, lass, not against your will," he whispered, slowly lowering his head. "But perhaps against your better judgment."

His mouth covered hers, and within her chest a shower of sparks rained down. This was so different, this kiss. So different from the one before. He was now a man with all the time and all the patience in the world. At first the kiss was light—coaxing, shaping, and exploring. Then, as his hands shifted, drifting down her spine to draw her closer, his mouth became possessive. Lost in the kiss, Maria moved her hands inside his shirt, over his chest and broad shoulders, and then she wrapped her arms around his neck.

The moment she molded herself to him, his mouth opened further, his tongue becoming more demanding. Maria felt herself shaking with the power of his touch.

His muscular leg moved between hers and pressed against her intimately. Her hands traced the strong lines of his back.

John's hand slid inside her cloak, covering her breast, caressing it through the bodice of her dress, while his other hand swept restlessly behind her, cupping her buttock and pulling her tightly against his aroused body.

Maria pushed her hips against his powerful frame and felt his hot arousal nestling against her. As Maria moved with him, all thoughts of resistance she had conjured up before exploded in an instant. Instead, her body strained for more of his touch.

When the Highlander finally broke off the kiss, Maria found herself floating weightless in a pool of light. Somewhere in the distance she could hear the pounding of hoofbeats, racing in a wild and endless race. How odd, she thought vaguely, to hear the sound of hoofbeats—here at sea. Reluctantly, the young woman focused her consciousness on the sound until it became more distinct. Recognizable. Not horses, she smiled to herself. Rather, the sound of a heart. Hers? She wondered. As her senses slowly cleared, Maria perceived that she was standing in the circle of his arm, her head resting against his chest, and she knew whose heart she was hearing. His. Rapid, solid, and true.

But as she tried to make sense out of what was happening to her, she realized that her own heart was undeniably racing in tandem with his.

John slowly raised her chin until their gazes locked.

"Against your will or against your better judgment, we don't seem to be able to get enough of one other." His voice was husky. "So, lass, what are we going to do about it?"

Maria stepped back from his embrace, shaking her head, her face burning. She couldn't. She just couldn't.

"Do?" she whispered, her voice cracking as she reached for the latch. "Nothing! We can do nothing, Sir John. I will not see you again."

The commander laid his hand on hers, preventing her from raising the latch. "This is a small ship, Maria."

"Please don't make it harder than it is." Pushing his hand away, Maria opened the door and stepped inside the cabin. Once across the threshold, she hesitated, keeping her eyes averted as she turned back toward him. "I'll stay inside these walls and you must stay outside."

The Highlander placed his big hand against the door as she moved to close it.

"That isn't what you want, Maria."

"Please!" she repeated, the hint of panic in her voice evident to them both as she pushed the door closed. "Stay away!"

Chapter 9

The glare weighed heavily on the sleeping woman.

In her dream, she could feel the weight pressing down on her. She had found herself running, falling, the weight overwhelming her, crushing her, smothering her.

Janet Maule's eyes flew open, and—unable for a moment to get her bearings—she stared at the blue cap with the feather that lay on the pillow next to her head.

"David?" the young woman whispered in alarm as she jerked to a sitting position. The early dawn's dim light was making a weak attempt, at best, to brighten the small cabin. Janet peered first at the closed door, squinting her eyes as she attempted to survey the rest of the room. Her progress halted on the blurred image of a person sitting silently in the far corner of the cabin.

"David!" she called quietly, pulling the blanket to her chest. "Is that you?"

"Nay, hussy. The foul thing has gone!"

The young woman's hand flew to her mouth as she recognized the chill tones of her stepmother, Caroline.

"How long have you been sitting there?"

"Long enough." Caroline Maule lifted herself off the three-legged chair and walked slowly toward the small bunk. "Aye, long enough to hear you proclaim your own disgrace."

The woman's shawl slipped from her hair down onto her shoulders. She shook her head with disdain.

"Calling his name out." Caroline stopped beside the bed, glaring down at her stepdaughter. "Ah, the shame of it. Your father, the old fool, was heartsick with worry over you last night. And for no reason, so far as I could tell. Little did *I* know, come to find out. But it mattered nothing what I might say to him. Sir Thomas wouldn't rest until I agreed to come check on you. And it appears the man knows his own daughter. Aye, quite a surprise, you are!"

Janet felt her limbs go cold at the words. Last night she had bid David good night outside of her door. Her face flushed at the memory of that first kiss. The tingling pleasure had remained on her lips for quite some time before she had finally fallen asleep. Later, in her dreams, they had been together. But that was only in her dreams. Those happy moments had only been a vision—a vision crowded out by the crushing weight that had pursued her, oppressed her, and finally awakened her.

And that had been the extent of their involvement. David had never so much as stepped inside these walls. She was certain of that.

But then, where had his hat come from? Her eyes locked on the colorful cap, the jaunty feather. It could belong to no one but David. Janet reached out quickly to grab the hat. She must hide it. But Caroline's hands snatched it away.

"Too late to hide the evidence, slut."

Janet watched, bewildered, as her stepmother seated herself on the edge of her bunk. Caroline held the blue bonnet with one hand while the other slowly caressed the long feather.

"You father must see this, of course."

"My father?" Janet swallowed audibly.

"I'm sad to say, I believe he suspected this all the while." Caroline's eyes were accusing and direct. "Why else would he have asked me to come to you at this god-awful hour of the morning?"

Janet sprang upright in the bed, tucking her feet under her. "Nay, Caroline! It isn't as it seems. I can't explain the cap, but . . ."

The tall Scottish woman stood up slowly, still holding the navigator's hat in her hands, and walked to the tiny window.

"There will be bloodshed," she declared, keeping her

back to Janet. "There will be shame on our family, but the foul demon will pay for it with his tainted blood." Caroline whirled on the younger woman. "Aye. He'll pay! Of that you can be certain."

"Bloodshed? Why?" Janet stared at the twisted shadow of the other woman. She wished she could see her expression, but Caroline stood beyond the limit of her weak eyes. "For what reason? Why do you talk this way?"

"Talk? This is not mere talk, hussy. If the Macpherson won't take action against the vile creature for such a flagrant crime against our family, it will mean a fight to the finish. And knowing your father, he'll not rest until the knave is dead."

"David? Dead?" Janet asked with horror. "But why? Why should he want to fight David? I've told you, he has done naught wrong. Nor have I!"

A smile crept into Caroline's face. A smile that she knew Janet could not see. "Stealing the innocence of Sir Thomas Maule's only daughter is not simply wrong, Janet. It is a vile and evil sin. It is a crime the overreaching swine will suffer dearly for!"

"My innocence!" Janet repeated, dumbfounded. "Caroline! He has done no such a thing. He . . . David is a man of honor. He has . . . well, he has done naught improper."

Angrily, Caroline raised her voice. "So you call spending the night in your cabin, in your arms, the 'proper' thing! You call sneaking out of a maiden's room at the crack of dawn the 'proper' thing? Do you call leaving this proof to damn you both, the 'proper' thing?" Caroline waved the hat in the air before her.

Janet jumped from the bed and ran to her accuser. "Please, Caroline, please!" she pleaded. "Everyone on the ship will hear you. Please don't accuse him of such things. If I could explain this—"

"There is nothing to explain." Caroline sneered, her face dark and ominous. "Not to me, at any rate. Aye, once your father sees this, once I tell him that I saw with my own two eyes the filthy sneak stealing from your cabin this morning—"

Janet grabbed at her stepmother's cloak. The tears now streamed down her face; her voice shook with fear and anguish. "Please, Caroline. Please don't do this. You must believe me when I tell you that David never came to me during the night. All I know is that he kissed me good night and then left me by my door. That's the last I saw of him. And now . . . and now . . ."

"Kissed you?" Caroline looked down at the younger woman, her expression of loathing enough to force the weeping Janet to her knees. The miserable thing was still clutching at her cloak. Caroline snapped out her words. "Get ahold of yourself!"

Janet tried to contain her wretchedness, but only managed to reduce the outward signs of her distress to violent sobs that wracked her body.

Janet Maule knew her father. She knew his temper. If Caroline did, in fact, say these things to him, there would be no opportunity to explain anything to him. He would go after David. And then one of them would most assuredly be hurt. Or killed.

Since her mother died, Janet had only had her father. Volatile of temper and possessive by nature, Sir Thomas nonetheless loved her deeply. She knew that. Throughout the difficult grieving period, he had kept her near him, and they had helped one another through the worst of it.

Until his recent marriage to Caroline Douglas, Janet's father had always cared for her, loved her. But now he was changed. His possessiveness regarding the things—and the people—he thought of as his was becoming a driving force in his life. Distrust and jealousy, she knew, now weighed on his mind, surfacing at times with an irrational violence that made Janet tremble.

And David, dear David, who treated her with such affection, was the only man who had ever made her feel beautiful, intelligent, and desirable as a woman.

But now, because of her, one of them—perhaps both of them—would be hurt. *My God,* she wept, burying her head in her hands. *How could I have allowed this to happen? One of them will certainly be killed. My God! My God!*

The sharp knock on the door jerked the distraught young woman to her feet. Caroline was eyeing her coolly.

"Janet! Caroline!" Sir Thomas's angry voice boomed outside the door. "What is going on in there?"

Janet felt herself shaking uncontrollably. As if the deadly chill of winter had settled in her bones, she trembled violently, turning her wild-eyed gaze to her stepmother.

Caroline's voice was a low hiss in her ear. "You will do as I say, do you understand me?"

Janet gaped uncomprehendingly into the eyes that were piercing her soul.

"Caroline! Open this bloody door!"

"If you want no bloodshed, you will do as I say." Caroline took hold of Janet's arm and pushed the blue cap into the younger woman's face. "Do you understand?"

Sir Thomas was pounding furiously on the door. Dazed, Janet nodded, tears streaming down her face as she stared at David's cap.

"Clean your face, you little fool," Caroline sneered. "I'll do what I can to save your wretched skin . . . and the skin of your filthy commoner."

"If you'll not open it, I'll break the bloody thing down. I'll—"

Caroline lifted the latch and the door swung inward. Then she stood calmly before the burly volcano, a look of blank innocence on her face.

Sir Thomas took a step inside the cabin. His eyes quickly scanned the interior.

Janet, pulling herself together, walked quickly to her bed, picked up a blanket, and wrapped herself in it.

"What in hell was going on in here?" the knight demanded. "Everyone from here to Rome could hear the sound of you two fighting."

Before opening the door, Caroline had tucked the cap

carefully into an inside pocket of her cloak. Now she took her husband's elbow.

"We women don't fight, my dear." She gently tried to turn him toward the door, but she may as well have tried to turn Edinburgh Castle. "Aye, we might disagree, at times. But to answer your question—aye, we did have a wee variance of opinion this morning. But isn't that the way with new family?"

"Aye, but . . ."

"I knew you'd understand," she continued. "And you'll be happy to know, you old bear, that the disagreement has already been resolved. So if you'll be kind enough and let two of us be, we could—"

"I'm not going until I know what you were fighting about." This time the old warrior addressed Janet. Sir Thomas's gaze locked on his daughter's face, and on the tears still drying there.

" 'Twas naught important, Father," the young woman blurted quickly. "Truly not anything at all. And I *am* fine, Father. Believe me."

The man remained where he stood, perplexed by his daughter's last words. "Of course, you're fine. Why wouldn't you be, lass?"

"My very words, Thomas," Caroline broke in, her tone becoming more insistent. "Now be on your way, and stop your pounding on doors at such an hour. We don't need to be bringing more attention upon ourselves than we have already."

Sir Thomas opened his mouth to object, but he was quickly silenced by his wife's fingers pressed to his lips, followed by a peck on the cheek.

"Mothers and daughters have a right to disagree sometimes, husband," she cooed, her hands lightly caressing his barrel chest. "And Janet and I both told you that everything is just fine between us. So be on your way, you big bear. Janet and I need to finish our talk."

The man's eyes narrowed as she hugged his arm tightly to her warm body. Caroline had never been one to show such open affection.

"If you'll go back to our cabin," she purred seductively, "I'll meet you there in just a moment—after we're finished here. And I'll tell you everything you want to know."

Seeing the sultry look in his wife's eyes, Sir Thomas immediately succumbed to the suggestion.

"Aye," Caroline nodded meaningfully. "Everything."

As the door closed behind her father, Janet watched apprehensively as her stepmother turned and silently advanced on her, a malicious smile of victory on Caroline's face.

Janet Maule shuddered with fear.

"Checkmate!"

"Twice in a row. And no mercy for an injured woman!"

Isabel stared with dismay at the exquisite ivory-and-ebony chessboard sitting beside her on the covers. Lifting her eyes, she glared menacingly at the handsome commander sitting on the chair next to the bed.

"If this is your way of trying to impress me, young man, then you've got a serious flaw in your judgment."

"Impress you?" John repeated with a smile. "Nay, Lady Isabel, the thought never entered my mind. And why would I wish to do such a thing, anyway?"

"Lord knows," Isabel retorted grumpily. "Considering you don't have a chance of succeeding."

John busied himself putting the carved pieces back in place, glancing up occasionally to answer the scrutinizing glare of the old woman.

"What do you have against me?" he asked, reaching for the black queen that lay half hidden in the folds of the bedclothes.

"What are your intentions?" Isabel countered. "Regarding Maria?"

The Highlander ran his fingers over the cool surface of the ebony chess piece. He began to place the queen beside the king on the board, and then stopped, silently eyeing the carved figure before turning his attention to Isabel.

"Very simple, Lady Isabel. Friendship."

"Bah!" Isabel scoffed. "Friendship is anything but simple, Sir John. But even if it were, you don't seriously expect me—a woman of the world—to believe such a thing. Maria is far too beautiful, and you are far too handsome for anything so 'simple.' "

"Ah, m'lady, you are so generous in your compliments to such a leather-skinned sea dog as myself," John quipped.

"You are a fool if you think I'm complimenting you." Isabel pulled the blanket higher on her chest. "I'm telling you what I see, and what experience tells me to beware."

"I take it we are done playing," he said, quickly returning the queen to her place on the board.

"For now," the woman answered.

The towering Highlander stood up and moved the chessboard to the far end of the room. Isabel's midday meal lay on the table, and the commander scooped up the tray and returned with it.

As she watched him, Isabel was more certain than ever that something had happened between Maria and this warrior last night. The injured woman had been drifting on the edges of sleep after their evening meal when the sound of Maria leaving the cabin had jolted her into consciousness. Isabel had remained in her bed, concerned about her young charge and forcing herself to remain awake. She knew the young woman's purpose in going to Sir John. Maria had given her word to the Highlander before, and in order to cancel their agreement, the young queen would naturally go to speak with him again.

The haze of the medicine clouded her memory, but Isabel could vaguely recall seeing Maria standing in the dimly lit cabin, her back against the closed door, staring into space. And Isabel had awakened once again, for just a moment, at the first light of dawn, and had seen the flickering glow of lamplight beneath Maria's cabin door. She had seen the shadow of her young niece pacing back and forth beyond the door. Maria had obviously been up for most of the night.

Something had transpired between the two, and Isabel had a good idea what it was.

The arrival of the ship's commander this morning soon after the departure of the young serving girl clinched it. The Scot hadn't asked about Maria, but Isabel was no fool. The man simply lingered about the cabin, playing the nursemaid, engaging the older woman in conversation. And every now and then, when Isabel knew he thought she was not watching, the Highlander had glanced surreptitiously at Maria's closed door.

Now just past noon, Maria continued to keep to her cabin. But Isabel was certain that her young niece was well aware of the presence of the Highlander. The thin plank door between the two rooms could hardly muffle the sound of his rumbling laugh and his bell-clear voice. But Maria continued to stay away.

Isabel ignored the tray of food and peered warily at the black-haired giant. She needed to find out more. She was older and more clever than both of these young people together. She would find out more about their little game. After all, her responsibility as Maria's aunt dictated it.

"Drink this," he ordered, lifting a cup from the tray.

Isabel looked suspiciously at the mug that the Highlander held in his outstretched hand.

"What is it, a love potion to make me like you more?"

"Now, there is not much chance of that, is there?" John answered, matching the faint smile of the old woman with one of his own. "Nay, it's poison."

"I should have thought as much." Isabel took the cup and sniffed it. "It must be, at the very least, a sleeping potion. One that will make me unconscious for days so you can have your way with my niece."

"It's barley water and naught more," John answered, ignoring the pointed remark. "It will help you regain your strength . . . if not your good humor."

Isabel brought the cup to her mouth. "What makes you think I ever had any?"

"Strength?"

"Humor."

"Your age, Lady Isabel. You must be near . . . forty?"

"Sly boy . . ."

"And no one could possibly survive their youth being as irascible as you." John gazed innocently at the woman as a wry smile crept across her face.

"You *are* a devil, aren't you!" she responded, waggling a finger at the smiling Highlander. She brought the cup again to her lips.

"But on the topic of getting you out of my way—"

The woman stopped suddenly. "It *is* poison, isn't it?"

"Nay, it isn't, I tell you." He shook his head at her. "But I do need to talk to Maria. Naught more, just talk, in private."

Isabel sipped the cup slowly and studied him. He hadn't gotten much sleep the night before either, she guessed. "Is that the reason why you've been playing nursemaid to me all morning?"

"Nay, I've a rare interest in being verbally abused, humbled, and degraded, as well as being talked to as if I had the wit of a wee lad. That's the reason."

"I am glad we understand one another." Isabel nodded with satisfaction.

John opened his mouth to continue, but then realized the wisdom in yielding the field—for the moment.

"So, you said you would like to talk to my niece in private." Isabel acknowledged the nod from the Highlander with a serene smile. *"What for?"* she shouted, nearly upsetting the tray of food.

John glared at the woman. "Lady Isabel, notwithstanding what I just said, have you always been this pleasant, or has this wound to your shoulder simply added to your charm?"

Isabel ignored his remark. "Stop barking at me like some cur and answer my question."

"I'm the one barking . . . ?" John's eyes narrowed on the woman's face. "Why don't you mind your own business and stop poking into other people's affairs?"

"Affairs! You've chosen the right word, there!" Isabel huffed. "I'll not change my ways simply because of the threats of some Scottish pirate."

"Aye, you will," John answered. "Maria is twenty-three-years old, for God's sake. If the woman lived in Scotland, by now she'd be nursing her sixth bairn and managing not just her own affairs . . . er, business . . . but her husband's and children's, to boot. And if she were married to a laird, she'd be happily managing the business of everyone living in the village as well."

"Wait a moment!" Isabel broke in. "Are you calling her *old*?"

"Nay, I am calling *you* a meddler!"

Isabel started, and then plunked her cup down hard on the tray. "Maria is my responsibility. I need to look after her."

"A bairn needs looking after," John argued. "A grown woman doesn't."

Isabel bit her tongue. As great as the temptation was, she couldn't tell him the truth about Maria. That as a queen, as the emperor's sister—regardless of her age and situation, Maria needed looking after. She was quite tempted to tell him how dangerous a game he was, unwillingly, playing.

"Isabel, you seem to be an intelligent, worldly woman—"

"Don't humor me," she snapped, cutting him short.

"Very well, I won't," John answered. "Isabel, you are a crafty, suspicious, shrewd duenna."

"That's better." Isabel straightened the blankets on her lap. Seeing his raised eyebrows, she nodded calmly. "You may continue."

"Thank you. What I was trying to say—if you are done interrupting me—is that with all your worldly knowledge and all your great insight, you fail to see beyond the end of your own nose. Aye, you fail to understand Maria, at all."

"And you do, I suppose!"

John raised a hand in a plea for silence. "Let me finish."

"Very well. This should be very entertaining!"

"My coming here this morning, my desire to see your niece is as much for her sake as it is for mine. And don't, for one moment, think I would come to *you* if I were looking for a mistress in Maria." Seeing the tightening of her lips, John knew he at last had Isabel's attention. "I've only known Maria for a few short days, but during this time I've been able to see a side of her that I think you have obviously failed to observe after a lifetime of being with her."

"I doubt that," Isabel interjected.

"You would. Because you don't want to see the truth." John leaned down and rested his elbows on his knees. His eyes bore into Isabel's. "Maria possesses both rare beauty and extraordinary intellect, but she retains the fears of a bairn. She seems afraid, uncertain, lost. She is clearly unprepared to face life. I am willing to wager, just from what I've seen, that Maria, rather than staying and overcoming obstacles that face her, always sees it safest to run away from them. After seeing you, Lady Isabel, and noting your protectiveness of her, it is not too difficult to see that she has always been allowed to run from her problems. That is, those problems that you don't resolve for her."

"That's not—"

"Let me finish," John cut in. "Put yourself in her place. Treat her as you would want to be treated, if you were her age, in her position. That's all I am asking. Don't forget a bairn never learns to walk until you let go of her hand."

"But she could fall."

"Aye, and then she gets up and learns to walk," he answered.

"Some children cannot afford to fall."

Isabel paused and fell silent for a moment. She herself had never been protected from life, as Maria had. But she herself was only an aging aunt of the Holy Roman Emperor.

"You've said enough," she said quietly. "If this is not my business, it is even less yours."

"Perhaps, m'lady," John continued. "But there is more. Maria is unhappy. We have spoken, Isabel, and I believe she has never been truly happy. Ever."

"She had a . . . good marriage," Isabel argued weakly, knowing even as she spoke the words that Maria's marriage had little to recommend itself in the areas of happiness or of love.

"I know that she was married. She told me that. And I know what kind of marriage it must have been, when after four years with the man, she carries in her heart no sense of loss for him. I know what kind of marriage that is, Isabel. It is the marriage that families arrange to better their own interests."

"Did she tell you this?" Isabel asked, her shock evident in her face. No wonder Maria had spent a sleepless night.

John nodded. "She needs a friend, Isabel. And, for a few days, anyway, I would like to be that friend."

Isabel stared at him for the longest time. He was going to great lengths to convince her of his good intentions. A man of his rank and his looks might have picked a different approach, one that would have not involved dealing with Isabel.

"It is true, we don't appear to be going anywhere in this fog, but why should you waste your time on Maria, Sir John?" she asked curtly. "Unless you admit that you have other motives?"

"What 'other motives?' " John asked calmly.

"You don't fool me, young man. Things . . ." She waved her hand in the air. "Things that happen between a man and a woman. I haven't reached this advanced age living behind the walls of a convent, I want you to know."

"I'm certain that you haven't, m'lady. But then I'll be asking you why you're treating Maria as if she should be living behind those very walls?"

Isabel stared, unable to answer his question.

"Lady Isabel, it's clear that Maria relies on you. But for once, stay out of this and let Maria stand on her own two feet. I only hope to talk her into spending time with me. I'll introduce her to those aboard who have some redeeming quality to them. As you say, this ship is going nowhere in these mists. What harm can it do, for the time we are onboard, amongst strangers, to exchange a few friendly words?"

"She has a reputation," Isabel interjected. "And it . . . well, it isn't the exchange of words that I'm concerned about."

As much as he hated to admit it, John knew exactly what she was talking about.

"I'm attracted to the lass, but I'll also give you my word that while we are at sea, I'll not whisk her away to my cabin, and I'll not take her to my bed."

His bluntness and his offer silenced Isabel at once. He had made the promise that she had wanted him to make. "Your word?"

"My word," he repeated.

The old woman contemplated his words. Looking at his face, she had no doubt of the sincerity of his vow. She had called Maria a fool the day before for falling victim to his words. And now she was doing the same thing. She was allowing herself to be charmed by him.

But he had a point. Maria was unhappy. She had always been unhappy. That sadness had been the reason why Isabel had made the trip from Castile. To come and save her from herself, and from her brother. *Oh, let me burn in hell for it,* Isabel swore silently. If this Highlander had the power to make Maria smile, and to make her happy, even for a few short days, then so be it. For Maria had always been living in a kind of darkness, she realized, never really allowed to feel the sun on her skin or even the rain on her face. What the future held in store was far too uncertain, but Isabel knew that the odds were overwhelming. Soon, Maria would take her place as queen, if not among the Scots, somewhere. This was, perhaps, her one opportunity. Here in the mist.

"Aye, show her a bit of life." Isabel nodded.

Chapter 10

The young woman curtsied before tucking the coin inside her apron and backing hurriedly out of the room.

As the door closed softly, Caroline moved easily off her bunk. Tossing her blanket of blond hair over one shoulder, she moved to the high table where she'd carelessly thrown the ring and gold chain a moment earlier. With great effort Caroline had avoided showing the serving lass how keen she was to learn whatever information was available about her adversary. After all, the prices would only go up if she showed much interest. Caroline smiled smugly, thinking how cheaply she'd gotten away with this. The young sneak had believed Caroline's little act completely. So far as the young woman knew, there was no value whatsoever in what she had stolen from Maria's cabin, and Caroline had paid her accordingly.

Picking up the ornate ring and chain, Caroline brought the band close to the flickering lantern light. It looked to be a wedding ring, but designed to be a sealing ring, as well. The intricate engraving, so striking to the eye, was a coat of arms that Caroline had seen before, but could not immediately identify. Bringing the golden object closer to her eye, she couldn't help but admire the rampant, crowned lion set against a ring of meticulously carved foliage and flowers. She stared again. The shield on the lion's chest featured another symbol. She squinted her eyes. A double-headed eagle.

Many a family in Europe used these animals in their coat of arms, but this one was quite elegant. Wracking her brain, she tried to recall where she had seen this combination, but to no avail.

Well, it was a start, she thought, letting the ring dangle from the chain. Gathering the ring and chain up in both hands, Caroline smiled. She would find out more. She was only getting started.

"What do you mean, we have company?" Maria asked in shock, eyeing the new gown Isabel had somehow managed to change into. The deep maroon color of the fabric had brought some color to her aunt's complexion. Isabel looked the best she had since being injured.

"There is a lovely dress for you, thanks to our hosts, sitting next to the chessboard. I recommend you change into it." The older woman directed the young serving lass to get it. "I am tired of seeing you in that same thing, day after day. And if I were you, I would hurry. I need your help, and there is not much time left until our dinner company arrives."

Maria watched in amazement as the servant jumped to her aunt's commands. From her cabin, she had been surprised to hear her aunt ordering the young girl about but, entering Isabel's cabin, Maria had never expected to walk into a commotion such as this. The room had been rearranged, and an extra table, laden with bread and fish and pastries, had been brought in and set up in one corner. The serving girl stood behind her, but Maria focused her attention on Isabel.

"You are a different woman than you were last night," Maria said accusingly. "But as far as this dinner! Entertaining! Isabel, you don't know anyone on this ship. How could you invite them to dinner?"

Maria waved her hand at the elegant dinner that awaited. "This is not your—" Maria was about to say "your palace in Castile" but caught herself, remembering the presence of the other woman in the room. "You're a guest! And not to mention, the wound in your shoulder is hardly healed enough to—"

"I don't want to hear any more of this, young woman.

Now be on your way. Go. Change. Make yourself attractive. I don't want to do this alone."

Maria stood her ground. "How did this thing ever get started, anyway? This has something to do with Sir John's visit this morning, doesn't it?"

"Were you listening at the keyhole, Maria?"

"There is no keyhole!" Maria shot back in denial. A light blush spread quickly to her cheeks as she thought of the serving girl listening to all of this. "You know I would never do such a thing."

"You knew he was here, though."

Maria nodded. "Of course. I made out his voice when he first came in, but I certainly didn't eavesdrop on your argument!"

Isabel smiled. "So you heard us quarrel?"

Maria, blushing furiously, glared at her aunt. "Just answer my question, Isabel. Is this grand dinner tonight the result of your visit with Sir John?"

"Take her away," Isabel ordered the young servant, ignoring Maria. "Take her away and help her dress. And while you're at it, see what you could do with her hair. Put some life into it, will you?"

Maria paused a moment longer, unwilling to surrender the field. Then, hearing the knock on the door, she watched in utter amazement as the door opened to her aunt's command, and Christie marched in with two sailors carrying a number of platters of fruits and bottles of wine.

"Be on your way, Maria," Isabel directed again.

Backing out of the bustling cabin, Maria turned and moved swiftly into the quiet of her own smaller room. The serving girl had already spread sets of underclothing and the dress on the small bunk.

"I can manage this myself," Maria said gently to the young girl. "You will be of much greater use to my aunt than to me."

As the woman politely curtsied and left, Maria remained where she stood, thinking over this new turn of events. She had been bound and determined not to see him again. And she hadn't lied to Isabel in saying she had not eavesdropped on their conversation today, though it had been difficult to ignore their raised voices.

Last night had been a long and trying night. She had lain awake on her small bunk for hours, haunted by conflicting feelings of duty and freedom—and by other things, as well. With her eyes open to the flickering glow of the lantern, her mind's eye had been on him: John Macpherson and his magical touch, his soothing words. Lying there, she could almost feel, all over again, the incredible passion of their encounter. Why was it that she had never before known desire such as this? How could it be that she had never even known that such feelings could exist? A lifetime of discipline, of doing the correct thing, of controlling all emotions, had been upended in a single moment. He had made her forget, and had made her feel. The chaotic tumult of emotions battered at her reason, but still a ragged line of defense remained. She could not allow herself to capitulate so completely. Her future was too uncertain. The plan for her future lay too close . . . too close to him.

Exhausted, she had only started to drift off when the first gray hints of dawn had crept into the eastern sky. She knew she had good reason—even after being awakened by the soft, captivating burr of his voice in the next cabin—to stay away. But now, seeing the affair being readied in Isabel's cabin, she wondered if she had done the right thing.

Maria pulled apart the laces that held the front of her dress together and stepped out of the garment. Who could possibly be joining them for dinner, she wondered. The Scottish noblemen and women who were aboard seemed to spend most of their time at cards in the galley, or chatting with one another in the narrow corridors. From what she had observed, few of the Scots had displayed much interest in the two of them, though Janet Maule had from the very beginning been warm and solicitous of their needs. Certainly, none of the others had sought them out. Looking at the soft, cream-colored dress lying on the bunk, Maria wagered inwardly that it had been Janet who'd supplied it. And as far as the dinner company went, Maria knew that—other than Maule family—neither she nor Isabel had met anyone in the Scottish delegation.

Changing her shift, Maria suddenly felt a chill race through her, though the cabin was snug enough against the damp outside. She quickly stepped into the soft wool dress.

As she absently tightened the laces in the front of the low neckline, Maria considered the possibilities. They were few. Aside from the physician, whom Isabel did not seem to care for particularly, there were, perhaps, only the Maules.

Her blood ran cold to think of sitting and dining with Sir Thomas. The Scottish knight had seen her in Sir John's arms. He assuredly thought her a loose woman. And then there was Lady Caroline Maule. Last night, she had been naked and quite willing in the Highlander's bed. Caroline Maule *was* a loose woman. Maria wondered vaguely what penalty adultery carried in Scotland. And then there was Janet. Dear, thoughtful Janet. Maria finished tying the laces of her dress. She would like to know Janet better.

Perhaps David Maxwell would come along. The handsome Scot would make a witty addition to any company. Maria knew Janet Maule would have no objection to the navigator's presence.

Beyond that, there was only John Macpherson.

Maria leaned her head to the side and started to tame her long, tangled mane with brisk strokes of her brush. She could feel the heat in her face, the tingles moving down her spine. As much as she'd like to deny it, the mere thought of the man set shivers through her.

Sweeping her black hair behind her, she straightened up and paused. Yes, he would be there. She would see him again . . . tonight. Suddenly, she was conscious of the pounding of her heart in her breast, and she looked down, wondering with a mild sense of panic how she would look. Then, slowly, the absurdity of her train of thought sank in, making her smile. One moment she was complaining about what Isabel had done, and the next she was shivering with excitement at the prospect.

Walking toward the looking glass the serving girl had placed by the window, Maria scrutinized her image. Her unbound, black hair swept down over her shoulders, unbraided and unadorned. The cream-colored dress had simple geometric forms worked in gold thread into the material, but the overall effect of it was one of simplicity. There were no buttons of pearl or gold arraying her gown; there were no jewels adorning her skin. There was no façade of grandeur or majestic splendor hiding her from the world. In a moment of unshackled joy, Maria gazed at herself and, for perhaps the first time in her life, relished the sight that met her eyes. Looking into the mirror, she saw a woman. Simple, plain, unadorned . . . and real.

The young navigator's fist banged forcefully on the door. He knew Janet was in there. She hadn't been in the galley with her father, and she wasn't above decks.

"Mistress Janet!" He raised his hand again, but before he could knock once more, the door was swung open on its hinges.

With a single glance at the tear-stained face of the young woman, David's anger disappeared, and he stepped into the room, pulling her into his arms.

Janet Maule went gladly into his strong embrace, a vague feeling of comfort and security washing over her as he wrapped his arms about her. For the entire day she had locked herself away, praying desperately for some inspiration, some insight that might guide her through the nightmare she was sure was about to unfold.

"Please close it," she whispered, her tone muffled. "I won't let him stab you in the back in my own doorway."

"Stab me?" David responded, his eyebrows arching in surprise. "Who's to stab me, lass?"

"My father," Janet whispered forcefully before pulling suddenly away. Pushing past him, she peered nervously down the hallway, and then closed the door.

David watched her long, white fingers tremble as they fastened the latch.

"What has happened, Janet?"

She turned and faced him, leaning her back heavily against the cabin door. "By now, Caroline has most assuredly told him that you were here last night."

"Last night?" David repeated. There was no one in the corridor when he'd kissed Janet good night. "What of it, lass?"

The young woman reached up and wiped away the tears running down her cheeks. "David, why couldn't you have stayed away." Her voice was ragged with anguish. "What made you think to come back here while I was sleeping?"

"While you were asleep?" David was beginning to feel like the village idiot, repeating everything she was saying, but he hadn't any idea what she was talking about.

"It was so humiliating to be discovered like that," she continued through her tears. "Caroline treated me as though I were some tramp—"

"Just a moment, lass." David shook his head. "This isn't making a bit of sense. If we're sailing into heavy weather . . ."

Janet moved away from the door and edged her way around him. Her face had taken on a wild, frantic look.

"She saw you, David. She *saw* you!" She was nearly choking on her tears. "And I am certain she will tell my father, if she hasn't already." The young woman lunged toward him, grasping both of his hands. "David, you must hide! Is there anywhere you can go? One of the other ships. You must get away. My father's temper . . . you mustn't let him find you!"

"Hold on, Janet!" David nearly shouted. "I don't run from anything. And why should I, lass?"

"My father! Sir Thomas will—"

"I'll take care to straighten things out with your father, Janet. But first, I need to know what it is that needs straightening out!"

"You have to be gone, David. We can't let him find you here!"

"I'll only be staying a moment, my sweet. Your father's just sitting down to his supper, so we've plenty of time for you to tell me what this is all about. Now, sit yourself here." David led the distraught woman to the bunk, and they sat hand in hand while Janet composed herself. "I'll stay just long enough for you to tell me what's happened."

Janet nodded gratefully, and he smiled back at her.

"Now, what is this about Lady Caroline treating you poorly? Nay, we'd best start from the beginning. Who saw me? And where? We've done naught we need to be ashamed of, Janet."

She stared at him in confusion. "But you were here last night."

"Aye, lass. In the hall. There's naught in that."

"Nay! You were in *here.*"

"I wasn't, Janet. And you know that as well as I do. I left you in the hall." David looked at her steadily. "Have you forgotten that already?"

"Nay! I haven't forgotten," she exclaimed, flushing scarlet at the memory.

David smiled. "I didn't think you would."

"But when you came back, Caroline saw you, and . . ."

"Came back? I didn't come back, Janet."

"That's not what Caroline claims," she responded, wringing her hands. "And then, there was your hat!"

"My hat?" he exploded. "What about my hat?"

"It was here on my bunk when I awoke this morning. On the pillow beside me."

"Janet, I didn't come in here last night." David forced himself to consider what Janet was telling him. His hat. Why, he'd thought he had left his hat in Sir John's cabin, though it hadn't been there this morning. "And the last time I saw my hat, I was in the commander's workroom. That was yesterday, lass. Now, I don't imagine he's been paying midnight visits to you, so I suppose we need to figure out just how that bonnet found its way in here."

Wide-eyed, Janet stared into the young navigator's face. "Then you didn't come to me last night?"

"Of course not, Janet. What do you think I've been

telling you?" David's eyes roamed her pretty face. "Though, to be honest, I'm certainly guilty of wanting to. But nay, lass, I never stepped foot inside this cabin until now."

Janet threw her arms around him and sank her head into the crook of his neck. David held her tightly for a moment, and then, untangling himself, coaxed her to tell him all that had taken place from the time she'd awakened this morning—from the time she'd discovered his hat on her bed. Once she got started, the knot began to unravel for him . . . and for Janet.

"Caroline! But why?" Janet wondered. "From the first moment my father brought her home, I have treated her with the utmost respect. I have never given her a reason to dislike me. Certainly, never a reason to want to hurt me."

"I don't know, lass." David caressed the soft skin of her hand as it rested in his. "But I think I may be the one she is after."

Seeing the bewildered expression on her face, the young navigator continued. "Aye, Janet, it's true. I have done naught to wrong her, either—so far as I know. But I serve the man whose attention she appears determined to get."

"Sir John?" she asked, aghast.

"Aye." David nodded. "And I think, yesterday morning in his cabin, the lines were drawn. The commander made it clear in front of witnesses that he had no interest, and no intention, to see her again."

"Witnesses?"

"Aye, Lady Maria and your humble servant. We were both there. And Caroline limped away licking her wounds."

"But that would be adultery!"

"Aye, Janet. Though some hold that a sin, others are less inclined to think on it so harshly."

Janet stared at her hands in disbelief. "And you think she would try to make us pay the price of her humiliation? You and me?"

David saw the tear well up, quiver, and trickle down

her soft cheek. Reaching up, he wiped away the glistening track with his thumb, only to see a second droplet follow the path of the first.

His voice hardened. "What did Lady Caroline ask you to do? After your father left?"

"Nothing," Janet answered, surprised at his question. "She just told me to be prepared to pay, but she was very vague about it. And then she left, making a point of taking your hat with her. I was certain she would go straight to Sir Thomas."

David stood up and began pacing the length of the room. His mind raced as he tried to think of a way to head off Caroline's attack. If he only knew what her plan was. He paused and gazed at Janet sitting on the bunk and gazing steadily at him. "I spoke briefly with your father around midday, and he was actually quite civil."

"Then she could not have told him, yet," Janet put in with certainty as the young man began to pace again. "But what could she be waiting for, then?"

"Your father." David came to a stop. "Does he suspect anything . . . between us, I mean?"

Janet stared at the handsome young sailor, and suddenly she realized what was at the heart of their trouble. She hadn't discussed David with her father. She couldn't. She knew how Sir Thomas would view her relationship with a commoner, and his wrath could be terrible. All of David's qualities would amount to nothing on account of his lack of rank. In her father's view, David Maxwell was a commoner and would never be anything more.

"My father is a good man, David, and he loves me. But since his marriage to Caroline . . . and especially since we boarded this ship . . . he's been cross and distracted. In any case, he hasn't given me a second glance since we left Scotland."

"I can't say I'm unhappy about that, lass."

"Nor am I, David. But to answer your question, the last person he'd expect me to . . . to be with . . . would be . . . well . . ."

"A sailor," he said curtly, finishing her sentence for her. "A common sailor."

"Aye, David," she responded quickly. "My father's a proud man."

"Aye," the young man replied, turning away.

As far as David could see, the world was full of proud men, but few of them had daughters the likes of Janet Maule. His lips were a thin line as he stood with his back to her, his arms folded across his chest. What was he expecting? He *was* a commoner, and the reality of it struck him hard—harder than he'd ever felt it before. He wanted this woman, more than anything he'd ever wanted. But in the eyes of the world—in the eyes of her father—David Maxwell was dirt for them to trod upon.

David's mind raced as he thought about Janet. He knew she harbored no feelings of superiority over him. She cared for him as he cared for her. But Lady Caroline clearly intended to use their feelings, their secret, to blackmail her stepdaughter. Why, he didn't know. But he would give her no opportunity.

Janet rose from the bunk and moved to his side. Tentatively, she laid her hand on his arm. "I am sorry, David. I don't care about those things—"

"There is no need to apologize," he answered. His voice sounded harsh even to himself, and he tried hard to soften it. "Janet, we have done naught improper. If I were simply to walk out of your cabin and never look back, then there would be naught she could accuse us of—naught your father could hold against you."

Janet felt the cold steel drive deep into her heart. He was going to walk away, leave her. This was to be the end of her short-lived happiness. She turned away from him, unable to hold back the grief that was welling up inside. Her breath was so thick in her chest that she thought for a moment she might suffocate, and, putting her hand out, Janet leaned heavily against the cabin wall. Though she wanted to cry, her tears would not come.

David turned and gazed at her slender back, watching her shoulders heave as she tried to take in air. Torn between his desire to hold her, comfort her, and his need to protect her, he stood, undecided and unable to move.

And then he knew he couldn't stay away from her any longer. He was a fool to think that he could. His arms encircled her waist, and he gathered her to him, burying his face in her hair.

Janet quickly turned in his arms. Like dew in the morning sunlight, she reached up for him. "Please don't go."

Her simple request was all he'd ever wished for. Crushing his lips to hers, he showed her how impossible it would be to go. He couldn't. It was already far too late for them. Whatever Dame Fortune held in store, she held it for both of them.

Chapter 11

John nodded to all except two of his serving men to depart, then moved to the side of the bed, extending his hand to Isabel.

The older woman first smoothed her dress before accepting the outstretched hand of the handsome Highlander. Pulling herself to her feet, she tightened her grip on his arm as a sudden attack of dizziness passed over her. But in a moment, it was gone.

"Are you certain you feel up to this?"

"I've been confined to that bed for too long." Isabel turned to scowl at him. "But, if you think you can get rid of me this easily, by simply feigning compassion for my condition . . ."

"I wouldn't dream of it."

Helping her walk the few short steps to the table, he pulled back her chair and waited as she lowered herself gingerly into the seat.

Isabel gave the table a cursory look and tried not to show her wonder. The feast before them and the finery that adorned the table were indeed a match for the best houses in Europe. She would have to remember to commend the ship's cook on his skill.

"I'll need that shawl for the draft and some pillows for my back."

"At your service, Your Highness," John responded in a humorously obsequious tone, and bowed low before doing as he was ordered. *This had better work*, he thought to himself. *She'd better come out of that little refuge of hers or I may just knock down the door. There is no way in hell I am going to spend an entire evening alone with Isabel, being treated like a cabin boy.* John smiled wryly as he returned with the items. He liked the old woman, but enough was enough.

Maria stood with her hand still on the latch and watched the handsome Highlander place a pillow behind her aunt. She stared at his back, at his powerful shoulders, and at the hands gently wrapping the blanket around the old woman. Remembering those hands on her, she drew in her breath as a surging heat coursed through her.

Isabel was sitting with her back to her as two men with a number of platters busily prepared for the guests at one end of the room. Maria contemplated the notion of backing out of the cabin and returning when the rest of Isabel's guests had arrived. It was so much easier to be lost in a crowd. So much safer.

She made no sound, but John seemed to sense her presence. He turned abruptly and stopped.

Suddenly, for Maria, nothing in the room mattered but John Macpherson. The Scottish commander was quite dashing in his impeccably fitted Highland clothes, in his white linen shirt with the tartan crossing his broad chest, in his kilt and his soft, high boots. She simply stood there, gazing at him, unconsciously allowing her eyes to travel the length of him, drinking him in, absorbing him.

And then she stopped. In an instant the sight of him loomed up before her, filling the breadth of the room, of her senses—and pouring into some unknown, unnamable void in her heart.

An eon seemed to pass, and then Maria forced herself to breathe, somehow managing a half-smile and feeling the heat about to burst through her skin. But John's smile, a dazzling response to her own feeble attempt, tore at her chest and she closed her eyes reflexively. Stunned and panic-stricken, she could look at him no longer.

Not once—from the time he had entered manhood to the present—had John Macpherson ever given heaven more than a passing thought. Not once had he ever thought to consider the existence of angels on earth. Not once.

Until now.

In an instant, the pagan was converted, the heathen subdued, the savage tamed. Gazing at her as she stood quietly in the cabin door, John knew what heaven looked like, what the sight of an angel can do to a man's soul. Clothed in ivory, Maria emanated elegance and beauty. Her hair, free from its usual bonds, cascaded in ebony waves to her waist. Looking on the black tresses, the Highlander recalled the memory of its silken feel and its fragrance. His gaze took in the soft lines of her throat, the milky skin that led from her angelic face to the tops of her full, high breasts rising above the simple, crossed laces of the dress's square neckline. His eyes did what his body could not do. They devoured her.

John let his eyes roam shamelessly over the sculpted perfection of her features, over the womanly curves of her body. For once, he knew he wanted her to feel his gaze. He wanted her to fathom the extent of his need, of his desire. He wanted her to feel the fire that was consuming him. The fire that could consume them both.

A shudder coursed through her as she followed the path of his gaze. She watched as his blue eyes unlaced the ties of her dress. Her lips parted as she felt the power of his stare draw her gown from her shoulders. Layer by layer, he undid her. He unraveled her. She felt as if she were standing before a looking glass, but it was as if in a dream. She could see herself through his eyes, and there was no gown, no material to hide her body— there was no lock to safeguard her heart. She stood naked and unveiled. But deep within her, Maria felt something else. She felt wanted. And though reeling a bit at the thought, she welcomed the response.

"Well, could it be Maria, at long last?" Isabel called out, her back still to them. She knew full well the prolonged hush could mean nothing else.

"Aye, Isabel," Maria replied, her voice a whisper as she let go of the door and stepped farther into the room.

"It's about time you joined us, my dear. I don't know

how much longer I could have withstood his company alone. It's quite a vexing task, you know!" She waved her hand over her shoulder and turned slightly. "Come. Come. The two of you. The physician's brew will probably put me out again in a moment or two. And that will be the extent of my enjoyment for the evening."

Maria caught a glimpse of the fleeting expression that crossed John's face, and she smiled. It was clear that, as far as John Macpherson was concerned, Isabel could have been put to bed hours ago.

Courteously, the ship's commander moved toward the young woman and reached for her hand. The clean wrap minimally covered her palms, now, and her fingers were free and functional. Somewhat to her own surprise, though, she didn't even hesitate before placing her hand in his. But when he brought her fingers to his lips, pressing them there, the flush of heat raced up her arm and coursed through her once again.

"I thought I asked you to stay away." She whispered the words to him alone. She could feel his warm breath on her skin. Pressing against her consciousness was the recollection of his full lips upon hers. She tried to push away the memory, but it persisted, and she found herself yielding to its allure.

Reluctantly, John lowered her hand, but he refused to let it go. "So you did," he whispered back. His gaze was locked on hers, his fingers caressing the softness of her hand. "And I would have . . . stayed away. If only I thought you meant it!"

She tried to move away, but he wouldn't let her go. Instead, he held her beside him and spoke to her as they started for the table.

"What are we going to do about this, Maria?"

His words were a caress. She felt as if she'd been kissed.

"And don't tell me nothing." He pulled a chair back for her to sit. "I'll not accept it."

"What won't you accept?" Isabel asked bluntly, trying to hide her amusement with the obliviousness of the two young people.

Like one waking from a trance, Maria regained awareness of her surroundings. She'd been so enraptured with John's presence that she had nearly forgotten Isabel. Blushing, she sat down on the chair that the Highlander offered. Looking for something to hide behind, she immediately picked up the crystal goblet sitting before her. She brought the glass to her lips.

"It's empty!" Isabel reported to her niece before turning to the Highlander. She repeated her earlier question. "Well, what won't you accept?"

John filled Maria's cup and took his seat across from her, giving her a reassuring wink as he settled into the chair. She was quick to bring the drink back to her lips. He turned to the older woman. "I will not accept her demand of taking me to her bed."

Maria choked on her drink, sputtering and coughing.

Isabel looked at him menacingly from where she sat. "And why is that?"

This time John was the one who would have choked, had he not been growing increasingly accustomed to Isabel's bizarre sense of humor. His composure remained intact. "Because she doesn't mean it. She is just planning to use me. I am not one to be so obliging, only to find myself discarded. My reputation ruined."

The elder woman considered John's words. "Ah, I see. Your reputation. So quite against all rules of courtly etiquette, you refuse to bed this young woman."

Before answering, John first glanced at Maria to make certain she was still breathing. Indeed she was. But while her complexion had the subtlest hint of color to it— something close to the shade of poppies—her eyes sparkled green and alive, and they danced with amusement back and forth between Isabel and himself. John turned his gaze back to Isabel.

"Courtly rules be damned," the Highlander growled. "I see, Isabel, that for the purposes of being deliberately contentious, you've conveniently forgotten the promise you forced out of me. Well, if you'd prefer, I'm willing to consider that arrangement finished, and, if need be, I'll agree to yield to her wishes."

Though she shook her head definitively, Isabel's sardonic look was answer enough, and John raised the decanter.

"More wine?" he asked the older woman brightly.

"What promises?" Maria injected, breaking the silence that followed. Their rough banter, she knew, made it safe enough for her to let down her guard. And though the answer to her question was obvious, she saw her opportunity to make them feel awkward—if it were at all possible to make these two feel awkward—for discussing her as if she were absent.

Neither answered. For a moment Maria thought the Highlander was about to, but after receiving a threatening look from Isabel, he simply smiled impishly at Maria.

"Shall we eat?" Isabel asked gruffly, motioning to the waiting men to begin serving.

"Won't there be others joining us?" Maria asked.

"Others?" Isabel huffed. She waved a knife at John. "This one thinks the party is already too large by one, I believe. Nay, my dear, I'd wager our good host, here, would prefer not to share the vision of your beauty and pleasure of your wit with any others."

John smiled innocently and speared a filet of fish from the gold platter that his man held. What Isabel said was true. Beyond all the repartee, he really didn't care to share Maria with any of the others onboard. He wanted her all to himself.

"You see, Maria? He doesn't deny it," Isabel said, raising her wine to her lips. "Is this *Spanish* wine, m'lord? I wouldn't have thought you had the good taste to keep Spanish wine."

"The truth is, lass," John said bluntly, ignoring Isabel, "I didn't think it appropriate to subject the nobles of the delegation to your aunt's foul temper."

"That was quite thoughtful of you, Sir John," Maria replied with a smile.

The Highlander leaned back in his chair. "Generous is a better word. We have, after all, been stranded here for a number of days, and I wouldn't want the entire delegation jumping overboard as a result of your aunt's treatment of them."

"Hmmph!" Isabel groused, continuing to eat.

Maria smiled down at her plate, unwilling to risk a glance at Isabel. "I can see, Sir John, that you've made the most of your good fortune in spending time with my aunt."

"Good fortune?" John responded, raising his eyebrows. "We're talking about Lady Isabel!"

"Aye?" the older woman put in, waiting expectantly.

"Certainly, 'good fortune' is too trifling a phrase to capture the true spirit of what I have . . . experienced."

Maria could tell, watching Isabel stifle a wry smile that, in spite of their gruff talk, the commander had indeed won her aunt's affections.

"My apologies, m'lord," the young woman responded. "It has, I'm certain, presented some difficulties for you. But beneath her ruined exterior—"

"Who is 'ruined'?" Isabel exploded.

"But beneath that damaged façade, there beats a very fine heart!"

"Well, that I have yet to see," John returned, giving Isabel an appraising look. "But to think that musket ball to her shoulder almost took away the only choice part!"

"It's true. It would have been a dreadful shame," Maria replied as she took a serving of fruit.

"I think I've heard just about enough out of you two." Isabel picked up a long yellow fruit from a proffered tray. "How is it that a barge like this one has Jerusalem apples at this time of year?"

John leaned toward Maria. "Aye. To think, we might have been sharing this dinner alone. Only the two of us. Such a pity!"

Maria gazed across the table into his deep blue eyes. The light of the candles reflected in them, giving his face a hint of the rogue within. Just the two of them, she thought. He didn't even know the extent to which his words produced chaos inside of her.

Isabel looked from one to the other, each enthralled

by the other's charms. "That's enough entertainment at my expense. Find a different subject of discussion."

As the dinner progressed, Maria toyed with the food on her plate and occasionally glanced up. John was continuously watching her—that she knew—and her blush deepened each time their eyes met. Isabel was clearly working hard to steer the handsome Highlander into more mundane discussions on a variety of matters, and Maria listened attentively, occasionally contributing. Everything he said interested her, but the young woman was far more eager to exchange silent looks that moved across her skin like caresses. Though John Macpherson mainly directed his words to Isabel, the commander continued to stretch his long legs beneath the table, pressing his knees—unintentionally, of course—against her legs.

Though there was a dreamlike quality to the way Maria felt, she knew that this was no dream. This man wanted to spend time with her. She knew that he had chosen to make her the center of his attention. She knew that, if she chose to allow it, she could soon be feeling his strong hands holding her body, pulling her close to him. She could soon be feeling his full and sensual lips devouring hers.

"Don't you agree, Maria?" Isabel's voice jarred Maria out of her reverie.

"What did you say, Isabel?"

"What I said was, in all my travel across these waters, I have never seen more comfort and amenity in a single ship than I have seen on the *Great Michael*. I'd be quite tempted to say that Scottish seamen are, by far, the most spoiled sailors on the German Sea. Wouldn't you agree?"

Maria looked at the naval commander's expression. He gazed at her, as well, awaiting her answer. "As you have said often enough before, Isabel, I am no sailor. And I have not spent as much time as you aboard such a variety of ships to know what comforts their sailors do or don't enjoy."

"Well, child, that was certainly a diplomatic answer."

Isabel turned toward John. "She doesn't get that quality from my side of the family, let me tell you."

"I wouldn't have guessed," John responded, never taking his eyes from the younger woman.

"It's just that I am certain Sir John is far better qualified to inform us whether the *Great Michael*'s comforts are standard for Scottish ships—or for any others, for that matter." Maria hoped he would not pursue Isabel's reference to family with any further questions. She was enjoying herself so much, and she didn't want it ruined by conversation on that particular topic.

"Well, Sir John?" Isabel asked. "Would you care to enlighten us?"

John looked from one woman to the other. As curious as he was about Maria's family, he sensed from the quick warning glance she gave her aunt that Maria was still quite hesitant to discuss her family. Perhaps some other time, he thought.

Indeed, there was no danger in revealing the truth of his commission to these two women. After all, half of Europe knew of the upcoming union, and there was no secret about the *Great Michael*'s charge.

"This warship has been specially fitted out for this voyage, Maria. The *Great Michael* and the three vessels accompanying us are indeed the grandest ships in the Scottish Navy, and this ship is the largest and the finest in the world. But a warship's value is all a matter of the size of her sails, the speed she can travel, and the number of guns that she carries. As far as the comfort and luxury which you see on this journey, this is hardly the way my men and I generally travel.

"I don't know how much of this you may have already heard," John continued, turning his attention to Isabel. "But since your refuse to tell me if you have any friends or connections in Antwerp, it's possible that you don't know. At any rate, these 'amenities' as you so well describe them, have been brought aboard this ship to welcome and comfort the chattel that we'll be conveying from Antwerp back to Scotland."

"Chattel!" Isabel exclaimed in amazement.

"Aye. Is there a better way to describe royalty?" John asked innocently as he turned to Maria.

She hid her hands in the folds of her skirt and tried to keep an even expression.

"Royalty?" Isabel asked, trying to draw the Highlander's attention away from Maria. The young woman's pallid expression would surely give them away. "You are to provide passage for a member of the royal family?"

"Aye," John answered, "Mary, Queen of Hungary. She is to wed my king, James of Scotland. Didn't you hear of the match?"

Isabel was quick to answer. "I am afraid we don't have much to do with the business of royal courtship. I think I can speak for both of us when I say that the world of politics is not one we care to move in."

"Aye, there's wisdom in that," John replied. He paused as a thought occurred to him. "But do you know her . . . or know of her?"

"Of a queen?" Isabel snorted, rolling her eyes. "My boy, you do us great honor to think we travel in such high circles!"

"What I meant was—even though you haven't said as much—your accents are Spanish." He was directing his comments to Isabel. "And from what I know, the Queen of Hungary is a Spaniard, as well."

"España is a large place, Sir J—" Maria began.

"You'd best check your facts before you greet her, Commander," Isabel interjected hotly. "Her blood may be royal, but she is far from being a pure Spaniard."

"Really?" John asked, feigning ignorance.

"That is correct," Isabel continued. "She is the daughter to Philip the Handsome, a Burgundian, and the granddaughter of Maximilian I of the Habsburgs, Regent of Flanders, Holland, Zeeland, Hianault, and Artois. Now, her mother is Juaña of Castile, and her grandfather was Ferdinand of Aragon, so it's true, she has some Spanish blood. But the girl wasn't even born in Castile. She was sent there as a child to be raised until her first marriage contract could be consum—"

Isabel came to a sudden stop. One glance at Maria told her that the young woman was about to pass out.

"Aye," John nodded reassuringly. "It sounds as if I was correct to assume that you know her."

"Know *of* her," Isabel cut him short. "Only *of* her, my dear."

She pushed her plate away from her and pretended to stifle a yawn. Perhaps she might have her lips sewn shut.

"And now I am tired," Isabel continued. "And my shoulder is tormenting me dreadfully. So before you push me into an early grave with your endless chatter, you might consider being a gentleman and escorting me to my bed. Maria will see you and your men out."

"But the night is young," John protested, helping Isabel to her feet.

"And I am old," Isabel answered, gesturing for Maria to stay beside her.

Maria took her aunt's arm, and glanced briefly at the Highlander. His eyes were smiling as they met hers.

"Hardly," he replied meaningfully, turning his attention back to the aunt. The men were scurrying about, clearing away the remains of the dinner, and he caught the eye of the nearest man. "Go and fetch the serving lass."

"What do you need with her?" Isabel queried sharply.

"I don't need her," he replied. "You do. I am taking Maria on deck for a walk."

"Are you asking permission?" Isabel asked as she turned and settled onto the edge of the high bed.

John looked directly into Maria's eyes. "Aye, I'm asking, Isabel. But I'm asking her, not you."

Maria's breath caught in her chest. His gaze never wavered until she at last nodded her acceptance. When he smiled and looked away, a rush of excitement washed over her.

The serving girl entered the cabin behind them and quickly crossed to the bed to help the older woman retire.

John bowed politely to Isabel. "I'd like to thank you, Isabel."

"Well, don't think we want you in here every evening." The older woman smiled and nodded after the retreating Maria. The Highlander turned to watch her as well.

Isabel was struck by the sureness in Maria's stride. The older woman grunted to herself, thinking to herself that it was about time.

Chapter 12

The mist was gone.

The fresh sea breeze lifted Maria's cloak behind her as she stepped out onto the deck. Her hair whipped across her face, momentarily blocking her vision. Reaching up and twisting her black hair into a thick rope, she tucked it inside her cloak and pulled up the hood. The air was clean and cool, and the night black. It was good to be on deck.

Maria had expected resistance by Isabel. But there had been none. It surprised the young woman that there had been no hint of protectiveness on the part of her aunt, no second guessing at all. Maria's decision to go had been sufficient. No questioning look, no knowing glance that spoke volumes about motives or outcomes. Maria wondered if her aunt had any idea how much that meant to her.

From what she could see in the darkness there were just a few men at their watch, posted here and there. Maria watched the commander's back as he moved toward one of them—the sailor standing by the solitary lamp that hung from the mainmast. She didn't need to hear what he had to say to the man. She knew. All night they had wanted to be alone. Now it was possible. During dinner, she had hardly thought of anything other than how it would be the next time they could be by themselves. She had even wondered if he would begin to court her all over again. If the appropriate behavior might involve some ritual she knew nothing about. Perhaps there was something that needed to be said before he could take her once again in his arms, before he could begin to rekindle the passion they'd begun. That would be gentlemanly, she supposed. But then again, she thought with a sigh, perhaps John Macpherson would be more of a rogue.

Looking up, Maria gazed at the moonless sky, stars as bright as diamonds spread across its black satin. Tearing her eyes away from their sparkling welcome, she climbed the few steep steps to the high stern deck and moved across the dark deck to the railing. Beside her, the long-boat that she had rowed lay overturned and secured along the rail. As she reached out in the darkness to touch the rough wood of the longboat's keel, her knee bumped against a cask that had been lashed to the rail.

Beneath her the sea, jet black and powerful, rolled along the ship's hull. As she scanned the distance, the line between water and sky seemed nearly indistinguishable—only the twinkling stars marked the boundary. And far off, beyond the ebony void that surrounded the *Great Michael,* Maria could see the lamps of three other ships.

And then she felt him behind her, the warmth of his body, the strength of his presence.

His hands encircled her waist and pulled her tightly against him. She let her head fall back against his chest as he took hold of her hands and wrapped them around her. She loved the feel of him holding her, the power, the gentleness. He hadn't said a word to her since they'd left the cabin, but she knew that they both had been waiting for this moment. A moment simply to embrace and to take pleasure from the touch. They could remain at sea forever, so far as Maria was concerned. And to-night there would be no fighting the feelings within her, no uncertainty, no coyness.

"The mists have cleared," she said quietly.

His hands tightened their hold. "Aye, lass. We'll be setting sail at first light."

"For Antwerp," she whispered.

"Maria, I have—"

"Please, John. Not now." She turned in his arms. He didn't release his hold on her. With her hands pressed to his chest, she found herself gathered tightly in his embrace. Looking up into his eyes, she thought she could see beyond the stars. "How long will it take . . . before we arrive?"

"Depending on the wind, perhaps two, three days." His arms pulled her closer to his chest as he felt a shudder wrack her frame.

"So soon," she whispered quietly, her chin resting against his broad chest. The wool of the tartan brushed softly against her high cheekbone. She could feel his hands moving across her back, warming her to her very core, bringing her ever closer, making her a part of him. She closed her eyes and felt his lips press firmly against her forehead. Caressing her.

With a tinge of sadness, Maria turned her face, and she could hear his great heart beating. Why was it that even Nature had united with the forces against her? So unkind, she thought, the power of fate! For the first time in her life, she had been on the edge of an exciting new discovery, of a new horizon—a new world—that beckoned with a promise of feelings as new to her and as unknown as the forces holding the stars in the sky. And she was willing to take the step, to go beyond the ledge, and to fall if that was what lay beyond. Aye, with a certainty that she felt to her very core, she knew she could risk it—for she could feel his arms around her. She was quite willing to risk losing the only life she had ever known, the one in which she had no voice, the one that held the future that she seemed destined to live. Aye, she was more than willing to leap from that ledge in the hope of finding the force that would buoy her, that would fix her in the new and brilliant firmament that she could see beckoning to her.

And mocking her.

For the mists had lifted. She rubbed her cheek softly against his chest, swallowing the sorrow she felt for the little time they had left between them.

"It doesn't need to end in Antwerp." He leaned down, his hand pushing the cloak's hood back off her head. He softly kissed her black tresses. "You can stay with me,

lass, while I take my new queen back to King James.
The journey back should be fairly quick. I'll take you to
Denmark. I could meet with your family—"

Maria reached up and placed her fingers against his
lips. She didn't want to lie. No more. They had only
these few, short and precious days at sea. She would
gather a lifetime of dreams from these few days. Raising
herself on her tiptoes, she followed the path of her fingers with her lips. She kissed him softly and then let her
hands encircle his neck, her mouth tasting his full and
sensuous lips.

"Maria, I want to spend more time with you. To get
to know you—"

Her mouth silenced him once again. She teased him,
running her tongue across his flesh. But he held back.
Waiting. She was not about to give up. Maria let her
lips move to his neck and kiss their way to his ear. She
bit at his earlobe. He growled in response. Smiling and
feeling bolder, she kissed a path back to his lips. The
kisses were gentle yet persistent, simple yet seductive.
She let her tongue play across their fullness again, and
this time they opened for her. Hesitantly, her tongue
delved in and began its voyage of discovery.

John leaned back against the railing, fighting to retain
the degree of control that her touch threatened to destroy. She was driving him mad with desire, but he knew
he couldn't allow himself to go where she was leading
him. Yet he couldn't bring himself to withdraw, either.
Something inside told him that she needed to take control of this moment. That here in the darkness, she could
find the confidence to explore her feelings for him. Here,
under a black and star-studded sky, she could discover
the fiery passion he knew she had.

John reached deep inside of himself, though, to remind himself that this moment must have its limits.

Maria let her fingers work themselves inside his shirt.
She touched the crisp hair covering his chest, all the
while her mouth sought more.

John tried to think of sea battles that he'd fought, of
blood, of rough seas and burning ships. Anything but

the softness and beauty of the woman in his arms. His muscles were tight as a stone, and his manhood—aroused and throbbing—ached with the primal need of the male.

His eyes were cloudy and his expression grim when Maria pulled back, peering in the near-blackness at his face. His hesitation in taking charge as he had done before puzzled her, and she shifted her gaze uncomfortably. "Has your interest in me disappeared with the mist, John?"

The Highlander filled his great chest with air and let it out before pulling her hips tightly against his hardened arousal.

She paused for a moment as the sensation registered. Well, there was an interest. Quite a large interest for that matter. Smiling at her own inexperience, she pressed with a shy but irresistible curiosity against him.

"Then why . . ." She stopped, unable to bring herself to say the words.

He leaned down and kissed the bridge of her nose, then placed another kiss on her cheek. His lips were now only a breath away from hers. His fingers cradled her chin. "Because I gave my word to your aunt that I will not take you to my bed onboard this ship."

His voice was strained, and she thought he sounded as if he were in pain. Maria bit her lips to stifle her laugh. My God, she hadn't even thought about what would follow. But as he spoke the words, she knew that their love play would have to end up in a bed. A bed. She tried to remember. Her marriage bed had not been such a memorable place for her during those four years of marriage. But then again, kissing her husband had not been particularly notable, either.

"So my aunt made you give her your word."

He nodded as he leaned his forehead against hers. "Aye, lass. I gave her my word."

"And you honor your word."

John pulled back and gazed into her eyes, deep green and magical and, seemingly, lit from within. His words were barely more than a growl. "Until the end of time."

Maria now understood why Isabel had not objected to the two of them leaving unattended. Her fingers stroked his hair. She stretched up and placed a kiss on his brow, trying hard to swallow the disappointment she felt at having to end their play. But the Scot was an honorable man and that she must respect. "So does that mean you're ready to return me to the cabin?"

The Highlander paused and turned his gaze out to sea before answering. Then, abruptly, he sat down on the cask beside them and maneuvered Maria between his legs. His hands held her there firmly. Their eyes were now at the same level.

"Took me a lifetime to get you away," he rumbled, bringing her closer and brushing his lips across the skin beneath her ear. "It might just take me a lifetime to get you back there."

"But you just said . . ." She tilted her head to give his lips better access.

"I just needed to let you know that there are limits."

"Limits?" she repeated vaguely as his lips suckled her ear.

She turned slightly in his arms as his hand found its way inside her cloak. His fingers cupped the roundness of one breast, and her breath caught as he stroked the nipple through the soft wool of her dress.

She edged closer into the angle of his muscular legs, pushing against the cloth of the kilt until she felt his arousal press intimately against her thigh. She pressed her lips into his hair as he pulled at the laces that held the low neckline of her gown together.

"Tell me more about these limits," she whispered. "How far—"

Her last words came with a sharp intake of breath as John's fingers pulled open the dress, exposing one of her breasts. She sank against him as his hand touched her bare skin.

A shudder rushed through her, searing her with an excitement unmatched by any sensation she'd ever experienced before. As if from afar, she watched with wonder as he parted the front of her cloak and lowered his mouth to her breast. Her body flared, and she rose to his lips, her hands gripping his hair. A liquid heat poured through her, igniting a fire deep within. A fire soared and danced at the very core of her womanhood, and Maria had no knowledge of how to contain such magic. And she had no thought of trying.

John tasted and teased her breast. Moving deliberately from one to the other, he forced himself to go slowly, to lose himself only to a degree in her sweet taste and her abundance. But Maria wouldn't stand still. Her hands were everywhere, her firm body now pressing intimately against his loins, her thigh rubbing provocatively against his throbbing manhood. But he refused to let his desire take control. He couldn't have her. He wouldn't have her. Not onboard his ship. But that didn't mean they were finished.

Maria welcomed his hand as it roughly gathered her around the waist and pulled her even closer into his embrace. His mouth never paused as he continued to suckle her flesh, but she gasped in shock as his other hand pulled up the front of her skirts and reached in beneath them. She closed her eyes, her arms clasping him tightly to her chest as his fingers pulled at her hose. Royalty be damned, she swore wildly, praying his fingers would find their mark. Her body screamed for his touch.

It was an appealing sound. Her undergarments tore away in his hand, and Maria almost cried aloud as she felt his touch.

As his fingers delved into her moist opening and began their stroking play, the Highlander tried desperately to close his ears to the sound of her moans. There were limits. That's what he'd told her. But those limits had been only set for him. That had been all he'd agreed to. Giving her pleasure, bringing her fulfillment, had not been part of their agreement. He could give—he *would* give—but not take.

This was not as Maria had ever guessed it could be. She bit hard on her lower lip as she felt his fingers pushed deeper inside. Unaware of anything now but the sensations that were vibrating through her body as he stroked her sensitive flesh, she rocked against his hand, opening more and more to his touch, and to the rhythm that was steadily obliterating all conscious thought. And deep within her, a desire was growing for something she could not even name.

His mouth was rough as it covered her lips. He muffled her cries as his fingers continued to slide within her. She was so close now. So close to letting go. Her breaths were coming in short gasps, her moans were quick and wild. Like a bird impatient to take flight, her slender body arched in his arms. And then she soared.

Torrents of liquid light and color—scarlet reds and brilliant yellows—burst in fiery waves before Maria's eyes, melting in a lava flow of passion and ecstasy. Wave upon wave thrilled her to her very core, illuminating a world that had been shuttered and gray, stripping away every vestige of restraint, every trace of control. Maria was free, truly free, and she ascended unencumbered, gliding on the currents, her life unfettered, her horizons limitless.

Wrapped in his arms, Maria continued to shudder with rapture. Moments passed, but she was unable to fix upon such trivial things as time or space. But then, eventually, conscious thought gradually returned to her. As the blazing power of the moment gave way to a sublime and amber glow, a melancholy thought occurred to her. Maria realized that never once in her marriage had she felt such bliss. Never once had she even thought it possible to feel such ecstasy. And then Maria smiled and the thought was gone.

As he slowly lifted his mouth from the swollen peak of her nipple, Maria continued her descent to earth. John's hands caressed her back, and his lips rested in the sweet, clean softness of her hair. But his brain was on fire, and his heart slammed mercilessly in his chest. His loins were screaming for release, but he tried to ignore the animal instincts that were threatening to take him where he'd vowed he wouldn't go. And, for a moment at least, the Highlander was certain he would prevail. But then, pulling one arm free, Maria lowered her hand to his thigh. Slipping her hand beneath his kilt, she wrapped her fingers around his erect shaft.

Maria gasped as John brushed her from his lap as if she were no more than a feather. A whirlwind of action, the giant drew his dagger and slashed through the ropes that held the casks. Then, throwing off the cover, he lifted the barrel high over his head, dumping the cold water over the top of his head. Astounded, she watched as he reached for a second cask.

"Old Highland custom," he said simply, emptying the second barrel.

Maria peered through the dark at his face, dripping with water. His hair was plastered to his head; his shirt was soaked, as well, and clung to his heaving chest. But the protrusion beneath his kilt was enough to make her heartbeat race all the more.

"It's not working," she said, stifling a giggle and shaking her head. "The custom, I mean!"

"More cold water, lass." John looked about him. "I need more water."

"Perhaps I can help . . . while you're looking." There was undeniable pleasure in watching him struggle. Moving close to his side, she wrapped her arms around his waist, her body pressing tightly against his wet torso. "This is only the month of March, remember. The sea air is cold. So while you are looking, perhaps I could keep you warm."

"Maria," he threatened as she pressed her lips to his neck. Resolutely, John placed his hands on her shoulders, but when it came right to it, he couldn't bring himself to push her away. Instead, his hands gathered her in. Biting her earlobe, his voice was a low growl. "You are playing with fire, woman. But in spite of what I'm feeling at this moment, I will do the honorable thing."

"Aye," she sighed. "I'm certain that you will."

She raised herself on her toes and kissed him.

John gazed deep into the smoldering depths of her eyes. Drawing her lips to his, he kissed her back with a passion that threatened to ignite once again the molten waves that lay at her very core. Angling his mouth over hers, he sought out the deepest recesses of her soft sweetness, his tongue thrusting and tasting until he felt all tension go out of her body. His own body could not take much more. He had to stop. Releasing her, he watched as she pulled away a bit, breathless and unsteady on her feet.

"It's time to go." His voice was hoarse. "It's time I took you back to your cabin."

Chapter 13

In the bright morning light, the tall, blond woman stood ramrod straight by the railing amidships, her eyes boring into the twosome standing so close together on the high deck far to the stern. To a casual observer's glance, Caroline Maule was merely gazing backward at the clouds of white sails billowing over the two stern decks rising above her. But the truth was that if her eyes could unleash arrows, then Death would command the *Great Michael*.

"You left the cabin without this, lass." The booming voice of her husband approaching her from behind brought a sneer to the woman's face. But before turning she was quick to plaster on a smile in its place. "You're a hardy woman, to be sure, but this is only the month of March. We've a fine stiff breeze this sunny morning, and I can't allow you to catch a chill now, can I?"

The man's burly hands wrapped the leather traveling cloak around his wife's rigid frame, and he looked past her at the ship's commander, standing on the top stern deck with his arm around the shoulder of the pretty young thing that they'd picked out of the sea. Smiling broadly, Sir Thomas pulled Caroline tightly to his side and looked into her face. The wind was cold, but it was a fine, clear morning indeed.

"We'll make Antwerp in no time with a good breeze like this, my dear." Sir Thomas turned and gazed forward beyond the high forecastle deck toward their destination. There was no land in sight. Flanking them on both sides, he could see the warships that made up their expedition. The ships were rising and falling only slightly as they plowed through the wind-whipped white caps. The aging knight took Caroline's hand as he leaned against the railing. "I still say, old warriors like me belong on a strong horse, a lance in one hand and a shield in the other."

"Old warriors, as you say, are renowned for such sentiments." Caroline's voice was cold and passionless, as she looked out at a pair of gulls hanging over the blue-green sea.

"Eh? What was that?" Sir Thomas's gaze narrowed.

"Nothing. I'm not feeling quite myself this morning."

"Hmmph," he grumbled, unappeased. "Well, if you're feeling ill this morning, lass, then perhaps rushing out as early as you did was a wee bit ill-advised. Why, you left our warm bed before the sun was high enough to wake a curate's housekeeper."

"I don't know how anyone could have slept through all the caterwauling these sailors were making this morning." The ship's crew had leapt into action at first light, unfurling the sails and getting the *Great Michael* underway.

"I thought it comforting lying abed, listening to the sound of competent men plying their trade."

Caroline fought to keep herself from responding to that. Turning her eyes away from him, she glanced involuntarily to John Macpherson and the Spanish wench. A wave of revulsion swept through her at the sight of the protective and affectionate grip that the Highlander had on her arm.

"I felt ill," she complained. "I still do. I've already lost everything I ate yesterday. I'm just not used to traveling at this speed."

"Aye, you're a lass that enjoys a good hard ride, yourself." Sir Thomas smiled at his own joke, but looked away when he saw Caroline's chilly gaze upon him. "Ah, Caroline, it won't be so long now. We're almost there. Two days, three at the most. And then we'll be enjoying the comforts of one of the finest palaces in Europe. They say the Emperor Charles has fifty servants to attend each of his guests. And until we arrive, I'll stay right by your side, holding your hand . . . or your head if need be. I'll do whatever you need done, just to make your journey more pleasant."

To most women, the older man's tender words would have brought comfort, but Caroline hated hearing them. She hated him. She hated the whole lot of them. Her husband, the daughter, and the group of useless nobles they traveled with. She had tried to spread the seed of suspicion among them, ignite some feeling against the two tight-lipped Spaniard women, but not one among them had shown even a glimmer of interest. Dolts, every one of them.

As her husband's hands continued their attempt to comfort her, roaming and kneading her back affectionately, Caroline tried to hold back any sign of her disgust. John's arms were the ones she wanted around her. His words of endearment were the ones she wanted to hear. Again, she lifted her eyes and cast a disdainful look at the Highlander's attentiveness to the woman standing so close beside him.

"I wonder what the Queen of Hungary would say if she were to find out that the cabin set aside for her royal use had been so readily given out to some straggling sea—" Wenches, that's what Caroline wanted to say, but she caught herself short. She was not stupid; she would not openly display her hostility in front of the old man. No, it was much better to go on and have him think that the sea travel was not to her liking.

"I can't see Queen Mary minding much," Sir Thomas answered. "Of course, you never can tell about royalty. But the lass hasn't married King Jamie yet; we've still some details to work out. And I don't think Sir John has any intention of bunking her in with the two women occupying the cabin now."

"A fortune was spent on this ship to make it perfect for a queen," Caroline snapped, unable to hold back her anger any longer. "Now if you think the sister to Emperor Charles does not find dishonor in such a slight, then you're a fool, and I am certain the Earl of Angus will see it differently."

"My dear, you may be feeling a wee bit ill, but I'll ask you to keep a civil tongue in your head. And I'll tell you this, if you think John Macpherson would do differently just for fear of Angus's wrath, I'm telling you you're wrong. He is one who will do as he pleases, regardless of what Angus—or anyone else—might think. He's the master of this ship, and no one here is about to challenge his decisions." Sir Thomas softened his expression and drew his wife gently to his side. Frankly, he was delighted that the Macpherson was showing such interest in the Spanish lass. "You wouldn't truly have expected Sir John to throw them back to the fish, now would you?"

"Pulling them from the sea is a long way from treating them like royalty," she sulked.

"Come now, lass? What else was he to do? Let them fend for themselves with the sailors?" Sir Thomas clucked and shook his head. "They needed proper attention."

"There are three other ships with us," Caroline huffed. "Considering the importance of this mission, he should have done differently. And, say what you will, there will be the devil to pay once Angus finds out about this."

Sir Thomas chuckled as he pulled her closer. "Ah, sweet, you just don't understand the ways of men. Angus couldn't care less what goes on before we reach Antwerp. And considering the lass's obvious charms, he'd be the last one to begrudge John Macpherson a bit of dalliance. Surely, I'd not be the one to do it."

Caroline's temper boiled dangerously to the surface, but her voice was like cold steel. "Being a member of Douglas clan yourself, you have a responsibility here. It is disheartening to see how frivolously you take such a serious matter."

Sir Thomas tried to sober his expression. He didn't want to hurt his young wife's feelings. "My dear, I've just said that Sir John doesn't give a tinker's damn for what others think. It's true I've known him only a short time, but the man is—"

"You forget that I know him well." Caroline shrugged off her husband's embrace and turned to face him. "In fact, you've forgotten that I know him very well." She smiled slightly as the older man's face darkened. "You seem to have forgotten a lot of things. But again at your age that's only to be expected."

"Caroline!" the man's cry was fierce and threatening, and carried in it the sound of a wounded bull.

"Aye," she said coldly, using the word as a weapon, driving it deep into his chest.

Stunned, Sir Thomas stared at the stranger who stood before him.

"That is quite enough," he growled, forcing down the feeling of impotence that was washing over him. "You will go below. I think you would do best to stay to our cabin."

The blood pounding in his temples, Sir Thomas watched his wife turn slowly and walk away from him. The cold wind that he felt in his bones seemed to touch only him. Caroline Maule glided away, her cloak, her hair, her expression impassive, unperturbed, untouched.

Maria tried unsuccessfully to tuck her hair inside the hood of her cloak one more time, but the wind whistling across the high stern deck once again thwarted her efforts. Determined, she gathered the loose strands of her hair in her hand and fiercely pulled the silky black rope to one side. Frustrated, she glanced up, only to see the ship's commander smiling down at her. Even his eyes, blue and sparkling, smiled.

"I must look like some sea serpent tangled up in the weeds."

"Nay, lass. Though I might say you look like a beautiful princess who has been a bit rumpled by that sea serpent."

"Rumpled?" Maria asked in dismay, trying vigorously to straighten her appearance.

"Aye, by that sea serpent." John nodded before reaching over to assist in tucking in her hair. He had been looking for an excuse to touch her. The need to feel her hair, to place his lips on her soft skin had kept him up most of the night.

"Sea serpent?"

"When I was a wee lad, my father told us tales of sea serpents and princesses," he answered, taking his time in smoothing Maria's ebony hair. "When we'd playact the stories, I always got to be the creature. Rumpling the princess has always been my favorite part."

"Well, you're quite good at it." She smiled, trying to not think of the irony of what he'd just said. His fingers brushed against her lips. As a shudder raced through her, Maria felt the urge to press her face against his chest and close her eyes to the world—and to everyone and everything in it. Everyone but him.

As if reading her mind, he took her arm in his and pressed it tightly to his side. She gave her arm willingly, but as she did, she glimpsed the tall blond woman striding toward the door leading belowdecks. Even from this distance, Maria could see the look of disdain Caroline Maule was directing toward them. "I think we might be putting on a scene for our fellow travelers."

"Fellow travelers be damned!" John growled huskily. As he eyed the white patch of skin beneath her ear, it occurred to him that nothing would please him more right now than to place a kiss there. But sensing her hesitation, he drew back and leaned against the railing, stretching his arm protectively behind her. "I don't stand around all day gawking at what they do. Why should they? You have nothing to do with them, so they can keep to their own business."

Maria couldn't help but agree. She *was* none of their business, and she never would be if Fortune would smile on her, for once. God willing, never again would she let her life be directed by men like her brother Charles. She tucked a wayward wisp of hair behind her ear. Perhaps if she had shown enough courage and confronted her brother early on, her life might have taken a better path. But then, if she had, would she have ever met John Macpherson? The melancholy that the thought caused her was sharp and sudden.

Maria peered hesitantly about her. The men perched amid the sails aloft were busy at their tasks, and Caroline had disappeared below. There were no other eyes on them. A few of the ship's officers could be seen moving along the decks, calling up to the men above and overseeing the tasks of those working on deck, but they were far too busy to pay any attention to the two of them. None of the Scottish nobles seemed to show much interest in being abovedecks, and there wasn't a soul enjoying the bright sunshine now. Except one: A solitary, thick-bodied man, standing with his back to them. He was leaning heavily on his hands and staring out to sea.

"Sir Thomas Maule," John said, having followed the direction of her gaze. "I don't think you've been formally introduced to him, have you?"

"Nay, I haven't," she replied. "Someday, perhaps— but not now—I'd like to thank him in person."

"Thank him?" John asked curiously. "For what?"

"For breaking in on us as he did two nights ago." She turned her bright green eyes back to him for a moment before laying her hands on the railing and looking out at the shimmering sea. "If it wasn't for him showing up at your cabin when he did the other night, you would never have kissed me. We would never have . . ."

Maria paused, flushed and self-conscious in her thoughts of the previous night. Of what he'd done to her, standing in the dark, here on this same deck. The recollection was heavenly, but still too embarrassing to speak of aloud.

John laid his great paw gently on her slender hands. "With or without Sir Thomas and his felicitous sense of timing, it was only a matter of time before I would have kissed you, Maria. I know that, from the time I set eyes on you, I looked forward to tasting your lips."

She shuddered at the feel of his warm fingers caressing her cold hands. She gazed up into his face and smiled wryly.

"Is this the customary way you treat all of the women you find drifting at sea?"

"You know, it's quite odd, lass," the Highlander responded, smiling back at her, "I have sailed the seas for more than half of my life, and you are the very first woman I've ever found floating in the sea." Her eyes were a bewitching color, no longer jade, but emerald. They drew him in, stealing his breath away with their depth and vibrancy. And now the glow in her face only added to her incomparable charms. She was obviously pleased with the answer he'd given her.

"I am glad," she whispered. "I am glad to be the first one."

His hand tightened around her fingers.

"And you . . ." she continued. "You are the first . . . as well."

"The first?" he questioned.

"The first," she said haltingly. "Well . . . to treat me . . . as a woman. The first to desire me . . . to cherish me. You gave me such pleasure that I felt fires exploding within me. I thought I'd been lifted among the stars."

John's fingers tightened around her shoulders. He didn't care that others were around. That they were standing in the open, in the daylight. "Your husband? Didn't he ever . . ."

She shook her head. "What you did to me last night"—she paused, trying to build her courage—"I never felt such . . . I never thought it could be possible . . ."

He could wait no longer. Taking her hand roughly in his own, he started for the steps.

"Where are you taking me?" she asked, hurrying to keep up with his long strides.

"To my cabin."

"But you said last night . . ." she hushed her tone, looking cautiously around her. "You haven't changed your mind, have you?"

He didn't break stride. He neither turned to answer nor even acknowledge her question. Feeling her excitement grow as she moved quickly beside him, Maria found herself hoping desperately that he had changed his mind. For too long she had accepted the child's role in her life. She would live the life of a woman, now. Whatever he had in mind for her in his cabin was more than acceptable to her. There was only one thing that mattered now and that was being with him.

Just him.

"Come, come, come, tell me, girl. Who is he? What is his name? Does your family approve of him?" Seeing the deep blush on Janet Maule's face, Isabel kept up the gentle assault. "Perhaps I should ask, does your family *know* of him?"

Very little went unnoticed with Isabel. Holding on to the younger woman's arm, she had led the way back and forth the length of the room a number of times. The physician, visiting Isabel earlier, had seen nothing wrong with her wish to get up and move about more. Her shoulder wound was healing nicely, and with the exception of some stiffness in her joints, Isabel was feeling more herself every day.

"Silence is a very becoming trait in young women, but when it is accompanied by flickers of smiles and then deep blushes, an experienced woman always knows." Isabel stopped pacing and turned her full attention on Janet. The older woman watched with a keen eye as the sandy-haired girl's complexion took on the hue of a harvest sunset while her gaze locked on her hands.

Janet then peered hesitantly up into the older woman's face, unable to loosen the knot in her tongue.

"Your mother—she has passed away, hasn't she?"

"Aye," Janet replied simply.

"Maria likes you. She talks about you quite a bit. She is the one who told me of your family and your new stepmother. It must be difficult not having anyone you can confide in. Let me tell you something; Maria has had much the same problem for most of her life. I think that's one reason why she has really taken to you."

"Did her mother pass away, as well?" Janet asked quietly.

"Nay, she is alive," Isabel replied, shaking her head. "My sister is still very much alive, but she might as well be dead. She has an illness, and that, together with some rather difficult family circumstances, has kept her from her children since they were babies. Maria wasn't even a year old when her mother was taken away. Bah, I don't know how I got started on that. This is not the time for sad stories."

"I am sorry," Janet responded. "It must be very sad for Maria . . . and for your sister."

"It does no good to talk of my sister's woes, child. Let's talk about your problems. Things we can mend." Isabel started for the table and chairs placed by the small, open window. Janet followed in her wake. The cool breeze flowing in the opening was fresh and clean.

After seating herself in the chair, Isabel gestured for the younger woman to do the same. "Now tell me, child, what is troubling you this morning. I have been watching you since you came in here. You seem cheerful enough on the surface, but I see those looks. There is something weighing on you, now isn't there?"

Janet lifted her eyes to meet Isabel's. It had been only a few short days since she had first laid eyes on the older woman, but there was something in her manner, in the firmness and authority that one could hear in her words. One perceived the sense of caring, of promised friendship, that made a new acquaintance want to trust her, to share her troubles—and heartaches.

What Isabel said was true. Janet had no one. No one to turn to for counsel, for advice. And right now, with all she was feeling for David and all he felt for her, the young woman needed good counsel. Someone devoid of malice. Someone with a sense of balance, of compassion, and reason.

"Let me guess, your distress has to do with a man. You have done something you think is wrong or you are about to do something you think your father might think is wrong." Isabel paused. "Am I close?"

Janet nodded, blurting out her words. "Aye. It's true. I am in love. But my father . . . my father, never . . ."

"Let's forget about your father for now. Tell me again

about this love of yours. Do you *think* you are in love or—"

"Nay, I *am* in love. I am certain of it. He is all that I think of. He is all that matters. And we haven't done anything wrong. But . . . but the way we feel for each other, I am afraid . . ."

"You are afraid that it's simply a matter of time before you do something wrong. Is that it?"

Janet just stared. She had been ready to give herself to him the night before, but he'd somehow put a stop to their passion. David had said they could not make love. Not until the time when she could stand in his arms with no guilt and sorrow over whatever consequences might follow.

"Does he love you, as well?" Isabel asked gently.

"Aye, much more than I deserve." Her hands entwined in her lap. "He is a good man, and an honorable one. He is a hard-working man, and he has earned his place in the world by dint of his own talent and not by any title or wealth passed on from his ancestors."

"Then he has the means to support you. But will he marry you? Provide you with a home and, more importantly, the happiness to furnish that home?"

She nodded tearfully. "Aye, all of that . . . and more."

Isabel placed her hand on the young woman's arm. "Then what is holding you back?"

Janet wiped away her tears with the back of her hand. Turning her gaze toward the open window, a corner of her mind cleared, and all of the torment, all of the confusion suddenly came into focus. Life at court amid her father's noble friends meant nothing to her. Never in her life had she coveted—or even longed for—the finery that accompanied her family's rank. Perhaps David couldn't provide all those things for her, but she didn't care. Those were things she'd never sought.

There was one thing, though, that did matter.

"My father's blessing," Janet said quietly. Her gaze was steady and her voice calm as she looked back at Isabel. "I wish I could have his blessing."

Isabel had the first thought—for the briefest of moments—that perhaps she shouldn't have said anything to this young woman. Without question, she had already single-handedly uprooted her own niece and destroyed any chance of her continued respectability within the courts of the Holy Roman Empire. But then, recalling the sight of Maria, bright and happy as she'd left their cabin this morning, Isabel knew that it was all worthwhile. In her twenty-three years of life, Maria had never looked more beautiful or more at ease than she had looked today.

Oh, forgive me, Virgin Mother, Isabel prayed, returning Janet Maule's gaze. *This young women needs happiness as well.*

Isabel nodded. She would do everything in her power to make sure Janet received her father's blessing.

Chapter 14

Honorable intentions be damned, John thought.

Nay, he argued, continuing the silent debate. You can't just take her, after giving your word. Though that injured aunt of hers was certainly no one's keeper, still—John reminded himself—he had pledged his word. And Isabel, in return, had kept her end of the bargain by arranging their little dinner. He would not be standing here, looking at Maria, if it had not been for the trust Isabel had bestowed on him.

"Perhaps you'd care to let me in on the argument," Maria suggested with a wry smile. She sat with her back straight in the chair, her eyes studying every detail of the handsome commander pacing before her in the room. The changing expressions of his face, especially around his eyes, showed the internal battle being waged. "Perhaps I can help."

John stopped his restless pacing, and leaning back against the open window casing, he gazed at her. Her hair was now tied loosely in a black, silken knot at the nape of her neck. The skin of her throat cried out for his touch, his lips. It only took one look at her and John's blood was again roaring in his veins.

This was going to be difficult. Very difficult.

When they'd left the upper deck, John Macpherson had every intention of taking Maria to his bed as soon as they reached his cabin. She was willing, he knew, and when she'd told of how she'd felt the night before—how he'd made her feel—his loins had caught fire. He wanted her.

But their journey below had been interrupted by

fifty . . . no, a hundred trivial matters as his officers, the
whole of the noble delegation, even the drunken sot of
a physician had found it absolutely essential to waylay
them, carrying on endlessly. Frustrated, he finally had
pushed past the last of them, storming below with Maria
in his wake.

Now, thinking a bit more clearly, John Macpherson
thanked God for the interruptions. If there hadn't been
those delays, he decided, his promise to Maria's aunt
would have been honored more in the breach—in a
manner of speaking.

Maria continued to watch him as he folded his arms
over his broad chest.

Though awkward at first, it had immediately become
quite interesting to stand behind John and watch him
attend to his duties as master of the *Great Michael*. She
knew he was impatient to go below—as was she—but
the manner in which he dealt with his men, and with the
Scottish noblemen, was fascinating to her. This was a
world of men, a gruff and plain-speaking world in which
the pleasantries of courtly language and manners held
little weight.

John Macpherson ran his ship with a firm hand and a
mind obviously well skilled in the art of the seafarer. He
was so competent, so clear thinking in everything he
said. She'd seen the looks in the men's eyes. The looks
of conviction, the looks of belief in the man that stood
before them. Just accompanying him, she herself had felt
the strength, the power that surrounded him. Maria
knew why his men followed him.

There was something about the life at sea that infected
a person with a sense of independence. Perhaps, she
thought as she'd watched him give his orders with such
confidence, it was the knowledge that the only thing
standing between life and death, between safety and the
danger inherent in the sea, was a person's own ability.
If you were a competent sailor, then you had good reason to be proud and confident. And you had good reason to feel lucky. Moving behind John through the ship,
Maria too had felt strong and confident, even happy with

herself. She knew she was living for today. And the sense of freedom she was feeling sent her spirits soaring.

But now they were alone, and she felt as if her heart was in her throat. She had tried a bit of humor to dispel the intensity that surrounded them, but that had apparently failed. Every time he directed her a look, she could feel the heat of his gaze, and her chest pounded with anticipation. The expectation of what was to come, the tension, the undeniable need that burned within her body, caused her brain to whirl.

Maria paused and gazed at the chart that lay open on the worktable. She didn't know how it had happened or even when, but she knew somewhere in the past twelve hours, a new threshold had been crossed. She was no longer just attracted to him. No longer could she think of him simply as the most handsome man she'd ever met in her life. Now her heart swelled for him. At the very center of her being, Maria ached for him. There was enchantment, anticipation, passion. Maria looked down into her healing hands. There was love.

John walked over and came to a stop before her.

She looked up into his face. His deep blue eyes were boring into hers. He hadn't said a word since they'd entered the cabin, but she knew he was ready to talk now.

"Maria, you don't know me."

She could hear the strain in his voice. His furrowed brow made her heart tighten in her chest. He was going to end this, she thought with a start. That was it. They were finished. What else would he be trying to do? Virgin Mother! Maria thought, panic-stricken, what did I say on deck? What did I do?

She stood up and faced him. "What do you mean by that?"

"You don't know enough about me. Who I am."

"I know more about you than you know of me."

"That's so. But I'm talking of different things now," he protested. "What I know of you is sufficient, for the moment."

"How so?" she argued softly. "How is it that the little

I've told you of myself is sufficient, but all that I've seen in you is somehow insufficient?"

John glared at Maria, at the stubborn set to her jaw, at the flash in her eyes. He had wanted to speak his mind and just be done with it. To tell her the things that lay heavily on his heart and his conscience. He had no patience with deceit or trickery. He wanted her to see him for who he was before she gave in to the hot-blooded passion he knew lay in store.

"I am waiting for your answer," she challenged, facing the Highlander, her chin raised in the air. For a moment she wondered how well her bravado would hold up. She wondered if he could hear her heart pounding in her chest. She didn't know if disappointment lay ahead, but this new Maria would not accept defeat without a fight.

"Maria," he began haltingly, "I have spent a lifetime at sea. It is difficult . . . I have lost the ability . . . well, women are . . ."

John cast about, searching for the words. Turning toward the window, he placed his palm on the smooth wood of the casing. "Maria, I am a third son. This is something you don't observe, but that you must know." He looked for a change in her, a reaction, but none was apparent. "Do you know what that means?"

"I am the fifth child," she answered. "And nay, I don't know what that means."

John stared at her. She hardly reached his chin, but the way she addressed him—she had the presence of a giant. "It means that I am in no position to inherit titles. I have wealth, it's true. But no position. I will never be laird of my clan, I will never be lord of any region—"

"Is that important to you?" she asked quietly, interrupting him. "It bothers you that you'll have no kingdom to call your own?"

"It's no kingdom that I am after, lass. And it is not a lairdship nor earldom that I desire. None of these things mean a straw to me."

"Then why do you bring it up?" She gazed steadily at him. "What does it matter?"

John scowled at her. "Because though you're a widow,

you're still a highly marriageable young woman. I know these things mean a great deal to you."

"To me?" she cried out in shock. Now her frown matched his. "Why should titles mean anything to me?"

"For God's sake, Maria, though you don't say so, it's obvious you are a woman of family and rank. A bonny lass, at that. I'm a man past his prime, and your family, I'm certain, has much better prospects in mind for you."

Her heart skipped a beat. For someone who didn't know anything about her family, the Highlander certainly had a clear picture of her brother and his plans. "We are discussing you and me, not our families."

"You're still a noblewoman," he pressed.

"And?" She raised an eyebrow and continued on, not waiting for an answer. "Is that to be held against me? Would it have been better if I'd been something else? Perhaps I should have pretended to be lowborn. A peasant girl. How would that have altered your feelings for me?"

John shook his head. "Maria, what I feel, I feel for *you*. And you could pretend away your life—pretend to be the Queen of Hungary, if you like—it wouldn't change who I know you to be, nor how I feel about you." He took a deep breath. "But this is not why I began all this talk. I needed you to know . . . I didn't want my lack of worldly titles—"

Maria put up one hand, interrupting him again. "Just look at the person who is standing before you. See *me*, John. It's me."

The words vanished from his lips, blown away by the fresh, spring breeze he felt sweeping through his soul. Her sparkling green eyes encompassed him, drawing him in with their beauty and with the goodness reflected from within her.

John Macpherson stopped. The woman before him was not Caroline Maule. Gazing at her, the Highlander realized that he was seeing this woman for the first time, and his heart leapt at the sensation. He had been so focused on himself, on his own shortcomings—his age, his position in life, his failure to live up to the expectations of . . . whom? John rubbed his chin with his knuckles. He had prepared himself to face the same complaints he had heard from Caroline. About his lack of position. He realized he was expecting from Maria the same charges that Caroline had leveled against him. Against his pride. He stood, gazing at this lass he'd found floating in the mist, and found himself completely lost for words.

Maria saw the lines around his azure eyes soften. The heavy clouds that had darkened his mood lifted, and Maria took a step toward him.

"Nothing you've just said changes the man I know. Nothing. Rank, power, and all the wealth in the world—I can turn my back on these things without a moment's hesitation." She paused and dropped her gaze to her hands. She was in love with this man. He was the only one she didn't want to turn away from. But how could she tell him this, declare herself, when she would be walking out of his life forever the moment they reached Antwerp. Maria lifted her eyes to his and smiled. She was not prepared to confess her artifice, but something within her drove her to share a piece of her past. "Anyway, you've confessed your life. But you still haven't answered how is it that you've been content knowing so little of mine?"

As she looked up at him from beneath her thick lashes, John felt the stirring in his loins once again. She looked more enticingly beautiful than ever. She was a vixen . . . no, she was an angel. As she lifted her chin, and her eyes flashed like emeralds, the Highlander thought her more ethereal than any time he'd seen her. John thought back on what she'd just said, on turning her back on all that other women sought in men. His hands lifted to gather her close, but then he stopped. He had to finish what he'd started.

"What is important about you, lass, I already know," he said quietly. "But I want to know more about you."

"Then tell me, what is it that you do know?" Her question came out as a whisper. She wasn't sure how far she was going, but she realized—absently, without concern—that her heart was quickly taking over her reason. John had revealed some of his past; she wondered, vaguely, how much of her own she dared to reveal.

He looked deep into her eyes and then, unable to hold himself back, he reached out and took hold of her hands. It was true what she said, there was so much he didn't know about her. Turning her hands in his palms, he looked down at the new pink skin on her healing wounds. She had removed the bandages today. "Let me see—you are a quick healer. That much I know."

She nodded, encouraging him to go on.

His thumb caressed her palms lightly and then lifted them to his lips. "You have the softest skin of any woman I've ever met."

"No exaggerating to make me feel more . . . cordial toward you." She smiled. "No lies. Only facts, if you please."

He nodded noncommittally. Placing her hands around his neck, he gathered her close around the waist. "You have the most magical eyes—"

"Only physical description, m'lord," she interrupted, tightening her hold around his neck. A rush of excitement ran through her as her body pressed against his chest. "There is no magic in my eyes."

"I can only tell you what I see, lass."

"Perhaps you only see the light in your own eyes reflected in mine."

"You are very clever. But nay, your eyes are the color of rare gemstones, and the light in them comes from deep within you."

"Tsk, Sir John. Exaggerating again." She lifted herself on her toes, and grazed her lips lightly against his mouth.

His arms were like steel as they pressed her tightly to him.

"You are passionate, quite a bonny creature, smart, and undeniably good-hearted." As she opened her mouth to object, he silenced it with a brushing kiss. His voice was but a whisper against her lips. "And you are unwed."

"Do you think a convent is the place for widows?" Seeing his eyebrows rise, she smiled.

"Some, perhaps," he answered. "But not all."

"But you seem to think a woman should fear for her future."

"Aye, but you're not afraid of what I don't have to give you. You don't seem to concern yourself, overly, with what tomorrow might bring you."

Her fingers combed through his long black hair. Her body arched against his. "And you find that an attractive quality?" she cooed.

"For the moment I do." His hands caressed the length of her back, rising to the laces at the nape of her neck. "But I believe the time may come when I will suffer for it."

She drew her hands back and began working her fingers inside his shirt. They were two days from Antwerp.

"Then let's enjoy this moment that we have." Her hand found his skin. "And when we arrive at that other time, I'll suffer along with you."

"Maria," he whispered, lifting her in his arms. She wrapped herself around him as he carried her toward the bed. Her mouth roamed freely, tasting the skin of his face, his neck.

He stood her on her feet, and leaned back against the high bed. Pulling gently, he loosened the laces of the dress, and it fell to the floor, pooling around her feet. Maria, covered only by her thin linen chemise, stepped closer to him, drinking in the sensations that were racing through her. His lips played over hers, while his hands cupped her backside, pressing her hips intimately against his aroused manhood. Feeling bolder as he deepened the kiss, Maria's body rocked against his, while her hands sought more of him. Her fingers fought to remove the barriers between them. The thought of his skin against hers, of seeing him lying naked beside her, made her nearly frantic with desire. But the Highlander pushed her hands away.

This was sheer madness, he thought. To promise one thing, and then to make them both crazed by such behavior. He felt, for a moment, like some boy at the abbey school, playing games with the cook's daughter.

But feeling Maria's firm flesh against his, John could not quite bring himself to halt so abruptly such a moment of pleasure. He slid his hand up over her firm round buttocks.

Hell, he thought, at worst they were only two days from Antwerp. And with the way the Emperor's warships patrolled this part of the German Sea, this might be the last moment he and Maria would have together. Besides, he was in control. This was all such harmless play. Vaguely, he wondered how much more speed he could squeeze out of the *Great Michael.*

As she reached for the brooch that held his tartan in place, John pushed her hands behind her back and held them there.

"Why don't you let me touch you?" she complained softly.

"Because of my promise," he growled, his attention drawn to the full, round breasts that strained against the tight linen of the chemise. He could see the points of the hardened nipples pushing through the fabric. "One touch from you, love, and I can't say how fair a job I'd do keeping that promise."

Her breath caught as he pulled her closer and kissed her pulse that fluttered beneath the skin of her throat. His lips moved lower and she arched her back as he pressed his lips to her heart. She opened her eyes and gazed at him when he drew back. Using one hand, John pushed first one strap of the chemise and then the other off her shoulders. She closed her eyes and let her head fall backward as he started to peel the chemise downward. Maria shuddered as the soft linen pulled gently at her breasts before it fell to the floor.

John's lips closed on a rose-colored nipple, his tongue darting, laving, tasting. His hand lifted the weight of her breast, squeezing gently as he suckled.

"John," she gasped, continuing with a voice ragged with desire, "I care nothing for that promise. I want you to lose yourself in me as I lose myself in you."

"In time I will . . . in time . . ." The Highlander sat back, releasing his hold on her, his words evaporating

as his eyes swept over her naked body. She did nothing
to hide herself. In the dark of the night on the deck, he
had not seen—nor had he guessed—the extent of her
beauty. She had the presence of an angel. Her skin
shone, shimmering and as snowy as puffs of clouds in
the midsummer sky. His eyes moved lower. Her breasts
were high, full, beckoning for his touch. The curve of
her hips and the dark triangle that hid the splendor of
her womanhood tempted him further. Her legs were
strong and lithe. His eyes returned to her face, now covered with a deep blush.

"By God," he growled, "you are beautiful."

She had never thought it possible to stand this way
before any man. She had never thought it possible to
feel so cherished by anyone. His eyes were dark, smoldering with desire, and they bore into hers.

"Take me," she whispered, fearing nothing. She knew
the truth. She belonged to him as she had never belonged to any other man. John Macpherson would be
the first and the last.

The Highlander's hands shook when he reached for
her again, drawing her back into his arms.

"I never have felt such weakness, such attraction for
a woman," he whispered the words as his hands roamed
over the smooth skin of her shoulders, her breasts, her
belly and hips.

"Why . . ." Maria shuddered beneath his touch. "Why
must we consider attraction a weakness."

"I brought you here to give you pleasure, knowing
that I myself must wait—until we reach Antwerp, at
least. But you've washed away my defenses. You've bewitched me, spun a web, taken away my discipline with
this spell of your beauty, of your goodness."

"I am no witch," she answered, breathless. "I've only
returned the spell you yourself have cast. Your charm
that has stripped me of *my* reason."

Maria took his hands and pushed them to either side
of him, pressing herself against him and kissing his throat
where she could see the throbbing of his pulse. Resting
her head against his shoulder, she felt his hands encircle

her, the bare skin of his knee sliding across her thigh. She lowered her hand to his muscular thigh.

I am in control, John told himself. *I can wait.* He knew he had kindled a volcano between them. And now his body was taking over his mind. *But I will not give in to my desire.* John lifted her into his arms and placed her on the bed beside him.

She watched him beneath half-lidded eyes as he moved next to her. The contrast between them—him fully clothed in his white linen, his tartan, and kilt, the thick leather belt crossing his chest; her, naked against the deep green of the bedclothes—the difference was so strange to her, so exciting. She reached for him, grasping the buckle of the belt. He moved on top of her.

She gasped at the feel of his weight upon her, at his arousal, large and heavy, pressing so intimately against her inner thigh.

He closed his eyes and rested his head against her forehead, trying, for a moment, to catch his breath. *I am in control,* he told himself over and over. Maria lifted her knee, opening herself to him as he settled deeper between her legs. *I can stop this any time,* he thought vaguely as her hands slid over his back.

She moved beneath him and smiled at the sound of his loud groan. Her hands caressed his lower back and moved past his waist. Her body was on fire, her womanhood, moist with desire, ground restlessly against him. His buttocks were like rock beneath her probing fingers. Slowly, ever so slowly, she started gathering his kilt upward.

"Maria," he rumbled, searing her mouth with a kiss. Taking hold of her hands, the Highlander pinned them over her head.

Maria gave in to him breathlessly. His mouth had never felt so wonderful, his tongue probing, thrusting. His free hand never stopped—stroking, caressing, sending shivers of pleasure into the very core of her. Their legs were entwined, and when John moved down her body to take her breast into his mouth, her gasps of pleasure filled the air. His hand fondled her breasts while his tongue swirled around one nipple. When he finally began to suckle, a white-hot flame of need began to engulf all conscious thought in her.

John raised himself a bit and slid farther down her body. His control was slipping badly, and he knew he needed to do something, focus on something . . . other than burying himself deep within her. Do this, he threatened himself. You are in control.

Maria moved restlessly beneath him, her hips responding to the love dance that was emanating from within her. Aware only of the blaze that was consuming her, her desire to touch him, to taste his body the way he tasted hers began to emerge from some dusky corner of her mind. But the sensations coursing through her were so raw, so new, that she had no way to control them. Her gasps turned to moans as his lips moved lower across the sensitive skin of her belly. And then he moved lower. Still lower.

Maria nearly came off the bed when his tongue sank into her. Gripping the sheets, she became wild as his lips and tongue found the source of all pleasure. Her moans became shrieks as a world inside her exploded in molten streaks of reds and white. As wave after wave consumed her, Maria clawed at the bed, wanting him to stop, begging him to keep on.

John knew there was no going back. Her cries of ecstasy, her liquid heat, the love scent that filled the air—all of these things combining to destroy any remnant of his control. Discipline, promises, every vestige of civilization—gone, washed away on wave after wave of primeval desire. Pushing her to the peak of pleasure, John held on as Maria's hips lifted in an arching moment of bliss. Hearing her cry out his name, the Highlander moved on top of her, gathering her in his arms.

"There will be no more waiting, love," he murmured as she fought for breath. He bit at the velvety lobe of her ear. "I want to, lass, but I . . ."

Her hands pushed him over on his back, and he went willingly as she tore at his kilt and reached beneath it. Her fingers encircled his throbbing arousal, stealing his breath away. John groaned deep in his throat and dropped his head onto the bed next to her as Maria's hands stroked and kneaded him.

"I've never done any of this," she whispered raggedly, pulling herself onto his chest. "But again, there is so much I have to learn."

John watched her breasts swing free as she raised herself up and began tugging at his shirt.

"Maria," he growled.

"John," she answered. Her green eyes sparkled as she exposed the bronze-colored skin beneath his shirt.

"This is no time to toy with me, lass."

"I agree, it is not." She lowered her mouth to his stomach, running her tongue over taut muscles of his belly. "But I've just learned something, and I intend to put it to use."

I'm in control, he told himself.

And then she moved lower.

David nodded to the grizzled sailor by the cabin door. "Have you seen Sir John, Christie?"

"Nay, sir. Only Mistress Janet in there."

"Oh?"

"Aye, I heard the bonny thing say she'd be only staying a wee bit, but I believe she dropped anchor."

Before David could bring himself to respond, the cabin door opened and Janet stepped into the narrow corridor.

The silence that struck the two upon seeing one another did not go unnoticed by either Christie or the woman standing just inside the door. Isabel smiled to herself at the ways of love. These two were like helpless babes—gazing into each other's eyes and oblivious to anyone looking on. *No one teaches these children anything anymore. The art of love is an art to be studied,* Isabel thought wryly. And these two really needed a few lessons. She coughed to get their attention.

"Lady Isabel!" David jumped, blushing as he noticed the older woman.

"Are all Scots in the habit of lurking behind doors, or is this a quality only you possess, sir?"

"Lurking?" David asked at once.

"Aye, lurking," she continued. Isabel cast a glance at Christie. "But, of course, it's not just you. We have this decrepit creature skulking about here. So it must indeed be a national trait."

"Skulking . . . ?" Christie muttered hotly from behind David.

"I wasn't . . . I don't know . . ." David stammered the words.

"Who's she calling 'decrepit?' " Christie grumbled.

"I was looking for—"

"Mistress Janet?" Isabel asked, hiding her amusement. "Of course, dear. As you can see, Mistress Janet stands before you."

"Aye, I mean nay!" he blurted. "I was looking for Sir John."

"Sir John?" Isabel questioned. "You don't know his whereabouts?"

"I don't! Nay, I mean I do. Well, I will." David shook his head. What was it about this woman that made him sound like a blathering idiot? "I've just begun looking for him."

"So you came here." Isabel gave the young man one of her most scornful looks. "All I have to tell you is that you'd better find your commander at once. And I want my niece found, as well. I don't like the sound of this at all. On your way, navigator."

David only nodded resignedly and bowed to the two women. With a quick and gentle look at Janet, the ship's officer went off down the corridor.

"Nice young man," Isabel said sweetly to Janet.

"Hmmph," Christie put in, slouching against the bulkhead.

"I shouldn't loiter down here, Janet, with the likes of this one hanging about." Isabel gave the aging sailor an icy look and then shut the cabin door with conviction.

*   *   *

"Aye, David. Stay the course." John's command was terse, and Maria watched his broad back as he blocked the partially open door. David was clearly concerned about the sails that had been sighted on the horizon to the south. "I'll be on deck in a wee bit."

John closed the cabin door and turned to her. His blue eyes swept over her, as if the bedclothes that she hid beneath were as transparent as air. A liquid heat pumped into her veins, and Maria felt almost wanton at the thought of being so affected by his simple glance. It was, undeniably though, *his* look that stirred her so.

John took a deep breath as he walked toward the bed. Maria had buried herself beneath the blankets, and she now peeked out from one end. Though it had taken a moment to clear his mind and grasp the fact that someone was at his door, the pounding had sent Maria skittering away in a panic. He smiled, because in a selfish way, her response had made him quite happy. Her comfortable responses extended no further than his own door. Gazing at her as he approached the bed, a wave of possessiveness suddenly washed over him. A thought came into focus that had been lying half concealed in the recesses of his mind. He wanted her only for himself, and he had no intention of giving her up. Not today, not tomorrow, not ever.

"You have to go," she said quietly.

"Aye, lass. They need me on the deck," he said as he sat beside the bed and pulled the blankets away from her face. As she pushed herself up on her elbows, the bedclothes settled provocatively over the tops of her breasts, and John felt the embers of desire stir once again. He shook his head to clear the notion. He looked into the sparkling emerald of her eyes. "From here, we'll be running down the coast to Antwerp, and with the number of guns we carry, it's important that no one see us as looking for trouble."

She just nodded in agreement. She had heard everything David said.

He lowered his mouth and kissed her, thoroughly. Drawing her up in his arms, the Highlander caressed the cool, smooth skin of her exposed back. He pulled back, leaving them both breathless.

"And perhaps you heard," he whispered. "Your aunt is looking for you."

"I heard." John could hear the husky note of passion in her voice.

"You and I have a wee bit of unfinished business to tend to, you know."

"I know. But you didn't break your promise," she said quickly.

He laughed, pulling her and the blankets onto his lap. "Aye, and spoken like a fine man of law! Acquitted of all charges! Though, if the truth be told, it wasn't for lack of trying." John pulled her tight and kissed her again soundly. Drawing away, he returned his steady gaze. "But it won't be long now, Maria. Once we reach land, there'll be naught to stop us."

Her hands encircled his neck, causing the blanket to fall away as he crushed her to his chest.

"It's very likely, lass, that I'll not see you again—alone—until we tie up in Antwerp. But once we do, you and Isabel will stay in the cabin until I come for you."

She hid her face in the crook of his neck and said nothing in response. There was so much that he didn't know. He assumed that they had no one waiting for them in Antwerp. That Denmark was still their destination.

Maria let out a long breath. Deliberately, she had been avoiding any thought of what was to come. Avoiding any thought that the only happiness she'd ever known was coming to an end. Avoiding any thought of leaving John Macpherson and disappearing into the dark. Into the mist. At Antwerp.

Chapter 15

The breeze from the open window raised gooseflesh on the old woman's neck. Vaguely, she recalled a lesson from childhood. The westerly wind's like a monarch gone mad, driving his courtiers to shipwreck and death. Shivering involuntarily, Isabel looked out into the growing darkness, shook her head, and exerted her will. I must be getting feebleminded, she thought, to let such foolishness prey on me.

Turning her attention to Maria, the older woman glanced from her niece's face to the young woman's hands as she busily changed the shoulder dressing. Maria showed real ability in the task. Her face was all business and her fingers worked nimbly and competently on the linen wrapping. How different, Isabel thought. So much had changed in the young woman since the two of them first set foot on the *Great Michael.* What Isabel had tentatively hoped to achieve in taking away Maria from the bullying of Charles seemed to have been accomplished almost overnight. Right before her eyes, the girl had bloomed in body and in spirit. Suddenly, Maria was so independent. Oh, certainly Isabel had seen her niece play her role of queen, wearing the imperial guise that professed power and feigned indifference. But now . . . now there was a reality to her confidence. Never had Isabel seen Maria so comfortable with herself.

Isabel chuckled to herself, thinking back on the conversation that they'd had when Maria returned to their cabin. The look her niece had given her had actually been enough to stop her from questioning Maria on the time she'd spent alone with the handsome ship's com-

mander. It appeared she and Maria had crossed a new
boundary, one that moved their relationship into a new
realm. Isabel had an idea that Maria was no longer going
to be so submissive to an authoritative tone. In fact,
Isabel thought it would be quite nice to develop a more
compassionate and harmonious relationship with Maria.
Perhaps they had both changed on this journey, Isabel
thought.

"I heard that we may reach Antwerp as early as tomorrow night," Isabel offered.

"That's what I heard, as well," Maria put in quietly.

Isabel waited for her niece to say more, but the young
woman appeared to be concentrating on her task. Isabel
waited a few moments longer before continuing.

"Have you given it any thought? What you will do, I
mean, once we come into port?"

"I'll not go back to Charles or to the palace," Maria
stated decisively, lifting her chin combatively. "That
much I am certain of. But if I'm to accomplish that, I
might just need to jump overboard before we drop
anchor."

"The water is cold, child. You'll die of a chill for
sure."

"True," Maria agreed. But then again, perhaps that
was a better fate than being handed over to her brother.
"Well, I suppose an alternative plan would be to cut my
hair, or alter my looks somehow, and just hope that I'll
not be recognized in the city. Perhaps I could mix in with
the common folk . . . find a place for myself, perhaps."

A smile crept into Isabel's face. "It won't work, my
sweet. What would you do? You are far too pretty—far
too healthy—to be taken for a harbor wench. And I
don't think you're considering what the good Sir John
might think of such a plan. I believe he'd most likely
skin you alive if he ever saw you living in such a condition. He knows you are no commoner."

Maria's hands left off their task, and she sat abruptly
in a nearby chair. She could feel the heat rise in her
face at the thought of John Macpherson feeling somehow protective of her. Already it was like some dream

to think on the moments of passion they'd shared. Embarrassed, she realized that her aunt was sitting quietly before her, watching her every move. Maria knew her emotions played across her face. She feared that Isabel had most likely guessed what was going through her mind. But there was no mockery in her aunt's expression. No hint of disapproval, no censorious look. Maria stood up, and finishing changing the bandage, helped her aunt pull her dress over her shoulder.

"I need to think of *something*, Isabel. I wish I had friends in Antwerp. Someplace to hide, someone to go to. But I haven't any. I don't even know the city all that well. You know, the only times I've ever visited Antwerp were the two times when Charles brought me in to ship me off—the gilded bride. I was only at the palace a month before he trundled me off to Hungary. And then this time . . . well, I simply sulked in my apartments before you helped me run away."

Isabel remained silent as she watched her niece struggling with her dilemma. After the divine power saw fit to have them rescued when they'd lost their first ship, Isabel had wondered if it might not be for the best for Maria to return to her brother Charles. Let fate lead her where it would. But then, this new turn of events—this obvious infatuation which Maria had developed for John Macpherson—complicated everything. Then again, perhaps fate was taking a hand after all.

Maria sat down again and gazed out into the deepening twilight. She couldn't keep him out of her mind. He was around her; everywhere she turned, she could feel his presence. She wondered briefly if he felt her absence the way she felt his. Probably not, she thought. He had his work, his ship to occupy him. The responsibility of all their lives. The responsibility of his mission. She let out a silent sigh, thinking of his beauty. No doubt he'd had so many women in his life. But the way he'd shuddered beneath her lips when she'd kissed his body, when she'd returned his touch. He'd seemed almost in awe. He'd delighted in her. In her—Maria of Nowhere! A castaway, a nobody. No tall, fair-haired Scottish lady.

Just . . . Maria. He delighted in her body, with a passion that she shared. But was there anything more in what he felt for her? She considered that for a moment. Their conversations were so comfortable, so enjoyable. But even if his feelings did not equal hers, perhaps, someday, he'd care for her the way . . .

Maria shook her head and bit at her lip. What was she doing? No, the future was impossible, and here she was, giving herself hope. An impossible hope.

Turning her eyes away from the young woman, Isabel tried to weigh what good would come of Maria returning to her brother. She knew that the young queen's future with the King of Scotland was finished, but how far reaching would Charles's wrath extend? At best, Maria would spend the rest of her life in a convent. At worst . . .

Suddenly, Isabel didn't need to take any more time to know what she herself must do. Another look at Maria, and Isabel decided. They had to push forward with their original plan. There was no other way.

"I have friends in Antwerp," Isabel said energetically, breaking in on Maria's melancholy thoughts. "People who can help us. But I just can't take you to them. They'll know you immediately. And even if I could convince them to put their loyalty to me above their loyalty to the Emperor, they know that their lives would be forfeit if they were caught defying his wishes. But I do have an idea."

Maria's eyes brightened, quickly catching her aunt's enthusiasm.

"Has John Macpherson learned anything more about you?"

Maria looked at her steadily, feeling the blush creeping into her face. "You mean, about my true identity?"

Isabel nodded.

"Nay." Maria shook her head emphatically. "There was no way I *could* tell him."

"That's good," Isabel responded. "This makes it easier for us to get away."

She paused, considering the ramifications of her plan.

She would be leaving Maria on her own. Glancing at the young woman, Isabel knew it was worth the gamble.

"Come, Isabel," Maria prompted impatiently. "How can I make a decision until I hear your plan?"

Isabel smiled. She very much liked this new Maria.

"Janet Maule visited me here this morning," the older woman continued. "And while we were talking, she passed on an interesting bit of news. One that we can use to help you escape."

Maria slid her chair closer to her aunt's.

"Janet mentioned that when this Scottish delegation reaches Antwerp, the nobles will be taken to Charles's palace, but that John Macpherson will be staying elsewhere. Apparently, his older brother is the diplomat, Ambrose Macpherson." Isabel peered at Maria's expression, but there was no flicker of recognition. "Of course, you wouldn't know of him. I've never seen the man myself, but when Janet mentioned the name, I recalled a number of women speaking of him. They all thought him quite handsome, if my memory serves me."

"Very well, Isabel. Please get on with it."

"Well, Ambrose and his wife, who is a sculptor or something outrageous. . . . Nay, I remember. She is a painter—you've *got* to love her—well, the two of them have holdings all across Europe. And, as it happens, they also have a place in Antwerp, and that is where John will be staying."

Maria sat restively, her heart thudding in her chest. She hung on Isabel's every word.

"Aye, I thought this plan might interest you." Isabel nodded, smiling knowingly. "This is the way I see it. We ask the good ship's commander to put you up when we reach port. After all, that's understandable, considering he thinks you have no one there and, after the ship being sunk, have no money. Once you're ensconced in his brother's house, you'll be safe—for the time being. There is no way Charles could even guess of any connection between you and Sir John Macpherson, Lord of the Scottish Navy."

All Maria could do was stare.

"It's absolutely the *last* place your brother would think to look for you!"

Staying with John, Maria thought, no longer confined to the promises binding them aboard ship, the possibility of . . .

Maria let out a long breath, trying to clear her mind. She couldn't think about it now. But then just the two of them, alone, even for a short time. She fought to quell the rising heat that was emanating from deep in her belly.

Isabel continued laying out her plan. "Now, I'm certain that Sir John will need to proceed to the palace with the rest of the delegation immediately upon entering port. So, as soon as we arrive, I'll think of some excuse and leave you. I'll go to my friends' house and get them to secure passage for us on the next ship to Castile. Since you won't be with me, there will be no way for them to assume who it is I am trying to help. They'll trust me that far. Assuming they're in the city—and they should be with the court in residence—it shouldn't take me more than a few hours to see to the entire task. If there's a ship leaving for Spain on the morning tide, Maria, we could be sailing with it."

"But what of my brother Charles?" Maria asked. There were a few problems with Isabel's plan. "Don't you think he already has put a price on your head for helping me flee the city? I don't think there was any question in his mind who helped me escape Antwerp. It's possible, Isabel, that your friends already know the truth. It would be their duty to surrender us to him."

Isabel shook her head with assurance. "I know your brother much better than you think, my dear. He would never—and let me say it again—*never* admit in public that his own aunt, never mind his own sister, could ever do anything contrary to his wishes. For him the Habsburg blood creates an unbreakable bond. I won't be surprised if he has already had his ministers invent a totally reasonable excuse for your disappearance. In fact, with the exception of that Count Diego fellow, even those closest to him probably think that he has sent you away himself."

"How about the sinking of our ship?" Maria asked. "He must have heard of that."

"He had no idea of where we were going, or if it was by the way of land or water that we left. I only hope he doesn't think you are still hiding in the city."

"But he must have known we would head for Castile," Maria argued.

"True," Isabel nodded. "In which case he would guess we were traveling by sea. But aboard which ship? There are 100,000 people living in Antwerp, and there are dozens of ships that pass through the port every day. There is no way he should connect us with that particular ship, or any other. Don't forget, my dear, I was the one who planned your escape."

"So you don't think that he'll know of our return."

"Even if he knows of that ship going down, he'll assume that we are either dead, or worse, in the hands of the French."

"In either case, he won't expect us back in the city."

Isabel nodded in response. "Certainly not in the company of the very people you were trying to escape. And I'll make sure that my friends will not reveal having seen me in Antwerp. It's not so uncommon for me to come and go at my leisure, but I'll see to it that they tell no one."

"What *do* you think Charles will tell the Scots when they arrive looking for me? It will look quite odd when I am not there to greet them."

"Bah, he and Count Diego are bound to have come up with something." Isabel shook her head. "I imagine it will be something along the lines of him having sent you off to pray. Meanwhile, a whole fleet of the Emperor's new galleons is probably bearing down on your poor mother at this very moment. He's sure to have her questioned as to your whereabouts."

"Juaña la Loca can hold her own," Maria put in. "Mother is the only person that Charles truly fears, I think."

"It's true. You know, it's quite odd that she's so content wearing the title he has given her. Joanna the Mad, indeed. The woman has better use of her faculties than any of us!"

Maria tried to think through everything they'd just devised. With Isabel's plan, there was hope, a slim hope, that perhaps someday she could see him again. Perhaps if he valued her, or somehow grew to love her as she loved him now . . . well, perhaps someday he could come after her in Castile. She would leave him a letter. She would try to explain everything. Once he knew the truth of her situation, once he knew her motives and her reasons for running, he would understand. He had to understand. There was hope. In spite of the years that might intervene, Maria knew that there was hope.

"I want you to understand, Maria, that finding passage to Castile is not the end of our troubles," Isabel added. "No question, Charles's men will be there before us, and once we reach Spain, we will still have to deal with them. But there's no sense worrying about that now. We have enough to contend with here."

Maria only nodded in response. She no longer could hear anything her aunt was saying. Her mind was on John Macpherson. On leaving this ship to be by his side. And on the difficulty of walking away the next day. But it might, perhaps, only be a short time, she promised herself. He'd come after her. She knew in her heart that he would.

"Do many Scottish ships make it to Castile?" Her hand flew to her mouth. She hadn't meant to ask the question aloud.

Isabel stared at her for a moment. When she spoke, her voice was gentle.

"Maria, you must resign yourself." Her aunt's words, softly spoken, still had the effect of daggers sinking into an open wound. "You will never see him again!"

Maria stood and went to the open window. The salt breeze filled her lungs and stung her eyes.

"Resolve yourself to the fact, child. And then make the best of what remains of your time with him."

Maria whirled around, opening her mouth to argue, to reason with her aunt about the future that she and John might still share, but then she closed it again. Isabel stood and walked stiffly to her, taking the young woman's hands in her own. Maria knew her aunt had more to tell.

"I don't know what your understanding is of the kind of man John Macpherson is, but you should know what Janet Maule told me about Sir John." Isabel led her back to the chairs and sat her down, keeping hold of her hands. "John Macpherson has a faithful following of seamen and nobles who worship the ground he walks on. According to what Janet knows of him—through her father, I expect—even those who disagree with his politics respect him and admire him. But at the core of those politics, John Macpherson has for years been the hero, the champion, and the devoted supporter of the Stuart crown. His prowess as Lord of the Scottish Navy is the sole reason that philandering pig, King Henry of England, has never attempted to control the coasts of Scotland."

Isabel leaned back in her chair. "Every king, every emperor has men like him. They are the true powers behind every throne. They are the fighters behind every cause." Isabel looked steadily at her young charge. "Sir John is the kind of man who will sacrifice his life without a second thought for what he believes in. He is a man who, while still no more than a boy, took a sword in his hand and stepped into the fray beside his king at the Battle of Flodden Field. And he is the man who, as an adult, will do anything to further the interests of that ill-fated king's son. Maria, John Macpherson will never be anything but a man for Scotland, and a man for the Stuart kings."

"I am not asking him to change who he is or what he believes in!"

"But don't you see, child?" Isabel argued. "That's exactly what you are doing. This marriage between you and James V was not contrived solely for the benefit of your brother and his wild dreams of ruling the world.

This marriage is as much for the benefit of the Scots. I might not be completely up to date on what has been taking place in that corner of the world, but since the death of this king's father at Flodden Field, Scotland has been a country in complete disarray. This boy-king you are . . . you *were* to marry hasn't yet taken control of his own land. A kingdom held by factions of nobles, each vying for power, will never thrive."

Maria held back her tears, but the knot that was burning in the back of her throat would not go away.

"Your marriage would have united Charles and the Scots against Henry of England. It would have given the Scots a position for trading with the rest of Europe. France, their old ally, is becoming more and more alienated from the rest of the world. The Scottish people need a new ally, and your marriage would have provided that. Now, I'm not saying that it is possible for you to change what we have done, but you mustn't fool yourself into thinking that you can have a future with John Macpherson without the man turning his back on all that he believes! On the king that he has dedicated his life to serving."

Maria closed her eyes and took a deep breath. Life was so complicated; every turn tore at her insides. She opened her eyes and gazed steadily into her aunt's.

"Isabel, I will never again be a sacrificial lamb for some other land's prosperity. No matter how much Charles desires it or how badly James V needs it, they will have to find another way . . . or someone else. It won't be me. I won't do it."

Isabel reached and held on to Maria's hands. "Don't misunderstand me, my child. I concur with all you say. You have already done more than your share for the Holy Roman Empire—and for your brother—by marrying Louis of Hungary. You have already paid a high price for your freedom. Now it is someone else's turn."

"Then why do I feel a guilt that is about to crush the breath out of me? Why do I feel like a deserter and a fugitive?"

Isabel paused a moment before she spoke again. "It

is difficult to turn your back on your brother. You care for him—perhaps more than he deserves. But now, at least, you understand why he treats you as he does. An empire needs a ruler like Charles. As he is." Isabel squeezed the young woman's hand. "But we need not let him ruin our lives now, need we?"

Maria shook her head. "But, to be truthful, all that you've said about Scotland . . . and about John . . . worries me more."

"I would hazard to guess that you worry about what he will think of you once he learns the truth?"

"I already know the answer. He'll hate me," she whispered, turning her head away from her aunt. "He'll never want to see me again."

"But you don't really want to change John Macpherson, do you?" Isabel's fingers gently took hold of Maria's chin and turned it to face her again. "Don't plan for the future, child. As it stands now, what the future might bring is out of your hands. You must plan and act on your own behalf, and you must plan for a future without him."

Maria could no longer hold back her tears, and they coursed freely down her cheeks.

"Enjoy what remains of your time with him," Isabel whispered. "Live all you can today, because tomorrow you'll need these memories—of each moment you spend with him—to take you through all the days of your life."

Chapter 16

The wharf beside the *Great Michael* seethed with the energy of a thousand human onlookers. Lashed soundly to the end of the stone quay, the giant warship was indeed a spectacle for the people of Antwerp, and the shifting horde quayside pushed and shoved for a better view of the Scottish leviathan. Rows of armed sailors stood at the foot of the gangplank keeping the townspeople at bay, while dockworkers carried crates and trunks of gifts for the Emperor Charles and the Queen of Hungary to carts waiting nearby. Aboard ship, the gaily dressed Scottish delegation awaited an escort to the palace. The gray light of day was fading into darkness, and a light rain was beginning to fall.

From the uppermost stern deck, John Macpherson gave a satisfied nod as the *Eagle,* the last of the Scottish warships, was safely tied off beside the *Toward.* He could see the Scottish nobles had already assembled on the deck of the *Christopher.* Glancing out into the wide mouth of the River Scheldt, he stared through the gathering gloom at the four galleons that had been escorting them since the previous day. They had taken up positions in the harbor that would allow them clear shots at the Scottish ships, should the need arise. John could feel the eyes of the galleon commanders on him at that very moment.

"Another day, lads," he muttered to himself, turning his attention quayside.

Antwerp had an impressive port. The walls of the city rose up in the distance, and beside the well-traveled carters roads that he could see leading up to city gates, there was also an extensive network of canals for barges running from the long row of quays lining the bank of the deep river up to and into the city. Merchant ships, many good-sized and many armed, crowded the wharves, and many more lay at anchor in the harbor.

The Highlander peered into the noisy crowd, past the huge, smoky dock torches that were sputtering to life. A young man was fighting his way through the throng of people, trying to make his way back to his commander as quickly as he could. When the lad looked up, John saw his navigator wave over the heads of the milling assemblage. In a few moments, David worked his way to the ship and quickly climbed the gangplank and steps to the stern deck.

"There were two Flemish ships that they know of what went down last week," David said breathlessly as he reached John. "Word is, the Emperor's galleons spotted a number of French warships in the German Sea, but the French refused to engage, preferring to run. However, the rumor is that the French sank the two merchantmen. And there could be more. They just didn't know yet. A number of ships are up to a week late coming in, though that fog we were stuck in may be the cause. At any rate, that's all I could find out. But the sailor I talked to said we could probably get more news—or rumor, anyway—at the Bourse. He says that the exchange opens every day for an hour in the afternoon and will open again for an hour in the evening. I saw a number of merchants coming off ships and heading directly into the city."

"Aye, no doubt heading for the exchange." John considered for a moment.

"Aye, the Bourse seems to be the center of activity." David glanced at the Scottish nobles on the deck. He could see Janet Maule standing with her father and Lady Caroline. The navigator forced his attention back on his commander. "Would you like me to go there next?"

"Nay, we haven't time," John answered, looking out at the commotion of torch-carrying men entering the harbor area. The escort, he decided, eyeing the troop of armored horsemen at the head of the line of soldiers. He had hoped to get some quick news for Maria and Isabel about any survivors of their ill-fated ship, but now he supposed it would have to wait until morning. He turned away and faced his navigator. "I would like you to escort Lady Maria to Hart Haus. Elizabeth and Ambrose sent a message ahead of me, so the house should be in readiness. The steward Pieter knows you, but be certain he knows that Maria is my special guest, and is to be treated as such. And as far as Lady Isabel, take a few men with you and deliver her to the home of her friends. She said she couldn't recall the name of the place, but she assured me she knows the way."

David nodded to his commander.

"I have to accompany this delegation to the Emperor's palace. As soon as I can get away without offending our host, I'll go straight to Hart Haus."

"Do you have any idea how long our stay will be?"

John looked down at the escort. The leader of the contingent was jerking hard at the reins of his spirited mount in a display of mastery over the animal. The Highlander shook his head and frowned. How long? He didn't want to admit it aloud, but he would have no objection to a prolonged visit. In spite of all the nonsense associated with this Queen of Hungary and the marriage, he was really looking forward to spending time with Maria, and staying here in the city gave him that chance. "I won't know until we meet with the Emperor and his sister—or at least with the welcoming delegation."

The attention of the two men was drawn to the scene on the quay, as the leader began shouting at one of his soldiers who had made the mistake of trying to quiet the headstrong steed as the courtier dismounted.

John chuckled at the display. "Well, it looks as if the forces of the Empire have everything under control here!"

"Aye," David chimed in, grinning. The navigator's face grew serious. "Sir John, will she going back to Scotland with us?"

"I surely hope so," John answered, watching as the leading noblemen of the delegation made their way down the gangplank and toward the courtier. "I'd hate to think we made this journey only to go back empty-handed."

"What?" David asked, shooting him a questioning look before comprehension dawned. "Nay, sir. I didn't mean Mary of Hungary. I was talking about Lady Maria. Will *she* be coming back with us?"

John looked steadily at his man. He hadn't asked her—not officially, anyway. But there were many things between them that were understood without being said.

"She is going back with us," the Highlander growled. There was no reason why she shouldn't.

"If you're looking for a place to hide," Isabel offered, looking into Maria's cabin from the doorway, "you'll need to do a better job of it."

Maria swept her ebony hair back over her shoulder as she knelt upright and frowned at her aunt.

"Very funny." She surveyed the small cabin for the thousandth time, then looked again at Isabel. "That large wick lamp in your cabin. Would you be kind enough to bring it in here? Perhaps with a bit more light . . ."

"What on earth are you looking for, my dear?"

"I am looking for my ring, Isabel."

"Your ring?" Now it was the older woman's turn to frown. "You never wear a ring, Maria!"

"My marriage ring," Maria responded, going back to her search. "I wear it on a chain about my neck."

As her fingers carefully searched the spaces where the wooden planks had separated, Maria crawled along the floor. Isabel shrugged and retrieved the larger wick lamp from her room. The older woman held it over Maria as best she could. The small cabin was considerably brighter with the additional light.

"Thank you, Isabel," Maria said, adding vaguely, "I wonder what's beneath us?"

"I thought you stopped wearing that ring when Louis died."

"Nay, I didn't." She had considered it carefully. When word came of the Hungarian army's crushing defeat— and of her husband's death—Maria had retreated to the solitude of her tower chamber in the grim, stone castle at Budapest. There, she had thought hard about her future. And about the death of Louis.

Theirs had never been much of a marriage. But, as she held the ring to the fading light, Maria had wondered what the union had brought her. The intricately carved insignia had cleverly combined the crest of the Habsburgs with the crest of Louis's family. The goldsmith had done exquisite work in creating the new design. Far better, she had thought with a pang of guilt, than she and Louis had done in creating an heir. But with the Ottoman Turks advancing from Mohács, Maria had had little time for either guilt or self-pity. Deciding that the marriage had at least given her *some* sense of identity, she had strung the ring on a gold chain, hung it about her neck, and used it as a seal.

"I didn't put it away," she repeated. "I've kept it with me as a seal for my letters."

A bit earlier, when she was putting together the few things that they had acquired while aboard the *Great Michael,* Maria had noticed, for the first time, her ring's absence.

Isabel sat on the edge of the bunk, still holding the lamp. "Are you certain you didn't lose it before we were picked up by the Scots?"

"Nay, I was wearing it when we arrived."

"Then tell me, when was the last time that you saw it? And where did you last put it?"

Maria sat back on her heels and looked up into her aunt's face. "I removed it from around my neck the first day we arrived. And I thought that I placed it . . . nay, I'm certain that I placed it on the shelf. Here." Her hands moved up and touched the empty surface of the wooden ledge. "But I have not been writing any letters, so I haven't thought to look for it."

Isabel looked casually about her in the cabin. "Well, it doesn't seem to be around any longer."

Maria pushed herself to her feet as she gave one last look around the room.

"You don't suspect anyone of taking it?" Isabel asked.

Maria shook her head. "There is not much value to that ring. It is gold, but there are no gems set—"

"Not much value?" Isabel choked. "A gold ring given by a king to his queen! And now you tell me it bears the royal seal? I don't think you have any idea of what constitutes wealth, my dear—particularly to people who don't have it!"

"Excuse me. I stand corrected." Maria took hold of Isabel's free hand. "Perhaps it would be more appropriate to say that my ring could not bring a thief anywhere near the worldly wealth that one of your rings might bring."

Isabel looked dumbly at the exquisite array of jewels on her own fingers. Finally, she nodded, mumbling. "What you say is true, my dear."

"And you're missing none of your rings?" Maria pressed.

"That is also true. I have not lost a single item." Isabel nodded again. "And I must admit, I was quite careless about them when my shoulder was hurting the worst. And even since I've been feeling better, I have left them unattended over and over again."

"Correct," Maria said, casting one last look on the floor. "We have had no thieves stealing about our cabin, Isabel. The ring must have slipped right through these planks. And I think it's gone."

Maria stood and helped Isabel to her feet. Together, they moved into the larger cabin, taking the lamps with them. As the older woman plopped herself into a chair by the table, the younger crossed to the partially open window. She could see the flaring torches on the quay the ship was tied to, and things being carried from other ships docked farther down the harbor. Even in the darkness, the port was a bustling place.

"Would you like a bit of wine, Maria?" Isabel asked,

pouring herself a goblet. "It is far too fine to waste, I'd say."

"Would any of Charles's advisors come aboard?" Maria asked, shaking her head at her aunt's offer. "Do you think Charles himself may come?"

Isabel stood and moved behind her niece, peering out over her shoulder. "In this instance, I believe we benefit from your brother's imperial arrogance, my dear. My guess is that he'd love to come aboard a ship as magnificent as this, but he will need to be begged before he'll do so. However, I'm sure, come morning, the palace will send ministers—perhaps even Count Diego de Guevara himself—to begin seeing to your comfort for the journey."

Maria turned her face and looked at her aunt's amused expression. "But I'm not there."

"True, child. But the palace will not be admitting that there's any problem . . . yet!"

"Hmm . . ." Maria looked back out at the dark hulks of ships stretching out into the night. "Charles does, indeed, love large and powerful ships. I believe the *Great Michael* is larger than any of his new galleons. He's sure to come."

Isabel tossed her head back and strutted around the cabin, putting on the airs of a pompous monarch. Maria turned and stared at her, wide-eyed.

"The world shall come to me and kneel before my throne." The Emperor's aunt placed a hand on the back of a chair and struck a royal pose. "I am the worthiest of all kings, Holy Roman Emperor by the hand of a pope I installed myself. And you . . . you in that, ahem, passably good-looking ship . . . you are all nothing more than lowly Scots. And my future subjects, at that, though you don't know it yet."

Maria smiled and pushed the window shut. "We may already be guilty of treason for defying his wishes, but I don't think it will do to give away state secrets."

"Charles's ways are no secret to anyone, child. But to answer your question, we'll be long gone before he condescends to pay a visit to the *Great Michael.* He'll certainly not come with night falling."

Maria stared at her aunt for a moment and then crossed the cabin to the peg where her cloak hung.

"We are not ready to go, yet," Isabel said. "We have to wait until that lovely young navigator comes to escort us."

"I know . . . I know," Maria answered, unable to shake the thought of how far away they would be when night found them again. She wrapped the cloak around her with a shiver. "But suddenly, Isabel, I'm feeling a bit cold."

Chapter 17

The erupting fireworks out on the Groenplaats drew Maria once again to the window.

From her window of the elegant upper-floor bedchamber that she'd been shown to, the young queen peered out at the carnivallike atmosphere on the crowded green. No doubt the good clergy in the darkened cathedral across the way were cringing in horror at such festivities in the middle of Lent. No, she realized with a laugh, there was the cardinal himself, surrounded by his entourage, clearly enjoying the noise and the multicolored bursts.

Pieter, the Macphersons' rotund little steward, had told her that the merchants in Antwerp had arranged for this display as a welcome for King Jamie's delegation. In the short time that Maria had been in the city before her thwarted escape, she had seen a number of these fireworks displays from the palace windows. She squinted her eyes to see through the smoke resulting from the last blasts, looking toward the spot near his statue, where the Emperor liked to watch the fiery exhibitions. The breeze quickly dispersed the cloud, and Maria could just make out the royal party. She couldn't see John though, and a pang of disappointment struck her.

"Don't be a fool, Maria," she muttered quietly to herself, continuing to scan the crowd. Picking up the brush she had laid aside, she drew it through her still damp hair. One thing about the citizens of Antwerp, she thought, they are happy for any excuse to celebrate. And certainly, the fanfare this time must have been favored by the Emperor. He was, most assuredly, quite delighted for this diversion of his guests while he continued to search for the object of their mission.

Absently, Maria began to weave her hair into a thick, black braid as she watched a young man climb a ladder to the top of the tall wooden post that held the next round of fireworks. After a moment during which Maria watched him exchange laughing remarks with the crowd below, he finished his preparations and scurried to the ground. Taking a long-handled torch, the young man ignited the fireworks and retreated with the scattering throng that encircled the post. This series of explosions was deafening, and the windows of Maria's room rattled violently. When the blasts ceased, Maria smiled as she espied the young man bowing to his appreciative audience before running off to the next pillar of explosives.

The trip from the harborside into the city to the Groenplaats and the Macphersons' town house had been, to Maria's delight, quick and uneventful. She had never any cause to enter any of the huge, stone houses that lined the open square, and Hart Haus, the Macpherson home, was an exquisite surprise. As Maria had stepped into the foyer beyond the massive oak door, the sight of the huge marble statue of a deer, his antlers spreading a good three yards, had immediately conveyed to Maria that the owners of Hart Haus were extraordinary people.

Though modest in size compared with the palaces and the castles she had lived in, Hart Haus was easily the most comfortable and most sumptuously furnished home she had ever seen. Even the Emperor's private chambers were austere in comparison. Besides, though Maria had never been impressed with the showy grandeur of a palace, there was a warmth that suffused this home, and that warmth had nothing to do with its rich furnishings. There was a sense of harmony, a happiness that seemed to fill Hart Haus, and Maria felt it the moment she entered its walls.

When they arrived, David had spoken briefly to the steward and then taken his leave, ushering Maria's aunt through the growing crowds of townspeople. Pieter, the portly steward, proved to be a kindly man with a slight hunch to his back and a sparkle of wit in his eye. Scattering the onlooking servants before him with jovial commands, he led her from the entryway into a large hall, no doubt where members of the household gathered for meals as well as most other activities. At the end of the room, a crackling fire warmed the air and lit up the whitewashed walls.

As Pieter escorted her to the wide stairs leading up from the Great Room, Maria gazed at the rich, vibrantly colored paintings that adorned the high walls. Ambrose and Elizabeth Macpherson had more paintings than the Medicis, she thought, ascending the steps. She would have loved to take the time to stop and study them.

They were everywhere, she realized, looking at the works that graced the walls of her bedchamber. In the stairways, the corridors. All through the house. Magnificent paintings. Only as she sat soaking—courtesy of Pieter—in an ornately carved wood tub, luxuriating in the warm, jasmine-scented water, did Maria realize that these paintings that so impressed her were all Elizabeth Macpherson's work. The importance of what Isabel had relayed to her, about Elizabeth being an accomplished painter, had not truly sunk in until she had entered Hart Haus.

Now, dressed and feeling quite human again, Maria stood and watched as the last of the fireworks were exploded. The aroma of warm bread and fish wafted into the room, and the young woman was suddenly conscious of a rumbling response in her belly. A serving girl knocked softly at a side door, and led Maria into an adjoining sitting room, where a table had been laid with platters of food, fresh fruit, and wine.

Pieter greeted Maria, clapping his fleshy hands together with obvious delight. "Ah, Lady Maria! How lovely you look!"

"Thank you, Pieter."

The steward ushered his guest to the table, where a group of servants waited to serve her. The treatment she was receiving was fit for a queen, Maria thought. And no one knew it better than she. She wasn't sure what David had said of her to these people, but Pieter was making sure that no effort was spared to ensure her comfort.

A part of her wished she could wait and take her meal later, perhaps with John, but she knew there was very little chance of him returning soon. She knew all too well the ceremonial affairs of her brother's court on the arrival of important foreign visitors. There would be, no doubt, a number of lengthy speeches that John would have to endure before Charles was done with him. And he would never be able to escape the dinner and subsequent entertainment. It being Lent, Maria was fairly certain that some dreadfully somber morality play would conclude the evening. It would be very late before John returned to Hart Haus.

As she accepted the proffered chair and sat at the table, a stab of regret shot through her at the thought that she might never see him again. Isabel had said that they might be leaving with the morning tide. If that were so—and if John were held up at the palace—then she had seen John Macpherson for the last time.

For the last time.

"Are you well, m'lady?" Pieter's voice was filled with concern.

Maria glanced up and forced down the knot in her throat. "I am well, Pieter."

The dinner was as exquisite as the setting, and Maria felt a bit guilty enjoying it as much as she did. Reluctantly, at first, Pieter sat with her when she asked him. But Maria had many questions to ask, and he proved an affable dinner companion.

"How wonderful Lady Elizabeth's paintings are, Pieter!" Maria said sincerely as she finished her meal.

"So true, my lady. We are blessed to be surrounded by such treasures."

"Does she sculpt, as well?" She sipped at her wine. "The statue of the hart in the foyer—it is so lifelike."

"Indeed it is, m'lady. It is the work of a sculptor

named Pico, a protégé of Michelangelo himself. It came directly from the studio of the maestro in Florence." The steward beckoned to a waiting man who trotted to the table with a crystal decanter. "Would you care for more wine, Lady Maria?"

"Oh, I can't. Thank you so much, though." Maria smiled at the man. "She is so talented a woman!"

The independence she must feel, Maria thought. To practice openly the art of painting. To act as she thinks she should, against all odds. To fight tradition, to practice what few if any women had the courage to do. Maria had never heard of another woman painting, and these things amazed Maria. She, herself, was a queen—sister to the Emperor. Her word had never been questioned; her wishes served as the minister's commands. But she had never been able to step away from the obstacles of tradition and the restraints of habit, at least not enough to make a real difference. Not in her life and not in the lives of those around her. Maria had ideas, but she'd always lacked courage, it seemed to her now. Seeing Elizabeth's work drove that message in deeply.

But that was in the past, she thought resolutely. She would make a difference in the future.

"Would you like to see her studio, Lady Maria?" Pieter was smiling at her, his eyes twinkling.

"She has a studio *here,* in this house?"

"Of course! And I believe she would like you to see it." The steward pushed himself to his feet. "Give me just a moment to ready everything. If you'd be pleased to make yourself comfortable here, I'll return for you."

With a quick bow, Pieter crossed the room and disappeared into the corridor, moving quite nimbly for a man his size, Maria thought. Leaning back in her chair, she gazed at the portrait of an elderly couple. The woman, sitting in the foreground, was still quite striking in her looks, and the man, ruggedly handsome in his Highland gear, stood behind her, his hands affectionately resting on his wife's shoulders. Maria smiled. No doubt John's parents—he resembled both of them. The two looked so real. She wondered, vaguely, what the rest of his family were like.

From what she'd learned already, since the birth of their young children, Ambrose and Elizabeth could only manage, at most, three or four visits to Hart Haus each year. The demands of the diplomat's life apparently took on less importance as his family grew. But the house in Antwerp—as was the case with many of their other holdings—they liked to keep open year round, offering its warmth and hospitality to family members and friends who might be traveling to this center of culture and trade.

It would have been a pleasure to meet this Elizabeth Macpherson, Maria thought sadly. But the way everything seemed now, that meeting would never occur. Even more than the warmth and hospitality that surrounded her, Maria felt the same loneliness that pervaded her entire life up to this point. And it was the same loneliness that she saw in a bleak and empty future.

Once again she busied herself in the study of Elizabeth's artwork.

The quiet shuffle of an elderly serving man entering the room drew Maria's attention. He made a half-bow from the doorway and held out his hand.

"A letter for you, m'lady," he croaked, crossing to the table as Maria stood. "A messenger delivered it only a moment ago."

Maria's heart sank. It must be bad news, she thought. Perhaps John had confided in her brother about finding two women at sea! Taking the note from the servant with an anxious nod, she quickly broke open the wax seal and scanned the letter's contents. Letting out a sigh of relief, she sat back in her chair. It was from Isabel.

There was nothing wrong. Isabel's tone was reassuring. But there was a slight change in their plans. Isabel's friends had left the city, but were expected back inside of a week. Maria was to stay where she was until their return, and Isabel herself would stay at her friends' house. In the meantime, Isabel would attempt to find out what was occurring at the palace, and try on her own to secure passage for them.

Maria read her aunt's letter again. There was nothing to worry about, she told herself again. Just use caution and avoid public attention—there were many in the city who might recognize Maria as the Emperor's sister. That was all Isabel had recommended.

A week, Maria thought. A week.

Maria folded the note and carried it into the other room. Glancing around for a good place to keep it, she espied the great canopied bed and quickly slid the letter beneath one of the billowy down-filled pillows. Running her head over the smooth linen of the bedclothes, the young woman considered her aunt's words. Common sense told her that this shift in their plans was not for the better. But her heart told her this gift was a godsend. This was a chance she'd dreamed of. It was her chance to be with him.

Feeling brighter than before, Maria was delighted to find the steward waiting for her as she reentered the sitting room.

The tour of the house was a sheer delight for the young queen. With the pride of a lord, Pieter showed her the many rooms. From the Great Room with its high, art-covered walls, to the library with its book-lined shelves, the steward led the young woman, answering her questions and pointing out the treasures that Ambrose had collected over the years, as well as indicating the family members that showed up so lovingly in Elizabeth's innumerable paintings.

Thoroughly enjoying herself, Maria followed Pieter up yet another flight of stairs. The steps were following the slope of the ceiling here, and the young woman knew their tour was nearly at an end. Throughout the house, the steward had had candles and wick lamps lit, and this upper room glowed, as well, with a golden light. Stepping through a narrow door at the top, they finished their tour in Elizabeth Macpherson's studio.

Enthralled, Maria circled the room. Wide, thick rolls of canvas, stacked in a far corner of the room, sat beside piles of wood strips. The young woman picked up one of the many framelike shapes that were constructed of the wood. It was lighter than she thought it would be. She wondered how heavy it would be with a piece of canvas stretched over it. Putting it down gently, she lifted the tops off a number of small casks that filled the shelves of an entire wall. They contained drab-colored powders that hardly looked like the bright hues of Elizabeth's paintings.

Pieter read the puzzled expression on her face. "When the pigments are mixed with oil," he told her, tapping one of the large barrels that stood nearby, "the colors come to life. Lady Elizabeth is a genius at mixing colors to produce the right shade. Truly a genius!"

"I can see that," she replied solemnly. Maria walked to a huge glazed window that had been set into the sloping ceiling. Peering out, she could see nothing.

Pieter's eyes twinkled again as he pointed to a thick cord dangling by the door. "I'd hoped you would wish to see out." Taking hold of the rope, he pulled on it, and the large wooden shutter that covered the outside of the window rolled away.

Maria gazed in wonder at the city that stretched out before her. Beyond the next rooftop, the open square lay far below, the torches still lit from the earlier celebration. In the distance, she could see the city walls and beyond, the harbor. The mist that had greeted their entry into the city had cleared away now, and the stars shone brightly in a black velvet sky.

"This is incredible," she whispered.

"After marrying Lady Elizabeth, Sir Ambrose had a room like this added to every one of their holdings. She is so very talented, m'lady. And with her excellent reputation spreading as it is now, she finds herself eagerly sought after for royal portraits everywhere." The steward's voice was brimming with pride for his mistress. "She and the children always accompany Sir Ambrose on his trips."

Walking past a small child-sized easel that stood beside a larger one, Maria paused to feel the soft bristles

of the brushes that filled a bowl-shaped table nearby.
Against the far wall there were at least two dozen paintings leaning one behind the next in three rows, each row
carefully covered with a tarp.

"May I look at these?"

Pieter smiled happily as he removed the coverings. "I
know Lady Elizabeth would be delighted."

Maria took her time and studied every painting in detail. "How many children do they have?" she asked. She
knew she was prying, but there was so much about these
people that fascinated her.

"Three," the man answered. "One girl and two boys.
Though their daughter, Mistress Jaime, is as much of a
handful as the two boys. She has got a lot of spirit, that
girl. Just like her mother. Ah yes, this one . . ." The
steward pointed to a portrait. "This one is of Jaime with
her baby brother, Michael, in her lap. This was, of
course, before little Thomas was born."

Maria looked over the painting, but then smiled with
pleasure. The little girl's dark and beautiful eyes were
flashing with mischief, but her facial expression showed
her self-restraint, as the little boy attempted to crawl all
over her.

"We had a devil of a—" Pieter stopped. "Excuse
me . . . a very difficult time getting them settled enough
for Lady Elizabeth. They have great energy, the children, and are a source of constant joy—and work—for
us."

The steward smiled, continuing to talk about the children while Maria's mind drifted to the thought that here
was another thing she would never experience. Mother-
hood. She knew she could not bear children. After four
years of marriage to Louis, she'd been declared barren
by the royal physicians. Before now, she had never
grieved over her inability to produce offspring. But now,
standing in this house, feeling the sense of family that
surrounded her, seeing the happiness that suffused these
works, she felt suddenly at a loss.

"Ah, this fortress in the background here, m'lady, is
Benmore Castle. The clan seat of the Macphersons,"

Pieter was holding a painting in his hand. "I've seen it only once, but it is a magnificent place. Strong and quite comfortable with its modern renovations."

Maria gazed at the building in the painting. "Tell me . . . tell me what you can about the Macpherson brothers, Pieter."

The steward stared at the young woman for a moment. Then, he replaced the painting and began to talk to the three brothers.

Maria listened intently, amazed at the bonds of love and loyalty that tied the three brothers together. She also learned that in what John had told her regarding his position as the third son, the *Great Michael*'s commander had grossly understated his own worth. John Macpherson had been the only one of the three sons who had followed in their father's footsteps. The only one who shared in the old man's love of the sea. And John had made a fortune in following that path. But none of that mattered a bit to her. It perplexed her, though, to reflect on Caroline Maule's inability to appreciate him for who he was. Maria shook her head, reminding herself that she should thank God for the woman's lack of judgment.

When the steward had finished speaking, answering Maria's questions cheerfully and directly, a comfortable silence fell as she continued to admire Elizabeth's work. She paused at a portrait of a young queen praying before a cross. The cross had white and red climbing roses curling up the rough wood, and a trio of magnificent angels hung in the air, watching over the scene. Maria sighed deeply.

"Do you think Lady Elizabeth would mind, Pieter . . . ?" she asked hesitantly. "Do you think I might just have a few moments alone up here?" The solitude, the refuge that the room offered was what she needed right now.

"I am certain Lady Elizabeth would be quite content to know that you asked to spend time up here. She herself spends many hours up here." The steward started for the door and then stopped. "I believe the mistress—in a way—draws strength from this room."

After Pieter had closed the door quietly behind him, Maria stared out through the glazed panes at the city before her. The cityfolk were, no doubt, crawling into their beds for the sound, untroubled slumber of honest souls. She looked out at the thousand darkened buildings, and sighed again.

The young woman turned and surveyed Elizabeth's workplace. Something about the studio struck a chord in Maria's soul. It was a place where another woman—a woman perhaps not so different from herself—created masterworks of art. Maria wandered about, enraptured both with the idea of the artistic effort, and with the place itself. Other than some simple drawings that she'd done in Hungary to pass the time, the only kind of representative art she'd ever done was the collaborative stitchwork that eventually became huge tapestries. But it seemed that fewer and fewer women were doing that kind of work. She pondered that for a moment, lifting a brush and running the soft bristles over the palm of her hand. Maria had always been impressed with people who could create images, whether in word, or song, or picture. Perhaps she, too, could learn to paint. Indeed! After all, who knows what talents she might have lying dormant within her?

Glancing into one corner of the room, Maria spotted a row of canvases that she hadn't looked at, leaning against the wall. Pulling off the tarp, she looked at the first two. They were unfinished. All of the paintings in this group were unfinished. Curious about the creative process, Maria studied the way Elizabeth constructed her compositions. There were quite a few works here. Looking at them one by one, she marveled once again at the different types of painting that Elizabeth obviously took on for the challenge. She certainly didn't seem to limit herself only to portraits. Maria stared at a flower jar and a bouquet of fresh-cut spring flowers, then she moved on to look at a number of battles scenes, then to a wild-looking landscape with a castle and a breaking storm. Even in their unfinished form, each of the paintings showed superb artistry, and Maria could feel the incredible power that emanated from each of them.

She came, finally, to the last painting in the pile. Her heartbeat quickened as the looked into the deep blue eyes that so much resembled John's. Though the background was the only thing left to do in this portrait, Elizabeth had truly captured the essence of her subject here—the man in the painting was obviously enchanted with the painter. Maria's gaze took in the softness that showed around his eyes, the half smile that tugged at his full lips. She decided that this had to be a portrait of Ambrose. With the exception of the scar on his forehead and the blond locks which differed so from John's jet-black hair, the resemblance between the two was undeniable. Maria's eyes surveyed the rest of the painting. Ambrose was dressed only in a kilt, one high-booted foot on a boulder, his muscular arms resting on his knee, massive sword held loosely in one hand, its point lying on a shield at his feet. Behind him, Elizabeth had begun a castle that loomed on a hill in the distance. He had no shirt on, and Maria's eyes ran the length of his impressive build.

"He is taken. On the other hand, I am not."

Maria whirled around excitedly at the sound of his voice. Quickly, she searched his face for some indication of what had occurred, some sign that might betoken his evening's exchanges with Charles. But there was no hesitation in his voice nor in his deed as he opened his arms to her. "I missed you," he growled.

They met in the middle of the room, their arms encircling one another, their bodies molding as one. His mouth slanted over her upturned lips and their kiss ignited in a frenzy of desire.

John leaned his head against her forehead and smiled. "I couldn't wait to get back. I've been bewitched, I know it. Your eyes were before me everywhere I looked. When I conjured your eyes even in the Emperor's, then I knew that I had had enough—I needed to get back to you."

"And that's why you are back so soon?" She breathed

into his ear as his lips grazed her neck. "You found yourself becoming attracted to the Emperor?"

"Aye, my sweet. He's a bonny lad, indeed," John answered as his hands started undoing the laces at the back of her dress. He had to restrain himself from ripping the gown off her body. He could feel the warmth of her body pushing against him. Her hands were pulling up at his kilt. "But truly, love. I have great news."

Maria glanced at the door. It was closed. She knew what he wanted and she wanted it, as well. They would make love here, she thought joyfully. What better place? "Tell me your good news," she said, unpinning the brooch that held his tartan in place.

"We'll be here a fortnight, at least." The Highlander slipped the leather belt that crossed his chest over his head and dropped it to the floor.

The tartan billowed around their feet, and she pulled his shirt out of his kilt and pushed it back over his shoulders. She covered the sinewy muscles of his chest with kisses.

"Our future queen, in all her reverence, refuses to travel with Holy Week approaching, and has decided to seclude herself until after Easter." The laces undone, John pulled her dress down to her waist, pinning her arms. "The saintly lass would not even see us."

She gasped as he dropped to one knee before her and suckled her breast through the thin cloth of her chemise. Running his hands over her buttocks, he pulled her hips against him. The restraint he had shown before, he now cast to the wind.

"I was not certain how I would feel about her before," he said hoarsely as he reached up and peeled the chemise from her shoulders. As her full breasts emerged in the candlelight, John ran his fingers over the velvet skin, tenderly kissing the subtle curves. Maria gripped his hair and his lips took a hardened nipple, eliciting a groan of pleasure deep in her throat. His hands stripped the dress and chemise from her, and as she stepped from the clothing, the Highlander encouraged her to kneel, as well.

"Aye," he continued vaguely, running his hands over her skin, smiling at the small shudders that his touch evoked, "I know my feelings for her now."

Maria allowed him to lay her head back on the pile of clothing beneath them. As her eyes watched him remove his kilt and boots, she shook out the thick braid of hair. He was magnificent. The most beautiful thing she had ever seen. Her breath caught in her throat as her gaze locked on his arousal. "How . . . how do you feel about her. Tell me."

John paused, his look washing over this vision of perfection. Maria's ebony locks tumbled like a wave over one breast. As she looked on questioningly, he abruptly turned and crossed the room, blowing out all but one of the candles lighting the studio. He moved with the grace of a huge cat. Finally, he turned the portrait of Ambrose to the wall and returned to her, a wry look on his face.

"She is shy and hesitant, I am told. Just a wee thing, they say." He lowered himself onto her and moved between legs that opened to him. Her body was warm, her arms inviting. "A woman of few words . . . and fewer passions beyond her solitude and her prayer beads."

She wrapped her arms around him, loving the feel of his weight. The intimacy of his manhood pushing against the juncture of her thighs felt so right. She moved beneath him, almost unable to breathe with anticipation of what was to come.

"Couldn't . . . couldn't a woman have many passions?" she asked breathlessly.

Surprised by her question, John lifted his upper body and looked into her face. "Of course. A real woman will indeed, lass." Sliding his weight downward, his tongue flitted teasingly at first one breast and then the other.

"Then you don't like her?"

John slipped off Maria, and lay his head on her breast. He could hear her heart drumming in her chest. "Nay, Maria! I've decided I like her very well!" His hand followed the curve of her breast, down past the rippling lines of her ribs, over the downy mound of her womanhood, and into the soft fold, already wet with desire.

Gently, he stroked her as her fingers dug into his broad back. "With those interests, Maria, she'll be a far cry different from those in power now. Aye, she'll do quite well as my Queen. And . . . she's given us a fortnight here together!"

Maria closed her eyes as the waves of excitement began to build within her. John's lips were now latched to her breast. She could feel his tongue swirling about the nipple as he suckled. Deep within her, molten tremors shook her with their force. She lifted her hips with a sharp cry as a shower of colors filled her brain.

"Take me, John," she whispered raggedly. "Please, take me!"

The Highlander drew back and stared into her fiery eyes. "I love you, Maria."

Her heart soared at the sound of his words. His eyes, clouded with passion, carried as well the intense truth of his avowal. She had to force back the tears of happiness that were about to spill from her eyes.

"Before we make love, I want you to know my feelings for you."

"Aye, John Macpherson. I love you, as well." Her voice trembled as she spoke. "And I want you to know my feelings, whatever tomorrow might bring."

"Only happiness, my love. Only happiness," he said as he lifted himself onto her once again.

"Only happiness . . ." she breathed, lifting her knees and opening herself to him.

Maria could feel his throbbing manhood pressing against her moist opening and lifted her hips to take him in. In a single motion, he buried himself completely within her.

It seemed for so long he had waited for this moment, for this sensation of her closing around him. His vow aboard the *Great Michael* had kept him from this, and now his spirit soared. Never in his life had he been a man to wait patiently for anything. Indeed, John Macpherson had always taken what he wanted. But the torturous, delicious, maddening delay that his promise had brought about only served to intensify the thrill of this moment. Raising himself on his hands, he gazed down on her perfect body, into her eyes, so filled with desire. John fought the urge to withdraw and thrust, again and again. To fill her with the essence of his manhood.

Instead, the Highlander withdrew, though not completely, sliding from her with deliberate, excruciating care. John wanted—no, needed—to go slowly, to give them both the chance to enjoy this first time, but he felt the flames of need licking incessantly at the edges of his control. Ever so slowly, he strained, probing, sliding into her with short, steady strokes. Her breaths were coming as pants, now, and her low, throaty moans were beginning to tear at his shredding discipline. He nibbled hungrily at her earlobe, shaking with his efforts to hold back, but the tightness of her, sheathing him, was nearly too much for him to bear.

Deeper and deeper he drove with each stroke. Maria wrapped one leg around him, taking in as much of him as he would give. Her nails raked at the muscles of his back. Her body rose to his, her hips moving rhythmically with every thrust. Waves of white, pulsing heat were washing through Maria now, flashing and exploding within her as he drove deeper and deeper, trying to touch her innermost core. Higher and higher, together they climbed, teetering at last on the edge of ecstasy, of oblivion. Together then, they soared, their climax taking them into a realm of crystalline bliss.

In the volcanic blast of heat and color, Maria was no longer conscious of the room about her—only of him. Like never before, she and her love simply floated in a sparkling world of warm, fluid air and golden light.

Moments later, she nestled against him as he talked. Though she already knew quite a bit, he told her of his family, of Benmore Castle, and of the Highlands. He told her of where they'd go once they arrived in Scotland, of what they would do once he'd accomplished his mission. He spoke of taking her back to Denmark to make arrangements with her family.

When John asked her about her relatives, Maria spoke as much of the truth as she dared. Of her parents, she

told him that her mother was the only one still alive.
But when he asked her whom he should visit—to ask
for her hand in marriage—Maria could no longer hold
back the emotions that had lain so close beneath the
surface.

John held her close, thinking them tears of happiness.

Maria let herself weep, for she knew they were the
first of many tears she would shed for the two of them.
For the future they would never share.

And then he gathered her into his arms and carried
her to her bedchamber.

Chapter 18

Janet hardly knew what it was that induced her to follow Caroline. Gliding through the elaborate halls of the palace, Janet kept to the shadows, avoiding the passing servants and officials. As she passed one gathering of guards, the young woman smiled innocently and continued on. When she again caught up to her stepmother's fleeting shadow, Janet realized the other woman was simply returning to her bedchamber. But why had Caroline acted so mysteriously in the hall at breakfast?

The change in her stepmother's manner had been as abrupt as it was enigmatic. Watching as Caroline disappeared into her chamber, the young woman considered what she'd seen. Seated between Janet and her father, Caroline had been expounding on the greatness of the Douglas clan, sprinkling her speech with words of praise for magnificence of the Emperor's liberality, when suddenly Janet had seen Caroline's eyes rivet on something on the wall at the far end of the hall. Caroline's silence was complete, and Janet peered at the thing that had diverted her so entirely. In spite of her nearsightedness, the young woman could see her stepmother's eyes had fixed upon a decorative shield that hung atop a crossed pair of brightly colored banners. Janet had glanced around the hall. There were perhaps fifty such decorative shields on display in the hall, so she had looked again at the shield, trying to make out the crest. It hadn't been a Scots coat of arms, of that she was certain.

When Caroline had complained of a "sudden illness" and marched from the hall, Sir Thomas, to Janet's surprise, had showed little interest and no compassion toward his wife's sudden infirmity. The young woman, mumbling an inadequate excuse of her own, had followed her stepmother shortly thereafter.

Now, Janet squinted at the closing door. Her room and the one occupied by her father and Caroline were adjoining, and a door connected the two chambers. Once Caroline was safely in hers, Janet slipped quietly into her own chamber and eased the door shut. Something was amiss, and Janet knew it. Caroline's abrupt departure had nothing to do with illness, and Janet was determined to find out what her stepmother was up to. Moving quickly toward the heavy door adjoining the chambers, Janet carefully lifted the latch and pushed the door open a crack. As she peered in, her mind raced, looking for some excuse if she were caught.

On the far side of the chamber, Caroline bent over a trunk. The tall, blond woman was searching for something and tossed her cascading hair back in anger as it impeded her efforts. Suddenly she stopped, and Janet knew she had found what she was looking for.

"Ah, there you are." Caroline's words were soft but distinct.

As she straightened up, Caroline was oblivious to everything but what she had before her. From this distance all Janet could make out was something dangling from the other woman's hand. Janet squinted her eyes, trying to make out the object. A thin chain, she decided, with something at the end. Seeing Caroline lift the bauble at the end and slide it over a finger, Janet knew. A ring. A ring at the end of a chain.

Caroline studied the ring for a moment and then gazed contemplatively into space. Janet watched in silence as a cold smile crept over Caroline's face. There was malice in that look; Janet Maule had seen it before. Slowly, the blond-haired woman poured the chain and ring into one palm and closed her hand into a fist. Then, with a quick movement that nearly caused her onlooker to cry out, Caroline strode to the huge chamber door. Recovering her composure, Janet listened as her stepmother stood just beyond the threshold, calling out impatiently until a serving man came running. Though she strained to hear, she could make nothing of the whispered instructions.

As the servant ran off and Caroline reentered her chamber, Janet drew back a bit and hid behind the door. She heard the door close, and Caroline's low laugh rang hollowly in the empty room.

"Dear Queen Maria." A chill ran down Janet's back. "You are mine!"

"It is simply out of the question, John." Maria tried to roll away from him and off the bed. "Don't ask again. I simply cannot do it."

He wasn't about to let her get away that easily. The Highlander's strong hands grabbed her around the waist and pulled her back to his side.

"You are being unreasonable, Maria. I'm quite certain the Emperor would love the opportunity to see another new face. Particularly a face as pretty as yours."

"Take someone else," she responded vehemently. "I won't go." She didn't know how to tell him that taking the missing queen back to her brother's palace for this dinner would most definitely be perceived as a serious breach of etiquette. Maria was quite certain that Charles would be a stickler on the point.

She again tried to squirm away, but he held her tight.

"I will not take someone else." He pushed her hair away from her neck and began to kiss the small lumps on her backbone. As he reached her neck, he continued with his kisses, knowing that she would sooner or later loosen her death grip on his arms. With his lips and tongue he teased, laved, and kissed the velvet skin beneath her ear, continuing with this torment until, at last, with a sigh, she gave up her grip on his arms and angled her head to give him better access to her neck. Breathing into her ear as he brushed his lips across the lobe, John felt her body soften in his arms.

"You are the only woman I want by my side, for now and forever." His hands moved up from her waist and molded one breast. He felt her nipple harden between his fingers. "I love you, and I will be very proud to have you by me. Maria, I want *you* by my side. No one else will do, love."

Maria felt his words of tenderness go directly to her heart, but her head knew the impossibility of the situation. She tried, in vain, to think of excuses that he could not argue with. What did other women say when they found themselves in such a dilemma? She tried to think what her female companions might say. She shook her head. *You are a fool,* she thought. *What other queen would work herself into such a predicament? None,* she answered silently. *Only Maria of Hungary.*

"I wouldn't have the slightest idea what is expected of me."

"I will show you what to do." His fingers caressed her breasts, his thumbs making small circles around the aureole. "I am a fine teacher, lass, and you've proved yourself an excellent pupil already."

She tried to ignore the hint of sexual intent in his words, but it was becoming more and more difficult. "Nay, John, I'll embarrass you terribly."

"You'll be a support to me." His muscular leg entrapped hers.

She loved the feel of his strong body wrapped around hers. She could feel his arousal now pressed intimately against her buttocks. It was impossible to think straight. "I have nothing to wear."

"I do like the sound of that," the Highlander whispered, his mouth continuing to graze across the skin of her neck. "But if you insist on wearing anything, I'll clothe you in gold."

She bit her lip, trying to force herself to concentrate on coming up with some way to make him understand. Cloth of gold. Her body was betraying her. It had happened during the night, and it was happening now. Every time he touched her, Maria's body erupted in an orgy of sensuality, and all reason disappeared. John Macpherson had a way about him that was impossible to ignore.

"Maria, come with me." He commanded, biting on her earlobe. "No more excuses. Just come."

She turned in his arms to face him. She gasped as his
fingers slid downward over the skin of her belly and into
the moist folds of her womanhood. She had been about
to say something, but whatever it was, it was gone now.

"I've already told Pieter to have a seamstress ready
by noon." John pushed her onto her back and moved
on top of her. He paused, gazing down into her beautiful
but troubled eyes. "You need a new wardrobe, dresses
to wear. So if that's the problem—"

"Don't, John." Maria placed her fingers against his
lips and then pulled his face closer to hers. Nibbling at
his lips, she arched her back, pressing her breasts against
his muscular body. He was trying to overwhelm her, kiss
away her defenses so that she would just give in and go
to the palace. But two can play that game, she thought
happily. Encircling his neck with her arms, Maria clung
to him tighter, thrusting her tongue against his and deepening the kiss.

John growled as she devoured his mouth. The way she
was responding—the teasing dance of their tongues—
was driving him wild. He pulled back just long enough
to whisper the words, "We'll make love until noon." He
rolled to one side and she followed. His hands caressed
her breasts, her sides, her hips. His manhood lay heavily
on her inner thigh. "And then, after the bloody seamstress has gone, I'll drag you back here, and we'll make
love some more." John's hand moved between her legs
and stroked at her flesh. "Then, after our dinner—at the
palace—we'll come back and make love all night."

"I have a better plan," she breathed. Her hand moved
between their bodies, as well. "We'll make love all day,
and we'll have Pieter bring us lunch here." Her fingers
wrapped themselves around his thick shaft. She smiled at
the way his whole body responded to her touch. "We'll
dine here, in bed. As we are now. Making love as we eat.
Perhaps I could use you as a platter for my food." She bit
his shoulder, and his head sank onto the pillow.

John couldn't wait any longer. Her fingers were sliding
the length of his throbbing arousal, guiding the tip to
her moist opening. Taking hold of her hips, he pushed

her hand roughly away as he rolled her again onto her back. Then, in a single motion, he drove powerfully into her tight sheath.

She let out a sharp breath as her body opened to accept him. "Then . . . then we'll continue . . . into the night." She gasped as he withdrew and plunged into her again. "Perhaps we'll share . . . oh, love . . . a bath."

John's hands dug into her hips and he lifted them as he continued his deep and potent thrusts. Her body was already moving in tandem with his, and the image of their bodies together in the water was exhilarating to them both.

"Your body . . . slick and shining . . . gliding over mine," he whispered raggedly. "We might . . . never . . . never surface."

As the tempo of their love dance increased, Maria's breaths became shorter and shorter, and she knew her body was about to explode. "You'll surface . . ." she offered, her responses punctuated with moans. "You'll have . . . dinner . . . palace . . ."

"We . . . will . . ." His words were spoken through gritted teeth.

"Nay." Her fingers clawed his back. "I'll . . . be resting . . ." Her legs were now wrapped around his waist as their bodies rocked in perfect rhythm. "Waiting . . . for you. Oh, John . . . John!"

"Aye!" he growled as their climax lifted them once again into the heavens. "Oh, God. Maria!"

Maria was the first to speak, and her body continued to shudder as his body draped exhaustedly over hers. "We'll . . . have a long night ahead of us. I'll wait for you here."

"I am very sorry, Lady Caroline, but a private audience with the Emperor is impossible just now. And since you refuse to confide in me . . ."

Janet pressed her back tightly against the wall of her bedchamber. She could hear everything that was being said, and there was no need to peek inside to know the identity of the speaker. She'd recognized his silvery voice immediately as belonging to the Emperor's trusted minister, Count Diego de Guevara, the man who, the night before, had greeted them with such courtesy prior to the Emperor's appearance.

Whatever the message was that Caroline had sent the servant off with, it must have been important, for the minister had arrived in a very short time.

"I have information that the Emperor *must* hear, Count Diego. But it is for him alone." Janet could hear the sharp edge in her stepmother's voice. "I assure you the Emperor will be very grateful to you for conveying me to him."

"I am certain what you say is true, señora. But the answer is still the same. He'll not have time for a private audience." The man cleared his throat. "On the other hand, since your information *must* reach the Emperor, I would suggest that you speak with Sir John Macpherson. I know that the Emperor intends to speak with him as soon as—"

"Wait!" Caroline cut the minister short and glared at the minister. Surprised at the vehemence of the outburst, Count Diego simply stood and stared back at her.

The silence stretched so long that Janet Maule began to panic with the thought that she had been discovered. Just as the young woman pondered making a dash for the corridor, she heard Caroline speak.

"You are treating me so dismissively because I am a woman."

"Hardly, señora. I am simply being—"

"How dare you!" she snapped. "Haven't you any idea who I am?"

"But of course. You are Lady Caroline Maule, a member—"

Her voice had the cold, hard edge of fury in it. "I am Caroline Douglas, cousin of Archibald Douglas, the Earl of Angus. *We* rule Scotland, and it is only through our good will that this marriage will take place at all. We, the Douglas clan, can make this alliance work . . . or crush it. Do you understand me? Now, I *will* see the Emperor!"

When Count Diego spoke, his voice no longer had the silvery quality it had manifested earlier. "I certainly *do* understand you, señora. And I know who you are. It is the reason why I came here to begin with. But now, since you refuse to listen, I will take my leave. I again suggest you speak to Sir John."

"What if I told you that this marriage hinges on the Emperor having the information I have to convey? What if I told you that this information will incriminate your good Sir John?"

Janet strained to hear what would come next. The minister was clearly considering Caroline's words carefully.

"It is not in our interest to meddle in Scottish politics, m'lady. However, if what you have to say concerns the safety of the royal family . . ."

"I will say naught more . . . to you!"

The pause was short, but ever so pointed. Janet heard the count move away toward the door.

"Very well, Lady Caroline. I believe I've stayed far longer than was warranted. If you will pardon me, there are other matters that need my immediate attention."

"Wait!" Caroline ordered. "Didn't you hear what I've said? Are you such fools here that—"

"I've heard!" Count Diego retorted sharply. "But then, you should hear yourself, your own foolishness! How dare you expect the Emperor to respond as if he were some stable boy, waiting to be summoned! I am a fool? Let me tell you who *I* am. I am Don Diego, Count of Guevara and Oliveres, Minister of the Household and trusted advisor of Charles V, Holy Roman Emperor, master of Europe and the New World, and by the hand of the Pope, Protector of the Faith. I come to you in good faith, and in return, you talk nonsense."

"Nonsense?" Caroline's angry voice faltered ever so slightly.

"Nonsense!" he returned decisively. "Your entire Scottish delegation of nobles has nothing to say but words of praise for your commander. A man known to the world for his loyalty and his integrity. And here you stand, puffed up with false pride, and accuse him, John Macpherson, Lord of the Scottish Navy, a fellow countryman for God's sake, of some vague treachery—and without a single shred of evidence. And then, in the same breath, you again demand a private audience." The man's voice was growing louder as his patience continued to disintegrate. "You are very lucky, Lady Caroline, that you don't live in this court. Now, I'll be on my way."

Janet heard the door in the other chamber swing open.

"I know the whereabouts of your queen!" Caroline's voice was low but clear, and it stopped Count Diego dead in his tracks.

"Our queen?" the man asked calmly. "Queen Isabella is in—"

"Nay, not Queen Isabella," she continued coldly. "Mary, Queen of Hungry. Though, as you know, she simply refers to herself as Maria. Now tell the Emperor that I need a private audience."

"Good day, m'lady."

"Stop!" she shouted. "Are you deaf? I know where she is hidden."

"Nay, I am not deaf," Count Diego answered. "And you are wasting your time. We have no need to learn of her whereabouts because the Emperor's sister is not missing."

"Then what is this?"

Putting her eyes to the small opening of the door, Janet watched in horror as Caroline extended her fist and let the ring fall, dangling between them at the end of the chain.

"So Maria of Hungary is not missing, you say?" Gloating self-satisfaction saturated her tone. "Then you tell me how I came upon this."

Count Diego reached out and glanced briefly at the insignia on the ring. With only the slightest pause, the minister turned and closed the chamber door.

"Now, let's begin all over again." Caroline smirked. "How soon will I see the Emperor?"

Chapter 19

The man was as stubborn as a mule.

Maria had considered the matter settled. But now, watching the white-haired seamstress and her two assistants flutter about, she knew she'd been wrong. These women had specific instructions, and nothing she said seemed to make any difference. They had been directed to make her a formal dress first, undoubtedly for dinner, she thought, and they were determined to make the best use of what little time they had. John must have had Pieter offer the women quite a reward if they could produce the gown in time.

When they'd arrived, Maria had insisted that they begin with a travel garment, but they only smiled and chattered among themselves. Maria understood Dutch fairly well, but their understanding of *her* Dutch seemed to be curiously lacking. Standing in her chemise on a low stool in the middle of her bedchamber as the three workers buzzed about, alternatively poking her, measuring her, and ignoring her, Maria began to wish that John would return. But this time, words of love were not exactly what she had in mind to use in greeting.

Just before noon, he'd been called to the *Great Michael*. Just a preliminary tour of the warship that would carry the queen, the messenger had said, but the young man had also told John that Count Diego de Guevara, himself, would be leading the officials from the Palace.

Maria scowled as one of the women draped a gold cloth over her shoulder. John had not been fooling when he'd said he'd clothe her in gold, she realized. So stubborn! But as she ran her fingers lightly over the fine gold threads of the brocade, something touched her deeply, and in her heart, a sense of joy overcame her annoyance. The gifts she'd received in the past had never meant much to her. After all, she had always had everything one could desire, and more. But John's generosity, his desire to provide for her, meant so much more to her. This dress was not to be a gift for a queen. This gown of gold was to clothe his beloved.

The quiet tap at the door and the entry of a serving girl drew Maria's attention.

"M'lady. You have a visitor," the girl whispered.

Maria paused, sliding the material from her shoulder. Perhaps a messenger from Isabel, she thought. "Does he bring a message? A letter, perhaps, that you could deliver to me?"

"It's not a he, m'lady," the servant chirped in response. "It's a lady. A Scottish lady. And she has no message that she'll leave. Pieter told her that you were quite busy at the moment, but she insisted on waiting in the front hall. She asked to tell you that it is essential that she see you in person, at once."

Maria quickly handed the gold fabric to the seamstress and reached for her dress. "Did she tell you her name?"

"Aye, m'lady," the girl answered. "Mistress Janet Maule."

Maria felt a wave of relief wash through her. The thought of facing Lady Caroline, for any reason, held no appeal for her. But Isabel had told her briefly of the dilemma facing Janet and David Maxwell. Most certainly, this visit had to do with that. She reached behind her neck and began to lace her dress, but one of the seamstresses jumped to the task.

"Thank you," she said before turning back to the serving girl. "Could you show the lady in here?"

"But m'lady," the seamstress was quick to put in, "to have your dress ready for tonight, we still have so much to do."

Maria addressed the serving girl first. "Please show Mistress Janet in."

With a quick glance at the white-haired seamstress, the girl disappeared into the corridor. When she was gone, Maria turned her attention back to the trio and addressed them all. "As I tried to tell you before, I have no need for a dress tonight."

"But Sir John gave specific instructions, m'lady. The steward has expressly—"

"And *I* am giving you even more explicit instructions." Maria smoothed a hand over her skirts. "We are finished here, but I thank you for your trouble."

"Very well, m'lady." The woman's eyes never stopped in their appraisal of her figure as she gestured for her helpers to gather up their cloth and equipment. "I think we have all we need."

"Please understand that I appreciate the position you are in, but as far as the gown is concerned—"

The woman smiled and laid a kindly hand on Maria's arm. "It is no problem, m'lady. You will have a beautiful dress by this evening."

Maria paused, thinking of what she might say to make these three understand, when the door to the bedchamber opened and Janet Maule followed the serving girl into the room.

Maria opened her arms and smiled at her friend. "I am so glad you are here, Janet. Perhaps you can help me communicate my wishes—" The young queen stopped midsentence. The full curtsy that Janet gave her made her throat tighten. When the young woman stood up again, she remained where she was, silent and her head bowed respectfully.

"Leave us," Maria ordered the others without taking her eyes off her visitor. "Leave us now."

The note of authority in her voice left no room for debate. It took only a moment for the room to clear. Once the door was closed quietly behind the departing women, Maria moved to Janet and took her trembling hands in her own. The young Scots noblewoman still would not lift her eyes.

Maria knew what was wrong before she even questioned her friend. But she still had to ask. "Tell me what's happened, Janet?"

Janet's eyes lifted only briefly to her face. "My stepmother Caroline. She has your ring."

"My ring!" Maria repeated. "I couldn't find it before we left the *Great Michael*. I assumed it was lost."

"She knows who you are."

The two women stood in silence.

Maria looked into Janet's face, searching for some indication of the young woman's feelings toward her. For anger. But Janet had not come to vent her hostility for Maria's actions. She had come to warn her. She had come as a friend.

"I should have expected as much!" She whirled and crossed the room to the window. Below, the Groenplaats was bustling with vendors and townspeople. Maria considered the ring itself, with its intricate insignia. The combined coats of arms of her family and her husband's family had been used on several portraits and decoratively throughout the palace. What a fool she had been to think she could stay in the same city and avoid being caught. A company of helmeted soldiers, their long spears flashing in the sun, marched across the center of the square. "Do I have any time, Janet?"

"Not much, Your Majesty. I—"

"Oh, please don't call me that, Janet," Maria cried, turning and coming back to the young woman. She took her by the hand. "I am Maria to my friends. I will always be Maria to you." Janet nodded tentatively, and the young queen smiled. "Now, tell me everything so that we can decide what must be done."

Leading her to a cushioned bench, Maria drew her friend down beside her. "Tell me what you know, Janet."

"I . . . I was hiding in my chamber. In truth, Your Maj . . . Maria, I had followed Lady Caroline to spy on her." Janet smiled shyly and received a nod from Maria. "I could hear everything. She knew from the ring that you are the Emperor's sister. Indeed, a minister came when she sent for him."

"Which minister?"

"Count Diego de Guevara. I recognized him from our arrival at the palace last night. When he came to her chamber, Caroline demanded to meet with the Emperor immediately. They argued, but when she produced the ring, he agreed to her wishes."

"She's seen the Emperor?" Maria leaped up in alarm and went again to the window. "They could be on their way! I'll be taken—"

"Nay," Janet cried out, following her. "It was impossible to see the Emperor. In fact, I don't see how he could know anything about it, yet. He left the palace in the middle of the night!"

"Left?" Puzzled, Maria turned around to face Janet. "Why?"

"Count Diego said that Queen Isabella gave birth to a child late yesterday." Janet continued. "He told her that the earliest she could possibly see the Emperor would be tonight after the welcoming feast."

"A child!" Maria couldn't keep the pang of worry out of her voice. "Isabella was not due for nearly a month. And have you heard of any news of them? Did she fare well with the delivery?" Maria had her differences with Charles, but she had always admired and respected his wife, Isabella of Portugal.

"From what I could gather, it sounded as if the mother and daughter are both fine."

Maria sent off a quick prayer of thanks for this news.

"Count Diego said they've named the child Maria— for you—though I don't think Caroline was overjoyed about any of it."

Maria couldn't help the smile that brightened her features. *That devil, Charles. He would try to soften her like this.* But that thought quickly passed as she thought of Caroline and Count Diego.

"Then Count Diego knows I'm here." Her brother's minister was an efficient man. He would come for her, himself. She involuntarily glanced out the window again. "Do you think Caroline knows where I am?"

"I'm certain she does," Janet answered. "Everyone in the delegation knew Sir John was staying at Hart Haus."

"Then the minister knows where I am, as well!"

"I don't think so," Janet said slowly. "Caroline refused to say where you were. And she didn't say anything about your . . . relationship with Sir John. She is determined to deal with your brother in person. But she assured the minister that you would be going nowhere, and I think he believed her."

Thank you, Holy Mother, for that, Maria prayed. Count Diego was a good man, but if he thought for an instant that Maria would slip through his fingers, he would have Caroline tortured on the rack without a moment's hesitation. Well, whatever happened to Caroline Maule, she had brought it on herself.

"That might work to our favor," she said, thinking aloud. "Perhaps, then, there is time to find Isabel, time to leave on the next ship."

Looking at Janet, Maria saw the look of alarm in her expression. "What else, Janet? You are not telling me everything, are you?"

The young woman paused, struggling with what she wanted to say. "You know that Caroline is after Sir John."

Maria stared at her young friend. "She wants him for herself, you mean."

Janet looked steadily at Maria. "She will destroy him if she can't have him. I know that."

"And you think she plans to disgrace him."

"Aye, Maria. At the very least. You don't know her the way I've come to know her. She is evil. Just from what I heard this morning, I am certain she will accuse him of wrongdoing. Although she chose my father, I know that she will never be happy with him. And I know that he already hurts inside because of her. And I also know that she will not stop, will not rest, until Sir John is found guilty of some crime. You are to be the wife of

King James. You are to be Scotland's queen. I don't
know what the laws are here, but in Scotland . . . Sir
John's betrayed his vow. By helping you to escape, by
spending . . . time with you, his life is forfeit, to be
sure. That's why I think she insists on meeting with your
brother face-to-face."

Maria shook her head. "But it can't be. He is innocent
of these things. I never told him who I was, or that I
was trying to escape an ill-gotten marriage to your king.
He doesn't know the truth even now. As far as he
knows, I am no one."

"But she has your ring," Janet pressed. "All that she
needs beyond that is proof that you were aboard the
Great Michael. But even if she didn't have the ring, everyone aboard that ship saw you with him. Perhaps Sir
John's men will keep silent, but the rest—the nobles who
were aboard—they'd gladly prefer to have his head displayed on a pike over Edinburgh Castle rather than their
own. And when the delegation returns without you, the
Earl of Angus will be looking for someone to blame.
John Macpherson is not of the Douglas clan. With Caroline's encouragement, they'll stab him in the back without a moment of remorse."

The laws of the Holy Roman Empire were not so
different from those of Scotland. Though Charles would
never harm one of his own blood, John Macpherson was
another matter. If the marriage contract were to be abro-
gated, the Emperor would surely treat John Macpherson's actions as a capital offense. And he would punish
him brutally. John would never have to worry about
what would happen to him in Scotland. Maria began to
pace back and forth in the room, her mind awhirl with
what she could do next. This was all her fault. John's
life was about to be cut painfully short, and she alone
was to blame.

Maria stopped before the window and leaned heavily
on the casing. She would not sit back and let Caroline
destroy John. That would not happen, not so long as she
lived. And then Maria knew that she could no longer

leave Antwerp. The price of freedom was simply too high. The price was John Macpherson's life.

"How did you get here, Janet? How did *you* know where I was?"

"I sent a message to David. He couldn't come—the people from the palace were expected aboard the *Great Michael,* but he sent several of his sailors to accompany me here."

"Aye, it's Count Diego who is with Sir John right now." Maria considered for a moment. "Janet, do you think Caroline might realize that you've come to me with her plans? Or that you know anything of her vile little plot?"

Janet wrapped her arms around her middle. "Nay, Maria. I don't think she does. But this morning, after Count Diego left, I remained hidden in my room, wracking my brain for a way that I could contact you." Janet took an deep breath. "It was then that Caroline must have noticed the partially open door to my chamber."

"Did she discover you there?"

"Aye. She yanked open the door and stormed into the chamber. She demanded to know how long I'd been there."

"And?" Maria asked uncomfortably.

"I told her that I'd just arrived and was only there to get my cloak."

"Did she believe you?"

Janet shook her head. "I don't know, but why do you ask?"

Maria walked over to the younger woman and gathered her hands into hers. "When I am finished with what I am about to do, Lady Caroline Maule may be more vicious and vengeful than ever before. I just want to make sure that you, my friend, will not be the target of her malice."

Janet's expression was one of worry as she looked at the young queen before her. "What are you planning to do?"

Pushing aside feelings of the brief moments of happiness she'd felt in John's arms, Maria gathered her strength. She'd sworn to herself she would never do it. Not for her brother. Not for the Holy Roman Empire. But she would do it for John. She had to.

"I am going back to the palace. To the Emperor," she announced. Her face was a placid mask, hiding the emotional chaos within. "I will be Queen of Scotland."

Chapter 20

The queen's cabin stood ready.

As Count Diego de Guevara inspected the furnishings of the room, John stood with his back against the wall and thought of Maria.

Never had he wanted anyone as fiercely as he wanted her. Each moment away from her dragged at his spirit, but the ache in his soul was only a reflection of the ache of desire that the Highlander was feeling for her right now. Glancing at the narrow door that led into the small cabin where she'd stayed, he envisioned her perfect body sleeping peacefully in the great, canopied bed at Hart Haus. He shook his head to dispel the image. She was not simply an image, she was a real woman, and he had no desire to shake Maria from the place she had taken in his heart.

When will this man be finished? John wondered impatiently. He had been present in body while escorting Count Diego and the rest of the palace delegation through their formal visit of the *Great Michael*, but not in mind. Thankfully, David had stepped in and led the tour, pointing out the improvements that had been made to the huge warship since John had taken over as Lord of the Navy. The young navigator, realizing his commander's attention was elsewhere, had been eager and quick to respond to the varied interests of the visitors. So John had not needed to dwell for very long on the few questions directed to him.

John felt the difference in him. He was not unaware of the watchful and appraising looks with which Count Diego regarded him. But the minister's estimation of

him mattered little. What had mattered so deeply a
month ago did not seem so important today. Though he
knew the *Great Michael* was impressive, it was almost
humorous to think that he simply did not care if this
delegation was awed by his ship or not. On the other
hand, as he had been striding down the quayside from
Hart Haus, his mind had been fully occupied with hopes
that Maria would be impressed by Benmore Castle, the
Macpherson clan holding. He knew that his family would
love Maria, but would she take to his home and his
parents as his brother's wives had done?

John's mind drifted back to the lovemaking that had
kept them up for most of the night. His life had carried
him all over the world, and into the arms of many
women, but his experience in the courtly art of love
paled in the light of her rich and joyous response. Indeed, there had been moments when he'd risen out of
the love mist only to realize that he'd been reduced to
little more than an eager lad. She made him feel sixteen
again—wild, uncontrollable, and driven with the buoyant
thrill of the first time—and proud of the ecstasy that he
had wrought in her.

But he would do better than that, he promised himself. After dinner, after they returned from the palace,
he would show her another side. He would make tonight
a feast she would never forget. But then, once they were
married, they would have many nights that they would
never forget.

As the tour continued on along one of the gun decks,
John heard Count Diego remarking on the German cannons that sat in readiness behind the closed gunports.
Something about the marriage of excellent firepower and
superb seamanship vaguely registered in the Highlander's brain.

Marriage! He would scarcely have believed it himself.
The thought of it had been a remote possibility for so
long. He had reconciled himself to the bachelor's life,
and was not distraught at the prospect. But now . . .
now a new life stretched out before him. One full of
promise. He wondered briefly if he might coax Maria

into marrying him at Benmore Castle right after they arrived. They could go to her people later—after the wedding. Aye, he would take her any place she wanted to go. They could swim in the blue seas off the coast of India. Lie in beds of silk in China. If she wanted, he would show her the wonders of the New World!

The sun was warm on John's face as they climbed into the bracing, fresh air of the forward deck. The Highlander looked up at the sails, tightly furled, and at the string of banners that flapped merrily in the spring breeze. His gaze lingered on the one that displayed the coat of arms of the Macphersons, with its rampant cat, claws outstretched. That same banner flew proudly over Benmore Castle.

His oldest brother, Alec, and his wife, Fiona, had settled in comfortably at Benmore. Perhaps Maria would enjoy life in the Highlands. It was a rough and wild country, but he would build her a new tower house of her own, with all the modern comforts. Of course, she might prefer to live at court, or in one of Europe's fine cities—Paris or Rome perhaps. But bairns were best raised in the country, John thought. Interestingly, he'd always thoroughly enjoyed the time he'd spent with his nephews and his niece, yet never had he ever thought of being a father himself. Until now, that is. He smiled to himself at the thought of a houseful of daughters with Maria's green eyes and her beautiful, ivory skin. However, perhaps he should warn her of the other Macpherson bairns. Other than Ambrose's darling daughter, Jaime, there had been only sons born to the line.

The Highlander sighed deeply, recalling how these very thoughts, voiced by other men, had sounded so trivial. So many times he'd looked on these things as weaknesses in those men. Frivolous, he'd once called these thoughts that now he eagerly embraced. What else matters more? he asked himself. What, indeed?

John followed Count Diego down the gangplank and onto the quay. The steel-helmeted soldiers came to attention. These were Spanish soldiers, and the ship's commander knew them to be a formidable fighting force.

Not that they had ever come up against an army of Highlanders.

He wondered if that was how Maria felt. There was so much that he was planning without ever speaking a word of it to her. John cursed himself. He had to make sure that she didn't feel bullied. The only thing that mattered was that she love him. Together they could plan the rest of their lives. Whatever she choose, whatever made her happy, he would be content with. So long as she remained by his side, his life would be perfect.

Count Diego de Guevara turned and gazed contemplatively at the handsome ship, his hand smoothing his graying beard. The palace men, despite their obvious efforts to restrain themselves, were clearly impressed. John caught a look from David that confirmed his observation. Then, with a word of approval—and one final glance at John—the minister mounted his black steed and led his party back into the city.

Not moments after their departure, John was ready. Ready to go back to Hart Haus. To Maria. After giving his final instructions to David regarding the crew, he turned to leave, only to have his navigator stop him and relay the message he'd had from Janet Maule earlier—about wanting to reach Lady Maria.

John shrugged off the incident. Most likely Mistress Janet was looking for more interesting company than the lot of boring gentry they'd brought along. John smiled, certain that the young woman had simply sought Maria's company. He, for one, couldn't blame her, as the friendship that had begun to blossom between Janet and Maria had been obvious.

But as the Highlander strode through the crowded and winding streets of Antwerp, he hoped their visit had ended. They'd had a long enough talk, he decided magnanimously, and as he walked, he prepared a cordial speech to start the young woman off for the palace. But by the time John arrived at the Hart Haus, he wasn't quite sure how civil he would be showing Mistress Janet to the door. He needed to see Maria. He needed to be alone with her. Climbing the stone steps, he thought his heart might burst if he couldn't soon hold her in his arms, if he couldn't look into her brilliant emerald eyes and lose himself in them. The few, short hours he'd been away seemed like ages to him now. Marching into the front door of the house, John called out her name.

Waving off the servants who approached him, the Highlander took the steps three at a time en route to her chamber. Shoving open the door without knocking, he stood in the doorway and scanned the empty room. Though his beloved was not there, he noted the beautiful dress of gold spread on top of the bedcovers. So, she was going to the dinner, after all, he thought happily. Backing out of the room, he headed up the stairs toward Elizabeth's studio. She had been so much at peace there; it was only natural for her to go back.

Elizabeth would like Maria, John was certain of that. There was something about Maria's unassuming ways that would make it hard for anyone not to adore her.

Reaching for the studio door, he opened it wide with one fluid motion and stepped inside. The silence and the darkness of the room slapped him in the face. This had been the room where they'd first made love. But the shuttered window blocked out all light and hid from sight any sign of his woman.

"Maria," he called out softly. John's eyes adjusted quickly, but the search was futile and a gnawing fear began to edge up his spine.

He suddenly thought of the sitting room beside her bedchamber. He backed out and hurried down the corridor. He'd simply passed the room in his rush to her chamber and never even glanced inside. The poor thing hadn't eaten so much as a morsel of bread this morning before he left. He hadn't given her time for it. Of course, Pieter would have laid out a fine meal for her. She was probably in that sitting room eating right now. Charging down the winding steps, he headed back toward the young woman's chamber.

He almost knocked Pieter down as he barreled onto the landing.

"Sir John, you are back."

"I am. At last." John placed a friendly arm around
the steward. "I am going to join Lady Maria. Tell the
cook that I am hungry enough to eat a boar. She's in
her sitting room, if I'm not mistaken."

As the Highlander released him and headed down the
corridor, the steward quickly fell in step with him.

"But m'lord," Pieter cried, "Lady Maria is no longer
here."

John came to an abrupt stop and whirled on the man.
"What do you mean, she is no longer here? Where else
could she be? Where? When is she coming back?"

The portly steward paled under the heat of the Highlander's angry glare. "I am sorry, Sir John. But I thought
you were aware of her departure. The Scotswoman that
came for Lady Maria was escorted by some of your
own men."

"Maria left with Mistress Janet?" John asked, confused. "Didn't they tell you where they were going?"

"Nay, m'lord. They said nothing." The steward shook
his head. "I was quite concerned, Sir John. One moment,
Lady Maria was happily arguing with the seamstress and
her helpers, seemingly as contented as one might hope
to be, and the next—it was immediately after she'd spoken with this Mistress Janet—Lady Maria became
deadly pale. She was clearly upset, but what could I do?"

"What was she upset about?" John asked impatiently.
The only thing that he could think of was that Caroline
had sent her some twisted message. But he dismissed
the thought immediately; Janet Maule was Maria's
friend. Surely the young woman would not play a part
in any deceit Caroline might cook up.

"I don't know, Sir John. Lady Maria said very little."
Pieter pointed to the open door of Maria's room. "After
speaking with Mistress Janet, she simply hurried about
her chamber, gathering her things." The steward's face
showed his distress as he trailed the distraught Highlander into Maria's bedchamber. "How could I interfere,
m'lord? Your men were waiting below. This Mistress
Maule seemed such a quiet and kindhearted young
woman. When Lady Maria said good-bye to me, she was

clearly leaving of her own accord, though I thought for a moment that she was about to break down and cry."

John felt every muscle in his body tightening. He had to restrain his temper to not shout at the man. "Did you ask her anything, Pieter? Such as when she is returning. Or what all of this is about."

Crestfallen, the man shook his head. "It happened so suddenly, m'lord. Just seeing your men, and this Mistress Janet, a Scottish woman from the delegation . . . I just thought . . . I never considered that you would be unaware of what was happening."

John turned away and surveyed the chamber. He shouldn't blame the man. Caroline had to be at the root of all this, and it wasn't Pieter's fault that he himself had bedded the most conniving woman alive for almost seven years. It wasn't this poor servant's fault that John had put himself in a position where Caroline Maule could possibly hurt the woman he loved.

"I am dreadfully sorry, Sir John," Pieter spoke from behind him. "I never thought . . . You don't fear for her safety?"

The worry in his voice made John turn around. The weight of his distress seemed to be bending his old back even farther. "None of this is your fault, Pieter. As you said, she left with Janet Maule and my own men. They won't let any harm come to her. It can only mean that Mistress Janet is taking Maria to the palace. But why? That is what I cannot understand. And without me."

"She left before the seamstress completed her gown," the steward put in, pointing to the dress lying across the bed.

John nodded vaguely and crossed the room to the great bed, with its canopy of deep blue damask. Lost in thought, the Highlander ran his fingers over the weave of golden thread. What in the hell was Caroline up to, anyway? What else could explain it? And what could Janet have said that might upset Maria so much? The oddest part was that Maria must have gone to the palace, in spite of knowing no one there.

Perhaps, he thought—trying to be more positive—perhaps the reason has nothing to do with Caroline. Perhaps this is all some elaborate surprise. After all, she had absolutely refused to go to the welcoming feast. Perhaps, he argued with himself, but not very likely.

"You are certain, Pieter. Lady Maria was upset when she left Hart Haus?" John asked again.

"I am absolutely certain, m'lord." The steward nodded. "When a person looks into those green eyes of hers, he can see clear to her soul. Besides, her hands were ice cold and trembling when she laid them in mine. Oh yes, and she even forgot to take her aunt's letter."

John stared at the older man. "A letter from Isabel? When did she receive this letter?"

"Last night, m'lord. It arrived during dinner. There it is." Pieter pointed at the envelope sitting on the small side table near the bed. "Perhaps Lady Maria dropped it in her haste. One of the maids found it beside the bed."

John turned and looked down at the letter. She hadn't said a thing to him about receiving word from Isabel. But again, the two of them had been occupied with other matters. "Thank you, Pieter. That will be all, for now."

"Will you be dining at the palace this evening, Sir John?"

He nodded. "Aye, and I'll be getting to the bottom of this, as well."

As the steward reached the door, he paused and looked back at the giant commander. "I truly hope you'll be bringing Lady Maria back with you, m'lord. She's a fine woman, if I may say so."

"Aye, Pieter. That she is. And don't you worry, I will be escorting her back."

With a small bow, the steward backed out of the room.

John stood for a moment, considering his next move. He had to go after her. That was, of course, the only way. Only when he found out what it was that Caroline had done could he straighten out the mess that she had somehow created. But he had to go now.

Suddenly, the Highlander became aware of the item his eyes had focused on. There, on the side table, lay

Isabel's note. Perhaps it wasn't Caroline. Perhaps something had happened to Maria's aunt. He considered, as he picked up the note, whether he should read the message. The parchment was thick and well made. Well, if he was to be of any help at all, he would need to know the problem. Whatever was written there, he would keep it in confidence. He smiled grimly to himself. How much more shocking could Isabel be on paper than in person?

John unfolded the letter and began to read.

Chapter 21

She never noticed the bitter scent of myrrh burning sharply in the air.

Maria continued to pray as she had for over an hour, oblivious to the clouds of incense hanging about the chapel altar. *Hail Mary, full of Grace.* The stone floor was hard beneath her knees, but the young queen felt nothing. *Blessed art thou amongst women.* Maria pressed her eyelids together. She would shut out the world. *Blessed is the fruit of thy womb.* A tear escaped and trailed unnoticed along the confining line of her wimple's starched linen. *Pray for us sinners, now and at the hour of our . . . death.*

She dropped her head into her joined hands. Her tears were plenty, but her sobs were hidden. Hearing one of the heavy doors of the chapel creak somewhere in the back of the church, she pressed her fists to her eyes, stopping the flow of her tears.

"Please, Virgin Mother," Maria prayed in a whisper, "help me through this. Let him go unharmed. If there has to be one who is punished, let it be me. I am the one who has sinned."

Maria heard the quiet steps of the man approaching. She picked up her prayer book and turned to look at the priest who now stood watching her.

"It's time, Your Majesty. He is ready for you now."

Rising from her place before the altar, Maria of Hungary nodded to the man and wordlessly glided past him to the door.

*   *   *

"These months have been trying, you know? Quite trying!" the Emperor barked angrily. "I am extending myself in every direction. I have to crush rebellion in Spain, contain the French king's egotistical land seizures, somehow hold the Turk's advances in the east, control Lutheran heresy in Germany, restrain the Pope in Rome! And on top of it all, I have to chase my own sister across the continent."

Maria's eyes followed the path of her brother's steps. He had been lecturing without a pause and had not allowed her to say a word since she'd stepped into the chamber.

"And *you*, of all people. The most amenable of the lot." He came to a stop before her. "Any of our other sisters and I would not have been shocked, not even surprised. Any of them could have done it, and I would have been prepared to react. Eleanor, Catherine, Isabella—"

"Our sister Isabella has been dead for three years now," Maria put in quietly.

"Don't you think I know?" Charles shouted back at her. With an effort, he controlled himself, grumbling, "God rest her soul. But now I have her daughters' marriages to worry about. What are their names?"

"Dorothea and Christina. And they are only babes."

The Holy Roman Emperor drew himself up to his full height and glared at her. "We have all been born to these God-given responsibilities, Maria. It is true that marital alliances and inheritance have consolidated the power of our monarchy. But as I promised when I received this imperial crown, either I or some member of my family will sit as a ruler or consort on every royal throne of Europe. This is the only way to fight back against that devil of a Turk, Suleiman, and that fanatic, Martin Luther. A united front is the only way! And God himself has chosen me to lead the fight." Maria looked steadily into Charles's face and saw his eyes soften. "Maria, it is not for us to change what God has willed for us. As you already know, my dear sister, we—and

I mean all the members of our family—must sacrifice ourselves to God's plan."

"Just as you have sacrificed yourself." Maria's voice was cool.

He quickly nodded in agreement and then, comprehending her tone, stared at her for an instant.

As Maria returned her brother's gaze, she knew he was considering the fact that she had never addressed him this way before. In fact, she doubted that she had ever so much as spoken to him without being asked a question first. And her answer had always been one of compliance. Well, it was time to shock even him further, she thought.

"Your sacrifice, though, my dear brother, has turned out to be a very agreeable one. As fate would have it, Isabella of Portugal turned out to be a most lovely and charming wife and queen, so please remember that 'sacrifice' encompasses a whole range of experiences, and not all so pleasant as yours."

Maria gave him a thin smile. She could see the anger beginning to emerge through his surprise. But she was growing tired of his speech on *God's* imperial ambitions. And at the same time, she knew she needed to shift the subject of discussion. After all, this was not the topic that needed to be addressed right now.

Her voice was soft as she continued. "And congratulations, Charles. The palace is buzzing with the good news. Once again you are a father. And a daughter this time." Her brother's green eyes told her that she had touched something in his heart. As hard as he wanted to hide his joy, Maria could see the smile creeping into them. "How fares the babe? And Isabella?"

The Emperor paused and looked away to regard the portrait of his wife. In the picture, she was holding their first boy. When he looked back at her, Maria could tell he was still trying to analyze her change in tone.

"The child has blue eyes," he said at last.

"We shall not hold that against her. All babes have blue eyes," Maria put in gently.

"She is feisty and loud."

"What else could we expect? She is *your* daughter."

"She is bald."

"Lucky girl." Maria smiled at his surprised look. "Perhaps there will be no suitors."

Once again Charles just stared, obviously trying to understand this change that he was perceiving in his sister. The young queen watched as a range of emotions flitted over his face, ending with suspicion.

"Where is she?" he asked threateningly. "She has taught you to pretend, hasn't she? You are to act indifferently to the knowledge that you must do your duty. But it won't work I am up to her game. Where is she now? Tell me that."

"Where is who?" Maria asked in a steady voice.

"Isabel!" he shouted. "Where is Isabel hiding?"

"I thought I heard you left her with the babe only an hour ago."

"Your humor is misdirected, Maria," he snapped. "You very well know that I am talking about Isabel, our aunt. Our mother's older sister. The shrewd, conniving, subversive troublemaker Isabel. The one who stole you away before my eyes. The one who has done her best to abuse your common sense from the day you were born. The one who has no courage to appear here before me now that her treacherous plan has gone awry."

Maria felt her temper warm her skin. "I will not allow you to punish her for something I initiated."

"She needs to be under lock and key. She is dangerous to herself and to empire."

"She isn't," Maria snapped, her emerald eyes flashing with anger. "She is kind and generous. And she is the only one with any common sense among us."

Charles opened his mouth to argue, but Maria was quick to continue. "Don't waste your time speaking out so rashly against someone who, despite your differences in opinion, we all know you respect and admire—"

"I despise the woman!"

She looked at him through narrowed eyes. "Then why do you continue to invite her back to court, despite all the times she openly defies your will?"

"I need to keep track of her. For all I know, she could be selling the family jewels to Henry Tudor," Charles huffed. "Besides, I never invite her. She just marches in as if she owns the place. Nay, I scorn her actions. I loathe her!"

"You are two of a kind, and you know it!" Maria pressed. "Otherwise, why is it that every time Mother stirs in Castile, Isabel is the first person you run to?"

"Because Isabel understands her. She is as insane as her sister."

"And why is it that before you lift a finger to plan one of your campaigns, you take her into your confidence?" She heard her pitch elevating to match his. "She is as valuable to you as the best of your trusted councilors."

"It's not true," he denied, his face scornful, but his eyes telling her she was correct.

"Admit it, Charles. You like her. You respect her. And you value her opinion . . . since she is the only one who has no fear of you. Isabel is the only one who has the courage to disagree with you when she knows you are wrong. When *you* know you are wrong. She is the only one who has the courage to speak the truth."

Charles tore his eyes away from Maria's face and moved to a long table before one of the high, arched windows. The Holy Roman Emperor would never admit that he took counsel from a woman. "None of what you said is the truth, Maria. I hate her!"

Maria was the one who paused now. She let her eyes roam her brother's profile. She let him feel the heat of her scowl.

"Charles," she said at last. "Lying is not becoming in you."

The look of shock of Charles's face, as he turned to stare at her, was priceless. She had never seen him so lost for words. He appeared to her like some foundering ship, his rudderless hull buffeted by some great wind. An unexpected wind.

The Emperor shook his head to clear it. "You've spent far too much time in her company." His tone had lost its fury, but his words were uttered with conviction. "I think you have become insane . . . like her."

Maria struggled to hide the satisfaction she felt in hearing what he'd just said. She took a deep breath. This was good. If it was easier for Charles to listen to her, thinking of her as crazed, then so be it. She would speak her piece. She knew the formula. Speak only half of the truth. Then ask for anything. That's what her mother had always done. That's what Isabel practiced, as well. And though Charles might call if insanity, he always listened, and generally acted to accommodate their wishes.

"I don't think insanity is catching, but think what you will, Charles." She gestured to the table and the chairs placed around it. "I have something to tell you, and it might take a few moments. But I can assure you that you will find it quite a bit less painful than the discussion we've been having."

The look of disbelief on his face and the shake of the head did not go unnoticed by the young queen. She remained standing by the table. She would use every inch of her modest height if it gave her any advantage.

"Let's start from the beginning," she suggested, folding her hands in front of her. The time for pleasantries was over; she needed to find out how much Charles knew of the situation. "Have you met with Caroline Maule yet?"

"Who the hell is this woman?" he asked, vaguely recalling the name.

"That's good." She nodded with satisfaction. "So that means you haven't spent much time with Count Diego since arriving at the palace?"

"I have seen the count," he answered. "I know everything you've told him. About the loss of that merchant ship you were traveling on. About being saved by the Scots. About them not knowing your identity. And I know very well about your damned thickheadedness regarding a perfectly well-conceived marriage to a handsome young king."

She ignored his last remark. The good count would never have spoken of her in such terms.

"This Caroline Mauve—" the Emperor continued.

"Maule."

"Very well—Mauve, Maule—it's of no consequence." He waved her off irritably. "This is the woman who insists on having a private meeting with me?"

"She is a conniving opportunist who thinks that by sneaking into my cabin and stealing a ring of mine, she can convince you to help her with some evil business of hers." Maria forced herself to keep the note of hostility out of her voice. She clasped her hands behind her back and tried to regain her calm.

"Well, perhaps we should have Count Diego lock her away in a safe place for a few years."

"Nay, Charles. That is not what I want."

"But it sounds as if she wants to dishonor you. I assume that you don't know this woman. Why is it that she wants to slander your name?"

"She is trying to settle an old score," she said calmly.

"Against you?" The Emperor's curiosity was ready to give way to his impatience. "Tell me what this is about, Maria. I was up most of the night, and—"

"Sir John Macpherson. Her vile plot is directed against Sir John, the ship's commander." She wanted to stop there. But from the look that her brother was giving her, it was obvious that she needed to explain more fully. "From what I heard while I was aboard the *Great Michael,* this Lady Caroline was an acquaintance—a close acquaintance—of the commander some time back. And . . . and from what I hear, even though the lady has recently married another man, she still had intentions of carrying on with Sir John."

"A lovely woman," Charles suggested wryly.

Maria hurried on, surprised that her brother was actually listening to her narration. "It is amazing the things you learn about fellow travelers onboard a ship. But, as I understand it, the commander's problems really started when he openly—in front of other people aboard ship—rejected the lady."

She paused and waited for her brother to absorb all that he'd been told. His look was one of annoyance when he looked up at her.

"So what does all this have to do with you, Maria? Or with me?"

"This Lady Caroline has taken the opportunity, after stealing my ring, to slander the commander's good name. From what her own daughter told me this morning, the lady is planning to use the ring to convince you that Sir John acted in a less than desirable manner with regard to me. That he—"

"Did he?" the Emperor asked seriously. "Did he mistreat you?"

She glared down at him from where she stood. "Look at me, Charles. Do I look like one who has not been treated well?"

"Well, you are different, Maria!" he said.

"I have learned a great deal since the death of my husband," she answered. "The experience of losing a ship, of not knowing whether we were to live or die, and then of being rescued by the very people that I hoped to escape—this has been a very eye-opening experience for me. I have learned that I can no longer be one who will simply accept the decisions that others make for me. I must live my own life. Aye, Charles, I *am* different. I have grown. I have learned to live. And I have returned."

Maria watched her brother reflect on her words. Then, abruptly, he lifted his green eyes and stared at her. "But are you back only in body, Maria? Will you continue to struggle against my will? Against the decisions I have made for you regarding this Scottish match?" Charles stood and took a step toward his sister. "Are you going through with this marriage?"

She let out a deep breath and looked steadily into his eyes. "I am here in body, Charles, because that is what you need to complete this alliance. I will not defy your will in this decision . . . I will not run from this marriage, if that is God's will, and if that is what is best for both the Empire and for Scotland."

Maria saw flashes of doubt darken her brother's features.

"You betrayed my trust once already. Why should I believe you now?"

"I am your sister," she whispered. "We are of the same flesh and blood. I may have made a mistake, but I have learned enough for a lifetime. I cannot change the past, and I would not if I had the chance, Charles, because I know I am a better person today than I ever was in the past."

The Emperor looked deeply into his sister's eyes. As Maria returned his gaze, she tried to decide whether he was looking at her as someone he'd never known, or simply as a sister he was now starting to understand for the first time. Perhaps it didn't matter which it was, as long as he recognized her now as a person, and not simply an item to be bartered for a parchment of promises or a few acres of farmland. She raised her chin and looked at him with an expression of cool composure.

"Trust me, my brother, and you'll benefit by it. This marital alliance was your doing, Charles, not of my choosing. So accept this act of good will on my part, or I'll be gone. And this time for good."

Charles took a deep breath and stared down at his sister. The Holy Roman Emperor was not one to be spoken to in ultimatums, and Maria could see the wheels turning inside his head. But whatever he decided, Maria knew she had already succeeded in what she'd wanted to do, and she would be satisfied. For even though he hadn't given her an answer yet, after this talk, Caroline Maule's words against John would amount to nothing but air with the Emperor. Thoughts of Scotland flickered through Maria's mind. If she could only be this successful there. She would have to be, for that would be the next place Caroline would try out her malicious designs.

"You'll join us for dinner," he commanded.

Maria looked at him as he stood awaiting her answer. He was content with what she'd told him, and that was more than she'd hoped for. She smiled and reached out for his hand. He grasped it warmly.

"I'll have Count Diego prepare a statement of some sort that will preserve our family's dignity. Perhaps something about Mother being ill—about you having to go to Castile. The rest they know."

"I never told them my identity while I was aboard their ship."

"Perfectly understandable." He shrugged. "The trauma of losing your ship, of being adrift at sea left you shocked . . . afraid . . . ill. You didn't know friends from foes."

Maria watched as her brother prepared himself to leave. Suddenly he looked weary from the past day's excitement.

"At least, beyond this family, I am still the Emperor. Whatever I say, they have to believe."

The young queen simply nodded, stifling a smile.

"As far as this . . . woman . . . what was her name?"

"Caroline Maule," she answered hesitantly.

"Yes, that's it. You go and see her for me. Do it before dinner. I don't want to be bothered by her during the welcoming feast." The emperor slapped his gloves in the palm of his other hand. "And Maria, give her a glimpse of my new *changed* sister. A quarter hour with you and I am certain she'll be packing her bags and heading for Scotland on the next ship out. And good riddance, but watch out for her once you get there. I think the Scots are all related to one another somewhere along the line."

Again Maria nodded. It would be a pleasure to put Caroline in her place. With people like her to deal with, Maria was reminded that being queen might have its rewards.

"Lastly," her brother said from the door. "We'll have to give the commander some type of honor—a medallion or a pension or something—for saving your life."

Maria returned his gaze, fearful of the words she knew were coming.

"You can handle that task, as well. At dinner."

Chapter 22

Count Diego effortlessly climbed the marble steps and strode into the Bronze Room.

"She is coming, Your Majesty." His eyes took in the profile of the young queen sitting at a small table composing a letter. A looking glass covered the wall behind her, reflecting the images of six bronze statues of Greek deities which filled the room and added to the impression of power that seemed to emanate from the young woman herself.

Maria lifted her eyes from the empty page before her and turned them to the count. "Does she have any idea with whom she is meeting?"

"I told her nothing, Your Majesty. As far as I can tell, she knows nothing of your return and believes that she is being escorted to a private appointment with the Emperor."

"Thank you," she whispered simply.

The tall man bowed as he began to leave the room, then as if having second thoughts, he addressed the queen again. "Are you certain that you don't want me to stay?"

She smiled gently at the man. "I believe I would like to handle this alone."

"She is quite loud, Your Majesty. From what I can gather, she tries to dominate everyone around her. Then there is a question of her character. I'm sorry to say that I know from my own personal experience with her that the woman is a thief and a liar." The man paused, searching for the right words. "Perhaps the best way to handle her might be simply to send her back to Scotland at once."

Maria pushed back her chair and stood up. "She is with the Scottish delegation that will escort me to my future husband. We will not openly treat her inhospitably nor will we expedite her departure. At least, not for the moment. But we can . . ." she mulled over her own words. Even though her own power permitted it, she would be wrong to punish Caroline when she herself had been partially responsible for the situation. "I will talk to her first, Count Diego. I'll advise you if there is anything more that we need to do to reinforce our position with Lady Caroline."

With an understanding nod, the minister bowed again and departed the room.

Now, left alone once again, Maria took a moment to survey the things that surrounded her. They all represented the height of refinement and taste, yet were so hard and unalterable. So regal, she thought sadly. Well, if that was the way of things, so be it. Her eyes drifted back to the letter she had been trying to write. It was no use, she decided, picking up the parchment and immediately throwing it back down. He would never understand. How could she ever be able to explain why she had withheld the truth, why she had sought his attentions and even gone so far as to seek his heart, knowing all the while that she could never have him. No letter could answer those questions satisfactorily.

No written word could explain why her heart was breaking.

When Count Diego announced Lady Caroline, the woman standing by the window never moved. The Scottish woman tossed her long, blond hair back over her shoulder and stared at the gleaming gold of the richly jeweled coronet. The short veil held in place by the coronet hid the woman's hair, and the mantle that trailed from her shoulders glistened with the embroidered gold design of the Habsburg coat of arms.

A moment passed and Caroline coughed politely to

attract the woman's attention. Caroline wondered if it was customary to see Queen Isabella before being ushered in to see the Emperor. None of this made sense to her, for the queen had supposedly delivered a daughter only a day earlier. It wasn't possible that she could be on her feet and receiving her here. And yet, here she was.

"Pardon me, Your Majesty. I am Caroline Maule," she announced as the woman before the window continued to ignore her. "If you are not well enough . . ." The woman at the window turned slightly. "I am here to see the Emperor. He has agreed to receive me."

As the woman before the window turned to face her, Caroline's gaze locked on the splendid necklace, the jeweled pendant, the gold-cord belt with its glimmering tassels that adorned and held her surcoat at the waist. Her eyes traveled down her dress. The precious jewels sewn into her gown were so large, so radiant—she had seen nothing like them anywhere. Without thinking, Caroline bowed her head and curtsied deeply before the queen.

Watching the bowed head of the woman before her, Maria tried to constrain her distaste for her and focus only on what needed to be done.

"The Emperor has asked me to receive you instead. Now, you may rise."

Maria watched with a keen eye as the other woman raised herself to her full height. She struggled to hide her amusement over the fact that Caroline had not yet discovered her true identity. The Scottish woman still had not looked her in the face, and Maria smiled wryly as Caroline continued to glance furtively at her gown and the adorning gems.

"I am told that you have something of mine that you'd like to return to me."

The sudden snap of Caroline's head, the gaping jaw that silently opened and closed, conveyed to Maria that she'd been recognized at last.

"I am told you have a ring. A ring that was *stolen* from my cabin." Maria made sure that the word "stolen" rang out clearly in the chamber.

Caroline was clearly in shock, and failed to answer.

Her body swayed slightly and her normally pallid complexion became ashen. She looked like one who had just come face-to-face with Death himself.

"We wish to make something clear to you, Lady Caroline," Maria said coolly, keeping her tone of voice low and even. "Even though you are a guest in our land, you are not protected from any punishments for such heinous crimes as you have either committed . . . or intend to commit. The Emperor is fully cognizant of your designs, and you are a fortunate woman still to be at liberty. And the punishment he has in mind . . ." The young queen dismissed the idea with a wave of her hand. "Well, Charles's punishments are always far too harsh to win favor with me. But in your case, it appears he may just insist."

"Nay . . ." Caroline shook her head, clasping her hands before her.

"Aye," Maria asserted. "You would make a fine example of imperial justice for the rest of the delegation to take home to Scotland. If the punishment and the dungeons of Scotland are anything like those we have here . . ."

Caroline continued to shake her head slowly from side to side. Maria could see her hands trembling slightly. She took a step closer to the Scottish woman, her low voice taking on an edge of steel.

"We will *not* be trifled with," Maria warned, her eyes flashing.

Caroline Maule sank to her knees in supplication. "Please, Your Majesty . . ." she stammered out. Maria fought down her pity—Caroline was still far too dangerous a woman.

"Stand, Caroline," she commanded, watching as the blond-haired woman rose unsteadily to her feet. Maria turned toward the window again.

"The Emperor may be having second thoughts about this union . . . because of you. How comfortable could he feel, Lady Maule, sending me to your land, knowing I will be surrounded by the likes of you. Imagine his feelings for a moment, if you can. People who steal from their future queen and then are conniving enough to try to ask for a reward from her own brother.''

Maria turned and looked on as Caroline gradually regained some of her color. Too much color, she thought. She could see that Caroline was searching the lines of the marble floor for the strength to attack. She waited, and the Scottish woman turned her venomous eyes on her in an instant.

"You were with Sir John," she hissed accusingly. "You can't change that. You were aboard the *Great Michael,* and you left the ship with his men to go to his house. You are his woman and a trait—"

"Don't!" Maria commanded, holding her hand up and shaking her head disapprovingly. "If you say any more, there will be no saving you from your fate, Lady Caroline.''

Once again, the woman's color drained from her face.

"It is clear to me that no one of any authority aboard the *Great Michael* esteems you enough to share any information with you, Caroline. The delegation has been informed, and my brother's ministers have already drafted a letter to King James, summarizing all that occurred and the reasons why certain actions had to take place. Though I certainly have no reason to explain myself to you, I can assure you that Sir John has continued to behave as nothing less than the gentleman he is, and he will be rewarded richly both here and in Scotland for his gallantry.''

Maria's eyes were direct as she took two steps toward Caroline. Her gaze was steady, but her tone took on a sharper edge as she continued.

"But since we are on the subject of 'rewards'—and since your attitude could hardly be described as repentant—did I tell you that the punishment for theft from a member of the Habsburg family is a hundred lashes—in public. A dishonorable spectacle for anyone, but for a noblewoman of your stature, Lady Maule . . .'' Maria paused, her green eyes burning into the woman before her. "But I suppose such a punishment pales in comparison to what would lie in store once you have endured that. Slander of a member of the royal family, the accusation of . . . what were you about to say? Treason? I believe the last person to speak in such terms was hung, before his disemboweling and dismemberment. In fact, his tongue is still nailed to the city gate. But perhaps I can convince Charles that a simple beheading might be more appropriate."

Maria took another step toward Caroline, her voice now a whisper.

"Which would you prefer?"

The visible shudder that wracked Caroline Maule's body made it clear to Maria that she had gotten her message through. The woman's mouth opened and closed a few times, but each time Caroline held back her words and remained silent. Only her eyes darted about like those of some wild animal trapped in a cage.

Caroline Maule will retaliate someday, Maria thought. But so long as John is not her target, then she would be satisfied.

"These are my conditions, Caroline," Maria said firmly, drawing the woman's gaze to herself. "You will return what belongs to me, and then you keep your distance. I have no wish to see you, to listen to you, or to hear of you . . . ever. In return, I will try to dissuade the Emperor from—at the very least—cutting out your tongue."

Maria waited, letting her words sink in. Then, seeing Caroline's gaze rivet on her own face, she knew that she would have to reinforce her message.

"Of course, you can reject my offer," she continued, not allowing Caroline to speak. "In which case, I'll call Count Diego and have his men escort you to your new quarters . . . where you'll await the rather unpleasant fate we've been discussing."

Maria gave her only an instant to make a decision, and then moved to the table where she'd been writing. Picking up a small bell from the table, she rang it lightly.

Before the young queen had time to replace the bell on the table, Count Diego entered from a side door with two steel-helmed soldiers at his heels.

As Maria moved toward the window, she watched as realization and sudden fear registered on Caroline's features. The woman's blue eyes now flitted wildly between Maria and the three men.

"Have you chosen, Caroline?"

The tall Scottish woman's hands trembled visibly as she reached inside one of her billowing sleeves, producing the gold chain and Maria's ring.

"You may put it there." Maria nodded toward the small table. "And about my other conditions?"

"Aye, Your Majesty. I accept your conditions."

The words rolled off Caroline's tongue too quickly, too easily for Maria's comfort, but she knew she had achieved a victory here. A small but important victory.

Chapter 23

"Isabel *will* accompany me," Maria insisted.

"Not so long as I am Emperor," Charles retorted.

The footmen swung open the great doors, and he and Maria stepped past them into the magnificent hall. All eyes were upon them, and as they passed into the crowd, the kilted Scots bowed stiffly on the right side of the room while Charles's courtiers did them homage from the left.

"I would be out of my mind if I allowed you two to spend any more time alone with each other, ever again."

"We will hardly be alone, Charles." Her eyes scanned the groups of Scots, but John was nowhere to be seen. "You are sending more attendants with me than the *Great Michael* has sailors. In fact, we'll probably double the population of Scotland the day we arrive."

"Make light of it as you will, Maria. My answer is the same. Isabel is not going with you."

Maria inclined her head slightly toward Janet Maule and a hawk-eyed Sir Thomas. Caroline was conspicuously absent from the welcoming feast. *I will need to speak with Sir Thomas one day,* Maria thought grimly. She took a deep breath and they moved on.

As they crossed toward the dais, she continued. "Very well, Charles. Have it your way."

"That is very kind of you, Your Majesty," he responded wryly.

"We'll summon Mother from Castile to accompany me."

The stiffening of his arm muscles beneath her fingers spoke of his displeasure with her words. She turned and looked at him from the side. His jaw was clenched, and his look of anger admirably restrained.

"I'd be quite happy to wait for her before sailing to Scotland," she continued.

"You know, my dear sister," he said, turning his green eyes on her, "I liked the old Maria so much better."

"I'm not surprised," Maria answered. "But I like *you* as I always have."

His eyes showed something new, she thought. He was truly seeing something in her that he'd never seen before.

"Well, Charles, you are the Emperor. I turn to you for your wisdom and your command. Which one will accompany me? Joan the Mad?" She paused. "Or Isabel of Castile?"

"Very well!" Charles nearly choked on his words. "Take Isabel if you must!"

Maria bowed slightly to him. She had thought the pleasure she would get out of this new relationship she was establishing with her brother would be quite gratifying. But it couldn't be while another relationship was tearing at her heart. Maria's eyes searched the crowd again, looking for him, as Charles led her onto the dais at the far end of the room. There, the two of them would receive the Scottish guests officially.

He was here, that much she knew. While she had been meeting with Caroline, the Emperor had met with the Scottish delegation and John Macpherson to relay to them his sincere gratitude for saving her life. He had told them the official account the two of them had agreed upon, and they had all seemed to accept his words without question. Maria had asked Charles of John Macpherson's reactions to his words. He'd said there had been none. But how could it be true, she'd wondered? Feeling her throat tighten again at just the thought of the hurt she must have caused him, she blinked rapidly to fight her tears. It would be very undignified if she were to weep before a crowd such as this.

*   *   *

John stood, silent and morose, leaning on the marble pillar against the far wall. The people around him carried on with their animated talk, asking his opinion on topics which he was deaf to. He had been taken for a fool, used, and then cast aside. He had been betrayed— or was it he who had done the betraying? What of his duty to his king? As he stood nodding absently to Count Diego's comment, he decided that the answer was the same.

What a fool she had taken him for! She had conquered him as quickly as the sea can claim a ship. Another victim . . . and destroyed as pitilessly. He wondered how many men she had allured with her charms. So practiced, the pretense of naivete, that innocent expression . . . and those lies. She must had thought the selection of men on *Great Michael* quite limited, since he had been the only one she'd dallied with. He wondered how many men she'd lured to her bed.

John glanced about. The long tables beneath the colorful tapestries were laden with fish and bread and fruit, but two servants had carried out the empty cask of wine he'd been drinking from. When were they going to bring another? he wondered with annoyance.

John knew that she and the Emperor had entered the Great Hall, and he'd deliberately moved as far away from them as possible. He'd paid his respects to the Emperor earlier. Congratulated him on the birth of his daughter. That was enough.

Daughters. The Highlander grew suddenly furious at the thought of his foolishness, his silly plans for their future. There was no future. And he was better off. Here he was, a seagoing man, a warrior—and one pushing middle age—and he'd deluded himself into thinking of children! Of all things! he thought, chastising himself angrily.

John recalled talk of the queen's barrenness. *There* was a blessing, he thought. To think that . . . with so many lovers! His face became black with rage. So many children might have . . . to think that he might have planted his seed in her! His hands fisted uncontrollably at his sides. Is this the treatment she gave all of the men she bedded? Simply walking away? Playing this ghastly game of a lass with no name, and then disappearing? He had seen her walk into the Hall, but he would be damned if he would approach her.

John's face burned at the ignominy of it all. A sense of disbelief raged in his brain. He was taking this woman to his king, to be his wife. The innocent James, his own friend, still merely a boy, and John was to deliver this . . . this experienced woman for the lad to wed. He wondered how she would play her game with him. John was certain she would, but poor Kit would not know the difference.

The Highlander's thoughts ran cold. This would only need to be a short-term situation. They needed to take her back to Scotland, so Angus would step aside and free King James. But once the marriage contract was . . . fulfilled, and once James was a free man, then an annulment could be obtained. With her inability to have a child, Kit's ambassadors could go to the Pope with a good case. A very good case, he thought bitterly.

Count Diego's comments continued to register only vaguely, and John tried to concentrate on the discussion that seemed to be drawing eyes more frequently on him. They were discussing him, he realized, and the minister was singing his praises regarding the fine treatment the queen received after the rescue. If he only knew just how fine the treatment *was* that he'd given her.

By the devil, how could he have been such a fool! He had slept with his future queen! Even though she had deliberately hidden the truth from him—had caught him in her web of deception—he was still guilty of a heinous crime against his host and against his own king. And it made no difference that, other than the servants at Hart Haus and his own men, no one could be certain of the extent of their affair. It made no difference. He himself knew, and he would not forget.

Aye, his people would keep silent, and she would, as well, the Highlander thought. From what her brother had said earlier, Mary of Hungary was thrilled to go to

Scotland and assume her position as queen. He wondered if the Holy Roman Emperor had any knowledge of his own sister's darker side. The commander of the *Great Michael* had listened silently as the Emperor himself had spoken of the queen's strict religious beliefs. But only a day earlier, John and this paragon of virtue had been lying together in her bed, and there had been nothing religious in what they had done to one another, he thought. Was the entire Habsburg family—the entire Imperial Court—as corrupt as the Emperor's sister? Or were they all just as taken in by her as he had been?

Count Diego's hand on his shoulder cut into John's thoughts.

"It's time, Sir John. Everyone is waiting."

John straightened up, looking at the man curiously. "Waiting?"

The Spaniard only gestured toward the path people were opening up before them. John's gaze followed the lengthening path. The groups of guests seemed to be stepping back and creating a passageway. There were whispers, murmurs, that he could make nothing of, but all eyes in the Great Hall were riveted on him. As he stood, unsure of his next move, the path—with the undulations of a snake—kept widening and lengthening, slithering toward its mark. When the people farthest from him stepped aside, John didn't have to look to know who would be standing at the venomous head.

Maria's green eyes locked on his from the far end of the hall.

Watching him, even from this safe distance, she still felt panic prickling in her scalp, burning in her face. What would happen if he didn't move? What would happen if he decided simply to leave the party? What would happen if he approached, only to tell her to go to hell?

Maria knew enough of his temperament to know that he might do any of those things without a second thought. Charles and his wonderful ideas, she thought silently as fear and sorrow struggled for dominance in her soul. Turning her eyes momentarily from the potential spectacle before her, Maria glanced at her brother, who had moved a few paces to the side. She could see in his face that he was looking on all of this with the greatest of interest.

Suddenly, it all became clear to her. He was testing her! Testing them! This way, Charles could witness how she and John would react to one another; he wanted to know how much of what Caroline had implied to Count Diego was true. Oh, Virgin Mother, she prayed, if Charles were to see anything that might confirm any suspicion he had regarding what had gone between the two of them, John's life would be imperiled.

Her face composed and cool, she turned her regal gaze back on the crowd, and took a short step to the edge of the dais.

John, too, was well aware of the Emperor and his minister, who now stood at his side. Both men's eyes were watching his every move as closely as they were watching hers. What he'd thought about her taking all of them for fools must be true . . . at least up to now. The Highlander considered leaving. Exposing her, even. So be it if she was disgraced before her own people, he thought. But then, that would be the end of the marriage and the end of any hope of freedom for Kit.

Damn her, he cursed silently.

"I am ready," he announced without emotion to the young page who had appeared before him. "Lead on."

Those looking on in the Great Hall could only see a man and a woman from different worlds. Mary of Hungary was a queen—soft yet regal, and utterly devoted to her family. Sir John Macpherson was a naval commander, a warrior—hard, fierce, a leader of men, yet entirely devoted to his king.

What those in the hall couldn't see was the surge of emotions—the guilt in one, the anger in the other. The sorrow in one, the hatred in the other. All these things lay hidden, buried just beneath the surface of their seemingly tranquil countenances.

John strode stiffly across the hall, his eyes fixed upon the woman at the far end. As he drew nearer, the Highlander could hear a herald recounting from the side of the dais a narrative of John's bravery and of the good fortune that had guided their queen miraculously to his ship.

More lies, John thought. Count Diego appeared at his elbow and began to whisper what exactly was about to occur. More face-saving foolishness. He couldn't wait to be done with the lot of them. He was getting closer now. He didn't try to hide his contempt as his eyes swept over her gown. How she must have laughed at him when he'd offered to dress her in cloth of gold. The jewels sewn into her gown seemed by their very design to heap scorn on his simple gift. Perfect, he thought. That gown was the perfect symbol of how inadequate she must have found him, of how inadequate he truly was.

Maria saw the fleeting but disdainful glance he gave her as he got closer, then he averted his eyes. Summoning all the courage she could muster, she steeled herself to the hot pokers that were punching holes in her heart. She had to get through this, she reminded herself. For him. She continued to watch him with a gaze she hoped appeared cold and reserved.

As he came to a halt, he bowed at the waist. Then, raising his gaze, he seemed to fix on something directly behind her. He was truly beautiful, she thought. His long black hair was tied back, and his face had the chiseled look of a god. His tartan and his kilt were dark and colorful in contrast to the brilliant white of his linen shirt. His muscular legs were spread at shoulder width, and the high, soft leather of his boots told of a man of wealth, a man of action. Maria gazed up into blue eyes that once had been so full of love for her, but were now cold and vacant. He stared through her as if she didn't exist.

The two stood facing each other, and for a moment, neither spoke.

She drew in her breath and tried to steady her trembling hands. Then, turning to the nobleman standing beside her, she picked up from a velvet cushion that the man held, a heavy golden chain and medallion and held it up before her.

They both knew what she had to do, but there was no way she could accomplish the task without his cooperation. Her green eyes pleaded with him, and he returned her gaze . . . but with a look that spoke of utter contempt. Then he lowered his head, allowing her to place the chain around his neck.

"Please accept this token of our gratitude for your service." Maria thanked God her voice was clear. She nodded in Charles's direction. "The Emperor himself has made arrangements to reward you amply."

The Highlander bowed at her in courtesy. His face was a mask, and he never took his eyes off Maria.

"I thank the Emperor," John said graciously, his expression never faltering, "but no more reward is necessary. You yourself, Your Majesty, have already rewarded me well."

He bowed again before turning on his heel and striding into the crowd.

If the Highlander had slapped her across the face, driven a sword into her heart, Maria's pain could not have been more grievous than the agony she felt as her beloved moved across the hall and disappeared into the night.

Chapter 24

It was a mistake to try to see him aboard the *Great Michael*, and Maria knew it, but she was desperate to have a moment alone with him. Yesterday, on their first day at sea, she had sent a messenger requesting his presence in her cabin, but he'd ignored her request and had never come.

Now, though, she had a valid reason to see him. News of Janet Maule's elopement had apparently spread like wildfire among the ship's occupants, but word of it had only now reached her ears. And Maria needed to find out from John whether Janet and David were, in fact, safe and had been adequately provided for financially.

Maria had known that it would come to this. From her personal belongings, the young queen drew out the short letter left for her by Janet at the palace. Maria glanced at the neat script of the young woman's hand. According to the note, Caroline had threatened to disgrace her before her father if she would not agree to certain conditions having to do with her future queen. Maria didn't need Janet's full narration of Caroline's intentions to know what the young woman was so discreetly referring to. But in Janet's own words, she knew that this would be only the first of many actions that her stepmother would extort from her in the days to come. And knowing also that her father would never understand her love for David Maxwell, Janet had written that perhaps the time was nearing for her to cut her ties with the past and seek her destiny at David's side.

Maria held the note in her lap. After their meeting, Caroline had not ventured from her bedchamber. But

Maria knew that the Scottish woman's deep hatred would not be restrained for long, especially when the woman realized that—given her stepdaughter's closeness to Maria—she had a way to strike back. From Caroline's point of view, Janet's friendship with Maria had to offer firsthand knowledge of the queen's romance. The fact that Janet had no prejudice against John would make her a very credible witness—to Charles and to King James. Maria had no doubt that Caroline expected her stepdaughter to cooperate "freely" and supply corroborating details of the affair between Maria and John.

But Janet had thwarted her stepmother's plans. At the side of her beloved, Janet Maule had eluded Caroline and fled to freedom.

Freedom. Maria put the letter away and allowed one of her attendants to open the cabin door. Moving quickly through the ship, the young queen stepped out onto the deck. As another attendant placed a cloak around her shoulder, Maria thought how unpleasant it was to be surrounded with servants and attendants every moment of one's life. For as long as she'd lived, this had been her experience, but she had never even noticed it. At least, not until she'd tasted the sweet nectar of freedom for a few precious days.

She simply couldn't breathe with so many surrounding her. Pampering her. Doing their utmost to please her. These young noblewoman were strangers to her, and Maria knew Charles had seen to it that this would be the case. Less chance for anything else happening that might jeopardize his plans. All strangers to her—with the exception of her aunt.

Isabel's presence on the ship provided Maria with the only agreeable antidote to the lethal doses of cheerfulness that these other women provided. Of course, listening to her, one wouldn't normally think of Isabel's conversation as agreeable. Cranky and difficult to the bitter end, the older woman had finally agreed to accompany Maria to her destination. But no farther. Whatever miserable port they put into, that port was the one she'd be departing from immediately. That was how she'd put it to Maria and to Charles. Indeed, her approach to her niece and nephew could hardly be described as subtle. Isabel made no attempt to hide her dissatisfaction with the new arrangements and with Maria's decision to cooperate with such blockheaded, old-fashioned diplomacy.

So the young woman had listened to everything Isabel said, and then warmly and mildly, thanked her for accompanying her throughout this ordeal. Though Isabel's contribution thus far would hardly be categorized as "moral support," Maria knew that if the time came that she needed her, Isabel would prove invaluable by her side.

For somewhere, buried deep in the recesses of her mind, the young queen was not yet willing to give up. She hadn't wed the Scottish king yet, so perhaps there might still be a chance to again join with John.

Maria breathed in the fresh sea air and moved casually across the crowded deck toward the railing. It was a colorful group on deck, and Maria sensed a bit of competition between the passengers for her notice. As she passed, groups of boisterous and restless nobles—both Scottish and Spanish—approached Maria, but she simply nodded to them and moved on, scarcely paying any attention to them at all. As she walked, her eyes searched for only one man. But the search proved fruitless.

He should be here, she thought. He was commanding this ship and the three others that she could see flanking the *Great Michael,* sailing them to Scotland without his best navigator, and John should be right on deck. But he was nowhere to be seen. Hiding the feelings of hopelessness and despondency that were washing over her, Maria gazed back at the high stern deck where she knew he preferred to keep watch over the activities of the sailors on deck and aloft. But he wasn't there, either. Then, letting her eyes drift toward the doorway leading to his cabin, she considered going below, storming in and demanding that he speak with her. She considered it, but for only a moment. Maria knew she couldn't go to his cabin. Any misstep now could prove fatal for him.

Well, she could wait, she decided, resigning herself to stay there for as long as it took to get even a glimpse of him. Maria leaned against a railing, pretending to enjoy the sun and the salty breezes, and watched as her dutiful attendants did the same.

Letting out a long breath, Maria caught a glimpse of someone else's eyes upon her. Not a tall and handsome Highlander, but a young sandy-haired lad was seeking her out—but shyly. She could see David's young brother, Andrew, standing not too far away beside one of the ship's officers, feeding line to the sailors who were repairing a section of rigging. The boy, obviously feigning indifference to the groups of nobles milling about on the deck, still peeked now and then in Maria's direction. The next time she caught his eyes upon her, she motioned to him to come closer. But the lad quickly turned his back, pretending that he never saw her gesturing to him.

Well, she certainly should be able to handle an eight-year-old, she thought. Speaking quietly to one of her attendants, Maria asked her to go and invite the boy to join her where she stood by the railing.

Maria watched the burly sailors pause attentively as the young woman approached them. Andrew and her attendant exchanged brief comments, drawing smiles from the onlookers. Upon seeing her messenger come back alone, Maria realized that perhaps this wouldn't be as easy as she thought. The message the boy had sent was that he was working and not allowed to rest in the middle of his shift.

This time Maria didn't hesitate an instant and went after him herself.

She fought back her smile on seeing the expression of terror in his face as he realized that she was coming after him. The sailors formed a circle as she entered their midst.

The boy had courage, she thought, noting that he was clearly fighting the inclination to turn and run away.

"Andrew," she said, stopping only a step away. She realized that a few more sailors working in the area had stopped their work and were watching the exchange with some interest. "I was hoping we could talk just for a short while."

He shook his head in denial, focusing on the rope in his hands.

She stepped closer and ruffled his hair with one hand, which made the boy pale and the sailors around him laugh.

"I thought we were friends. I've missed your company," she said quietly, leaning down and speaking into his ear. "I'll give you a choice. I hug you, a tough young man, in front of your fellow sailors, or you come and keep me company for just a short while." She straightened up and looked at him. "Which is it, Andrew?"

Maria knew from the look in his eyes, that he would have preferred death to a hug. After only the shortest of pauses, the boy dropped his chin to his chest and led his captor out of the circle of the grinning sailors.

Maria followed him to the railing, where she gestured for her attendants to give them some space to communicate privately. Andrew turned and sat against the gunwales of the ship, only to spring up again immediately as if he were on fire.

"What's wrong?" she asked worriedly, glancing at the railing.

The lad looked at her awkwardly. "I am not allowed to sit before you, am I, Your Majesty?"

"Of course you are," she answered. "I invited you to join me, didn't I?"

He just shrugged his shoulders in response. Maria pointed to a pair of casks not far from where they stood, and the two sat down, though Andrew still had the look of one being led to the gallows.

"You're angry with me," she said decidedly. "Why is that?"

"Who says I'm angry?" The young lad's eyes flashed with alarm only for a moment before he quickly averted them. Maria bit her lips to keep from smiling as he took in everything around them, but never turned his gaze back to her.

"I am not blind, Andrew. Have I done anything to you? Anything that has upset you?"

Again, he simply shrugged his shoulders.

"Answer me, Andrew. Or I swear I'll hug you right here."

He turned abruptly in her direction, wide-eyed.

"And kiss you, too, if that's what will get your attention."

"Queens are used to having their own way, aren't they?" he grumbled.

"Of course, but obviously not so much as you are accustomed to having your own way." Maria looked down at the lad for few more moments before continuing. He was wearing the same leather doublet and wool shirt that he'd been wearing on the way to Antwerp. His kilt was long, hanging over his roughly sewn shoes of sailcloth. "Are you warm enough, Andrew?"

The boy looked up, startled by her question. "Aye, of course, I'm warm. It's a fine day."

"It is, isn't it?" she said, her gaze sweeping over the sparkling expanse of sea.

"Aye, the wind is from the southeast, and we'll be home in . . . no time." His voice faltered as he finished.

"Tell me what has upset you so." Other than your brother David leaving the ship, she thought silently.

Andrew scuffed the painted wood of the deck, and squirmed uncomfortably.

"Is there something I can do to make you—"

"You've made the commander sad!" the boy blurted out suddenly, his eyes flashing. "And angry, too!"

The boy's straightforward accusation stunned her momentarily.

"I am angry because he is," Andrew continued with the bluntness of his age. "When Sir John heard that you were headed up here, he went below to his cabin. He didn't want to see you or talk to you. Well, what Sir John says goes for me, as well. I answer only to him . . . er, Your Majesty."

Maria just stared into the boy's large brown eyes. The fact that John avoided her so openly that a child could see it hurt her deeply. And the fact that Andrew had been left behind by his only kin hurt her, as well. But what else could David have done? she wondered.

"Sir John is a fine man to look up to," Maria whispered. "But whatever differences exist between Sir John and me now . . . well, I hope to mend them."

"It's not that easy, you see. With Mistress Janet and David, it was different. To make it work . . . well, they had to go away and leave me behind. But now, I'm left with the commander. And he is different than you. So . . . so . . ." The boy's voice trailed off, and he stared glumly at his feet.

So if we mend our differences, that means you'll be left behind again, she thought sadly to herself. With no one.

"Andrew, I just want peace with Sir John." She placed her hand on the boy's arm. He didn't flinch this time. "He'll keep you beside him. He will care for you. Your brother is a good man, and he left you in the care of another good man." She paused before continuing. "Have you any other kin?"

"Aye, I have an aunt who feeds me when we dock at Dundee." He glanced up at her defiantly. "But I'll be a sailor, not a farm lad."

"Of course," she replied gently.

"What you said before about David and Sir John"— the young boy looked down at his callused hands—"I know they are good men. David talked to me before he left. He told me that the commander had already offered to look after me, and David had accepted his offer. He also said that someday soon he and Mistress Janet would come for me. And as far as the commander, I know that he cares for me, too. I know that. Yesterday, when everyone figured out why Mistress Janet and David were nowhere to be found, I thought Sir Thomas was going to beat me, instead. But the commander put both Sir Thomas and his wife off the *Great Michael,* and stowed them aboard the *Eagle* . . . to protect my neck."

"No one has any right to punish an innocent for something others have done."

Andrew looked up into Maria's face. "Do you think what they've done was wrong?"

She shook her head. "Nay, lad. They've followed a path that leads to happiness. I think what they've done is very right."

Andrew nodded with satisfaction. "That's what Sir John said. He says they've done right, as well. Though I don't think Sir Thomas was even a wee bit happy to hear it."

Maria felt a knot rising in her throat. If things had gone differently—if John had known her true identity—would he have placed their love over what his duty required of him? Above his loyalty to his king? Would he have accepted her and loved her and been happy to turn away from everything?

She would have. She knew that. But she'd never told him. Perhaps, she thought, perhaps she'd never allowed herself the chance to tell him.

"That decides it, Lady Mar—I mean, Your Majesty," Andrew piped in. "Now it's two of you saying the same thing. Aye, I'm going to be proud of my brother and Mistress Janet." The young boy nodded vigorously. "After we come to port, Sir John said we may be going on to Benmore Castle. I wasn't sure what I would say about David when we arrived there. But now I know. I'll speak the truth of them."

Maria gathered the young boy's hand in hers and held it tight. He let her.

Was this truly the end? she thought. Had she crushed any chance of happiness for the two of them? The questions jabbed at her conscience. Had she done wrong from the first in not telling him the truth when they'd met? Nay, deep in her soul she knew that if she had, she and John could never have loved. His honor would not have allowed it. She splashed away a tear.

"Are you sad, Your Majesty?"

"Aye, Andrew. I am a bit."

"About Sir John?"

"Don't you be troubling yourself over it, lad. It will all work out for the best."

"May I go now, Your Majesty?"

Maria looked back at the young boy sitting beside her with his hand still in hers. She nodded to him as she let his hand go. "Thank you, Andrew, for talking to me."

"Thank you," he answered. "I'll tell Sir John that he doesn't have to avoid you. That you don't want him to be angry. I'll tell him that you are not going to run away with him, so he doesn't need to be afraid of leaving me behind."

"But Andrew . . ." Maria's mouth hung open as the lad sprang off his seat without another word and disappeared into the crowd.

Chapter 25

Scotland was a country in chaos.

Looking out from atop the flat roof of the Abbey of Holyrood, Maria pulled her cloak tighter about her and peered through the mist at the rain-darkened walls of Edinburgh Castle, rising on a rocky summit above all else at the far end of the town. The thatch-and-wattle town before her was new, rebuilt less than fifteen years ago, but she could see the still unrepaired damage to the castle walls where the English cannons had hammered away after the troops had burned the burgh. The English hadn't succeeded in taking the castle. Maria sighed deeply, considering the violence of men, and she wondered vaguely why the English commanders had spared the abbey and its unfinished royal residence.

But they had spared it, and had finally been pushed southward across the Borders. Relative calm had returned to the north country, and an infant king was now on the verge of manhood.

As the rain began to fall harder, Maria considered all that had occurred in the last week and all that she now knew of the months prior to their arrival.

On coming ashore in a hard rain at the tiny port village on the Firth of Forth, they had been greeted by no welcoming party. Only an armed company of warriors had been there to escort Maria and her attendants, without ceremony, to the Abbey of Holyrood. Without much fanfare, the Scottish nobles accompanying her from Antwerp had slogged onward through the muddy street to the formidable castle that loomed over Edinburgh. From the whispers that she'd heard from them, great changes had occurred in the two months that they were away, and the differences had been astonishing even to them.

From what she could gather, Scotland's ruling nobility had, for some time, been gradually separating into factions. Apparently, for almost a year the country had been on the verge of civil war, with some nobles loyal to the Stuart king openly hostile to the Douglas camp and to Angus, the Lord Chancellor. Maria knew before coming to Scotland that Angus had been married to Margaret Tudor, the king's mother, since James IV's death at Flodden Field. She also knew that he had struggled with her for power during the child-king's minority. But what Maria now learned was that while John Macpherson and the delegation were in Antwerp, the Pope's decree had reached Scotland, annulling the marriage of Angus and Margaret Tudor. There was even a rumor that Margaret had immediately married another nobleman, Henry, Lord Darnley. At any rate Angus, now lacking any legitimate claim to rule in the name of the royal family, had apparently imprisoned his former wife, placed the king in "protective custody," and effectively seized all power for himself.

Chaos indeed, Maria thought, turning her eyes to the south and the dark hills partially hidden behind the thick, low-hanging clouds. A cold, damp breeze began to pick up as she stood, considering the facts as she understood them.

Angus's marriage to the widowed Queen Margaret, and later his control of Scotland, had been largely supported by Margaret's brother, King Henry of England. But now, with Margaret's annulment granted by Rome less than a month ago, the Lord Chancellor must be feeling seriously threatened by the possible withdrawal of support by the English king. After all, Angus was no longer married to Margaret Tudor. Angus must have known that the annulment was coming, Maria reasoned, and he knew he would be needing a new ally—and quickly. The Holy Roman Emperor Charles was just the man he needed backing him, and Maria knew that Charles was not one to balk at an offer like this one.

And that brother of mine knew all this, Maria realized.
Charles knew that Scotland was about to be torn apart,
but he kept silent about it anyway. And then he sent
her on her merry way. Best of luck to you with your
new husband, Charles had told her, his face the very
picture of sincerity. From that alone, she should have
guessed the chaos that would be awaiting them. Well,
Isabel had immediately perceived that all was not well
and had offered to stay, and Maria was grateful for her
aunt's company.

For a week now they had remained at the abbey with
no word from the Lord Chancellor, and of course, none
from her future husband either. The abbot, a dry and
leathery-looking man who seemed to brighten only when
Isabel was present, had supplied the few facts they'd
been able to gather, and he had told them—well, he'd
told Isabel—that Angus had been forced to take a large
force of men to the Borders, to quell the rising tide of
outlawry and violence that was destabilizing the region
and threatening to bring English troops onto Scottish
land once again to settle matters themselves. From what
Maria could surmise, Angus needed to show his south-
ern neighbors that he could control the Borders as well
as the rest of Scotland.

Maria had not complained. The longer she had to wait
for this dreaded marriage, the less real it seemed. But
then this morning, the abbot had come to the abbey's
guest quarters and, sitting beside Isabel, had informed
them that the Earl of Angus had left his troops at the
Borders and was riding back to Edinburgh to greet the
future queen.

He was going to rush this marriage, she decided, considering everything. Angus needed to see that the marriage was consummated thus sealing the treaty between
Scotland and the Holy Roman Empire. Angus and his
Douglas clan were the ones responsible for this upcoming wedding of the Scottish king. And from all that had
taken place here in Scotland over the past month or two,
she could well understand the man's motives for seeking
to finalize his pact with the Emperor.

Maria turned and looked to the northwest, past the great hill and the castle. The Highlands were there somewhere. And Benmore Castle. Perhaps John was out there, standing in the same rain. Looking southward toward Edinburgh.

She had done her best to hide the fact that the abbot's news distressed her, but she wasn't really sure how successful she'd been. She already disliked the Earl of Angus. He was clearly an ambitious, power-hungry man with no sense of integrity. Curious, she thought, that Caroline Maule is a cousin to the man. Angus's message to the abbot had referred to the upcoming wedding ceremony. It would be conducted, the Lord Chancellor promised, as soon as the trouble with the Borders could be contained, and the King safely conducted to Edinburgh.

Maria wondered for a moment how much of what she heard was true. Some reports had it that both Margaret Tudor and her new husband were imprisoned in Stirling Castle. Others held that the Queen Mother's husband, Lord Darnley, was free in the Highlands to the north, gathering support from the clans there. It appeared to be common knowledge that King James was being held against his will at Falkland Palace, in spite of the Lord Chancellor's denials. Thanks to Isabel and the abbot, her aunt's willing informant, Maria was beginning to get a steady flow of news. Maria was truly glad Isabel had agreed to stay.

Isabel had taken one look at the confusion surrounding their arrival and had softened considerably to her niece's plight. She had apparently seen that the young queen had no one to support her. The delegation had quickly dispersed, and the four ships under Sir John's command had immediately set sail, reportedly northward to Dundee.

John Macpherson had gone, and nothing had been resolved between them, Maria thought with a pang of sorrow. Or perhaps, all had been resolved.

They had been settled into the royal residence at the abbey, a favorite stopping place for Margaret Tudor, the

King's mother. It was curious to Maria that even though she had never met Queen Margaret in person, she couldn't help but feel a sense of intimacy with the woman. Margaret, too, had been wed at a young age, and she, too, had an aggressive and ambitious brother who interfered and planned out her life for her. But now, after two marriages, she had taken her future in her own hands and had wed a man of her own choosing at last—only to be imprisoned by her ex-husband.

With a last look northward, Maria went down the spiral steps to her abbey chambers and, hanging her dripping cloak on a peg by the door, sat down by the small fire. After exchanging a few words with Isabel, who sat sewing, Maria sat back to wait for Angus's arrival.

Looking into the fire, she wondered if she were nothing more than a puppet. A fancy, expensive, elegantly dressed puppet bought to play a part and divert the people. Perhaps that was the role of all nobility these days, she thought, forcing down the anger that was threatening to push to the surface. Letting out a long breath, she ignored Isabel's questioning look and picked up the small volume of Scots poetry she'd borrowed from the abbot's collection. Opening it to her place, Maria went back to Blind Harry's exploits of a hero named "The Wallace."

Archibald Douglas, the Earl of Angus was an extremely unlikable and arrogant man, Maria thought, her smile plastered on her face. Even worse than she had imagined. Perhaps he wanted to impress her with his "manly" drive to rule, or perhaps he simply thought that because Maria was a woman, he could say anything. But whatever the reason, he blustered and bragged, strutted about the chamber, and tugged his long black beard— in all, making very little effort to hide his ambitions. Angus's behavior was appalling, but still she remained where she was seated, and tried to memorize his every word. She would not be so foolhardy as to give him any clue of just how insidious she thought his plans to be. Nay, she had already decided to play the simpleton and agree wholeheartedly to everything he suggested. But only for now.

The Earl of Angus had already imprisoned a king and a queen. She was not about to give the Lord Chancellor any reason to lock her up at Edinburgh Castle before the wedding took place. It was an act she really thought was not beyond the realm of possibility. She had played this game with her brother, and the Emperor was far better at it than this man. But she was not going to underestimate him. She knew how to play this game. And she preferred to play it from the relative freedom of the Abbey of Holyrood.

"In two weeks the Borders will be secured," Angus announced reassuringly. "Then I'll be bringing back our young king to Edinburgh for the day of the wedding. There will be no time for any troublemakers to disturb the festivities, and this whole affair will be settled. It will be a day of joy for you, Your Grace, and for Scotland."

Once again, she simply nodded.

"Of course, you do understand that I am relying on you, Your Grace." He paused, giving her a knowing look. "I am relying on you to convey to your brother immediate news of . . . well, of news that . . ."

Even though it would have given her great satisfaction to let him stew uncomfortably, looking for a courteous way to speak his mind, she knew the wiser course, at this point, was to help the arrogant boor through his difficulty.

"That the marriage is consummated?" Maria suggested, smiling sweetly.

"Aye. That's it." Angus nodded his approval. "Since you're barren, there is no point in waiting for a miracle to occur before your brother forwards the second part of your dowry to us. In my opinion, your words on the matter should be sufficient for all concerned . . . Your Grace."

It seemed impossible that he could not know how cruel he sounded. "That's very kind of you, Lord Chancellor."

"Also, in your letter to the Emperor, if we may, I'd

like you to mention the possibility of him sending some of his Imperial troops along with the dowry." Angus stopped by the window and stared out at the courtyard below. After a short pause, he continued, sounding like a man thinking aloud. "With these fools in the north acting up, a show of force by the Emperor would benefit us all."

This was more than Maria could believe. How could this man have survived in power all these years? She was not yet married to James, and Angus was already asking her to help bring in foreign troops.

"Could I rely on you to grant me that, Your Grace?"

"M'lord, I understood you to have excellent rapport with my brother. You surely do not need my help in such a trivial matter, now do you?"

"Aye, Your Grace. I do, I do. You see, I mean to send a letter to the Emperor after your wedding, with the same request. But a note from Your Grace in support of my petition—why, that would mean a certain response from your brother, I should think."

Maria couldn't agree more. Angus was inviting the wolf into the hen house, and Charles would jump at the opportunity, she was quite certain.

"Whatever you think best, Lord Chancellor," she agreed in her most vapid tones. "I don't know how much Charles reads of the lower-level correspondence, but I'm fairly certain he reads my letters. As you already know, these days are exceptionally trying for my brother." Reciting the Emperor's exact words, she continued with a pained expression, "My poor, dear Charles is extending himself in every direction. He has to crush rebellion in Spain, fight with the nasty French, hold back the Turk's advances in the east, control Lutheran heresy in Germany, even protect the Pope in Rome! Oh, my heavens . . . on top of it all, he will be extremely put out if he is summoned to Scotland."

"But perhaps, if you were to ask . . . ?" Angus suggested.

"Aye, if I were to ask . . ." Maria gave him a honeyed

smile. "The dearest thing will do anything if I were to ask. And don't fret, m'lord, I'll ask."

"Then it's settled!" The man rubbed his hands together and then smoothed his long beard reflectively.

Seeing the earl so content, she paused before asking her final question. "Once I am wed, though, I hope you don't expect me to spend much time in some hunting hovel."

"Oh, no, Your Grace. Though Falkland Palace may not be up to the standards you are accustomed to, it is quite comfortable. And once I've hammered the outlaws of the Borders into submission and secured the allegiance of the rebels to the far north, we'll devise a progress for Your Grace through the kingdom that will please you. And, of course, we could oversee the building of a new palace, if you care to." Angus tugged at his beard. "It's just that I have to . . . well, provide for the young king at one of the royal residences for a while yet." As an afterthought, Angus concluded, "For his own safety, of course."

"Of course," she repeated with another vacuous smile.

Maria watched as the Earl of Angus roused himself and rubbed his hands together. The man was clearly delighted with himself and his good fortune at finding such an agreeable queen.

"I have naught more to trouble you with, Your Grace," he announced, bowing to her formally. "I must return to the Borders for a fortnight, and when I return, we shall have a wedding to attend to."

"M'lord," she called softly, as if she were just recalling something, "with only a fortnight or so to the wedding, do you think there is enough time—" Maria brought her hand to her mouth, stopping her words, a look of mortification lighting her face.

"Enough time for what, Your Grace?"

"Before I left, my brother . . . the Emperor demanded that I forward him a wedding portrait of me immediately. And I've been here a week already and done nothing to honor his request."

"Your Grace," Angus said impatiently, "I assure you

there will be plenty of time after your wedding for a portrait to be painted."

"Well, then I suppose my letter to the Emperor will need to be delayed for at least that long, as well," she replied, a note of petulance in her voice. "But I suppose if I must wait that long to gratify the Emperor's only desired recompense for his efforts, I could send off for Charles's painter, Jan von Vermeyen. Of course, Vermeyen is always quite busy, and it might take him perhaps six months or so before he could come. Oh heavens, that brings us to winter, doesn't it. Oh, well. I guess he won't be able to come until next summer." Her voice again cheerful, Maria turned her bright green eyes fully upon him. "But you can wait a year or so for a few soldiers, can't you, Lord Chancellor?"

The look of horror in Angus's face was priceless, and Maria fought back her smile.

"Nay, Your Grace. I fear we can't wait that long. It . . . we simply can't. Certainly, your brother is a reasonable man. If you were to send a letter with the promise of a portrait to follow soon after."

"Clearly, Lord Chancellor, you don't know the Emperor's mind on such important matters." She turned the poutiest face on him that she could muster. "If you think I am going to send my brother a letter asking for a few pieces of gold and some soldiers, and not even do him the courtesy of sending the portrait that he so much desires, then you are mistaken, m'lord. Quite, quite mistaken."

"I am certain there is something we can do."

"Very true. We'll wait for Vermeyen." Maria brightened suddenly. "You know, Lord Chancellor, as well as I that I *should* wait for the best."

Maria again watched from the corner of her eye the struggle that Angus was going through. Charles had asked for no such portrait. As far as Maria knew, her brother couldn't care less for such a gift. But if she could use this ploy as a way of passing on the Lord Chancellor's rather despicable intentions to those who really served King James . . .

"I fear I have a headache coming on, Lord Chancellor," she announced, unwilling to give the man time to consider the matter. "I'm not accustomed to so much . . . so much *hard work* all at one time. So, since you agree, I'll forward a letter to Vermeyen and ask him to join us here next summer." She put a hand to her forehead as if checking for a fever. "With Charles and Queen Isabella redecorating the palace at Antwerp, I wonder if he'll be able to make it then. Perhaps two years might be more realistic."

"I assure you there is no need for you to wait that long," the Earl replied unhappily. "Scotland boasts one of the finest portrait artists living. Elizabeth Boleyn Macpherson's reputation is well-known."

"A woman?" Maria gasped. "A woman artist!"

"Aye. They tell me she studied with Michelangelo himself."

Angus ran a hand down his beard, obviously trying to think through what he'd just suggested. But it was Elizabeth Macpherson's name that Maria had wanted to hear all along. But she was not about to admit to the Lord Chancellor that she had knowledge of the woman. It was obvious from all she'd heard before that Angus didn't consider the Macphersons as allies.

"I have never met a woman painter before," she announced. "How exciting!"

Again, Maria noticed the doubtful look in the man's face. "But," she said with the look of one having second thoughts, "I don't think so. I've seen Vermeyen's work. And this woman's . . . why, she could be a fake. She could make me look horrible. Nay, Lord Chancellor . . ."

"She produces excellent work, I assure you. Excellent!" he emphasized.

"I don't wish to sound stubborn or condescending in the face of your obvious regard for this painter's work, but I have not seen any of her work and until such time as I might see some of her paintings and speak with her of her methods . . ." Maria shook her head. "I, for one, am not willing to risk postponing Vermeyen's visit for an *additional* year. Don't you agree, m'lord?"

She stared at him blankly, waiting for an answer. The furrows of the man's forehead seemed to be deepening by the minute. He was aging before her very eyes.

"Your Grace, if I could arrange a meeting with Elizabeth Macpherson in the next two or three days, would you be willing to speak to her?"

"I don't know, Lord Chancellor." She smoothed her skirt over her lap. "With little more than a fortnight to my wedding, I don't know if I have the time—"

"Lady Elizabeth has done portraits of Margaret . . . the Queen Mother, in a very short span of time. If I could convince her to come to you in the next couple of days, she would probably have your painting finished by the wedding." Angus gave a weary sigh. "Then perhaps, Your Grace, you would consider corresponding with your brother?"

Maria tried hard not to show her excitement at his words. Taking her time to answer, she pretended to be in deep thought. "Well! The work won't be as good, but perhaps Charles will be satisfied. He's very particular, you know."

"Aye!" Angus said happily. "Your brother's satisfaction will be ample reward in itself, Your Grace."

"Very well, Lord Chancellor. Have this Lady Elizabeth sent to me."

"I believe she and her husband are in Stirling, Your Grace. But you should know, the Macphersons are an independent lot."

Maria's face affected boredom.

"But she will be here in two or three days at the most. I assure you of that."

Maria nodded. "Very well, Lord Angus. Do finish up your business in that Border place, will you? You could be such a help to me here."

Angus began to respond, but then closed his mouth and bowed deeply.

"Aye, Your Grace. It is my pleasure to serve you," he said, backing away from her.

"Oh, one more thing," the young queen said as Angus paused anxiously. "Since I will not be meeting with King

James before the wedding. I wish to correspond with him by letter. As we've just been discussing, I am a devoted letter writer. Please see to it that I have couriers to deliver my correspondence."

"I will see to it, Your Grace. It will be done."

Chapter 26

A hush fell over the crowd of men gathered in the hall of Ambrose Macpherson's town house in Stirling. The circle of noblemen turned to receive John Macpherson, who was just descending the great stairs in the hall. The Highlander had only arrived within the hour after a hard ride from Dundee, where he'd anchored his fleet. His mud-covered clothes were barely shed when one of the servants had brought his brother's message, asking John to come down to his meeting. He didn't need to be told what it was all about. He knew the subject at hand.

Looking about the room, John grasped the hand of his eldest brother, Alec, as his friend Colin Campbell, the Earl of Argyll, stepped up and clapped him hard on the shoulder, the earl's fierce face belying the welcome in his eyes. John knew all of the six nobles assembled there. Besides his two elder brother and Colin Campbell, the other three—the earls of Huntly, Ross, and Lindsay—were all Stuart men and devoted antagonists of the power-hungry Earl of Angus.

As John stepped into their midst, some settled into large carved chairs as their discussion picked up once again.

"Is it true, Sir John? Is it true that blackguard Angus is forcing this marriage to take place inside of a fortnight?"

"Why do you ask the question when you already know the answer, Ross?" Lord Lindsay interrupted before John could speak. His voice was subdued, and he was shaking his head in annoyance. "Angus has already sent us the details and conditions of the marriage."

John's eyes fixed on the jeweled hilt of Lord Lindsay's dirk. It had been a gift of James IV, given to him by Queen Margaret just before they'd marched south to that fateful battle at Flodden Field. The queen. John's mind flitted to Maria. So this was it, he thought, fighting the anger that burned within him. She was truly to become his queen.

"Then tell us this, John. Is it true that he has asked you to accompany the King from Falkland Palace to Edinburgh?" Ross asked impatiently, glaring at Lindsay.

"Aye, tell us that, Sir John," Lindsay added, returning Ross's look coldly.

Turning from the animated Lord Ross to the flint-eyed Lindsay, John responded in a low tone. "I have received such an order. But the good Lord Chancellor is not so foolish as to let me bring the King without an escort of his choosing. A troop of five hundred of Angus's men are to accompany us on the trip."

"I am glad, at least, that one of us is going to accompany Kit." Huntly's voice, from the far end, drew everyone's attention. "John, with you away as much as you've been, Angus must think your mind is the least poisoned against him. We have to use that to our advantage."

"Angus asked my brother to go because he knows John will let no harm befall the King," Alec Macpherson put in. "And he knows the lad would follow John to the gates of Hell."

"And the purpose of the five hundred soldiers is to make certain that the two of them don't take that route." Colin Campbell, stretching his muscular legs before his chair, spoke through tented fingers. "With only ten days, Angus would prefer a direct route to Edinburgh."

"But why?" Lindsay questioned with restrained vehemence. "Angus is pushing this wedding along far too quickly. It goes against all that we thought we would do. With the Queen Mother under his thumb at Stirling, and the King of Falkland, he was what he wants—control.

We all thought he'd at least put off this damnable wedding until he could settle the Border affairs and secure the Lowlands for himself. I hardly thought he'd be so hurried and willing to step down."

"Bah . . ." Ross threw his hands in the air. "I can't believe you still put a whit of credence in his word of freeing young Jamie after this blasted thing." He whirled and pointed a gnarled finger at the King's friend, addressing him exasperatedly. "You, Sir John, you don't believe any of it, do you?"

John looked from face to face.

"It is all a lie," he responded simply.

With a satisfied look at Lindsay, Ross turned to Ambrose Macpherson, who had been standing quietly against the hearth, his arms crossed over a massive chest. "And you, Ambrose? What do you say?"

"John's right. It's a scheme." Ambrose pronounced the words with utmost confidence. "Angus and his Douglas clan will never willingly relinquish their rule over the King . . . or over Scotland."

"If we accept your view," Lindsay put in, "what are we to do? We've tried to push Angus before, and he's been more than ready to crush all opposition. We had six thousand men at Linlithgow only a year ago. We thought we'd free King James for certain then. I don't have to remind you of the price we paid? I don't have to name the good men who were hung and quartered at his order?"

The man held out his hands to the others. Their faces grew dark with the memory of Angus's brutal retribution. John could hear the note of frustration in Lindsay's voice as the earl continued.

"And naught is changed for the better, as I see it. He still has the King, and now he has the Holy Roman Emperor's sister to be queen. With James under lock and key, and this woman, Mary of Hungary, on the throne giving him support, who knows what will become of Scotland." The other men murmured their assent. "Aye. For that matter, who knows when Charles's troops will be pouring in."

"They'll be pouring in right after the wedding."

Everyone's eyes turned to Ambrose Macpherson, including John's. Ambrose straightened up and took a step forward.

"But at last we have something in our favor," he announced, putting a hand on Lindsay's shoulder. "We have a future queen who has taken our side."

John watched in silence, his jaws clamped shut and his mind a whirl of confusion as he waited for his brother to continue. The gathering suddenly grew animated, firing their questions at Ambrose.

"Aye, it's true," Ambrose said, waving them off. "My wife, Elizabeth, met with the queen yesterday at the Abbey of Holyrood. And the subject of their chat was not painting her wedding portrait as Angus's message had conveyed. Maria Habsburg only used that as a ploy to get a message to us."

Everyone started at once. John kept his silence. Was this another one of her tricks? Should he tell them she could not be trusted . . . whatever she said? Should he tell them of . . . everything? John pondered his brother's words. What if she truly was willing to help them?

"Quiet, friends," Ambrose shouted over them. "Do you want them to hear us all the way to Edinburgh?"

"To start with, Ambrose, I'm a wee bit surprised that Elizabeth and the emperor's sister could get along!" Colin Campbell stated. "After all, isn't Henry of England trying to divorce Catherine of Aragon—this Mary of Hungary's aunt—so that he can marry Anne Boleyn, Elizabeth's sister?"

"Let me put it this way," Ambrose answered. "Elizabeth went to Holyrood Abbey not expecting much. But when she returned, Elizabeth felt quite differently about Maria Habsburg. My wife told me that the queen's opinion of the English business is very much the same as her own. And apparently, neither felt compelled to defend or condemn the actions of their families."

Alec Macpherson's impatience began to show. "Then tell us the gist of their exchange. What did she convey that we don't already know?"

"She told Elizabeth that Angus is making an arrangement for the Holy Roman Emperor to supply him with troops immediately after the wedding. She also told her that the Lord Chancellor admits to his intention of keeping James under lock and key—in spite of his pledge to the King."

"We speculated as much, ourselves," Huntly put in.

"Aye, but there is more," Ambrose continued. "Maria Habsburg has a plan."

John couldn't remain silent any longer. "What are her motives for wanting to help us? What does she hope to gain?"

Everyone's eyes turned on him.

"You know her, certainly better than any of us," Alec answered bluntly. "Considering that you plucked the woman out of the sea, you've had more opportunity to spend time in her company than Elizabeth. Did you see anything in her behavior that bespoke what sounds like defiance to her brother's plans? Is this Maria a Habsburg only in blood and not in soul?"

John thought back over what he knew. Maria was looking forward to this wedding. She had been on her way to see to her ailing mother when her ship had sunk. The Emperor had spoken these words directly to him.

"There was nothing that I witnessed between the Emperor and his sister that bespoke enmity between them."

"John has a right to be concerned," Colin interjected. "We are ready to barter, but we know nothing of her price."

"Aye, we can't see in the fog," Huntly agreed. "She is a Habsburg. I am willing to wager that we cannot afford her price!"

The others began to murmur their own concerns.

"In league with us before the wedding," Huntly continued, "is no assurance that she will remain friendly once she is Queen of Scotland. With Angus gone, there is very little to stop her—"

"Not so fast, m'lord." Ambrose raised a hand. "Aye, Lord Huntly, you are correct to assume that she is after gain. And Colin, you too are correct to assume that there is a price to be paid. But I firmly believe that what she is after has nothing to do with controlling Scotland. I also believe that her plan for rescuing the King places her in as much risk as it does any of us. Perhaps more."

John's hard gaze fell on his brother, and his tone was severe. "What is she after, Ambrose?"

"Though I know, I cannot tell you any more of that than I already have."

"We can't bargain when she is holding back the truth," John pressed.

"She has spoken the truth." The two brothers glared at one another. "And she wishes to keep her intentions private."

In the awkward pause that ensued, John wondered briefly whether Ambrose knew of their affair. Nay, he decided. She would not undercut her own position with such an admission.

"Then tell us of her scheme, Ambrose," Huntly encouraged. "There is very little time to raise an army, but with the planting still a few weeks off, we might still do it."

"Her plan does not call for any army of warriors," Ambrose answered, turning to him. "Not for rescuing the King, at any rate."

"What do you mean by that?" Lord Lindsay asked. "How could that be possible? Angus has the palace at Falkland protected by a hundred cannons and the devil only knows how many men. How could we break through that without a massive force?"

"Let me tell you her plan." As Ambrose motioned for all to gather around a table by a window, John remained where he stood, Maria's face before him. What she intended, suddenly he couldn't be sure of. What did Ambrose mean when he said that her price had nothing to do with the control of Scotland? And how did Kit's welfare fit into her plan? What of their marriage?

And Ambrose had the answers, John could tell, glancing at his waiting brother. But knowing him, John was also certain Ambrose would never reveal the truth until Maria herself stepped out of the mist.

Chapter 27

Jedburgh Abbey, The Borders

Dismissing the wine-sodden physician with a wave of his hand, the Earl of Angus sank heavily into the hard wooden chair and picked up Caroline Maule's letter once again.

As much as he detested the miserable wretch, Angus saw little reason to doubt the physician's half-hearted support of his cousin's accusations. Perhaps there was something to her letter, he mused.

Nay, it's absurd, he thought, arguing with himself. When he'd first read her letter, Angus had first dismissed it as the work of a jealous woman. He knew, as well as anyone, that Caroline had set her cap on John Macpherson. When Angus had heard of her marriage to Thomas Maule, he knew it was no love match, but with the Borders in tumult and so many of the nobles once again in near open revolt, the Lord Chancellor had more important matters than the marital affairs of his cousins to concern him.

This letter had the definite sound of a woman scorned. To say that Sir John had knowingly seduced Mary of Hungary was preposterous. Angus had spoken with the Habsburg queen himself. Aye, she was bonny enough for the Lord of the Navy, but she was just a simple and fairly agreeable lass . . . all things considered. There was certainly nothing deep about the woman, at all, so far as he could see. Nay, she wasn't capable of conspiring with John Macpherson and keeping it so well hidden. And she was safe enough in Edinburgh.

Angus read through the letter again. Lingering over Caroline's warning that Sir John was not to be trusted, he considered the order he'd already issued for the man to convey the King to Endinburgh. True, he was to be accompanied by five hundred Douglas warriors, but . . .

He shook his head. In two more weeks of hard driving, he'd have these Border rabble under control. A few more key hangings, a burned village or two, and he could move the bulk of his army north. But if the King were not to reach Edinburgh—if Caroline's predictions came true—then all would be lost.

Throwing the letter down, the Lord Chancellor leaped from his chair. He was not going to take any chances. If John Macpherson, Angus thought with a sneer, had any idea of hindering the wedding of King Jamie and the Habsburg wench, then he'd personally see to it that the commander's head would decorate a pike at the wedding feast.

Striding out onto the landing outside his chamber, Angus began to bark orders at his waiting attendants.

"Get a messenger to Edinburgh Castle. I want Sir Thomas Maule to take a thousand men to Falkland Palace, and I want them there *now*!" He turned on his heel. "And get a cleric in here to write the message. I want no confusion over what I want done."

Chapter 28

The Abbey of Holyrood

For the past five days, every day, she had written a letter.

Quickly learning her habit, the abbot, on the orders of Archibald Douglas, the Earl of Angus, made certain that every morning a messenger waited at her door, while two more stood with their horses in the courtyard. Long before the monks filed in for their prayers at prime, three men spurred their horses out of the abbey gates, carrying with them a sealed parchment from their future queen to their king.

Maria placed her quill pen into its inkhorn and blew on the ink on the parchment before folding the letter. Another day, another letter, and still no sign of any movement. There were so few days left, and she wondered when exactly they were planning on carrying out her plan. It had to work. Maria's own distress over an unhappy future was nothing compared to the life of imprisonment James would face if he could not be freed from Angus's clutches before this dreaded wedding took place. And after the wedding, Scotland would soon bend to the dominating power of the Emperor Charles. This was their last and only chance.

Maria had met with Elizabeth every day for the past week and knew from her new friend that her first letter had been delivered into James's hand with no difficulty. Angus's armed warriors, encamped in the land around Falkland Palace, were accustomed to correspondence between the young king and the outside world. Hearing this, Maria breathed a sigh of relief. She'd desperately hoped they would not suspect three innocuous messengers arriving daily at the palace.

Maria held the sealing wax over the wick lamp on her desk and allowed it to drip onto the folded parchment. Removing her ring from around her neck, she sealed the letter.

"Come in," she called. As the door to the chamber swung open, she whispered, "Just in time."

Blowing onto the wax, she glanced at another letter that sat in the corner of her writing table—a letter she was almost finished with. The one she had written and rewritten . . . to John. But as she gazed sadly at the lines, she wondered if she would ever find the courage to give it to him. Even if she did, though, would he ever find enough forgiveness in his heart to read it? She pushed the letter carefully into the corner.

Rising from her seat, Maria pulled her shawl tighter around her neck and picked up the sealed letter. She turned to the man.

"Please thank your fellow riders for me." She came to a stop, realizing the hunched and brawny messenger had not even stepped into the chamber. The hood of his cloak kept the man's face in shadow.

The Highlander's great heart thundered in his chest as he watched her from the chamber door. He wanted to hate her, to remember her by her ambition, by her deceit. But seeing her sitting quietly at her desk, unadorned and demure, the picture of innocence and beauty, his heart leaped to her defense against all reason.

After this woman had left him, to John she had become the queen of darkness, the mistress of deception, a fiend to elude. But now, as she glided to within a few steps of him, a white veil covering her glorious hair, a simple blue dress hiding her angelic beauty, he could not believe her anything but Purity itself. He looked down, not daring to gaze on her for long. She was to be his queen, he reminded himself. And he was here on a mission to save his king. He had lost his heart to her once, drowning in the depths of her emerald-green eyes. He would not tempt his resolve. He knew he could not risk it.

"Aye, Your Grace," he whispered in a low, raspy tone that he hoped would hide his true identity as he reached for the letter.

Maria took a hesitant step toward him, then her heart leapt in her chest. His powerful arm, the callused hands. "Sailor's hands," he'd called them. Her body thrilled as she looked on the rough fingers that had so gently caressed her and loved her. Her eyes drifted up the tall frame to the face still hidden in shadow. As she looked at the Highlander, a sharp pain pierced her heart, driving out all emotions except fear.

"Why? Why does it have to be you?" Her strained whisper reflected the full realization of what she had proposed. A castle full of soldiers, a few men breaking in to carry out a plan that an army of thousands could not do. "Why can't they send someone else?"

John swore under his breath and backed up a pace. He should have allowed one of the other men to come up and get her letter, but his stubbornness had bested him. He had wanted to look upon her face one last time. He had wanted to remind himself of the reason for his anger. What he had not expected was to be overwhelmed by the innocence of her beauty. And he had hoped to avoid being recognized.

"Please, John. Please have them send someone else!" she cried out in near panic. "Don't let it be you!"

Her words stabbed at his pride. His eyes flashed with anger as he stepped into the room.

"I can assure you, Your Grace. There would be no purpose served in recounting the events of our . . . time together to the King." He stared right through her, trying not to be softened by her moistening eyes. "All that occurred between us I have buried deeply. So you need not fear your secret being revealed by me."

Her voice was raw with emotion. "Do you think I only fear for my safety?"

"What else does a viper feel—or a whore, for that matter."

"A . . . whore?" her voice was barely a whisper.

"My apologies, Your Grace," John answered coldly through clenched teeth. "I only use the term to indicate what a low point my bed must have proved to be compared to those you are accustomed to. But it *is* such a poor word. Wench is not much better. How does a courtesan sound to you? Of course, you must have heard such a colorful array of words! In Scotland, we say harlot . . . swyver . . . bawd! What is the word in Hungarian, Your Grace?"

Looking into his fiery blue eyes that aimed at piercing her soul, Maria felt her insides crumbling, her will shattered by his wrath. When she spoke, her words came through haltingly as sobs threatened to choke her.

"There . . . there were never any lovers. Never . . . not until you stepped into my life. And then there was . . . only you." She took a shaky breath. "So call me a cheat . . . a liar . . . a coward . . . a fraud. But don't call me what I am not."

John turned his head. He had to get away from her. He needed to close his eyes and ears to her. Like an enchantress spreading her spells, he could feel himself being drawn in. Looking at the floor, he extended his hand again. "The letter, Your Grace. This is finished."

Maria listened to his cold voice, then stepped back, holding the letter to her breast.

"You must listen," she pleaded. "This may be the last time we ever meet."

"There is no more to say." John took a step toward her, his hand still extended. *She wants to ease her conscience,* he thought. *Well, damn her.* He carried the pain day and night—and so should she. "I care to hear no explanations. Your letter!"

Ignoring his command, Maria turned and moved to her desk where she picked up the open letter she'd written to him. She saw his brow furrow angrily as she placed it in his hand before drawing back.

He glanced at the neat script. It was addressed to him. *John, I must speak of love. . . .*

Maria's words tumbled out. "John, I know I could

never hope to regain your love, nor even your respect, but it is crucial for me to tell you the truth."

John looked again at the first line, and then crumpled the parchment in his hands.

"You've never spoken the truth!"

"I was running away from *you* when you first found me at sea," she said quietly. "How could I speak the truth when I was a fugitive, fleeing from a royal command, trying to evade the very delegation who plucked me from the sea?"

"You were going to see your mother."

"That was just a story fabricated by my brother to avoid any difficulties. He did that to preserve the family's honor. To smooth the path for this wedding."

"Then I must say he is quite good at covering the truth. You have given him ample opportunity to hone his skill, I should think."

"Cut me as you please," Maria whispered. "But at least listen to what I have to say."

"The others are waiting for me in the yard," John said shortly.

"I think they will wait for you," she answered. "Do you remember how hesitant Isabel and I were when you first found us? If what Charles told you was the truth, what reason would we have for hiding our identities?"

"Perhaps to protect the lover you were running to?" John leaned heavily against the casing of the door. He didn't know how much longer he could keep this up. "I'm sure, the disappointment of that journey must have been devastating."

She bit back the bile that was rising in her throat. Maria reminded herself that it was better to endure the stab of his tongue than to have him walk away before she was done with what she had to say.

"It was devastating to be saved, but not because there were any lovers waiting for me. It was because once again, my freedom, my will, my ability to breathe on my own were being snatched away from me." Her hands trembled as she gazed down at the King's sealed letter. "You don't know how it feels to be caged like a bird all your life—never taking flight, never so much as seeing the sky."

John looked away as she turned her misty eyes of jade on him.

"John, they planned my life before I was even born. By the age of three I was betrothed to a boy of two. Do you know what is like to grow up without parents and have every day of your life dictated by the articles of some treaty?"

"That's the price of royal blood," he said as curtly as he could.

"Aye, the price," she whispered sadly. "But I mistakenly thought that I had already paid the price. I married Louis when I turned seventeen. He was just a boy of sixteen."

John watched a sad smile creep across her face. He watched her delicate hand reach up and quickly stab away a tear.

"You were the first man that ever made love to me, John," she murmured quietly, her eyes fixed on the letter in his hands. "He took me. As an act of duty, he came to my bed. I think he saw that act—as you say—as the price he had to pay for his royal blood. But after the pain of the first night, I felt nothing. And he felt nothing, either. A few short moments in my bed was, for him, just another of the rituals we were both brought up to endure. I suppose he wanted an heir, but I couldn't give him any."

John ground his jaws together, fighting the sudden urge to go to her, to hold her. The Highlander shifted uneasily in the doorway.

"They raised me to be a queen. To bear children for a king. That was all." She shrugged her shoulders despondently. "The one thing that I was expected to do . . . and I couldn't even do that. Louis became frustrated. He found . . . other things to keep him occupied. I would hear of . . . his other life, of conduct that was not befitting a king. I would hear of him, but I saw nothing of him. If I were the plague, he could not have avoided me more completely. For two years, John . . ." Maria stopped, gazing up at him.

He couldn't look away. The pain in her eyes tore at his heart and pierced his will.

"I was faithful, John. Please believe me, I was. I never thought to be any other way. Not even once, even after hearing endless tales of his wildness, did I even think of retaliating." Maria paused, looking deeply into his eyes. "Do you know, John, what it is like to be alone—completely alone—for so long?"

"I am not your husband, Your Grace," he said quietly. "There is nothing you need to prove to me."

"But I do, John. I do." She placed the letter on her desk and wrapped her arms around her waist. "Louis never loved me, nor even cared for me. But he knew me well. He trusted me. And yet you . . . you said once that you cared for me. But you don't trust me."

"I have reason for my distrust."

"You do." She nodded sadly. "I gave you the reason. There is no one at fault but me."

John watched the way she moved to her chair and sank into its seat. He wondered how simple it would be just to walk to her, to gather her into his arms, to put behind them all that had been said . . . and done. But instead, he simply stood and listened to her.

"Louis died in the battle of Mohács, fighting like a common soldier against the Turks." She stared at her hands. "It was suicide, many said. He was outnumbered by many thousands. But still, the sadness, the lack of love in his life, the unfulfilled desire for an heir—for something he never had, for something I could never give him—all this drove him to his death. And it was no hero's death. He drowned, John, being dragged across a marsh, escaping, wounded from a foolish battle *he* chose to fight. And he was only twenty years old." Maria lowered her head, and John watched her tears run freely down her face.

"Many lads die in battle," the Highlander said quietly. "And it is not for their wives or their mothers to carry the guilt for an act of war."

These were the first gentle words he'd spoken. She looked up, trying to comprehend the change.

"I had a reason for telling you of my marriage," she continued. "You mentioned the price that we all have to pay. Sometimes the price is too high for a life we have no voice in choosing. But you see, I was foolish enough to think that I had paid the price. That my time in Hungary had purchased my freedom. But I was wrong."

"You are talking of your upcoming marriage to King James."

She nodded to the window. "I left Hungary after Louis died. There was nothing for me there. Charles sent a cousin to rule the country—what the Turks left for him, at any rate. But suddenly, I had a future. If I were to move to Castile and live with my mother, the rest of my life might be spent sheltered and guarded in her castle, but I knew I could be happy with that. I saw people I loved again. Nieces and nephews, cousins, Isabel. Then, little more than a year later, my brother summoned me to Antwerp. I was to be married again . . . to another boy in a country Charles saw some use in having. It was too much for me to bear. I saw more years of loneliness ahead. I could not obey any longer. I had to get away."

She looked up, returning his gaze. "All my life has been sheltered. Men have never meant anything to me. My marriage was a disappointment—nay, a disaster. Never in my life has a decision been made that considered *my* feelings. Never has my brother considered what is good for me . . . or anyone else in the family. His decisions only encompass what is good for the power of the Habsburg dynasty, for his expansion of his Holy Roman Empire. So I ran away."

Almost against his will, John believed every word she spoke. But still, knowing his mission, she had allowed him to take her into his bed. His face grew dark.

"Once you came aboard the *Great Michael,* you should have kept away."

"I tried."

"But not hard enough."

"You courted me, John," she whispered. "You wooed me."

"You could have stopped me," he said harshly.

"I could have . . . if I was strong enough. If I were more experienced with men. I could . . . if I wasn't in love—"

"Stop," he snapped roughly. "You shouldn't have come to my bed when we reached Antwerp."

"When we made love, I thought I would never see you again. When we loved at Hart Haus, my plan was to go to Castile." She picked up the letter she had written to James from her desk. "It was wrong of me—I know that—but it was like a dream for me, a memory that I will carry all my life. We all need that, don't we? A dream? A moment of happiness? A memory to carry with us?"

"But you didn't go to Castile, after all. Isabel's letter said you were ready to go. But when the time came, you found you couldn't turn your back on the power that awaited you at your brother's side. You went back to him. You left me with noth—" he stopped abruptly. He had held back his emotions up to now. Maria was to be his queen, the Highlander reminded himself, and he was on his way to rescue his king. And the two would marry. It was not for him, John thought bitterly, to rebuke her for doing the very thing she had been brought up to do. And what would have happened if she had gone to Castile? Would he ever have gone after her?

As much as he wanted to deny it, he knew he would have gone . . . if he thought she loved him as much as he loved her. He would have gone to the ends of the earth.

But she was marrying his king.

"I am sorry, John," she whispered quietly as she walked toward him.

John could still feel the weight of her crumpled note in his hand. He slipped it into a deep, inside pocket of his cloak and watched her as she came to a stop only an arm's length away. His eyes roamed her face, so pale, so innocent. Her green eyes sparked with her tears. His arms ached to reach for her, to gather her to him. Perhaps she was no angel, but she was no demon, either. She was a woman.

A moment of happiness? He wanted to give her a lifetime of happiness. But she had chosen this instead. There was no changing that. She hadn't gone to Castile; she'd returned to the palace of the Habsburgs.

"Here is the letter." She held out the sealed parchment. John's large, rough hand reached out, but rather than taking the letter, his fingers closed around her hand. Their eyes locked. They couldn't speak the words, but each grieved their terrible loss.

"Did it have to be you? Delivering this letter?" she whispered. There was the slightest of pressures, a caressing by his thumb on her skin, and he withdrew his hand, taking the letter.

"The King trusts me," John answered simply. The feel of her soft skin beneath his fingers—that was a memory he would carry in his heart. "And he'll follow me, as he may not follow others."

She smiled bitterly. "You didn't betray your king, John. I did."

"You were only hoping for a dream," he answered, turning and disappearing into the darkness of the hall.

Chapter 29

The three riders had spurred their steeds on through the driving gale. The winding road, the stone-and-thatch huts that huddled sporadically by the wayside, groves of trees and the hedgerows, had all blended together in the furious blur of darkness and rain. Then, just before they'd reached Glenrothes, the storm had passed, and the stars and moon had pushed brilliantly through the scattering clouds.

Twice already, they had been stopped since crossing the Leven. Angus had spread his Douglas men a much greater distance around Falkland than had been reported. John had only expected a concentration of soldiers immediately around the palace. Angus was expecting something, John decided, pushing his horse ahead of his companions. Hopefully, he was not expecting this.

John glanced over at his mud-covered companions as they thundered into the forest that stretched from the Lomand Hills to Falkland. Their own mothers would not recognize the two Border Scots. One of them, Gavin Kerr, was a hulking giant of a man, broader of shoulder than John's own brothers, and one of the few trusted friends of Ambrose Macpherson. The other, Gareth Kerr, was the smallest of the trio, a cousin of Gavin and another devoted fighter for the Stuart crown.

Unless one of the earlier riders had been found out, the Highlander knew there would be seven of them to achieve the delivery of the King's freedom. The first four groups of couriers that had delivered Maria's letters had each left behind one man at Falkland Palace. Each one was a warrior loyal to the King, and more than ready to wield his sword in whatever difficulty arose.

Galloping furiously under the moonlit sky, the three men broke out into the open space just south of the royal burgh, and there they reined in their frothing and panting horses. In the rolling hills between them and the walls of the town, an army was encamped. John's gaze took in the horses, wagons, the scattering of tents, and the thousands of men huddled around sputtering fires.

To take on such numbers by force would surely be suicide, John thought grimly. But this would be their only chance to stop Angus and his plans. Maria had told Elizabeth that with Angus in power, the marriage would assure that the Lord Chancellor would receive from the Emperor Charles whatever troops he sought to safeguard his control of Scotland. But without Angus in command, the Emperor would have no interest in acting on his own.

Throughout the hard ride, John had thought of her over and over again, of the words she had told him of her life, of her actions. Thinking back on their discussions, he knew there were traces of truth in everything she had said. And then he had read the crumpled letter. It had confirmed her words.

John could see a pair of sentries eyeing them warily across the field.

"Well, lads," John said quietly, wheeling his mount. "For Scotland and King James!"

"Aye!" the two men responded heartily, falling in beside him as he spurred his steed toward the towers of Falkland Palace.

More horses and another large company of Highland warriors were waiting for the small entourage as they climbed out of the small boat that had ferried them across the Firth of Forth.

"I still can't believe you agreed to being dragged out into as wild a night as this simply on a whim!" Isabel complained, wrapping her heavy cloak tighter around her as she settled into the saddle.

"It wasn't a whim, Isabel," Maria answered, glancing to make sure their companions hadn't heard her aunt. "We should be thankful that Elizabeth and Ambrose came for us when they did. I, for one, would not have wanted to be sitting in the Abbey of Holyrood and waiting for Angus's wrath to descend upon our heads."

The two watched as the tall, blond Highlander with the jagged scar on his forehead leaped onto his horse and joined his wife, who had already mounted up. Spirited out of the abbey by Elizabeth and Ambrose Macpherson at the height of the passing storm, Maria and Isabel had been escorted by their friends—and close to two hundred soldiers—to the boatmen at Queen's Ferry. The group of warriors, at least equal to that number and crowding around like a company of fierce-looking shadows, had met them as they'd come off the sparkling waters of the Firth. Maria thanked heaven that the storm had given way to a night crystal clear and moonlit. A good night for traveling.

"There is no guarantee that those men can do what they have set out to do," Isabel whispered. "It could be that nothing good comes out of any of this. It could be that they all get killed before they even reach the King."

Maria felt a sharp pain tear at her heart on hearing Isabel's words. She had told her aunt everything—everything but the fact that John had been the one carrying the last message to Falkland Palace. Maria gripped the reins of her horse tighter in her hands. If something were to happen to him, if he got hurt . . . She couldn't think anymore. Trying to fight back the tears that were burning her lashes, Maria turned her face from her aunt. Please, Virgin Mother, keep him, she prayed. Save him. Bring him back. Even though he would never again come back to her. Even though he would never again want her.

Maria ran a quick hand across her cheek, wiping away any telltale tears before facing her aunt again.

Elizabeth and Ambrose paused only a moment as they passed. The dark-haired beauty reached out and took hold of Maria's gloved hand. "Are you ready to go on?" Elizabeth asked hurriedly.

"Aye," Ambrose replied for them with a nod, reining in sharply his heady steed, "I'll warrant these two can outride the rest of us."

"You are truly the diplomat, Sir Ambrose," Isabel commented.

"Aye, he is that," Elizabeth agreed. "But we've a long ride ahead of us, and we want to be far away when the sun rises."

"We're ready, Elizabeth," Maria asserted, receiving a squeeze of her hand in response.

"Then we're off," Ambrose said with a quick glance around at his men.

Without another word, husband and wife spurred their horses forward into the darkness, while Maria and Isabel followed suit.

"I shouldn't wonder if they've already found that we're missing," Isabel remarked decidedly, turning to Maria as they rode.

"I suppose so," Maria answered. "But they won't know where we are heading. Ambrose's plan was for the abbot and the rest to think we were kidnapped. With the rest of our delegation left behind, that may be just what they do think."

"Very smart." Isabel nodded curtly.

"Very kind, I should say," Maria countered. "If the plan f— If things don't go according to plan, they are providing for our safety. For when we return."

"You mean, *if* we return," Isabel retorted.

Isabel knew her well, Maria thought. She would not return. If this plan failed, if John got hurt, there would be nothing that would drive her back to the side of the Scottish king. She had already said as much in her letters to King James.

John hunched his back to make himself look smaller and pulled his hood of chain forward on his face, though with the thick mud that coated his face and clothes, he doubted anyone would recognize him.

The sour-faced Douglas man who had been roused to

take him up to the King, handed the torch roughly to John
and motioned for him to follow him up the tower steps.

"You two wait here," he commanded.

John nodded to his cloaked companions, and noted
that Gavin and Gareth casually positioned themselves
where each of them could dispatch one of the two surly
sentries should the need arise. The Highlander hoped all
would go smoothly—without bloodshed.

"Oh," the steward said, turning back to John, "disarm
yourself here."

"Aye," John replied, his voice low and rasping. It took
him only a moment to lay his sword and dirk against
the stone wall at the bottom of the tower.

Satisfied, the man led the muddy messenger up the
circular stairwell. At the first landing, John found no one
standing guard beside a stout oak door. There were a
few bedchambers for high-ranking visitors beyond the
entrance, and a corridor leading to the Great Hall. From
his past visits here, John knew that there was a heavy
bar on the far side of the door, but he had no way of
telling if it offered him an alternate means of escape.
The lack of a guard here, though, clearly indicated that
they thought any attempt at freeing the King would
come from outside the heavily manned palace walls.
Climbing the next winding set of stairs to the top of the
tower, the two at last reached the royal apartment, and
the man motioned for John to wait.

Before he could knock, however, the door swung open,
and two figures emerged from the King's chambers. John
backed away as he saw them, trying to hold the torch as
far away as possible where its light would not fall on his
face. The short, bulky man was holding a wick lamp.

"Ah! Lady Maule. Sir Thomas." The man bowed
slightly. "I didn't know you were with the King."

"Our business was with him, steward," Sir Thomas
remarked sharply. "Not with you."

"Aye, Sir Thomas," the man responded with a fawn-
ing tone. "My apologies, sir."

"What's this?" the elder knight demanded, waving the
wick lamp at John.

"A messenger with a letter for the King," the steward offered helpfully.

"At this hour? The King is ready to retire."

John kept his eyes on Sir Thomas's feet, and he could feel Caroline's gaze brush over him disinterestedly. He had no desire to kill Thomas Maule, but he was prepared to kill all three of these people in an instant, if either husband or wife recognized him.

"He is one of the daily messengers from Edinburgh," the man explained. "They bring letters from the King's bride."

"Bride . . ." Caroline muttered under her breath.

"Very well," Sir Thomas said with a glance at his wife. "We're finished here. Announce yourself, steward."

The man bowed before going to knock at the open door.

"Wait!" the knight commanded. "Why are there no sentries here?"

"I passed your order on to the captain of the guard, Sir Thomas. I don't know. . . . In the past, we're . . . I . . . I'll go to him immediately after speaking with the King, m'lord."

"See to it." Sir Thomas turned on his heel and started for the steps.

Even with his eyes averted, John felt the heat of Caroline's gaze once again before she moved off at her husband's side to the stairwell.

The steward's call "Your pardon, Majesty . . ." drew John's eyes upward for an instant, and the Highlander caught Caroline's last glance before she disappeared around the bend of the stairs.

Placing the torch in a wall sconce, John followed the steward into the well-lit chamber. He found Kit, dressed in a doublet of black velvet, standing by a writing table and holding a quill pen in his hand.

"Your Majesty, a letter from your bride!" the man announced. Then, turning to John, he ordered, "Place it on that table by the door. You've delivered it to His Majesty in person, as you were commanded. Now depart."

"It has been an honor to serve Your Majesty." The Highlander pushed back the hood from his head and, as he bowed deeply, John saw the young king's eyes focus on him. As he began to back out of the room, he halted at Kit's command.

"Don't go! Not yet." King James picked up the parchment from the writing desk and looked back at him. "Are you departing for Edinburgh tonight?"

"If that is your wish, Your Majesty," John answered.

"Very good. Then you will wait a moment while I finish this letter. I'd like it to be delivered to my bride immediately."

John simply bowed again in response as he watched the King sit down at the desk and begin to scratch busily at the parchment. Absently, the King waved at the steward.

"Fetch me something to eat," Kit said without looking up at the steward.

"Something to eat, Your Majesty?"

"Aye, this may take longer than I thought, and I'm hungry." King James looked up at John. "Are you hungry, soldier?"

"Aye, Your Majesty. Starving."

"Bring something for this good man, as well, steward."

"For this . . ." the steward looked at John askance.

"Are you deaf?" the King asked with a show of anger. "Go, steward! Now!"

The steward looked uncertainly from the King to the muddy messenger, then headed quickly for the door, leaving it open behind him.

"I don't think it was right for you to speak so slightingly of the queen before her future husband, Caroline," Sir Thomas scolded his wife.

"I only spoke the truth," she snapped. They were back on Scottish ground now. Maria could not shut her up as she had done in Antwerp, Caroline thought. She would speak of her name and character any way she wished. Let her try to stop her, she thought. Caroline was a

Douglas. They were on her turf now. "As her husband, this boy has the right to know how many men she has slept with before they marry."

Sir Thomas turned sharply at his wife. "As *your* husband, I wasn't told of *your* habits."

She gave a quick glance around them. There was no one at the first landing. "You knew about John," she sneered.

"But John wasn't the only one. Was he?"

"Perhaps he wasn't," she taunted. "But he was the best. The best lover I ever had. The best I have *ever* had. He made me feel like a woman. Even now, I see his magnificent body, so beautiful, coming to me in my bed. Even now, I remember the way I cried out in ecstasy as he—"

"Stop!" Sir Thomas grabbed his wife by her elbow. "Stop, Caroline. Before you drive us both to madness."

"Stop? Never!" she snapped, jerking her elbow free. "He is the only man I've ever loved. The only I've ever desired."

The older warrior looked imploringly into his wife's wild face. Every day, since they'd set sail from Antwerp, he'd heard these same words. Over and over again, at every opportunity, she had reminded him of his age, of his inability to match John's prowess, his charm. But as they'd neared the coast of Scotland, Sir Thomas had come to the realization that the problem lay not with the Highlander, but with his own wife. Her loss of John Macpherson was only part of it. Now, standing in the stone passages of Falkland Palace, Sir Thomas feared for her mind.

He had never appreciated the serenity that he and Janet had shared and enjoyed until Caroline came into his life. He'd been fooled by her youth and her beauty. He'd been fooled to think that his young wife would be a companion and a friend to his daughter. How wrong he had been. In the few short months since their marriage, he'd aged. He'd been blinded to the world around him and had, perhaps, driven his only daughter to run away.

And he'd been gradually withdrawing. He no longer lost all control at Caroline's abuse. A momentary flash of temper, and then he simply shut her out. He feared the darkness he now saw clearly within her. He hated the viciousness that was no longer hidden beneath her beautiful veneer. Caroline was now striking out at everyone around her. And who could know how far her cruelty would extend?

Sir Thomas wanted her out of his life. He wanted things to go back to the way they were before she came. But even as that thought crystallized in his mind, he knew it was too late. He had already lost his daughter. Looking blankly at the burning torch hanging on the wall, Sir Thomas felt old. Very old.

"Retire to your bedchamber, old man," she taunted, backing away a step. "Go rest your weary body and be sure to pray for your soul."

Sir Thomas stared at her. But now he could see through her. He saw the hollow shell of a person and nothing more.

"Aye. And you may do as you please," he muttered as he walked away, wishing her out of his life.

"Jack Heart, I knew you'd come." The young king leaped up from the writing table and crossed the chamber toward the Highlander.

John held up a hand and then glanced quickly into the hall. He wanted to make sure the steward wasn't lurking on the steps. Then, pushing the door nearly closed, he turned to Kit and put his hands on the young king's shoulders.

"We have very little time, Your Majesty. We have a large army gathering near Campbell Castle, and they are waiting for you to arrive before moving. The plan is to take you out of the palace tonight, disguised as one of us. They won't know you're missing until morning, and by then we'll be halfway to freedom."

"But the steward! He'll be coming back soon. He'll surely raise an alarm."

John quietly removed a sharp dagger from the inside

of his high boots and held it in his hand. "He will not be talking, sire."

With a grim look on his face, the young king nodded and quickly went to the massive bed, pulling a bundle of worn clothing from beneath. Pulling them apart, he spread the garments on the bed. They looked like clothes someone had stripped from a stable boy.

"I found these in my chamber this morning when I came back from working the hawks. I don't know who left them, but I knew something was about to happen."

"If you would put them on, sire, you'll draw far less attention when the time comes to pass along the roads."

Kit immediately started removing his clothes as John kept watch by the open door.

"They've doubled the number of soldiers around Falkland," the King said, pulling on a ragged tunic. "Sir Thomas Maule and his . . . and his wife arrived yesterday with a company of a thousand men. They told me you might arrive as early as next week to escort me to Edinburgh. Angus is surely thinking those loyal to me would once again use an army to try and free me. We are more clever than that! We'll smash him this time, won't we, Jack Heart?"

John smiled over his shoulder at the eager young man. Some of the nobles questioned whether King James would agree to leave the palace at all, considering the fact that his bride-to-be was already in Scotland . . . and a marriage was all it would take to test Angus's promise. After all, they'd argued, the Lord Chancellor had given his word to the King to relinquish his power after the wedding. But now, seeing Kit's unhesitating response to the plan to free him, John knew that he had argued correctly that the young king knew Angus to be a liar. What the Highlander didn't know was when exactly in the past months Kit had given up on the dubious hope the marriage offered.

"Aye, Your Majesty. *Your* time has come."

Caroline Maule watched her husband's back without emotion until it disappeared into their chamber. But the slamming of the door brought a sneering smile to her lips. She had hurt him more deeply than he'd shown.

At the sound of the footsteps coming down the stairs, she whirled, and, moving cautiously to the open door leading to the landing, she waited in the dimly lit corridor. There had been something odd about the man—the Queen's messenger—something that was nagging at her. Watching the reflected light of the flaring torch grow brighter as the bearer descended, Caroline was sure she'd remember if she saw him again.

The sight of the solitary steward coming around the bend of the stairwell brought a frown to Caroline's brow.

"Where is the other man?" she asked abruptly, stepping in front of the startled steward. "There were two of you up there."

The man, taken aback with the abruptness of her interrogation, raised the torch, looking for Sir Thomas. But there was no one else on the landing. "The King told the messenger to wait. His Majesty is writing a letter to his bride, and he wants the man to take it tonight."

"Aren't there other couriers available?" she barked, her temper seething quickly to the surface. After all that she'd told this foolish boy-king about his fraudulent bride . . . and he still had to write her a letter. Foolish, foolish boy, she thought darkly. He deserved to be locked up for the rest of his life. "When we arrived, my husband specifically told you not to leave the King alone with any strangers. He'll have your head on a pike if something happens to the King."

"But King Jamie wanted something from the kitchen sent up, m'lady—for himself and the man. There was naught else for me to do." The steward's voice took on a pleading tone as he scrambled for more excuses. "He is just standing and waiting, m'lady. The man left his weapons down the steps—"

"Have you seen this man before?" Caroline interrupted. "Is he one of your normal couriers?"

The steward shook his head slowly. "Nay, m'lady. I've never seen this one before. But then again, it seems every time they send someone else—"

"Did he give you a name?" she interrupted again. "Or what clan he belongs to?"

The steward ran his hand nervously over his bristly chin for a moment before lifting his face brightly to the woman. "Aye, m'lady. Jack Heart. One of the ones with him called him Jack Heart. Not a common name, I'd say, but as to his clan . . ."

Caroline face went white, but it was her hand clutching at his collar that made the man stare at her in terror.

"You fool," she whispered hoarsely. "It is a plot to abduct the King. Jack Heart . . . Jack Heart . . ."

Caroline repeated his name again and again and shoved the wide-eyed steward away from her. "Run and get my husband. Tell him John Macpherson is here. Tell him he has come to steal the King from under his nose. Then raise the alarm."

The steward bolted for their chamber as Caroline went quickly up the steps, a vicious smile on her lips.

"You are mine, John," she murmured bitterly, drawing a small dagger from her belt. "This time I have *you* at my mercy."

"The letters, John," the young king called at the last moment as they readied themselves to step onto the landing. He pointed to the pile of letters on his desk. "Get me those letters. I can't leave them behind."

John quickly moved to Kit's desk and picked up the few folded parchments from the table. They must be Maria's letters, he thought. But before he could make it back to the door, where the King stood pulling on a filthy cap, John saw her shadow gliding across the landing.

She moved behind Kit before the Highlander could reach them.

"Not so fast, John," she said in an peculiarly husky voice. He could see the small dagger she held to the side of the King's neck. "Isn't that far more pleasant than the last time we met?"

John glanced behind her at the landing, but there was no one there. His mind racing, he tried to decide if they

could disarm her. But one look at the crazed expression
in her eye and the sharp blade beneath Kit's jaw convinced him that the lad would be hurt if John rushed
them. Kit wouldn't have a chance: John needed to dis-
tract her somehow.

"You didn't want me. You practically threw me out
of your cabin, remember?" Her hand was shaking. "And
that paragon of virtue, our future queen . . . you were
kissing the slut, I believe, on the threshold to your
bedchamber."

John saw no reaction on Kit's face to her words, the
young man's face lacked all expression save the look of
one waiting for a chance to break free.

"Oh, His Majesty knows all about it." Caroline
laughed, seeing the direction of John's glance. "I've told
him everything—and Angus, too. Don't you think that
everyone should know that our good Lord of the Navy
couldn't keep his hands off our precious queen? And
our noble queen! Well, she just couldn't stay away from
your bed, now could she? Now throw down your
dagger."

John complied, gritting his teeth and fighting back the
urge to lunge for her neck, shutting her mouth
permanently.

"But this time, Jack Heart, she is not here to save
your unfaithful neck. She is not going to appear suddenly out of the mist—as she did at her brother's palace—and swear lies for your honor's sake."

John felt his whole body tense at Caroline's words.

"Aye," Caroline continued, her voice dripping with
bitter irony, "for *your* honor. She knew I would go to
the Emperor. She knew I would have your head on a
platter. Ha, you must have outdone yourself in her bed,
for the bitch to take such risks."

John recalled once again Isabel's letter. They were
waiting for a ship, and then Maria had disappeared from
Hart Haus. There was nothing to stop the two women
from sailing on to Castile. She had only gone back to
the palace for him, to save his miserable life.

Chaos reigned momentarily in the Highlander's brain.

He was a fool. How could he have been so blind? He had maligned her, acted such that he had put her in danger a dozen times. Pulling his scattered thoughts back together, he recalled the night of the welcoming feast in Antwerp. She had acted out of love; he'd acted out of hatred. The pain, the remembrance of her bright teary eyes looking at him when they'd parted at the Abbey of Holyrood now tore at the fibers of his heart.

"But I almost ruined you there, anyway," she cried out angrily. "I secured an audience with the Emperor, but at the last moment she appeared, looking like some bewildered innocent and swore lies through her teeth." She pushed the dagger closer to the King's neck. "She can't save you this time, John. She can't. No one can."

"Caroline!" John snapped, seeing the wild look in the woman's face. She was ready to thrust the point of the blade into the King's neck. "That's not Maria beneath your dagger. That is not my neck beneath the blade. That is your King you hold—God's anointed. Your fight is with me, not with him. There is no salvation for the murderer of a king. Let him go, Caroline."

As Caroline shook her blond hair back with a disgusted laugh, John saw Sir Thomas—his sword fully drawn—appear on the landing.

"The ever-so-loyal John Macpherson. I know he is the King, you fool. But this pathetic little boy is *your* king, not mine. . . ."

Caroline Maule never took her eyes off John's face as she pulled at the King's fiery red hair, exposing his throat more clearly to the gleaming edge of her dagger.

"You have me now, Caroline. There is no way I can get out of here alive. What else do you want? Let him go."

"That's too easy, my love," she cooed. "Your own death, painful as I'm sure it will be, is hardly enough. On the other hand, to watch someone you cherish so much die right before your eyes. To watch his royal blood drain away—with nothing you can do to stop it— now that's pain that you cannot bear. I know you all too well, Jack Heart."

"You are mad, Caroline! You can't just murder a king!" John took a step toward her. The sudden tensing of Kit's body showed that her dagger had pierced his skin. John stopped, watching the thin rivulet of blood run down the King's young neck. "You'll be disgraced, Caroline. Publicly tortured and hung. Your head will grace the pike next to mine. This goes beyond hurting me. In killing the King, you are killing yourself . . . and the future of Scotland!"

"Do you think any of this matters to me?"

The Highlander looked directly at Sir Thomas, who was now standing behind his wife. "Stop her."

Caroline gave a quick glance behind her shoulder at her husband. John watched for his chance, but she never eased the pressure of the blade on the King's throat.

"Ah, our aging hero has at last arrived. It certainly took you long enough. Where are the rest of our men?"

"The steward went after them." Sir Thomas's voice was deadly calm. "He is cornered here, Caroline. Release the King."

"The man of wisdom speaks," she said, laughing. But her laughter had a clipped, mirthless sound to it. "Well, I now am in charge here, my dear husband. So shut your mouth and do as you are told. Go and make him kneel before us. Make him kneel before his king."

"He is unarmed, Caroline," the knight said quietly. "There is no reason for any further action until the others arrive. Release the King, I said."

"You coward," she hissed, ignoring his last words. "You are afraid he'll kill you."

"That's what you really want, isn't it?" Sir Thomas asked in disbelief.

"Perhaps it is." She shrugged her shoulders and cackled wildly. "But you can't have everything you want, can you. Well, I'm not unreasonable. I might settle for less."

The young king now twisted in pain as Caroline's blade dug deeper into the flesh of his neck. The Highlander could see how close she was to the lad's vein. The next time her eyes flickered away from him, John decided, he was going after her.

"You are a Douglas, my dear husband. Contrary to what your treacherous daughter did, turning against me and warning the slut queen back in Antwerp, you've been forgiven of her sins."

"Janet?" Sir Thomas asked, confused.

"You fought at Flodden," John called to the knight. "You were loyal to your king. Don't allow clan loyalty to destroy your honor. Your allegiance is to the King above all else."

"Aye! Janet, that blind bat! The stupid, vicious creature you once called 'daughter.' If it wasn't for her, John Macpherson would be dead by now. But I took care of her. I drove her away."

"You drove Janet away?" Sir Thomas asked incredulously.

"Thomas," John interrupted. "Remember the blood, the lives we lost, to gain our freedom, our liberty? Can't you see what Angus is doing to us? To Scotland? He has already called on the Emperor to move in. Don't let this happen, Thomas."

"He will die, John. The boy will die," she announced. "And it won't matter to Angus, or to anyone else, if he dies. Angus will be king. At last, a Douglas will be king."

As if waking from a trance, Sir Thomas's eyes cleared and he took a step toward his wife. "Stop, Caroline. You are mad. You cannot kill the King. Release him now!"

"Stand back, you coward," Caroline hissed at her husband. "You've never been a real man—either in or out of bed. You don't have the stomach for a fight. Hide behind me so you won't have to see the blood. Or go to the landing, if you've less courage than I thought. Go ahead, coward, go and hide."

The two men both saw Caroline lift her wrist, poised for the thrust.

"Stop her, Thomas. This is not for one clan's wealth or honor. This is our king, our future. In God's name—"

Kit's hand caught at the dagger, but Caroline was strong, and the point sliced upward through the skin as they struggled. And then she stopped.

John grasped her wrist just as the sword blade tore

outward through the side of Caroline's chest, nearly catching the Highlander, as well, with the force of Sir Thomas's powerful thrust. The woman's body tensed for a moment, her eyes glazing even as she turned them back to her husband.

The King held the dagger in his hand as Sir Thomas allowed Caroline's body to slump to the floor. They all stared at the dead woman at their feet, the blood dripping steadily from the sword in the knight's hand.

Steps outside and then the sight of two men as they rushed into the chamber brought the Highlander's attention back to their mission. John shook his head silently, stopping Gavin from cutting down the knight.

"There was no other way, Thomas," John said as the older man stared wearily at his dead wife.

"Sire," Gavin said, addressing the King as the two men bowed quickly. With only one startled look at the woman's dead body, he turned his attention back to John. "Jack, we stopped the steward from spreading the word. But there is not much time. The others have fresh horses ready for us. But we have to go now!"

John gave a quick look at the young king who stood, dagger in hand, his eyes fixed on the unsteady knight.

"I'll never forget what you did here, Sir Thomas," King James said quietly to the knight, drawing the man's attention upward. "I swore long ago that, once I was free, every Douglas in Christendom would feel my wrath. You have taught me that I must reconsider that vow."

With a nod, the King moved to a washstand and wiped away the blood that had run down his neck. John placed a hand on Thomas Maule's shoulder.

"I am truly sorry," the Highlander said quietly.

"You were never the cause." Sir Thomas turned bloodshot eyes toward John. "She brought this on . . . and I did, as well. I was too blind to see it before. And now it is too late. A woman is dead, and another I love even more is lost to me."

"You don't need to lose her, Thomas," John spoke fast, sensing the edginess of his men. "If you ask her, she will come back—now that Caroline is gone. But you will have to accept a son, as well. That's a price your daughter will surely demand you pay."

The older man's eyes brightened a bit. "It's a passable small price. One I willingly pay. David's a good lad."

"Aye," John said. "You'll see. There's none better."

Moments later, the King and his rescuers started out the chamber door.

"Wait," Sir Thomas called before John could follow the other three out onto the landing. The knight hurriedly scribbled a message on a piece of parchment at the King's writing desk. Quickly, he folded it, addressed it, and sealed it using his own signet ring.

"Hurry, Jack!" Gavin called urgently from the chamber door. John shared Gavin's concern. The problems that lay ahead would be insurmountable if they had to start fighting their way out before even leaving the palace.

"Use this letter," Sir Thomas said. "It has my seal on it and I've addressed it to the Earl of Angus. If you get stopped, it should guarantee you a smooth passage through our men."

John moved to him and accepted the letter. Looking at the seal, he realized this meant the King's freedom. Sir Thomas's action meant more than the swords strapped to their sides. He put out his hand in friendship and the knight grasped it.

"What did you write in it?" the Highlander asked.

"Just this: That his time has come."

Chapter 30

Drummond Castle, The Highlands

It just can't be true, she thought as she ran.

By the time Maria reached the end of the long corridor, she could hold back her tears no longer. Shoving the door open, she rushed into her chamber and swung the heavy oak door shut behind her. The young queen stood with her back to the door for a moment, her unseeing gaze sweeping over the chamber's furnishings. Then, sinking to her knees, she began to sob uncontrollably, her tears flowing down her face.

She looked down at herself through the tears. There was nothing different about her. And yet, everything was different.

The quiet knock at the door was followed by the raising of the latch, and then Elizabeth slipped into the chamber as Maria quickly wiped at her tears.

Although Maria had run to her chamber in search of solitude, a feeling of relief and gratitude washed over her at seeing her friend's look of concern and support. The friendship they'd established in the Abbey of Holyrood had already deepened and strengthened into a bond Maria had never before experienced. With Elizabeth, she was not queen. She was simply Maria.

She had passed Elizabeth's room as she'd blindly made her way to her chamber. Elizabeth must have seen her and followed.

"Is there news?" Maria asked, looking up at Elizabeth.

"Nay, it's still too early to hear," she answered, watching the young woman pull herself to her feet. "Even assuming that all went well, and they were able to free him at Falkland Palace, there is no telling what resistance they may have met at Stirling Castle." Even though Maria had put a stop to her tears, her flushed face and her trembling frame spoke of continuing distress. Their eyes met, and then Elizabeth simply opened her arms to her friend.

With her friend's arms embracing her, Maria's tears began to flow again.

"What did Fiona's physician say, Maria?" Elizabeth asked. "Did he tell you what is wrong with you?"

Maria drew back out of the embrace and turned around, facing the room. She felt so foolish. One moment she was thinking what a disgrace she would be to all of them—to her family as well as to her friends. But then she was thinking that her condition now was so different than before. She *was* a different woman. A woman with passion and belief. She wanted to laugh and cry at the same time. But how to express that to Elizabeth . . . to anyone.

But at the bottom of it all, she cherished the news. It was a gift, a miracle. Four years as a wife and she had not been able to conceive an heir to a husband whom she had not loved. One night with the man she loved . . . and here she was carrying his child.

Her tears were of happiness for this chance and sadness for the fact that she could never tell John about their child. There would be no one she could share her joy with. She already knew what she had to do. Her only chance was to go to Castile and live out her life as her mother was living out hers. And she would raise her own child. Juana would help her there, Maria was certain of that. Her mother understood love, and she understood what it was like to have your loved ones taken from you.

Maria felt her friend's hands rest gently on her shoulders.

"You don't have to bear it all alone. Ambrose and I can help. Please let us."

Maria turned around and smiled timidly at her friend. "There isn't a thing wrong with me. The physician said I am fit. You worried for naught."

Elizabeth smiled gently before gathering Maria's hands in hers and taking her to a nearby chair. After Maria was seated, Elizabeth went and fetched a drink for her friend before returning to her.

"You shouldn't shoulder this alone," Elizabeth said quietly, standing before Maria and handing her the cup. "You should talk to him about it."

"Talk to whom?" Maria asked, startled. She had never spoken a word of John and their affair to Elizabeth. In their talks at the Abbey, she said that she would not wed King James and that she would do whatever she could to help free the young monarch. But she had also told Elizabeth of how John had saved her life when she had been running away from her brother the first time. How he had cared for her injuries. She had said nothing more of how he had won her heart. Had she been so obvious?

"You should talk to John."

Maria couldn't stop the heat that rushed into her face. "I don't know." She tried to clear throat. "I don't know what interest Sir John would have in my health."

Elizabeth looked for a moment into the face of the young woman before her. The overwhelming urge to protect Maria had surprised her at first. It was a different urge than she had experienced with her own sister Mary, a woman far more helpless and dreamy-eyed than Maria. But something in Maria's desire to determine and pursue her own happiness resonated in Elizabeth. Elizabeth knew what it was like to have your future dictated to you. And she knew what it was like to fight against it.

"I can assure you, John has a great deal of interest in you," Elizabeth said, pressing on. She was willing to play the chattering magpie if she could make Maria listen. And the color rising again in her friend's face encouraged Elizabeth to go on. "After all, John is very much a Macpherson. And I can safely tell you that when it comes to their women, all Macpherson men are alike. Ambrose and I have been married but four years; however, you can ask Fiona. She and Alec are going to be married twelve. Or you can ask Lady Elizabeth, their mother. She and the laird, Alexander, have been together a lifetime. She would be the first one to tell you that her sons might be the new generation, but their attitudes are the same as her husband's."

Elizabeth paused. Maria was listening to her every word.

"She will tell you that all Macpherson men are alike. They might search a lifetime for their soulmate, but once they have found her, they'll never let her go." Elizabeth felt a glow of happiness building within her as she talked. She was speaking of Macpherson men, but her thoughts were only on Ambrose, her own husband. "They have a way of folding themselves around you. They are always part of your life, always there, forever giving, forever loving. They draw you into their hearts and nestle you there. You feel their passions, you understand their beliefs and they understand yours. And after a while, they are like the air you breathe, they become a part of you. You wouldn't think to live without them— nor would they think to live without you."

"It must be wonderful to be loved so much," Maria whispered, unable to keep silent.

"It is heaven on earth. It is a more beautiful world that any sorcerer could conjure," Elizabeth whispered with a smile. "That's why I think you should talk to him. It would be fruitless to try and lock him out of your life."

"But . . . how do you know . . . ?" Maria couldn't continue. She couldn't ask the question without admitting what she and John once had felt . . . so long ago, it seemed.

Elizabeth placed her hand on Maria's. "You knew of me—of my family before we even met. You told me so at our first meeting, remember?" Maria nodded in response. "John would never have revealed so much unless he cared for you. Unless he thought of you as part of this family."

"We had days at sea," Maria argued weakly. "Perhaps . . . just to pass the time . . ."

Elizabeth acknowledged her words with a smile and a

nod. "Then let's talk about more telling things—more revealing than words." She took a breath and then continued. "Your eyes brighten, you blush continually, you stop whatever you're doing any time his name is even mentioned. Ambrose tells me John's condition is not much different. And when you and I talk, I see your thoughts drifting, so much like a woman in love. Another thing, John took you to Hart Haus in Antwerp. He has never taken any woman there. Nay, Ambrose and Alec both see a difference in John. A sadness, an anger, and yet a faraway look that is so new to his character—they believe their brother is in love."

Elizabeth paused, searching Maria's face for a reaction to her words. It was there; the young queen couldn't hide it.

"It took great courage on your part to defy your brother and run away as you did. But then, it took an exceptional love to drive you back to the palace at Antwerp. In fleeing, you had already done the unthinkable. So why didn't you finish it?" Elizabeth watched as Maria lowered her head, her eyes locked on her hands. "You don't have to speak the words, my friend. They are written across your face. They are in everything you do. You can't hide it, Maria, nor can John. He is with you, and what the two of you have shared has changed you and changed your destiny. Your lives can never be the same."

Maria lifted her eyes. "I've done him a great wrong. I know he has more hate within him now than he ever had love. He will never forgive me, Elizabeth. There is no future for us."

Elizabeth took hold of Maria's arm. "Don't underestimate the power of what you've already shared, of the words you've spoken, of the seed you've planted."

Maria looked up at her friend as Elizabeth rested her hand lightly on the young queen's stomach. "You knew, and yet you had me examined by Fiona's physician."

"It would have been difficult to ignore your condition, since we are sharing the same symptoms." Elizabeth didn't try to hide the smile that lit up her face.

Maria's face reflected the sudden radiance. "Does Ambrose know?"

Elizabeth shook her head. "Not yet. I've been through it twice already, so I know better than to tell him so soon. The baboon would have me bedridden for the next seven months."

"Twice? What about Jaime . . . ?" Maria stopped abruptly. She had no right to ask. "I am sorry, Elizabeth. It was wrong of me to pry. . . ."

"Don't be sorry." The young painter smiled. "I spoke without thinking. Now you are a part of our little secret, as well. To the world, Jaime is our daughter, but there is a very small number of souls who know she is really my niece. Aye, everyone thinks that Ambrose and I had a child long before we married. For a while it kept the gossip mill turning happily at court, but only for a while."

"Then who . . . ?" Maria asked.

Elizabeth shook her head. "That's a long story—and one I'll share with you during our long months of pregnancy together."

"Things are never as simple as they seem, are they, Elizabeth?"

"I don't know. Perhaps they could be."

"Nay, they can't," Maria answered seriously. "You have a husband; I don't. I can't stay in Scotland, and I won't return to Antwerp. In fact, I think sometimes it would be best if I disappeared from the face of the earth."

"You will not speak such foolishness," Elizabeth scolded. "You will stay here and bear your child. And I'll stay right beside you."

Maria shook her head. "I can't. When people learn that I am carrying a child—John's child—it will be the end of him. He'll be accused of high treason. I could never do that to him. Never."

"That might be true if you were to go forward and marry the King, but you are not."

"Still," Maria asserted, "I will not put John's life at

any more risk than I have already. And I will not allow him to shoulder this shame."

"And you?" Elizabeth argued. "What of the shame you must face—and face alone?"

Maria felt the knot rising in her throat again, but this time she forced back her tears. "I began this journey on my own. I made a mistake, and I did John a great wrong. I've brought him pain, Elizabeth, and I swear I'll never do that again." She took a deep breath. "I went in search of my freedom. I found John Macpherson. And I found love."

"Then he must know!"

Maria gazed steadily into Elizabeth's eyes. "I will not bring him any more suffering. I will bear the weight of this, and as our child grows I will live in joy knowing that John is with me always. These are consequences I can live with, my friend."

Elizabeth reached out, and the women hugged one another fiercely.

"What can I do, Maria?"

Maria considered for a moment. "Help to secure passage for me and Isabel . . . to Castile."

Elizabeth pulled back and looked into the younger women's eyes. "You are going to run away. You will never tell him."

"That's what is best," Maria whispered. For him, she thought. The best for him.

Chapter 31

Edinburgh Castle

The sun shone brightly on the town below as John Macpherson and the young king walked along the ramparts of the ancient fortress.

The Highlander paused and gazed at the Abbey of Holyrood at the end of the Royal Mile. He knew she was no longer there. She was safe with his family at Drummond Castle. But when he thought of her, a burning pain took hold in his chest. When he'd last seen her at the abbey, John had been so involved with the magnitude of their undertaking, and so angry with her actions in Antwerp, that he had been completely blind to the danger she was bringing on herself by helping them to rescue the King. But, sending a prayer into the flawless sapphire-blue canopy overhead, John thanked God for Elizabeth and Ambrose. They'd had the insight to move her to safety.

Indeed, Angus had sent his men after Maria immediately after hearing news of the King's escape from Falkland Palace. Whether he'd wanted to use her as a hostage for negotiating his terms, or whether a fury for revenge had possessed him, the Highlander was just grateful she had been removed. Whatever his intentions had been, the Lord Chancellor had been thwarted.

So much had happened since the night at Falkland Palace. Sir Thomas Maule's letter had worked like a charm in facilitating their movement through the burgh gate, as well as through the Douglas encampment. Then, west of Loch Leven at Campbell Castle, they'd met with an army led by Colin Campbell, the Earl of Argyll, the Earl of Huntly, Alec Macpherson, and the others who had met in Ambrose's Great Hall. They were prepared for resistance, anticipating a bloody battle with those holding Stirling Castle.

But a miracle had occurred. Upon seeing the King with his noble entourage, the gates at Stirling were flung open and men poured out in joy, welcoming the young monarch. The same scene repeated itself at Falkirk, Linlithgow, Blackness, and every village and town they passed. Like a gathering wave, the company of the King grew with every passing mile, turning over the land, burying in a tide of strength and justice what remained of Angus's support. By the time James reached Edinburgh, Scotland had spoken. Rising up, the people met him, cheered him, and followed him, overjoyed in the knowledge that at last a Stuart king would again rule their land.

The sweep from Stirling to Edinburgh had gone well, but they knew ousting Angus might not be so easy. Apprehensive about Henry of England's reaction to the forced removal of his puppet, the Earl of Angus, King James and his loyal nobles had moved with the swiftness of lightning. Tracking Angus to Tantallon Castle, the King had laid siege to the red-stone fortress. Then, in a display of justice and mercy, the young monarch had allowed Angus and his Douglas cronies to go into exile in England. By moving quickly, there had been no time for the English to intervene.

John watched as King James showed remarkable skill in his first acts as ruler. With the help of Ambrose Macpherson, a letter to Henry of England was drawn up, emphasizing James's good will toward his uncle, Henry Tudor, and identifying the reasons for his dissatisfaction—on behalf of the people of Scotland—with the exiled Angus. In this letter James also made known the Lord Chancellor's plan of using Emperor Charles's troops to aid him in running the country. Let Angus explain *that* to the English king, Kit said.

The orders of the King and his council were final. If Angus ever returned to Scotland, he would be imprisoned for life beyond the waters of the Spey. The presence of the Douglas clan would no longer be tolerated at court. The King's Council also directed Angus and the Douglasses to surrender their castles and belongings. The council's edict even proclaimed that any servant or friend of the Douglas clan would suffer death if they so much as stepped foot in Edinburgh. But amid all these charges of treason, one man and his family were excluded. By order of the King, Sir Thomas Maule became lord of Brechin Castle, a place of honor in the history of his family.

"My mother tells me that my father had plans for a magnificent palace to be built at the abbey."

Startled out of his reverie, John turned his attention back to the young king.

"The royal residence he did build is a fine place, sire."

"I know. Mother loves staying there, but perhaps someday I will make it over the way my father wanted it." Kit looked at the bustling town below them. "But not now."

John gazed at the young man who stood so comfortably before him. He was born for this, John thought.

"While I was locked away, Jack Heart, I made a promise—to myself and to the Lord. I promised that if ever I sat on the throne of Scotland—really sat on the throne—I would be the king of all the people—noble and commoner alike."

"It is the common folk who are the most in need," John answered with a nod. "And Scotland is their country, sire, far more than it is ours."

King James smiled at the Highlander. "I knew you would understand. But there are many who won't. Your values are strong and true, Jack Heart."

"You are king now, Your Majesty . . . in every way. You lead, and the rest will follow."

The King leaned against a broken piece of the wall and looked southward toward the Pentland Hills. "There were only three hundred nobles that I invited to welcome me and the Queen Mother to Edinburgh Castle. Many will be fearful—resentful even—that I didn't summon them to join us."

"Their fear is well-founded, sire, when you have every reason to doubt their loyalty. In time, you'll know whom you can trust and whom you can't. Many of those you excluded you may never want in your company."

"It's true. But John . . ." The young man paused. "I will always want you at my side, regardless of what the future brings."

John nodded. He understood what Kit was talking about. This morning, the council had dwelt for a considerable amount of time discussing the future queen and her courage in helping to free James. But conspicuous in her absence was Maria herself. John knew where she was and so did the King. The Macpherson clan had made their appearance at court, but had returned immediately to Drummond Castle. The Macphersons had come and gone, but—oddly enough—Maria had chosen not to come at all.

The rumors had immediately resurfaced then. Caroline Maule's poison was continuing to spread, despite her ignominious death.

John had wondered how long the King would listen to such talk. Before this morning, the Highlander had not given much thought to his own treachery—as Caroline had described his actions to the King—but he had given plenty of thought to Maria, and to her sacrifice in trying to save his life. Even now, speaking to the man he knew would soon marry her, pangs of love and regret coursed through him. John knew that no one could love her as he did. He knew he loved her more than he'd thought it possible to love another. But he also knew he didn't deserve her—she was destined to become his queen.

For many weeks now—since before leaving Antwerp—John had resolved to take whatever punishment King James or his council decided to mete out over the liberties he'd taken with the King's intended bride. He thought back over her words. Maria had said she was looking for a dream, and now he knew that he had been looking for one as well. The memory of all they'd shared would remain locked forever in his heart, whether it meant imprisonment or pain of death.

"Today the Queen Mother asked me the date of my wedding." Kit gazed at the Highlander. "Perhaps you heard some rumbling about it in council?"

John felt the pain, like a hot poker, push straight into his heart. And then he knew. The image of Maria in another man's arms was something he could never endure. Even if that man was his king. If death was not to be his sentence, then he had to go away. He had no ties, he lied to himself. He would give up his Lordship of the Navy.

"Sire, I—"

"Wait, John," the King interrupted. "I told Mother that I am not ready to wed."

The New World, John thought. Aye, that's it. He would sail to the New World. With enough distance and time, perhaps someday he might forget. . . .

I am not ready to wed. James's words slowly worked into his consciousness. He looked up, suddenly aware of the young king's knowing expression.

"You . . . you are not to wed?" John asked.

James shook his head. "Someday, perhaps I will, but not now, and—though I owe her a great deal—I'll not marry this woman."

John stood speechless.

"She wants neither me nor this marriage, Jack Heart. I would be honored to have her, but she will have no part of me. She is in love with . . . well, she loves another man."

John cleared his throat. "Sire, I think it is important for you to know, when I found this woman adrift in a longboat—"

James reached into his doublet and drew out five letters. "I know enough, Jack Heart. She wrote it all down for me. In these letters, she conveyed to me the events of her flight from the Emperor's palace right up to the point of her arrival in Scotland."

"She wrote you," John repeated. "And she told you . . . everything?"

"Well, I believe she may have left out a few . . . sensitive . . . details that might be considered incriminating to the Lord of our Navy. Truthfully, sometimes as I read her letters, I had to question her objectivity in viewing of your character."

"My character? Sire, I don't think—"

"Aye, Jack Heart. If you have any miracles up your sleeve, I believe the Pope will have to confer sainthood."

John shook his head. "She told you she . . . she wrote of her feelings for me?'"

"Nay, that she didn't," Kit answered cheerfully. "In fact, of her feelings she wrote nothing but praise for your chivalrous behavior toward her."

"Then how did you know . . . ?" John paused. "Caroline . . . you listened to Caroline."

"Of course." King James shook his head. "But she was a foe, and you are a friend. So to answer you, I heard what she had to say, but I considered it mostly falsehood."

"I did court your queen, but that was before I knew her identity."

The young king placed a hand on John's shoulder. "There is no one I've learned to trust more than you, my friend. I listened to Caroline's malice, knowing her intent, and I read Maria Habsburg's letters, understanding her affection. So in her twisted way, Caroline helped me to see what lay behind the praise. Maria Habsburg is in love with you, Jack Heart."

Standing there in the sun, a new world opened for the Highlander. But then the difficulties rose again, clouding his features.

"But what of the contract, Kit? The marriage contract between Angus and the Emperor?"

"Let *them* marry, it they want to! Our official position will be that the contract bears no legality. I've already sent a letter to her and another to Antwerp saying so. I signed no document, and we will defend Scotland against any action the Emperor cares to initiate. Nay, Jack. My feeling is that Maria is free at the moment."

Free! John's mind ran through any other potential problems. There were many.

"Sire, I will repay the dowry. The gold Angus received from Charles must be gone."

King James considered for a moment, and then nodded in agreement. "Aye, if you care to. I believe we'll take you up on that offer. Everyone knows that the Macpherson wealth exceeds even that of the Emperor."

John laid his hand on the castle wall. Maria was still at Drummond Castle.

"But there is still the question, Jack," the King continued, "of convincing the Emperor that you have any right to her hand. He may just have other plans for his sister. Plans involving another monarch somewhere."

John's eyes flashed, Maria had already paid that price. He clapped his hands on the young king's shoulders. "Farewell, Kit," the Highlander said warmly, starting abruptly for the castle tower at the end of the rampart.

"Where are you going, Jack Heart?" the King called with a smile.

"After a dream, sire," he responded and then, with a wave, disappeared into the tower.

Chapter 32

Drummond Castle

At first light, she and Isabel would start for Dundee. A ship would be waiting for them, Elizabeth had assured her. In a week or two, depending on the winds, Maria would be in Castile. Maria glanced down once again at the letter from the King abrogating the agreement between Angus and the Emperor, and releasing her from their betrothal. It was now time to leave, she thought, stabbing away a tear.

Fiona had proved the most gracious of hosts during Maria's stay at Drummond Castle, making Maria and Isabel feel like members of the family. They had both been surprised to learn that Fiona Drummond Stuart Macpherson was actually half-sister to King James himself. And she was a woman who emanated love for her children and for everyone whose life she touched. She had taken Maria to herself like a long-lost sister. And like three sisters, Maria, Fiona, and Elizabeth had learned much from one another, exchanging stories and gathering fond memories.

And for tonight, this final night of their stay, Fiona had prepared a gathering. All would attend. All except John. Alec and Ambrose were expected at any moment. Elizabeth had received word from Ambrose that John was busy with the work of the King's Council, but Maria knew the truth. He would sooner travel into the jaws of death than come to her. Understandably, he could not bring himself to see her again. But perhaps that was the best for all.

Standing, she placed the letter from the King on the side table and looked into the long looking glass Fiona had sent in for her. Her stomach was flat and hard. How was it that life could be growing in there? This was no time to be grieving past decisions, Maria thought, turning and slipping out the door into the torchlit corridor. She had a whole lifetime ahead to ponder what might have been, and a child to raise. Their child.

Coming down the spiraling stairway, Maria was nearly flattened at the landing by a giant of a young man who barreled into her with a black-haired girl on his heels. A steel-muscled arm helped her regain her balance, but she nearly laughed out loud as she realized that her assailant was still using her as shield against the attacking Jaime.

"Please stand where you are, mistress," the young man pleaded. "I'll be forever in your debt if you'll keep this banshee away from me."

Maria, staying between the seven-year-old girl and the towering young warrior, laughed heartily. "You can't mean this wee lass?"

"Aye," he replied, breaking away and taking the steps three at a time. "Fairy folk come ever so small, you know. But they're very, very dangerous."

Maria stood in front of the little girl, blocking her path. "Terrifying," she said, looking at the child.

"Excuse me, Your Grace," Jaime said, giving her a full curtsy and then trying to force her way around the young queen.

"Jaime," Maria said, staying in front of her, "I was hoping to run into you. I heard that besides the entire family, a great many guests will be here tonight, and I was hoping you might tell me the names of those I don't already know."

The little girl gave a wistful look up the winding stairs, and then nodded her agreement. Maria took Jaime's hand and turned her back down the stairs.

"Who is your young man?" Maria asked, seeing Jaime's reluctance about giving up on her prey.

"That's Malcolm," Jaime answered simply.

"Malcolm. Fiona and Alec's stepson?" Maria asked with surprise. Fiona had spoken so proudly of Malcolm

MacLeod, the young clan chief of Skye and Lewis beyond the Western Highlands. But for some reason, Maria had expected a young boy. Clearly, this was how Jaime thought of him, as well.

"Aye. We're going to marry when we grow up," Jaime announced matter-of-factly.

"Does he know this?"

"Of course. I told him first on my fourth birthday. But he doesn't believe me."

"And what you were doing just now? Trying to get his consent?"

Jaime looked down at her feet, scuffing the steps as she descended, and then lifted her mischievous, black eyes to Maria's face. "I just like chasing him. He always runs away, you know."

Maria smiled back at the child. The resemblance between Jaime and Elizabeth was startling. It warmed her heart to know that Elizabeth had revealed this secret to her. She could see that this little bundle of energy was a happy and well-cared-for child, and she rejoiced in her friend's trust. To be thought of as a friend! she thought happily. She'd never experienced such a relationship before.

"My cousins are a wee bit childish," Jaime said with an air of maturity as a swarm of children raced past them, heading for the kitchens. The little girl lowered her voice to a whisper. "But they have good hearts, I suppose."

"Thank you," Maria responded, hiding her smile. "I'll keep that in mind."

Jaime proved to be a wonderful escort and kept up a running commentary on Drummond Castle, its dependents, and its guests. Though she thought of Alec and Fiona's sons as mere children, the eldest, Alexander, was actually eleven and twice her size, while James, their second son, was nine years old and a head and shoulder taller than the young girl. And what she knew of the doings of the guests, servants, and townsfolk quite nearly shocked Maria.

As they approached the Great Hall, Jaime extricated

herself courteously from Maria's hand. With a quick glance toward the hall, where the merriment had already begun, the little girl dashed off toward the stairwell they'd just descended.

"Well," Maria murmured to herself, "at least Malcolm has a bit of a start on her."

Maria slipped quietly through the huge doors and into the hall, trying to avoid bringing any attention to herself. Standing on the side, Maria let her gaze roam the room, taking in its festive occupants. Though Alec and Ambrose had been expected in the afternoon, the two brothers had not yet arrived. Maria wondered what news they would bring of John. And she prayed she would learn something before she and Isabel left in the morning.

Hearing her aunt's snort of laughter over the revelry, Maria looked over at the dais where Isabel sat with the elder Macphersons. It had been amazing how Isabel's complaints about being dragged to Scotland had ceased the moment she'd arrived at Drummond Castle. In fact, her only criticism of Maria recently had been to complain about the young woman's hurry to depart. Maria had an idea she was planning a tour of the Highlands, with an extended stay with Alexander and Lady Elizabeth at Benmore Castle.

Fiona was the first one to spot Maria. Crossing the room to greet her, the red-haired beauty gathered Maria in a warm embrace as she brought her to the middle of the room. The immediate attention that the young queen received from those around her touched her heart and brought a lump to her throat. The merriment, the banter, and the love these people showed for one another clearly included her, wrapping Maria in a soft glow. Maria rejoiced in that light, and she hoped they would never consider her untrue. The way John considered her.

Inwardly, John kicked himself for the hundredth time for accepting his brothers' invitation of traveling with them for the remainder of the journey. That he had caught up with them en route to Drummond Castle should have alerted him to the fact that they would keep him from his goal. They were as slow as old mules on a hot summer day. He had told Alec and Ambrose as much, and in response they had slowed their pace even more. But now, at long last, they had reached Drummond Castle.

During their journey, John had thought over his approach. Was it best just to sweep in and take her in his arms, pretending that he'd caused her no pain? He was in love, but he was not a fool. Perhaps he should begin all over—court her, allow her to see his love, and then hope she might perhaps find it in her heart to forgive him for what he'd done.

Approaching Drummond Castle's Great Hall, John felt Ambrose's heavy hand upon his shoulder, bringing him out of his reverie.

"We'll give you tonight to make good, you blackguard," Ambrose said with a wry smile.

Alec's huge paw fell on John's other shoulder. "Show her your charm, your allure, your gracious courtesy, but be sparing with that ugly face of yours."

"We like her, John," Ambrose put in. "And if you lose her, there will be hell to pay with our wives."

"So, John, don't muck it up," Alec warned, slapping him on the back.

John glared at one man, then at the other. These two giants were treating him like a mere lad.

But neither waited for a response. With a wink and another shove, the two older brothers strode ahead of him into the hall.

He was here.

Maria felt her body tremble with excitement and dismay as she watched John step into the room behind his brothers.

The long benches emptied as everyone rose to welcome the new arrivals. Everyone, including Isabel. Maria watched in amazement as her aunt crossed the room to John and gave him an affectionate hug. The best she could do was to stand. One step away from the table and her legs would surely fold beneath her.

John looked up and their eyes met. His heart pounded in his chest as he devoured her with his gaze. Radiant, she stood behind the trestle table—clad in white, her silky black hair falling in waves around her. Isabel was whispering in his ear, but what she told him he already knew. His niece and nephews were using him as a climbing tree, but his eyes never left her face.

Maria noticed how the hall gradually quieted. The silence became pronounced as all eyes riveted on John, awaiting his next move.

Lifting his nephew Michael in his arms and handing him to Elizabeth, John moved purposefully through the crowd to Maria.

Her heart was beating so hard in her chest that she thought it would explode. His strides were confident, determined. His eyes sparked with that roguish glint she recalled from their first days at sea. He halted directly before her. Only the width of the trestle table separated them.

"Your Grace." He bowed. She felt her heart sink at his formality.

"M'lord!" She nodded slowly in return.

"May I have the honor of sitting beside you?"

She stared at him, trying to measure his mood. He talked one way, and yet his mischievous blue eyes spoke of something else. "Of course," she answered quietly.

Without hesitating an instant, John vaulted over the table and stood beside her.

With great effort, Maria lifted her jaw back into place. It seemed that no one in the hall seemed shocked at his move, and suddenly the young woman was conscious that the pause in the merrymaking was only momentary. The servants bustled, people talked, children shouted. Gradually, Maria regained her poise and then looked up into his eyes. He was standing behind her bench, waiting attentively for her to sit. Glancing at him over her shoulder, she took her seat.

Her look was clearly one of invitation, he thought. Exultant, John prepared to sit, but out of the corner of his eye, he caught his mother making her way past them to her seat.

"Maria," Lady Macpherson said softly to the young woman, "forgive this young scapegrace. I'm sure I brought him up better."

Turning to John, the older woman reached up to kiss her son and whispered, "Don't ruin this opportunity, my dear, or your sisters-in-law won't be the only ones you'll be answering to."

"It's very good to see you, too, Mother." John hugged her tenderly in his arms. "I always knew you loved me best."

Pulling away, she punched him squarely in the chest. "John Macpherson, you are a scoundrel."

Maria just watched in amazement as he took the seat beside her. She was seeing a different man than the one she'd last spoken with at the Abbey of Holyrood. But she could not assume he had forgiven her of the wrong she had done him. And she was not sure she could bear the disappointment of a false hope.

"A drink, Your Grace?" he asked.

"Very well," she said, lifting her cup.

John's large hand closed over hers, his fingers holding hers captive as he poured the wine.

She felt her face redden as the heat of his hand radiated through hers, but she could not look away from the smoldering look in his eyes. She put the cup on the table and cast about for something casual to say.

"How was the journey from Edinburgh?"

"Long, because of the slowness of my good brothers."

"Everyone appears delighted that you made it."

"And you?" John asked, absently reaching out and taking hold of her cup.

Maria nodded. "I'm thrilled that you came," she whispered. As she spoke, she felt his knee press deliberately against hers. She drew her breath in sharply.

"Have you had a pleasant stay at Drummond Castle, Your Grace?" he asked, the indifference of his tone belied by his soft caressing touch of Maria's cup.

"Very pleasant, thank you, m'lord," she answered, her eyes following the movement of his fingers.

"Has anyone showed you about?"

"I've been here for some time."

"I'd be willing to show you more." John reached up and casually pushed a loose strand of hair from her cheek. "One can experience so much in a new place."

His fingers scorched her skin where they brushed so lightly against her face.

"Can there be much more to experience here?"

John gazed at her lowered lashes. The soft skin of her face. His eyes drifted to her lips. "To experience a place fully, a traveler must be open to new things."

"And one needs the right guide, I suppose."

"Aye, that's it." He smiled.

She reached over to take her cup, and his hand wrapped around hers. Her eyes lifted to his face. "Are you offering your services, m'lord?"

"I am, if you'd have me."

She tried to ignore the sound of thunder in her heart. "I would," she said shakily, looking about the room. She wondered if anyone could see the excitement bursting within her. No one seemed to be paying the least attention to them.

"You know, this is the best time of the year to be here."

His voice drew her back to him. Beneath the table, his bare knee moved slightly against her leg.

It is, since you arrived, she thought. "It's paradise."

"Have you had a chance to stroll through the gardens in the moonlight?" He came closer to her side and whispered the words. "The roses should be in full bloom, and the night is quite warm."

She just shook her head, fighting the urge to close her eyes and allow his lifting whisper to beguile her.

A serving man placed a platter of food before them. She stared at the food, but her hunger was not for food. John served her first and then just stared, waiting. Hesitantly, she picked up a slice of pear and brought it up to her lips. She shivered involuntarily as his eyes followed the path of fruit.

He lifted his cup to his lips. "Have you been kissed in a garden of roses, under a starlit sky?" His words caressed her.

She swallowed hard and then brought her hands to her lap to hide their trembling. She shook her head. "Never."

His hands moved beneath the table and rested on hers. Welcoming his touch, she clutched them tightly in her lap.

John's words enthralled her as he leaned toward her, breathing the words in her ear. "Perhaps, when you are finished with your meal, I could show you the gardens."

"Aye," she said simply, her voice a ragged whisper.

"And perhaps, when you've had your fill of roses—the guide might kiss you under the stars."

She stared at her plate, his fingers now playing sensually against her thigh. She gazed up to his deep blue eyes and then at his lips. Leaning closer to his ear, she whispered her words. "I am finished with my meal, and I've had my fill of roses."

John held back the urge to sweep her into his arms and carry her from the hall. Taking her arm, he stood up slowly, waiting for her to rise as well.

As they moved toward the entrance of the Great Hall, Maria looked about furtively. They were the souls of discretion. Unseen by anyone, John and Maria slipped through the huge doors and hurried toward the gardens.

As the great doors closed behind the fleeing lovers, a cheer went up among those left behind.

It was passion, it was greed, it was a dream.

Under the quiet of an arbor, hidden away from people, and enclosed by darkness and aroma of flowers, they embraced.

She had thought this would only happen again in a dream. But, my God, she thought, he was real.

As John touched his lips to hers, he felt her hands

reach up and caress his face. Their lips brushed gently in search of remembrance.

With unspoken words, in a silent embrace, each sought forgiveness. In the tenderness of their touch, each spoke their love. And then, their passion soared.

As if outside herself, Maria felt her own body shudder as John's hands traveled her back. His mouth was covering hers now, and she opened her lips willingly to his.

As his tongue delved into the depths of her mouth, a heat coursed through her body, scorching her with a deep, consuming flame. Maria's hands flew up to encircle his neck. Her tongue, her mouth molded to his and her body ached with the need to follow. A boldness took control of her as her hands traced his back, his neck. Her fingers were raking through his hair, while her mouth answered the seductive rhythm of his thrusting tongue. This was all as she remembered. That exquisite dream.

John could see the passion in her eyes. She was in his arms, and she was willing. He wanted her. Remembering the passion they'd shared, John's mouth moved insistently against hers as a rush of wild desire directed his action. His hands roamed her back, cupping her buttocks and pressing her against his hardening manhood. He smothered her gasp with his kiss as she pressed her body to his.

"I've seen enough of roses," she pulled back breathlessly.

"Good, then perhaps I might show you my bedchamber."

She nodded, smiling.

As the candle flickered beside the bed, Maria looked one last time at the beautiful curve of his muscular torso stretched so naturally across the bed. A black tendril lay across his cheek, and she fought the urge to push it back and kiss his face for the last time. She thought of the love they'd shared by that candle's light. There had been great hungering need in both of them, but their lovemaking had known no hurry, and their tender touches no grief. She had known this would be their last night together, and she had savored each precious moment.

She had sighed out his name; he had made her tremble. They had not talked of the past; there had been only rapture, the pure and simple joy of drowning in the moment, in the night, in each other.

She gave him a last look and a smile. As she slipped out of his chamber, a tear marked their final farewell.

Chapter 33

The German Sea, off the coast of Dundee

The commander of the Macphersons' armed merchant trader, the *Elizabeth*, looked with satisfaction at the full sails billowing above and the bright azure sky beyond them. Time enough, he thought, directing his steps to the stern cabins.

As he made his way down the narrow passageway, he could make out the sound of crying coming from the partially open cabin door. It was a sound of a broken heart. He slowed his steps, trying to force back the pangs of guilt. He came to a stop outside the cabin and silently pushed the door open.

His eyes made contact with Isabel's and then came to rest on the sobbing figure in the older woman's arms. Gently, Isabel released the young woman and laid her head down on the cabin bunk. Quietly, she rose and moved across the space to the door and stepped into the passageway.

Without a word John stepped into the room and closed the door behind him, leaning his back against it.

"The first time, I let you get away," he said quietly. "But this time, lass, I won't be so gracious."

Her head shot up as she turned to face him. She was pale, her sorrow evident in her swollen eyes, in her pained features. She came quickly to her feet.

"How . . ."

"Stealing like a thief from my bed in the middle of the night." His gaze did not waver. "Not even the courage to say good-bye. You may think you had good reason the first time, but making love to me, whispering that you love me, and then disappearing forever?"

Her lips were parted, trembling with the effort to hold back the tears, but Maria's attempts were in vain. The tears spilled over onto her cheeks. The young woman turned, burying her face in her hands.

"Why did you come?" she said raggedly.

He ignored the question. "The last time I was a fool. But this time I was prepared." John stepped toward her. "Do you think I don't know how your mind works now? After all we've been through? You might despise the way your brother thinks, but you have much in common with him."

Her head snapped around. "I'm nothing like him."

"Your motives are different, it's true. But in the same way that he sacrifices himself for an empire, you sacrifice yourself for the ones you love."

In a futile attempt, Maria wiped the endless stream of tears from her face. John closed the distance between them and took her by the shoulders. His blue eyes gazed tenderly into hers.

"I know everything you've done. I know why you left me and went back to your brother in Antwerp. I know of your letters to King James. Aye, lass, I even know of our child."

Her eyes widened. She couldn't bear his pity. "Why did you come?" Maria pressed, trying without success to pull away from his embrace.

He held her until she ceased her struggle, and then framed her face with his hands. "I came because I love you. Because I know that you love me, as well. I came because of what we've shared, and the dreams we have to fulfill."

"And you came for the sake of our child," she said sadly.

"I knew nothing of the child. We were at sea before Isabel gave me the news." His eyes pierced her soul. "Our child we'll treasure, but you are what I came for."

Maria could hold back no longer. Throwing her arms around his neck, she laid her face against his chest and wept. "John," she whispered lovingly.

He held her for a long time until her tears subsided.

"Will you marry me, Maria? Will you put up with my stubborn pride?"

"I will marry you, John. And I will cherish whatever fate deals us."

He held her tenderly. "We still have your brother to deal with."

"Don't worry." She smiled, turning her emerald eyes upward. "He hates the new Maria. He'll be glad to hand me off at the first offer."

"And what of your mother?"

"Aye. And she'll love you, too, Jack Heart." Maria's eyes sparked with mischief. "She isn't mad, you know!"

Epilogue

Benmore Castle, the Scottish Highlands

> *The Queen o' Hearts,*
> *She made some tarts*
> *All on a summer's day.*
> *The Jack o' Hearts,*
> *Cared not for tarts,*
> *But stole the Queen away.*
>
> *The King o' Hearts*
> *Called for the tarts,*
> *He sent his fiercest men.*
> *The Jack o' Hearts*
> *Gave up the tarts,*
> *But kept the Queen again.*

Lady Elizabeth Macpherson finished her tale and sat back in her chair, her grandchildren spread around her feet. Jaime patted her on the knee.

"Is that a rhyme about Uncle John and Aunt Maria?"

"It sounds like it, doesn't it?"

"Will you make a rhyme for *me*, Grandmother?"

"Yours is next, my love."

Journeys of Passion and Desire

☐ **TOMORROW'S DREAMS by Heather Cullman.** Beautiful singer Penelope Parrish—the darling of the New York stage—never forgot the night her golden life ended. The handsome businessman Seth Tyler, whom she loved beyond all reason, hurled wild accusations at her and walked out of her life. Years later, when Penelope and Seth meet again amid the boisterous uproar of a Denver dance hall, all their repressed passion struggles to break free once more.   (406842—$5.50)

☐ **YESTERDAY'S ROSES by Heather Cullman.** Dr. Hallie Gardiner knows something is terribly wrong with the handsome, haunted-looking man in the great San Francisco mansion. The Civil War had wounded Jake "Young Midas" Parrish, just as it had left Serena, his once-beautiful bride, hopelessly lost in her private universe. But when Serena is found mysteriously dead, Hallie finds herself falling in love with Jake who is now a murder suspect.   (405749—$4.99)

☐ **LOVE ME TONIGHT by Nan Ryan.** The war had robbed Helen Burke Courtney of her money and her husband. All she had left was her coastal Alabama farm. Captain Kurt Northway of the Union Army might be the answer to her prayers, or a way to get to hell a little faster. She needed a man's help to plant her crops; she didn't know if she could stand to have a damned handsome Yankee do it.   (404831—$4.99)

☐ **FIRES OF HEAVEN by Chelley Kitzmiller.** Independence Taylor had not been raised to survive the rigors of the West, but she was determined to mend her relationship with her father—even if it meant journeying across dangerous frontier to the Arizona Territory. But nothing prepared her for the terrifying moment when her wagon train was attacked, and she was carried away from certain death by the mysterious Apache known only as Shatto.   (404548—$4.99)

☐ **RAWHIDE AND LACE by Margaret Brownley.** Libby Summerhill couldn't wait to get out of Deadman's Gulch—a lawless mining town filled with gunfights, brawls, and uncivilized mountain men—men like Logan St. John. He knew his town was no place for a woman and the sooner Libby and her precious baby left for Boston, the better. But how could he bare to lose this spirited woman who melted his heart of stone forever?   (404610—$4.99)

*Prices slightly higher in Canada

Buy them at your local bookstore or use this convenient coupon for ordering.

PENGUIN USA
P.O. Box 999 — Dept. #17109
Bergenfield, New Jersey 07621

Please send me the books I have checked above.
I am enclosing $_____ (please add $2.00 to cover postage and handling). Send check or money order (no cash or C.O.D.'s) or charge by Mastercard or VISA (with a $15.00 minimum). Prices and numbers are subject to change without notice.

Card #_____ Exp. Date _____
Signature_____
Name_____
Address_____
City _____ State _____ Zip Code _____

For faster service when ordering by credit card call **1-800-253-6476**

Allow a minimum of 4-6 weeks for delivery. This offer is subject to change without notice.